ODE OF THE CHIMERA

Serpent's Refrain

By

Hal Wintry

ISBN: 979-8-9999474-0-6 (ebook)

ISBN: 979-8-9999474-1-3 (paperback)

To those that helped me get this far

MAP OF KAZAR

Contents

PROLOGUE

Tears ran down my cheeks as I watched the light leave her eyes. "Mom… please wake up."

The ground vibrated as the crowd drew near with their blood covered weapons, and animalistic rage. I tried to hide, but was pulled out of my hiding spot and laid on the ground at the mercy of the rioters.

"He's just a boy, do we kill him too?"

The mob debated what to do with me, the last surviving human on the compound. I listened as some defended me, saying I was far too young, while others brought up my red hair.

"What are we *debating*? He's **his** son! Do you not remember Erélora?"

"The Scorcher of Erélora is dead, and so is his wife. Why do we need the boy?"

"Leverage, that's what the humans would do. We kidnap him."

"And bring him where? They'll tear Kore apart looking for him. He's a witness and decades from now, he'll be just like his father. We need to kill him."

I saw my chance while they were arguing, and made a run for it. One of them grabbed me by my neck and lifted me off the ground, I felt their fingers tensing around my throat. With all the strength I could muster, I punched them in their nose and fell to the ground, head first.

I jumped to my feet, and ran away as fast as I could. I ran until my lungs and chest hurt, and then ran some more. I ran blindly through the mazelike compound as they fired and screamed at me. A bullet grazed my leg and I stumbled, but I didn't stop running. I ran down every hall, crossed every corner, until I finally made it to the exit. I tried to read the red sign, but my neurolink wasn't working correctly. The word 'exit' was written, but some human letters looked like kazamite characters.

"I think he went this way!"

I'll take it. I approached the door panel, but it was locked due to the emergency shut down. I thought back to what my parents would say: control your breathing, reassess. I took a deep inhale, and then exhaled… and then punched in my parent's override. The one I've seen them do half a million times before.

The door opened and I let out a sigh of relief. All those nights spying on my parents through the vents finally paid off. The door began to slide open but then abruptly stopped. The lights in the hall cut off and the emergency lights kicked in.

"No no no no."

I put in the override code again but there was no power to the panel. I could hear the mob get closer. Power would be diverted to essential doors, like exits, so why was this door stuck?

The mob turned down the hall.

Without another thought, I turned sideways, and slid through the door crack into the dark room. Whatever was in here, was better than being caught by a mob of kazamites. People have wanted dad dead for years now, but nobody has ever acted on it. How did they know where we were?

I blindly stumbled deeper, and fumbled over rocks and thick grass until I saw a door that I could read clearly. I rubbed my eyes and hit my head and read a sign two more times.

"Wait…. If *this* one says 'exit' then…"

My thought was cut off by the low bellow of a thifrum. A thifrum? Here? But they're cattle, and would only be here as… fodder for the…kurous' den. I saw the eyes first, then came the low guttural growl. My heart dropped as the kurous raised itself to its full height. It glowed magma red, a sign of irritation and it roared.

I ran.

2

I looked back as the kurous let out a devastating breath of magma onto the thifrum near me. The thifrum was vaporized. I pumped my legs and arms faster. This time, I made it to the *actual* exit, while the kurous raged and thrashed.

I punched in my parent's code again hoping to override this door. Light crept in as the door **crawled** open. Behind me, I could hear how angry the kurous was as the ground vibrated. I dropped to the ground and crawled under the door, and dragged my body across the ground.

I stood to my feet and laughed as the sun's rays warmed me.

But I jinxed it.

The kurous charged at full speed. I dove out of the way just as the kurous broke through the door and took out half of the wall. Metal and rocks flew everywhere. I spiraled through the air and hit the ground hard. My head bounced off of a rock as I landed, blurring my vision. I tried to stand on my feet, but everything was fuzzy and spinning. I felt nauseous and dry heaved as my ears began to ring.

The ringing was loud, but the kurous' roar was louder. I looked up at the beast as it towered over me. Some of the kazamites that were already outside made an attempt to attack it, but were all met with the same breath of magma that killed the thifrum. More kazamites rushed over to subdue the kurous, but it was smart enough to know it was outnumbered. It stretched its scaly wings, and took to the sky. Dust was kicked up everywhere as the gargantuan reptile flew off.

"He's over there!"

The world was spinning, and I couldn't see past the dust cloud anyway. I watched as the silhouettes of the mob of kazamites charge towards me and then stop

"Look out!"

The ground began to vibrate and I heard the sound of a stampede of thifrums escaping, and running towards me. I tried to stand on my feet again, but my legs were just too weak. I slowly went to my knees and did the only thing I could: cry.

I'm going to die here.

As the stampede drew closer, I squeezed my eyes shut and tightened them as **hard** as I could. I tensed up, and readied myself to be run over. The ground vibrated more as their hooves battled to drown out the ringing and then... a loud thunder clap. The rumbling continued, but I couldn't hear the one that was leading the charge anymore. I opened my eyes but quickly shut them as dust, dirt and rocks hit my face. I stayed on my knees as the stampede continued around me. Within a minute, the herd was gone. I knew the herd was gone, but I could still hear them and the ringing in my ears.

I wiped my face and slowly opened my eyes and saw the silhouette of a person with one foot on the head of the thifrum that led the herd, and one on the ground as if standing on a trophy they hunted. I assumed it was one of them kazamites due to all the stories about them being demonically strong. The figure turned to face me, and I was stunned by the glow of white eyes staring down at me through the still settling dust from the thifrums. The glow of the white eyes was a dead giveaway, it was worse than a demonic kazamite: it was a bloodthirsty chimera. The dust settled and I saw it in all of its glory. It was a girl, no older than me but with soft violent skin and unruly blue curls.

"Hello," she said to me. It could *speak?* And it... it... *she* saved me. I broke out into tears and hugged her waist. "I'm Mandy."

"Mandy?" I asked through my sobbing.

Her head canted as she replied "I asked if you were mad at me. Chimera aren't normally given names. What is that coming from your eyes? I didn't know humans could create water."

I giggled and wiped the tears from my eyes and said, "I am Copernicus Hyperion Petrus, pleased to make your acquaintance."

"Is... is that a name?" Before I could reply, half a dozen red lasers appeared on Mandy's body. Several human soldiers in armor rushed to surround the both of us but all of the guns were aimed at her. All of the kazamites that were threatening me once before, were arrested or killed.

A soldier in regime proper dress, walked towards us from behind the soldiers. His boots echoed over the dirt and sand as the soldiers made a path for him to walk. Hate filled his eyes as he stared at Mandy. It's the same look he gives… *gave* my mom. He was my uncle, Alex.

"Subject M04, step away from the boy. You will be tried for the attempted murder of a military commander's child and the killing of a thifrum. Copernicus, come boy. Let us deal with this miscreant, this is no place for children."

The sound of charging guns echoed. "NO!" I yelled and jumped to my feet and in front of Mandy. I stretched out my arms attempting to cover her from the lasers. "Mandy saved me! The others were trying to hurt me after… after they got to my parents. But she saved me from them. And she's a kid too!"

"*Mandy?*" I could hear the disgust in his voice. "Boy move, that is a chimera, they do not **have** names. You name dogs, and pets, not those things. There are a handful of them we have named but they are given those names by the Primarch and the tribunal, not by children."

"But she's a kid too!"

"Kid? This 'kid' ran several yards, jumped over you and struck the thifrum in the skull, and *killed* it in a singular blow. **Move.**" I didn't budge, I was unwavering. "Subject M04, step around him, face away from us, and get on the ground." Mandy began to move obediently, but I stopped her by grabbing her wrist. Uncle Alex gritted his teeth. "You're strong enough to kill a thifrum, but not pull away from an eight year old?"

"She saved me; how would we look if we arrested all those who helped us?" It was Alex this time, who was unwavering. "Please…"

He groaned and said "Stand down. I'll honor your words, Copernicus. It's your lucky day, Subject M04, you live to serve the regime even further. I need to report what happened here. Keep them together, and if there is so much as a misplaced hair on my nephew after you escort him, you'll be put in front of the firing squad. Also, find me some medics." The soldiers all lowered their weapons and rushed to grab us. "And where is Subject J08?"

The soldiers grabbed the two of us and whisked us away to another building. There were arrested kazamites who spat and cursed at us, and even some that lunged while chained up. The more aggressive kazamites ignored us however, and instead lunged at the human soldiers. While some soldiers ignored the aggression and disdain of the kazamites, some responded with violence and slurs. "Filthy chameleons" was one of the many slurs from the humans.

As we approached the building, I grabbed Mandy's hand and held it tightly and said to her, "don't be scared, you're safe with me now. The humans won't hurt you."

I smiled as one of the soldiers looked at me. He spat at me and said, "your father was a traitor to true loyalists. Long live Primarch Leopold."

Mandy stood in front of me and said to me, "no human, *you're* safe with me."

We entered the building and inside were two more chimera sitting, a girl Mandy's age, and a young adult. The chimera man stood and nodded his head at the humans and tapped the girl for her to stand. Unlike Mandy, this girl chimera had mint green eyes and very faint pink skin. Her hair was in space buns and she wore a soft and welcoming smile to Mandy. The man wore a formal aketon that covered his umber colored skin and he had sunset orange eyes. He approached the soldiers escorting us with a polite smile, but they responded by yanking me closer.

"Hail fellow," the chimera man said. "Captain Trogz instructed the two of us to wait here." The human soldiers and the man began to talk, but they didn't loosen their grip on me. The little girl grabbed Mandy's hand and pulled her to the side while the adults talked.

"Who is that human?" Mandy, stunned and unsure how to answer, just stared for a second. "I am your pod leader, you **must** answer. It is what a lady outta do. That's what Chevalier says." The mint eyed chimera looked up at the chimera man, who spoke with his hands behind his back.

"He is Copernicus... and he called me Mandy." Mandy replied to the girl. "I think we're supposed to name our friends."

"What's a 'friend'?"

Mandy paused for a moment before replying. "I think you... and Chevalier are... so you need a name too, how about Historia?"

She gasped, but then her eyes lit up. Before she could reply, the door opened and the soldiers stood at the position of attention, and the chimera man named Chevalier, kneeled. The air in the room suddenly felt dense, as Uncle Alex marched in.

He walked over to Mandy and I and said, "I said before that it was your lucky day, but that was a severe understatement. The new primarch has approved one of his legendary boons, to the likes of you. You may ask for anything in this world, and he will grant it. I, Captain Alexander Trogz, will honor this."

Without hesitation Mandy replied, "an adaptive AI."

Everyone in the room tensed up, a couple gasped.

I could see the disgust on Uncle Alex's face. A vein in his forehead started to pop out and he asked, "how do you know about that? That's confidential."

"So it *is* real?" she asked. You could almost see steam coming out of Alex's ears. But before he had a chance to respond, she continued. "It would help me adapt. Each pod has some way they could aid humans on-world and off-world, I could lessen the burden on my pod. I would have a way to monitor myself, others, and playback events to offer more data. A chimera coupled with an adaptive AI, would make a statement. A loud one."

Alex thought about Mandy's response for a second before replying. "You have a valid point. The three of you can wait here until I send someone for you." He looked at me. "It's safer in here, than out there. Too much bloodshed for a child. Soldiers will be outside waiting, in the event one of the chimeras decide to act like their *true* selves. I'll be back with medics so that we can assess the damage to your body. Looks as if you've been rattled. I will get this AI for you as well, chimera."

"Cricket." Mandy said. "I will name the AI Cricket."

"Do not get ahead of yourself. Perhaps your AI can teach you your place, chimera. Copernicus, a word please." I walked over to my uncle and he kneeled down and sighed. "I am sorry for the life you will experience. I loved your mother and father, and I will do my best to honor what they wanted, and what you want but please understand I will stumble. But we will get through this, together."

"The mob, they spoke ill of my parents."

"They 'spoke *ill*'? You need to see a medic, this isn't how you normally speak. Your neurolink must be damaged, you could have a concussion. Copernicus I loved your dad, he was a great soldier that–" a soldier shifted uncomfortably. Aelx tensed up and sighed again. He took a deep breath and stood up. "We can't afford to show weakness when our enemies are actively hunting us. I will be back. Chimeras, do **not** let any soldiers enter this room that I haven't vetted."

Alex left with the soldiers in tow, leaving the chimeras and I behind. The chimera named Chevalier spoke first. "Master Copernicus, well met. I am Subject L09, but many refer to me as Chevalier. You already know Subject M04 and this is Subject M01."

"You called her Mandy… She gave me a name too. I am Historia!" said the green eyed chimera.

Chevalier looked puzzled at her before he spoke. "Chimeras can't name other chimeras. But, I do think the names Mandy and Historia are cute names for the two of you. Copernicus is a handsome name, as well."

"It's a terrible name," said Mandy.

"That's mean. You're not supposed to be mean to friends, or family," I replied.

"I do not have a family or know what that means."

"You can be my sister! I always wanted a sister, but I thought all chimera were family. It's ok, I'll be your first. Families do fun stuff together like giving each other nicknames."

"Ok, then from now on… I will call you–"

Chapter 1

A Haiku Of Oil And Water

Mandy, present day 20 years later…

"Nic…" The focus on my visor zoomed out as I sighed. Extremist groups have been popping up all over and what does Nic do? Gets himself captured. He's always in trouble.

"Is that Nic? *Here?* Does it feel like he's always in trouble?"

I turned my head to the sound of Historia's voice but shrugged her off as the scanner on my wrist mounted NUE pinged with the last bit of intel I was waiting for.

"Yea, he was *supposed* to be on pass, vacationing in another province." I said, turning to her. I watched with a smile as she struggled to get her helmet over her space buns.

"Humans don't really stick around this prefecture, he must've known he'd stand out like a sore thumb."

"He's a redhead that hangs out with us, he always stands out like a sore thumb."

Historia didn't reply, she was lost in concentration, too busy fiddling with her claret sash she was trying to tie around her waist. It looked like a stain clashing against her gleaming cream techsuit that sits beneath her armor.

"Glad I have your attention." I nudged her to get her focus. "Ok, my NUE came back with three sentries near the hostages. One guarding the hostages in the middle building, one guy in a mech and one near him. Chevalier, can you take out the lookouts around the area?"

Historia and I didn't need to communicate when we went on missions, we were always in sync. Chevalier feared he'd get in our way, so he entered from another part of the compound. And honestly, he's probably right.

"Of course, I am honor bound to aid you on this quest. I ponder, which one of you fair maidens will engage in combat with the mech?" Historia giggled. "Ah yes, I am the jester for even asking. Perhaps today, we heed caution and move **slower** without showboating?"

Before he could even finish his sentence, Historia had already rushed down the hill. She slid down the rocky hillside carefree with her sash flowing behind her. Once she made it to the bottom, she dashed across the open field without so much as glance her way and dove through a window. She covered 100 meters in five seconds; if you were looking that way and blinked, you would've missed her.

Chevalier was next. He trotted over to the sentries and one by one knocked them out with a bonk to the head. He hid their bodies and then gently piled them on top of each other. We were dealing with kidnapping extremists, and this man was concerned about hurting them.

The last sentry must have noticed the lack of sentries, and rushed to an alarm system. I raised my gun to shoot him, but Chevalier beat me to the punch. He tackled the sentry and then knocked him out. I shook my head as I listened to him over the radio trying to catch his breath.

"Cricket, were you able to remote into Nic's account?" Cricket was the best AI bar none. The humans had a bad habit of listening in to my conversations when I had my helmet and suit on, so Cricket came up with a plan. He'd make an ultrasonic chirp whenever he wanted to say something that could get me in trouble and would cut the feed so people couldn't relisten to my comms.

I copied how Historia slid down the hill as Cricket replied. "I have not finished but I did learn something. His heart rate is consistent, showing he isn't concerned for his well being. Maybe he isn't in danger, and never was."

"He's hiding something, Cricket. Learn anything else?"

"A shrimp is an Earth creature and its heart is in its head." I groaned at his stupid trivia. "Ah yes, you meant about Nic and the extremist. The regime has been monitoring this cell for months. The regime didn't see them as a critical threat at first because they were anti-kazamite, but they recently stole two weapon blueprints. They're now in possession of a storm generator which can be tweaked to rain sand and then heat up the falling sand, thus turning it into glass. The next blueprint is more theoretical, but it is a DNA and RNA bomb. It's able to target DNA or RNA and unravel it."

As I snuck around the buildings, Historia took out most of the remaining extremists. She took out one of the last ones just as I snuck up to the building where the hostages were being kept. I climbed through an open window and ducked behind cover. The room was big and dark enough that nobody in the room noticed I crept in. There had to be a couple dozen hostages all being monitored by one guard. What was Nic thinking? Did he plan on rescuing everyone in here alone? Ugh, he's in over his head… again. One of the hostages so happened to look over in my direction and saw me. She gasped. The guard turned his attention to my direction.

"Now or never."

I stood up and kicked the desk I was hiding behind at the gunman. He didn't even get a chance to raise his gun before the desk smashed into him. He and the desk flew into a wall and let out a loud crashing sound as his body slid to the ground.

"Hmm, and people claim chimeras don't have monster strength," chirped Cricket. "I'm sure all humans splatter when they're unconscious like that?" As Cricket finished his one liner, he displayed all the hostages' spiking heart rates on my HUD. I answered him with a groan and asked him to declutter my visor.

"I'm Mandy, is anyone hurt?" I looked around the room for Nic, but didn't see him. Cricket knew what I was looking for, so he turned on my visor's sonar vision which worked like an advanced echolocation but, still nothing.

"There was a redhead human here," I said to the group. "Where is he?"

"Why? So you could save him and only him?" A chained up kazamite girl yelled at me.

I walked over to her and broke her chains and said, "because everyone gets to be rescued, nobody gets abandoned."

I freed everyone that needed it and checked for injuries as I did so. The kidnappers were smart enough to not hurt anyone severely, the worst injuries were superficial. Once done, I asked everyone again about Nic. But I was met with silence. Cricket pulled up the heart rate monitor again and told me to ask people again.

"None of you saw anything? He has curly hair and is about my height." The crowd awkwardly evaded my glance and shifted uncomfortably. One of the prisoners caught my attention so I walked over to them. "Hi, I'm just looking for this human."

"I don't know any humans."

Their heart rate spiked on my visor. Ugh, what gives? I just saved them.

"I understand you aren't happy with humans right now, but he could still be in danger. Where is he?"

"I-I don't know any humans." The kazamite became still as a rock. Kazamite's were always fidgety or moving, unless…

I took a deep breath in, and let it out with a sigh at the end. "Please, where is he?"

"He… he's in the minotaur."

I gasped. I dashed out of the building and said into my comms, "he's inside the mech!"

"I know, I see him," Historia said as she backflipped over a tree that the mech threw at her.

Fighting minotaurs was always a pain in the ass. Whether it was dealing with their three foot long arc ax, or their towering height of eight feet mixed with their strength, it was never fun for me. The only good side about minotaurs, was that they looked cool like their mythological counterparts and were designed to help with farmland.

I raced over to Historia but before I could make it, the mech threw a tree at me too. I rolled out of the way effortlessly, but the tree crashed into the front door of the building where the hostages were.

"I got this!" Historia yelled.

I bolted for the building, removing the tree and debris from the door and did a quick scan for any injuries. The kazamites were shaken up, but none were in any real danger. And they wouldn't be with Historia taking point. I sucked my teeth as I glanced over to her fight and watched her get to let loose.

Historia slid, and flipped over everything the mech threw at her. With her dadao swords drawn, she closed the distance on the mech forcing it onto the defensive. It swung its great ax at her and even from this distance, you could hear the low hum of the energy from the blade.

She was a twisting flurry with her scarf and her tassels from her blades trailing behind her. She rolled under the mech and cut its legs causing it to collapse. In a last ditch effort to win, it swung at her one more time with its ax and tried to grab her. She parried the ax and then cut both arms of the mech off. The mech powered down and fell flat on its back. With one hand, she ripped the mech open.

Out of the mech, crawled a man with red curly hair. He sat up and said, "it seems today I am the damsel in distress. Thank you, Historia." She stepped back and replied with a curtsy.

I smiled and walked over to them. "You're an idiot Nic, but I'm glad you're safe."

He made an attempt to move a coil of hair from his vision, but it fell right back into place. "Ah, perhaps I thanked Historia far too quickly and should've credited this rescue to you. Hi, sister." He smiled at me while dusting himself off.

"And a good morrow to you as well." Chevalier joined us with his helmet already off. He gave us a smile and then bowed at Nic. "Master Copernicus, perhaps you can explain to us how you ended up in this scoundrelous affair."

"Unflappable Chevalier, indeed I can. I was simply vacationing and heard that the flowers here in this province *and* the sunrises were something pulled straight from the art gallery of the cosmos!" He threw his arms up with a big smile to add to his uncharming performance. We all had our helmets off at this point, so he could tell we weren't buying it. "Very well," he continued. "I've been trailing a clue for I believe that this group is part of something bigger. I believe the ones here are acting on their own, but there is something greater going on. There are blueprints to a weather like machine which I'm unsure could work, but the device can be turned into a massive power source. Or, an EMP."

"We knew part of this already," said Historia. "The other blueprint is some sort of genetic bomb, but it'd require scientists from that specific field to be operational."

He motioned to a few of the kazamite hostages leaving the building. "Recall the missing human scientist presumed dead for a moment. They had kazamite assistants with the same knowledge and I was able to track them. An all kazamite town not too far from here is where they were abducted. I shall add, I believe that there is an anti-regime organization that has created smaller factions over the months to confuse us. But in truth, there is *only* one cabal, that is gathering kazamites and humans under one banner, to dismantle the regime."

"Master Copernicus, what you're saying has grave implications. You aren't implying but stating kazamites are taking arms against humans. Kazamites have not openly fought humans in about a century, another quarrel at that extent, would be sudden death for them," Chevalier said.

"Wrong, my parents are proof of that. Today is irrefutable proof as well that there is a rising tide."

"But a whole organization unified? The regime won't tolerate this."

"I know, it'd be an egregious offense indeed. This faction I speak of, they call themselves 'Verrucosus' from what I have ascertained, and their leader is a kazamite named Lissax. I have evidence that she and her miscreants are responsible for raiding bases for weapons and attacking human convoys."

"I have already summoned the military; with the wind to their backs, they should be here soon. Historia, would you do me the honor of helping me with the hostages? They are surely troubled and you are better with people than I am."

"Of course!" She skipped away and plucked flowers from around the area and gave them to the hostages. And for those that were children, she knelt down to speak with them. Chevalier nodded at me and bowed to Nic and walked away.

I punched Nic in the arm and asked, "what were you thinking? You shouldn't have done this alone."

"Keep your ogre strength to yourself." He rubbed his arm. "I was thinking I had a lead, and I followed it. And there was no time to ask for help for I pondered a war between kazamites and humans, and the thought gave me fright. The kazamites would fall to humans, with chimeras leading the charge."

"You heard Chevalier, we haven't seen open conflict in years. You better have a **lot** of proof."

"I do. In several urban areas, people have spray painted waves, like the sea. My NUE is set to pick up certain trigger words on dark nets, 'low tide' keeps appearing. And humans living in kazamite areas are now leaving in hoards."

"Nic that's not nearly enough."

"Actually, I can corroborate this," Cricket chirped. "The University of the First Scholar has forums where people can challenge prefects, senators and military action. Would you like to be enrolled?"

"Hush you. Nic, you're talking about an actual revolution. Chimeras aren't death squads."

"I know this to be true, but not everyone thinks like this. I mean for a faction like this think they'd win, is simply foolhardy. They'd fare better if they simply left Kore! The thought of war is just sickening."

"Good to see you in good health and good spirits, Nic." Cricket chirped.

Nic snickered and said, "and you as well, Cricket. Perhaps you can assist me with getting Mandy to invest in colors and more style in her stodgy armor."

"I'll add it to my list. I'll put it right behind 'teaching Nic language from this epoch'. Is it safe to assume that all graduates of The University of the First Scholar speak with such jurassic vigor?"

Nic frowned and said, "as I live and breathe, the mouth on this mouthless robot. Glad there's only one of you, it'd be a nightmare if we had an army of you."

"As opposed to a nightmare of an army of you?" I asked Nic.

"Well if that gives you pause, the next thing I say will restart you. I want your help… I want to aid the kazamites against the regime."

"The *hell*–"

"Withhold your displeasure and discourse for but just a moment. It's no secret how humans treat kazamites and following this group of extremists it made me wonder, did *we* push them this far? I've been giving it thought, and when you look at *our* history books versus *theirs*, it's always muddy. We proclaim ourselves to be divine cosmic beings, we call ourselves gods. Because of what we can do, because of our technology. Because we can live twice as long as kazamites. Humor me, remember when kazamites first met humans?"

"Every conversation is humoring you. But yea, in the mangroves of the province of Kissax, the name of the first kazamite humans met. What's your point?"

"That humans aren't primordial beings and it's not our birthright to rule the cosmos or the planet of Kazar simply because we have traversed the stars. Yes, we are star walkers, but this doesn't mean we should be worshipped and by the **stars**, it does not give us the right to treat them the way we do."

"Yea, humans treat non-humans poorly, but that doesn't mean kazamites can just go around raiding places and kidnapping people."

"But if the regime pushed them this far, is this not the next course of action?"

"Murder? Uh, no. If the kazamites are unhappy, they can speak with a senator, a proconsul or a prefect. Or peacefully assemble."

"But *can* they? To file a complaint through their prefect, a kazamite has to give their full name and provide their address. And why are there only two senators that are kazamites? Why do humans have the right to ordain things out of our race? Kazamites should lead other kazamites."

"What are you saying? That terrorism like today is a knee jerk reaction?"

"Yes. I levy the question: why would the knee jerk if not tampered with? And now, they've been pushed far enough, a **bomb** is their next reaction."

"And what Nic? Because their feelings are hurt, they deserve the right to use a bomb? How can they want peace while literally reverse engineering a bomb? I'm not saying things are perfect, but kazamites in their entire species history are missing warfare, except in the last couple centuries. They have lived quiet and peaceful lives and this group is ruining the balance."

"A true statement. Enlighten me again, where did the blueprints for such a weapon come from? Follow up, what's the common denominator for when warfare first appeared in kazamite history? We aren't their shepherds, they aren't a flock needing to be tended to. This group is fed up with the treatment from the regime. **I'm** fed up. Are you not?"

I hesitated before answering. "You need to get to a medic, let me check your vitals. You're talking about treason, Nic."

He sighed and said, "victory sired by a hundred fathers, while I'm the bastard orphan of the surname 'defeat'. Forget it." His head hung and his shoulder dropped.

"Maybe I was too dismissive." I sighed and rubbed my temples before replying. "What… what did you have in mind? Join this group, reshape their morals and reeducate the regime?"

"No. We should not let the fear and threat of the minority rule over the actions of the majority. We cannot allow fear or this group to win. We should strive for a tolerant world of kazamites and humans, working together. Not a world where humans are gods that are feared."

"And where does this leave us chimeras?"

"I'm unsure. We created chimeras, so many would state we have claim over you. But I'm not sure if having claim over another sentient being is a life I want to live. As for my plan, a small outpost called Camp Frazier houses information of prisoner kazamites across a couple provinces. It'll provide evidence of unfair judicial punishments against kazamites and I have reason to believe that we can even delete the information. That might be aiming too high however. The next location is Camp Puban, it houses a plethora of mechs that have been deprogrammed and will soon be scrapped. I aim to troubleshoot their issues, and repurpose them for kazamites. Imagine, if kazamites had access to mechs as much as humans do."

"And you want to what? Break in? We'd need help and resources. What, we recruit anti-human kazamites that can keep a secret? Our first recruit would end up being a spy."

"I uh… have been conversing with several different kazamites already." I groaned and opened my mouth to reply but he threw his hands in the air. "Hang on, hang on, we could recruit Historia! I'm unsure if she'll join us, but I'm sure she'll at least cover for us. Perhaps we could recruit Ambrotos?"

"**No.**"

"Is it his sarcasm? He delivers sarcastic retorts more than midwives deliver babies. Nevertheless, I don't know a kazamite that is brave enough to do this plan of mine. But I do have a friend, Valen. The only person that speaks to machines better than him that I know, is Cricket. We have fought side by side many times, and we have saved each other's life twice as much."

"And you trust him with something, like this, Nic?"

"Well, he's in all the anti-regime group chats I've been in. That's where I heard of a woman named Vesalia. We have not met in person, but she can be our drawbridge into these extremist groups because I believe she is in one of them. I imagine you, Historia and I venture to Camp Frazier, then our journey takes us to Camp Puban where we could meet with Valen. We find ourselves victorious on both fronts, and then report our successes to Vesalia!"

Cricket interrupted and said, "the welcoming party has arrived."

"Look Nic, I don't think humans are as bad as you're saying, but it's no secret they can treat others better. We'll finish this later but promise me no more extremist talk until then."

"Mandy—"

"Promise me."

With a sigh, he said, "I'll hold my tongue about this. All I ask in return, is that you dare pull back the veil on humans and kazamites."

I nodded and hugged him. The soldiers arrived and immediately checked on the hostages, but treated them more like culprits than victims. There was another human prisoner, they weren't in the same building as the prisoners I had originally checked on. The humans took their time with them, and separated them from the kazamites.

"I-I just want some water." I overheard a kazamite say to a soldier.

The soldier shoved them to the ground and zip tied their hands behind their back and said, "how do I know you're not one of the anti-regime kazamites? You'll get water after you've been processed and catalogued."

It was as if the kazamites weren't saved, they just gained new captors. Thankfully, Historia was keeping the kazamites company. She spoke and played with the kids and a couple reptiles and bugs were nearby so she played with those as well. Chevalier reported immediately to the leader of the humans when they arrived and the rest of the humans set up a perimeter around all of us.

Not a second after Chevalier finished debriefing their commander, he said "everything here is evidence, bag it all. Sergeant Jean, take your scouts and advance to the town. Once there, set up in an overwatch position, and keep an eye out for any runaways. Lieutenant Zu and Lieutenant Byrd, you will be taking your platoons to set up a cordon around the entry and exit points of the town. Lieutenant Pointe, point as always. Chevalier, I want you with Pointe, Subject M01, you'll be with Sergeant Jean's recon squad. Orders given, let's move."

"What about me?" I asked.

The commander turned his attention to me and sucked his teeth. "You are standing dangerously close to a human, *chimera*. You clearly have a problem with touching and hugging humans, so you'll be with me. Alright men, you have your orders. Let's also get a mech to camp here and sappers to build up a temp fence around these hostages so they can't leave. And someone check this destroyed mech."

The hostages all murmured and gasped in frustration and fear. Chevalier was the first to speak up. "Wait," he said. "We're imprisoning the hostages? Hold a moment sir, does that not make us seem like kidnapers ourselves?"

"Sorry, an *adult* was talking. Didn't realize chimeras had the right to vote. Fall in line like the others, knightboy. Or get reassigned to a kazamite interrogation cell." Chevalier's chattered, but he bowed and walked away. It's dishonorable to disagree with a superior, so of course, he threw in the towel.

The scouts began to leave and after Historia got her fill of petting every wild animal nearby she could, she left with them. A few of the child hostages complained, so Chevalier walked over to them and told them stories of battles he won, but threw in a magical twist. I wasn't allowed to get too far from the commander, and wasn't even allowed to see what the medics were saying to Nic. All I could tell was they kept checking his head for any injuries. While the commander typed up his report and took recordings, I was forced to stand guard over him.

I groaned, how archaic? Imagine being a commander and having to use a computer, gross. All chimeras had wrist mounted NUEs, and so did special units and individuals. I guess he wasn't part of the cool kids.

"No NUE?" I asked him.

"NUE?"

"Neraform uploading equipment. The 'n' can be nanite too. It's the size of a rubber band, but can expand with a holographic screen and keyboard, for typing."

"Must be for special units."

"Odd, Nic has one." I turned my back with a smirk. I could *feel* his glare.

About a half hour later, the fence was built. There weren't any wires, but you could hear the low hum of electricity running from beam to beam. The corralled hostages were told they could leave at their own discretion, but of course none dared to leave. The one human was upset and complained that they were being roped in with kazamites, but they were innocent. The soldiers ignored their complaints just like they ignored the kazamites. They even had Nic rounded up and he complained and tried to use his rank to get out, but it was no use.

"Staggered columns, let's move!" The commander barked marching orders, and we began our walk towards the nearby town.

Halfway through our march, the scouts called up on the radio with their intel on the town. The town was just farmers with two mechs. Most kazamites living in small towns like this one, were farmers. Focused on crops or fishing, and they lived out here to avoid trouble. This town was one of the lucky ones, it took an act of primarchs to get a mech as a kazamite.

"Sir, what exactly is the plan? We saved the hostages and got the bad guys."

His face soured, as if disgusted with the idea of even humoring me.

"Kazamites can't be trusted," he said. "So we are conducting a thorough investigation. You will go into houses deemed too dangerous for me to enter, but may have value."

"And if we find nothing?" I asked, but already knew his answer.

"Then they're *lying*. An extremist anti-regime group with a bomb has *chameleon* webbed hands all over it."

"I don't think I like you saying that word, sir. No, no I know I don't like you saying that word."

"What you have a soft spot for these plum bloods?" He smirked at his own xenophobism.

"I just think xenoist words aren't necessary. But I could be mistaken and you could be putting on a show. Isn't that what primates were known for back on Earth? Their circus acts?"

He stopped walking and looked at me. "***Excuse*** me?"

"I said: I don't think that they are a threat sir, they're just farmers."

"You have an AI, yes? AI, replay the last 30 seconds."

Without skipping a beat, Cricket replied, "my storage is full, commander. Perhaps I can interest you in sounds of your home world that can help ease your mind and makeup for this discrepancy." He played sounds of a jungle with what I assume was the sound of primates in the background. I snickered as the commander began walking again and picked up his pace. Cricket hands down, is the freaking best.

Not too much later after Cricket's score, we arrived at the town. Everyone staged into their positions with the scouts pulling overwatch with their snipers. The town, if you could even call it that, was entirely kazamite. As the commander and I walked to the center of the town, all the kazamites cowered and hardly even looked at us. Due to humans being seen as gods, many kazamites feared upsetting them. Of course some were seen as minor gods, but most kazamites feared the regime, especially when they could walk into your home with guns.

The commander had a smile on his face, as if enjoying them lowering their gaze. He stuck his chest out and said, "a terrorist cell was found only a few miles from you all so, you are all being detained. We will conduct an investigation and we expect orderly cooperation. Bring me your town mayor and their deputy."

Almost all the kazamites were frozen with fear, and who could blame them? At first, nobody moved, but slowly one by one they all continued with their lives. I couldn't help but smile. Over the last decade or so, kazamites have been distancing themselves from humans; they moved out of city limits to avoid humans at all cost. It was their way of fighting back. Some fought back in other ways, but it always ended the same for brave kazamites.

The commander sighed and said, "the folly of man is his lack of follow through." He drew his pistol and shot a random kazamite with their child.

There was immediate pandemonium. Half of the citizens screamed and dropped to the ground, and the other half made a break for it. All the runners were tackled or shot in the leg and the now dead kazamite was being shaken by their son. Within half a minute, the air was filled with gunpowder, sniffling and whimpering filled the air.

"How sad you all have become so… disagreeable in public." The commander shook his head at the kazamites. A couple of the kazamites balled their fists and took a couple steps towards the soldiers. He scoffed and said, "please, you are not an aggressive race. You are a race with one more orphan however, because of your insubordination. I don't enjoy splitting up families like this, I have a child of my own and would move the heavens for them. Legacy is a beautiful thing in my opinion. So for me the scariest thing in the world would be losing them. Grab the child, subject M04."

"Sir?" I snapped my head.

"Go on. I have heard how much you love your friends and you wouldn't jeopardize them and that human boyfriend of yours by disobeying a direct order. Would it be easier if I used your fake name? Grab the child, *Amanda*." I didn't move. "What are you waiting for?"

"Amanda isn't my name, I assumed you weren't talking to me," I said.

"Ugh, I'm talking to **you**."

"Yes sir." My head began to throb from how hard I was clenching my jaw. I walked over to the crying child and grabbed them by the arm and brought them over to him.

"No more blood need be spilled as long as you all answer one simple question: where are the blueprints, boy?"

Nobody moved or answered.

"Very well, kill the boy."

I didn't move.

"**Kill** the urchin, or else your AI will be deactivated and Chevalier will be sent to a reloyalty camp again."

I still didn't budge, but one of my eyes twitched. There was nothing I hated more than reloyalty camps.

Cricket chirped, "Mandy, this isn't the fight we want. They'll just kill the boy anyway and then arrest you, Historia and Chevalier."

While looking at the commander, I picked the boy up by his throat, and threw him through a window of a building. The sound of the shattering glass made more kazamites quiver.

"I expect faster results next time. Now, is the leader of these people going to make an appearance, or do I need to kill more people?"

"Please, no more." A frail old kazamite walked over to us; his faded fins on his arms aged him somewhere in his 50's so he didn't have much time left.

"I am the commander of these forces and we are here on behalf of the regime. You will address me as sir. Who am I speaking with?"

"Greezor."

"**Sir**," the commander corrected.

"Greezor, sir."

"Yes, you certainly are a geezer. You're probably the oldest kazamite I have ever seen. We are looking for blueprints on a few weapons and intel."

The kazamite looked confused, but to be sure I had to have evidence. I put his heart rate on my HUD so I could tell if he was lying, and he wasn't.

"Fix your face Greezor, because it feels you're about to say something I don't want to hear. Think hard because someone here has answers. I need something."

"I am sorry, sir, but I have lived here all my life and I don't know what you're talking about. We are just farmers. We keep to ourselves so we haven't heard anything," said the old kazamite.

"I refuse to believe you're this stupid. I didn't ask for your backstory, I demanded answers and you're about to hear the sound of you losing your town and gunfire if I don't get some. Your choice."

The kazamite raised his hands in submission and lowered his head and replied, "I'm telling the truth. Please, we are only farmers, we don't even hunt. I don't know what you're talking about."

The commander backhanded the old man. The villagers gasped as the old man hit the ground with a loud thud.

"Disgusting lying urchin. How pathetic you are, groveling. You clearly aren't taking me seriously." The commander aimed his gun at the man and said, "your species is a mistake and don't deserve this world.

And yet, I'm expected to treat you like my equal. I think I'll be doing this parsec a favor by ending you and your hillbilly village."

"Let me handle him, sir," I blurted out.

He raised an eyebrow and said, "I don't know what you're trying to pull…"

"Intel. My AI paired with my NUE can tell me if he is lying. If he is, I can advance to where the intel is being stored and ping my location along the way or come back and clear houses."

"Very well." He holstered his gun.

"**Up.**" I grabbed the old man and threw him through the same window I threw the child from earlier. "This won't take long, sir."

I walked over to the window and hopped through drawing my sidearm. The man had cuts and bruises and was lying on the floor begging for help. Once he saw my gun, he tried to run away, but I stopped him before he could. I pinned him to the ground with my foot and aimed my gun at him.

He trembled under my foot and pleaded, "please… mercy…"

"Why have a settlement out here?"

"We have seen life under human rule; it's safer to struggle out here than in there. Please, we really don't know anything. How would you feel if you or your loved ones were being accused of a crime you didn't even know was a thing? Wasn't killing the boy enough?"

I grinned. "I've actually never killed anyone before. It's safe to come out now."

The boy I threw through the window earlier was hiding in the corner. He had scratches too, but he was fine.

"I hate how right Nic is. Cricket scanned this building earlier so I knew it had a cellar when I threw you both through it. Go to the cellar and get to safety, there is a tunnel that leads to I think a river. You guys have 30 seconds or less." I put my weapon up and walked away.

"Who are you?" the man asked.

"Mandy, good luck."

I jumped out the window I entered through and walked back over to the commander. He looked unhappy.

"You were in there for a while."

I had to stall him. "Interrogations aren't supposed to be fast, if done correctly. But he was telling the truth, he really was clueless and it only slowed things down."

"So why didn't you grab him? I think us humans have better interrogation tactics."

"My AI has access to forgotten interrogation tactics which we can and did use. We also studied kazamite anatomy so I was able to use that to my advantage."

"You did all of that in the time you were in there?" He crossed his arms and raised an eyebrow. I nodded. "Move sea witch. You're a liar, and a bad one to bat. Two one me." Two soldiers jogged over to us.

"Why would I lie? What you think they're just hiding in there under a couch?"

"I think you're stalling. You might think you're clever, but humans are the apex on this world. You two, shoot anything that moves in there."

Before the soldiers could move towards the building, I snatched a thermal grade off of one of them. I primed it, and then tossed it into the building. Historia, I hope you're not watching. The grenade made its usual sizzling sound and got louder, and then went silent.

The commander and the soldiers both were too stunned to speak. But after a few seconds, the commander found his words.

"What did you do? We could've still squeezed intel out of that geezer!"

Now was my chance. "I never heard of humans interrogating dead men. This way, the rest of the town is more submissive. My AI suggested it as part of those forgotten interrogation techniques."

"Hmmm… surprisingly good thinking. You will stay close to me, the rest of you, tear up this shithole excuse of a home. Today, we teach kazamites that going against the regime only ends one way. Today we teach the definition of powerlessness and loyalty. Any prisoners we bring, will be sent to a reloyalty camp."

And he delivered. It wasn't five minutes before there was gunfire. I stood powerlessly for half an hour as the soldiers rounded up the kazamites with some soldiers using minimal force, and others using too much force. But the kazamites weren't taking it lying down, and after the third person was shot, they fought back. They used anything they could: shovels, spades, pitchforks, and more. They fought back the soldiers with farming tools and they killed and maimed several, but the soldiers still had guns.

"Weapons free!" Barked the commander.

The soldiers unloaded on the kazamites with weapons, and the kazamites that were surrendering. Some still fought to the end, some surrendered and got on their knees but others made a run for it. But, it didn't matter to the humans, they shot at all of them the same.

"Something wrong, *chimera?*" The commander stood proudly looking at the carnage.

"Mandy."

"I don't follow."

"My name is Mandy. Not chimera, not girl, not Amanda, not another slur, it's **Mandy**."

"Your name is whatever the regime tells you."

"No, it's Mandy and you're a bully that gets off on cartoonish murder and genocide."

He scoffed and said, "murder? No, this is culling at its most efficient. We did it on Earth to all sorts of animals, deer, cows, sheep, what have you. I guess we could treat them like housepets and neuter them."

29

"It seemed like neutering humans would've honestly been the right answer for Earth, from what I hear."

"You are a rude and ignorant annoyance. We came to the planet Kazar and brought technology to these literal water-like creatures. Kazamites making it this far only proves that luck is real because I have never seen a more incompetent set of creatures in my life. They have weaponized incompetence and perfected it so well, they made it contagious and it's spread to humans. **Clearly**, it has spread to chimeras as well. They suckle the regime's resources, manpower, aid, time, patience and more and have for centuries. We **run** their country, the least they can do is get in line."

"You *took* their country, and their world. Kazamites were fine before you all came and set up governments. Not all humans, but humans like you are why there is tension especially when kazamites haven't done anything."

"Oh please, grow up. We have led them to greater heights and what do they pay our generosity with? Kyren's disease."

"That's not their fault, they can't control that. You're literally an alien to this planet, to this parsec, and this solar system. Of course you'd catch something, but that still isn't their fault and you hate them for what?"

"Because my species is still in space and this planet is big enough for us to colonize it, but we swore to not leave this country to avoid hurting the ecosystem. Chimeras like you and other kazamites, are unappreciative of all the help we have given, so there has been a change in the last few decades. One where we push order, one where we're given what we're owed: obedience."

A bleeding kazamite raised its hands to surrender. They were met with a kick to their chest by a soldier. The kazamite crawled away but the soldier kicked him onto his back and hit him with the buttstock of his rifle.

"This is what you envision?" I asked.

"What the *regime* envisions. Millions of humans have died just to get us on this world, and no kazamite is worth a single human life. Once kazamites get in line like the good old days, the regime will pull back. I'll show you and them an example, tell the kazamites to surrender, and we'll leave. And destroy their makeshift mech."

"I don't believe you."

"Doesn't seem you have a choice."

I sighed and walked over to a mech dressed in rust, if you could even call it a mech, and looked it over. Kazamites needed to request mechs, and if denied they sometimes would make one as best as they could. I stuck my arm in its chest, and ripped out its core. The mech sparked a few times, then fell to the ground and shattered into pieces. I dropped the core onto the ground and crushed it, as I walked back over to the commander.

Cricket pinged, "incoming."

I sidestepped out of the way as a pitchfork was thrown at me by a kazamite. He balled his fist and yelled, "death to the outworlders!"

I took a step towards him when I heard a scream and a gunshot. The pitchfork landed in the commander's stomach and he drew his sidearm and shot the kazamite in return. Everyone stopped what they were doing as we all watched the commander as he fell to the ground.

"KILL THE OUTWORLDERS!"

The kazamites rushed the soldiers again, but this time with more aggression than before. The kazamites overpowered several of the soldiers, and took their guns causing a massive firefight between both sides.

"The commander is still alive, Mandy," Cricket chirped. I ignored him as I took cover. "If he dies, the regime will come back with more men."

I groaned and rushed over to the commander, he was in bad shape. I scanned him to see the extent of the damages and he was lucky, he could make a full recovery. Or...

31

"Help me halfbreed." He coughed out blood as the words left his mouth. "Fucking kill them, kill them all!"

I broke a piece of the pitchfork off and stabilized the lodged portion as best as I could, but not without causing him as much discomfort as I possibly could.

While I tended to the commander, several kazamites tried to stop me, which thankfully Chevalier came to my rescue. He tanked their hits and shoved them and broke their weapons. He ran interference for me so I could focus and it helped me, but also helped the soldiers. Soon, the soldiers regained control and readied themselves to kill everyone. This, was Chevalier's limit.

"**Enough**." He brandished his cyan greatsword and raised it into the air. It was an arc weapon, so it spewed energy everywhere. Everyone stopped to stare in awe at the weapon.

"We have to leave soon," I said to Chevalier.

He nodded to me then turned his attention to everyone else. "My claymore can cut through steel as if it were butter, do not be foolish. Enough blood has flown today from both sides, we need not see anymore. Please do not continue this course of insanity, concede." Some of the kazamites dropped their weapons and surrendered, but not all of them.

"An arc sword doesn't scare me," a kazamite said as he walked towards us.

"I have an arc mace and a dagger as well. Unless kazamite flesh and bone are suddenly tougher than chimera's, then step back. **Yield**."

"I'm the one with a gun, I like my odds. I could kill the girl chimera before you got to me."

I snickered and said, "have you ever seen a chimera bleed? I like my odds that today you won't."

He sighed and dropped his weapon. Chevalier mumbled "thank you" to me as the soldiers barked orders. He hated using his weapon against humans and kazamites, but not because he was bad at it, but because he was good at it. Most of us had weapons and skills we specialized in, like Historia with her swords and martial arts, Sibil knowing humans weapons and tactics, and me with a saber. Chevalier was good with medieval weapons and he loved all their weapons from that era, but not many people today wore armor that could withstand his arc weapons. So, he refrained from using it in a lethal way.

While the soldiers ordered the kazamites around, medics came over to move the commander around and stabilize him. The medics rushed the commander away back to our last site, leaving behind his second in command.

"You two," the soldier named Lieutenant Pointe walked over to Chevalier and I. "I don't understand, what happened? Why did you hesitate to strike them down when you had your sword? Aren't you supposed to be on our side?"

"There was no need to escalate the situation, sir," Chevalier said.

"A knight is supposed to follow orders and is the sword of their king or leader, that's us. Go help round up the kazamites." Chevalier nodded, excused himself and walked away. "And you, thank you for saving our commander. Humans and chimeras are the only thing standing between kazamites and chaos, I'm glad we're on the same boat."

"Albeit a Titanic."

He frowned and said, "I don't know what is up with you chimeras, you guys should be more like Sibil. Chimeras are enforcers, you guys are supposed to help us reclaim some form of order or else the country and maybe planet will just unravel. Think hard how much humans have helped, and how we literally made you."

A soldier ran over to us and said, "sir, I have a report. We got orders to treat everyone in the town like a suspect and to strip every building. An intelligence company is coming here too."

"There's literally kids here," I argued.

"No, they're fighting age soldiers," he said. "And before you say just scan everywhere, it's not my call. If rounding them up and displacing them helps humanity, then it's simple math."

I sucked my teeth and walked away. I walked over to join Chevalier who was standing by a group of kids being separated from their parents. One of them dropped a toy and he bent down to pick it up and hand it to them.

The kid took the toy and said, "I'm tired of starting over."

"You shouldn't keep having to." Chevalier balled his fist and walked away.

I sighed. "Cricket…"

"I have already sent a message to Nic."

"Let's see what Nic has in mind, guess we'll see him tonight."

Chapter 2

HUMANE TREATMENT

By the time I joined up with Nic, both of Kazar's moons, Pala and Ven, were high above us and there was enough cloud coverage to mask our movements. The moons gave off a pretty color that contrasted perfectly. Normally, the illum from the moons would make us stand out, but thanks to the overcast, we were cooking with gas.

After terrorizing that small town earlier, I was punished for my 'insubordination' or something. I was forced to write a report about the events which of course I lied about, and then was put on clean up duty. Humans aren't slick, I know I was being punished for my personality. One of the soldiers also overheard Nic and I talking about getting lunch together later, cause we can't have that. Chimera and humans hanging out or having any resemblance of a relationship was taboo, especially a soldier and a chimera. The only reason Nic and I got away with it, was because we have been close for decades. People who knew who we were normally didn't press us, but our relationship has always drawn attention from Nic's higher ups and peers.

But, Nic said Valen was different. Valen had volunteered not only to help us, but run interference for Nic so that people wouldn't question him not being around. It also helped that Valen so happened to be in this province already, but many visited this province at least once in their life because it was known for its impressive mechs and tech. Which also helped our alibi since Camp Puban was in this province too.

"Exciting isn't it?" Nic asked as he threw his navy blue hoodie on.

"Cricket wasn't happy with me leaving my aegis behind; thought I was ditching him."

"Ahh, is that why you are wearing glasses? They record?"

"Mhm. He wants to analyze it once I'm back."

"Perhaps next time, he can help you fit all of your hair better under your hat and hood." He snickered while I rolled my eyes. "At least you were able to cover your skin fully."

Valen saw us first and flagged us down with a wave. He greeted me with a smile, and reached out to shake my hand; I couldn't remember the last time I met a human that wanted to shake my hand.

"You must be the infamous Mandy, hi. I've heard a lot about you." His teeth were glistening white and was a stark contrast to his soft maroon skin.

"I must be." I shook his hand and raised an eyebrow. "Hulpin tight grip." I returned the favor and tightened my grip.

"I didn't mean anything by it, just heard you guys could rip a mech in half with ease and I wanted to see how my grip fared. My bad."

"Stronger than any human I've ever met, that's for sure. Am I your first chimera?"

"No, I've sparred with Ambrotos before and from him I've heard about Sibil; feels like I practically know Sibil honestly. But you can't imagine how happy I am that you aren't like either of them," he chucked.

"You and me both."

Nic smiled and said, "and I am gracious and mirthful to have allies that I can burden with a secret such as this. I couldn't fathom not having the both of you in my life." They dapped each other up.

"Dope, now let's talk shop. I cometh with gifts." Valen said in a mocking voice, imitating Nic's… unique speech. I thought it was funny, but Nic didn't take too kindly to it. "Plug this into your NUEs and it'll mask where we are, trick cameras, sensors and scanners. Our NUEs and common sense should get us through most areas and for the few places that it won't work, I have some more party gifts." He patted his bag.

"A fanny pack?" Nic asked with a smile.

"You won't be laughing when they come in handy. The cameras are on a closed circuit so we'll have to get inside the control room. But from there, we can get to where the mechs are being housed. I scouted the area already which is why I pinged this spot. We can enter through that drainage over there. The sewer has several tunnels but one of the routes will take us near the server room. This shouldn't take longer than an hour and some change so if you guys are down to clown, let's go."

Nic and I smiled at each other and then nodded. Nic and I seldom got to do missions together so an off the book one was pretty exciting. The last mission we did together was an amphibious operation off the coast earlier this year. That's when I learned humans were terrible divers; they can't even hold their breath and swim for five minutes without issues. Thankfully this mission didn't require swimming, I'd have to drag Nic's ass.

We expected the sewer to smell like... well, sewer, but it didn't. They must have used mechs to clean the area and they only housed a skeleton screw here so there was hardly any actual sewage. Valen having a blueprint of the tunnels and compound also helped us avoid getting lost, so we made it inside the compound in a little over ten minutes. Our path took us right to a vent shaft in the bathroom and the bathroom was next to the control room.

"There's a control panel outside the control room, hang on," Valen said as we climbed out the vents.

He went into his bag and pulled out a few metallic balls and placed them on the ground. They grew legs and resembled spiders, and then they turned invisible as they left the bathroom. You couldn't see them but if you really listened for them, you could hear them. I didn't know where they went, but I could hear the panel by the door being messed with and then a click as the door opened.

"The hell?" The voice came from inside of the room. "Dave that you? What you took a shit after you went for a smoke?"

It was a guard manning the room, which means that there is another guard somewhere wandering around. He stepped out into the hall and looked around, but of course didn't see anything. We could easily take him out, but if we did, the other guard would know. The guard kept looking around but after not seeing anything, he turned his back and went back inside the room. Before he could close the door, Valen went back into his bag and pulled out a blowgun and blew a dart into the guard's neck.

"Catch him," Valen said.

I dashed down the hall and caught the guard before he hit the ground. I put him in a chair and crossed his legs and put his hat over his face to make it seem like he fell asleep on the job. Valen collected his spider mechs as he joined me, and Nic stayed by the door and kept watch.

Valen jumped on the computer and said, "this shouldn't take long."

And it didn't. It couldn't have been much longer than five minutes of him working before he told us he was done. He pulled files from their computer, scanned a badge so we had admin access to the compound, and fixed the cameras. We left the control room and made our way to where the mechs were being housed and it was a walk in the park now with the admin badge. Valen swiped his badge to the vault's door and inside we saw dozens no… well over a hundred mechs.

"Elves? Why were these deprogrammed and not retasked?" I asked Valen.

"Don't know," he said. "They're used a lot on the moons to help with daily tasks. We use them in stuff like training and them being seven feet tall helps keep us on our toes for sparring. I'm gonna see if I can get them on, be right back."

Nic shook his head and said, "vexing. Standing before us are enough mechs to help a small town, or aid a city and yet here they stand, idly. I understand why kazamites can't have sentries and minotaurs due to their combat rating and being armed. But elves? The logic escapes my grasp."

"Ditto," I said. "These could help the workload of so many people."

"And yet senators and their lap dogs, prefects, sit on this goldmine. We could help and save so many families. Think about what good this could do near the Afuera; it would give citizens peace of mind."

"Dreskin is a bit far and I'm not sure if that senator would go for it… but I think there's a prefect that supports kazamites in that province. Maybe…" I didn't finish the thought before Valen called out to us.

"Check this out. This hanger is full of two types of mechs. Most are elves, 160 to be exact. I wish I could take the credit, but I didn't do much. They were already programmed to help with: mining, agriculture, sanitation, and even an ability to work on oil rigs. Like underwater welding specifically." Valen showed me on his NUE as he spoke.

"They weren't deprogrammed, they were *already* programmed. The regime just never planned on giving them away," I said.

"At least not without a price tag, it's called leverage. These mechs aren't geographically locked either like how others are normally, so I can send them to any province or prefecture in a province. Any suggestions? I could send them to places that are pro-kazamite or hurting for workers. It'd take maybe weeks to get to all those places, but it's doable and under the radar."

Nic blurted out, "Demeter's Landing, Newlana, Hylo, and Pis Aller. That puts 40 mechs to each place."

"Done. Not sure I would have suggested Newlana, but I guess it could use a facelift."

"You said most were elves, what are the others?" I asked.

"Husk, TALOS husk to be exact, but there's only 10." He saw the confusion on my face. "Alright so, you can remote in or what we normally say, 'pilot', these. It'd have to be an AI designed to do a specific thing, for example you have an agriculture key AI and let it pilot the TALOS."

"I thought AI could pilot mechs already."

"Some models sure, but you're more likely to find the Milky Way with a telescope than that. Besides those few, mechs are designed to have an immediate killswitch when piloted in. We still get nervous at the idea of a mech uprising; can't have any dirty cyborg leading self aware mechs. So, they're made on different systems and with failsafes, it'd be like if I tried to connect my NUE to a 20th century game system; not only would it not work, it'd probably get fried."

"You figured all of that out just now?" I asked.

"I specialize in all things tech. It comes in handy at cookouts."

"Cookouts?"

"Firefights. Anyway, the takeaway is that mechs normally can't 'talk' with AI, it has to be specifically designed for that. These 10 were designed to 'talk' though and because the last tech guy working on them didn't clear their cache correctly, a good AI programmer could make an AI that can fish all the deleted files, restore them, and create a program that makes all the other husks follow suit."

"Or just a very advanced AI, right?"

He snickered. "Yea, good luck finding one. But yea, theoretically an advanced AI could pilot I guess two husks at once but that'd be kinda like how starfish or worms grow newer versions of themselves. An AI like that would have to be pretty damn smart."

"What's a starfish?" I asked.

"Dang my bad, it's an old creature on Earth. I guess some idioms and phrases aren't translated by Babylon so I'm sure this is all Greek to you huh?" He chuckled.

"What's Greek?"

"Killing me Smalls. Nevermind, you wouldn't get that one either. Maybe I've been hanging around Ambrotos' retpop ass too much. It means retro pop before you ask."

"I have an AI that I think can help. Cricket should be able to create a program himself and pilot them if I just ping them."

"You having an AI is daffy by itself, but I'm not sure he could do all of that. That'd imply he can pilot any mech or device, cover his tracks and learn from his mistakes and probably leave false tracks all within two tries."

"Cricket's the best. "

"Fucking wild. Alright, I can open up the door and disable the alarm and censors and send the mechs on their way. Your AI probably can pick up the influx of activated mechs then I'm guessing; just tell him to mask these mechs and their movements. He could probably also help you house the husks as well. As for getting out of here, we probably should exit the way we came."

"And what can we do to aid you?" Nic asked.

"It'd help if you both could help with the bypassing system. I'd like to keep it simple, slip a trojan in under a routine systems check. Trick the system into updating without raising any alarms but it'd take longer. Do either of you have experience working on thothian servers and network systems?"

"I don't even know if that's a word," I said.

"Perhaps something a bit more... unadorned," Nic said.

Valen chuckled and said, "both of you need to hit the emergency blast door release buttons at the same time while I focus on the control panel. Once I give you guys the thumbs up, hit it."

We nodded and went to our buttons. We didn't want to stand around and be useless, but I guess 'button pusher' is my job for the evening. A couple minutes later, Valen gave us the thumbs up. Nic and I hit our buttons at the same time and stepped back as the doors crept open. Nic wasn't kidding about Valen being some type of tech wizard because no alarms went off. The only issue was how loud the blast doors were, who knows the last time they were opened, oiled or inspected.

Valen joined us grinning from ear to ear and said, "I'm pumped. I've never seen mechs come to life and jump into action like this. Mandy, we'll have to talk about Cricket some other time. I've never heard of an AI as advanced as you said."

"I'm sure he'll love to meet a fan," I said.

"He has a personality too? Like a non-linear one? I gotta hear what else he's capable of, he sounds amazing. He could pilot a husk and join you guys for missions, you know."

"Cricket a working man?" Nic laughed. "Imagine him doing more than having sarcastic remarks and being Mandy's conscience."

We were all caught up on Cricket, that we almost didn't notice when the blast doors crawled to a stop and dropped.

"Watch out!" Valen instinctively threw his right arm up to stop the blast doors… and actually did. The blast doors began to rise again and fully opened without any issues. Valen then played with his NUE and the mechs began their march to their new homes.

How did he do that? He could only do it, if he was… "you're a syn…" The words trailed out of my mouth.

Nic punched my arm and said, "a morally erroneous statement from you, Mandy. He is **human**."

"Nah, she's right. Part of in-processing when you become a bion is learning to cope with depression and what you are now. They teach us about the Theseus' Paradox and how we'll all face it eventually. They make us face the reality of how many original pieces of me can get traded out before I'm no longer the original me? Ya know, human? I'm not sensitive about it and it's not a secret, you can ask me whatever," Valen said.

"I'm sorry, I didn't realize 'syn' was a slur. The news calls you guys syns and cyborgs, I thought those were normal words."

Valen shrugged and said, "syn is just short for synthetic and apparently back on Earth, it was considered cool to be a cyborg. I'm not sure what happened between Earth and here, but here, we're just bions."

"How much of you is synthetic?" I asked.

Nic shot me a look. "He owes us no such tale, Mandy." I could hear him speaking through his teeth.

"Nah, it's cool. I got hit with some fungus on Ven a lifetime ago. Didn't really have the meds to help, so I got infected and lost my right arm. Had to cut it off myself because the fungus was spreading. I put a tourniquet on and passed out due to the pain. By the time I woke up, I was in the hospital going in and out of consciousness. The fungus had spread to my liver, right kidney, right lung and gallbladder, so all were taken out."

"How the hell are you alive then?"

"Some redhead with a silly name. Thanks to your brother, I was given a second chance and was able to get synthetic organs. I mean physical therapy was a mess and not sure if you know, but the fungus also messes with your head. Most know it makes you hallucinate and sweat so you dehydrate yourself faster, but that's basic knowledge when you go to Ven. The scary part is that the fungus releases chemicals in your brain to delay your motor skills. The actual scary part is that we were wrong about that. The fungus doesn't simply break the connection from mind to body, it *erases* memory…"

Nic noticed Valen trail off and jumped in. "I was just assigned to a down aircraft rescue team, when he and I met, Mandy. This DART unit was unique, our team had specialties like: engineers and sappers, avionic specialist and mechanics, infantry, air traffic controllers and joint terminal attack controllers."

"And you were the traffic controller I'm guessing?"

"Indeed! On our way back to base, I picked something up on the net. We trailed the source and cleared parts of the jungle and found him. The soil was trying to decompose him, but we got to him in time and brought him back with us!"

"Is that why you extended your tour on Ven? To help him?" Nic nodded at my question. "Valen, you don't have to continue. I'm sorry you went through that."

"Nah, it's cool," said Valen. "How else can you learn about something if someone doesn't explain it? Clearly the media hasn't done bions or chimeras any favors. Anyway, I had to relearn certain things, manually. Like how to talk, swallowing after chewing and not before, what a 3D printer was and how half my organs were printed. I had to even learn what Earth was. With all that, my army tenure was going to be over but they gave me another option. The first woman praetorian told me that if they replaced my other lung, I'd get a pass to try out for a special unit and get to stay in the military. She told me how things were hard right now, but the military and regime would hate to lose someone like me. So I had them take the other lung and print me a new one. But I didn't realize that the special unit was a unit of bions. My training ended at Ven and I was sent to the other moon, Pala not long after. Been there pretty much since but it's not so bad, we got animals there from Earth."

"Wait, a unit of bions? I've never heard of a unit like that on Pala. Are they the ones who taught you to be good with machines and mechs?" I asked.

"Yea, that's kinda the point; it's a covert unit. Pala house's two units: The Hellfighters, and the Vanguard, I've been with the Hellfighters. Ven on the other hand has the First Regiment, which is the training unit, and the Last Regiment, the stationed unit. Sentinels is another unit that's combat rated there, but they stay mostly in space."

Nic cleared his throat and said, "while I do enjoy informative discussion between friends, I believe we should depart. The longer we dawdle, the higher chance of our capture."

Nic was right, so we left and made it back to where we all met up in no time. I'm not sure where they're getting their security from, but the guy on shift should be fired. We pretty much walked back the way we came and put minimal effort to escape. We didn't speak much on our way out, but all I thought about was how Nic never brought up Valen before, so it's strange they were this close. Am I shitty for not knowing all of my brother's friends? I brushed the thought off and figured I was looking too deep into it.

"It was nice meeting you," said Valen. "Hopefully we meet again cause I have some friends you might rock with."

"Bions?" I asked.

He chuckled. "Not all of my friends are humans or bions, I got a kazamite friend or two. Anyway, their names are Hela and Eyas. Hela is the girl I mentioned earlier, the one who recruited me. She's pretty unorthodox, but her strategic mind is a game changer. She's strong willed like you and Nic. And Eyas, probably the best pilot we have. He used to be a praetorian but after becoming a bion, he gave up his position to go back to the skies. They don't make them like him anymore."

"That'd be cool. I'm not sure if I'm ever in Ven or Pala's neighborhood, but if you're ever back on Kazar, swing by. We aren't all like Ambrotos," I said.

"Cool, and bring Cricket next time. Nic and don't always get to hang out, but when we do we have tons of downtime. So I'm surprised he's never brought up Cricket, but **everyone** knows about you. They have it set up where we aren't allowed to hang out with chimeras because of you guys."

"I'm touched. Living in people's heads rent free is my favorite pastime, at least that's what Historia and Cricket say. Actually, I think you'd like Historia. She always has questions about stuff and you guys would probably hit it off. If you give me your number I can—"

"We sully the night by speaking and not savoring this visage," Nic interrupted. "Look! The moons, the stars, the ring of Kazar. Let us observe and enjoy the night sky." Nic said, smiling towards the sky.

"Before we do, I'm curious about something, Valen. What was the most confusing thing when trying to relearn stuff?" I asked.

"Vehicles."

"Oh, had that one in the chamber huh?"

"Yea, been asked before and I didn't have an answer. Earth had terms for vehicles that we use differently but I was forced to learn them even though they don't exist anymore. Like shuttles are cars, we have arc jets, and they had regular jets. Monorails here are designed to travel across the continent, and I think a monorail back then was a train. But trains here are only for intra-city travel. And we have dockers for shuttles and they didn't. It was just a lot, earthlings were just weird."

We watched the moons glide across the night sky with Kazar's ring in the backdrop. We enjoyed the silence for well over half an hour before we decided to say our goodbyes. Valen invited me to train with him whenever our schedules would match, and then he gave Nic a hug and left.

After Valen left, Nic and I fished our bike out of some bushes. We had stashed our bike so that any roaming patrol or bandits wouldn't find it. I hopped on the back and smiled at Nic.

"I'm driving again?" He complained.

"Last time I drove us somewhere, you complained about my speeding. So, enjoy being tonight's chauffeur."

He groaned and then hopped onto the mako. Once he punched the coordinates in, he sped off. So much for *my* speeding. If we cut through the trees, Camp Frazier was a straight shot, but Nic would crash into a tree within seconds. So, we went south and then west. Our route took us through the open country side, which was a treat for me. Chimeras hardly ever got freedom to travel, so this was a treat.

I sat back and smelled the fresh air. The flowers in this area smelled like clean linen, and yet the cold from the air gave the aromas a nice crispness. I smiled and watched as the varns darted through the grass trying to avoid us out of fear we were predators; and then burrowing when we got too close.

"You spooked them!" I said to Nic as we flew past the rabbit sized creatures.

"Well they're going to be very spooked in a moment!"

Thanks to Nic's speeding, we woke up a herd of thifrums and spooked them. They moo'd awake and then stampeded alongside us. Their thundering hooves echoed probably from here to the moons and back again with only us to listen.

I loved night riding.

Few things in the world were better than going for a night drive. And only a few things could make moments like this even better, and I saw it. I smiled as a lightning bug landed on my arm. Humans brought these guys to the brink of extinction by accident, a human trait. But somehow, they survived and now they thrive.

The bug flew off of my arm and floated away. Nic turned and said, "I have an idea. Maybe once this is over, the three of us can go to the black beaches of Kadura."

"You, Valen and I?"

"No, you, Historia and I."

"I almost forgot to tell her we're on our way. I could use a break, it'd be nice."

"You'll come then? And... Historia?"

"Nic, no flirting with Historia. You're not her type."

"Egad Mandy! What do you think I am?"

"A nuisance."

"My schedule is full of more important things than courting your friends, Mandy. I'm appalled by your accusations."

"Save it, prince charming. Historia already told me how you've asked her for animal book recommendations. And how you've been talking about animals from Earth."

"I just enjoy zoology. Is it a crime to enjoy learning about my people's homeworld?"

"Save it." I shook my head.

"You defy me from seeing her and for what?"

"I'm trying to get you right, before you go left. One of you is too good for the other, don't make me answer which is which. Are there no theater kids that would be into you? That seems more in your league. Don't human women love theater stuff anyway? You could be their project?"

He scoffed then said, "irrelevant. What is relevant is that I may ask her to the military ball. As friends of course."

I snorted. "You're not her type, she has a type, a *specific* type. But, you can try if you want, I won't stop you. But when you enter stage right and then exit stage left, I'll be around to say 'I told you so'. I'm sure one of the other girls would go to the ball with you."

"**Wrong**. It's because I'm in cohorts with YOU. You ruin my chances with anyone because all onlookers view us as if we're a pair or think you'll hurt them. "

"I don't care who you date Nic, I just know Historia and you go together like mayo and peanut butter. Date a human, kazamite or chimera. You'd be the first human I personally know, in a relationship with a kazamite or chimera though."

"I don't need your blessing on my *dating* life. I at least put myself out there. Regale me: how many eons ago was your last partner?" He turned his head to face me and the bike wobbled.

"Alright alright, you win. Just focus on getting us there safely. I'm not sure what your angle is, but Historia already has a crush. Besides, I'm not sure she dates slow and shitty drivers."

"Oh *I'm* the shitty driver?"

I already drowned him out before he started his winded rant. It sucks that we didn't get to hang out as much as we used to but, we stole time wherever we could. We hung out a lot more back when he was infantry, but now we only hung out every three months or so. All that is that we antagonize each other as much as we can to make up for lost time.

Eventually, Nic stopped ranting and after half an hour or so, we saw Historia. She was kicking her legs and sitting up on top of a boulder when we pulled up next to her.

"Traded Cricket in for Nic?" She asked with a smile. She hopped off the boulder and gave me a hug. She wore the exact same dark outfit as me, but with the addition of a baseball cap and loose strands of hair leaking out from under it.

"Two Historia sightings in one day, truly a treat of the ages." Nic said as he smiled at her.

I groaned and spoke up before she got a chance to reply. "Have you scouted this place out yet?"

"Mhm. I even picked a lock to create an opening for us."

"Lockpicking? When did you learn that?" Nic asked.

"Oh, Ambrotos! I visited him a couple weeks ago and he taught me." She let out a sneeze as Nic let out a low groan; I doubt she heard it. "So here's the plan," she continued. "We'll have to sneak into the control room though and cut off the alarms and try to hack the cameras."

"I have a better idea." I synced my NUE to hers. "You should be digitally masked now. How close is our entrance to the computer with the prisoner locations?"

"See, that's the thing, I don't think this is a prison. I skimmed over the intel Nic gave me, but it had… consistencies… too many. It was like looking at the most perfect prison with the most advanced systems."

We both turned our attention to Nic.

"Preposterous, there shouldn't be an advanced system. Once inside, I'll check it. Roaming patrols?" He asked her.

"No, it's dead. I'm not sure this is a good idea…"

"We'll unmask the truth soon enough. Ladies, shall we?" Nic gave us a smile and started stretching his legs.

"Well I'm never second to the fun. Hope you can keep up!" Historia finished her sentence and then immediately dashed towards the compound.

I gave Nic a grin and took off after her. Humans aren't *nearly* as fast as chimeras, but it's always fun to watch Nic try to challenge or keep up with us. If anything, it made Nic better than most humans because he always tried to match us. But of course, it was rare for him to beat us in physical stuff, and tonight's no different. We waited several minutes for him at the edge of the compound. Once he finally made it, we hugged the walls to continue and even though we were safe from cameras, we still made an effort to avoid them. Thanks to Historia's recon, we made our way inside in no time. We bypassed all the cameras and made our way to the control room and shut off all the alarms. From there, we were able to find a computer that gave us access to the whole system within minutes, it all felt too easy.

After we pulled the files we needed about our alleged prisoners, I walked over to Nic and asked, "doesn't this feel *too* easy?"

"In some ways, but there are still friction points. While the system was not hard to get into, bypassing the firewall is. And it is testing my wit. Not everything must be an uphill battle Mandy, maybe this is just free chicken?"

"Or misdirection. Keep trying that firewall. Historia, let's do some digging."

Historia was right, this place was a mimic. It didn't *feel* like a trap, but it felt not normal, like it was trying too hard to not be a trap. Historia and I walked around to search for *anything*. But after 15 minutes, we came up empty handed. On our way back to Nic, we took a different hall and stumbled on an elevator... an elevator on a ground floor compound.

Historia used her NUE to interface with the elevator, but was met with a firewall.

"A firewall for an elevator? I understand an off the books basement storage area, but a protected elevator is a bit much."

"Let's go back to Nic and check the blueprints."

By the time we made it back to Nic, he was complaining about multiple firewalls and how there were now too many inconsistencies. We told him what we found and he pulled up the blueprints to show that there wasn't anything under us. However, there was an increase in blue collar contractors with higher security clearances for a period of time and it doesn't say what all they worked on but, we found a document with the word 'elevator' on it, and that was enough.

"There's something beneath us," we all said in tandem.

"But how would we get down and back up?" Nic asked.

"We jump down the elevator shaft and go fishing, come on," I said.

We brought Nic back to where the elevator was and Historia used her ONI to lock the elevator, in case it moves while we're snooping. We opened up the hatch at the top of the elevator and climbed out and looked down. Historia nodded and then walked over the edge and vanished into the darkness. Nic and I waited a couple seconds and then heard her hit the ground and then call up to us.

I looked at Nic and smiled. He shook his head and said, "have you *lost* your **mind**?"

I grabbed him and yanked him with me as I walked over the edge. I had to cover his mouth cause he let out a loud gasp and shriek, but we landed safe and sound.

"Not a **word**," he said and stormed off.

Nic and I stumbled around in the darkness looking for Historia or a light switch, but all we did was bump into tables. You could hear our steps echo around us as we made our way around in the dark and we only found a lightswitch, cause Nic stumbled into it.

The lights came on, row by row and I wished they never did.

Historia stood in front of a tank and was the first one to break the silence. "What... what is this?"

A dead kazamite floated in liquid inside of the vat. But it wasn't the only one. The entire floor was a science lab that was meant for testing... testing kazamites. We were surrounded by dozens of mansize cages, dozens of vats and dozens of operating tables. We drifted apart as we wandered around, unwilling to believe our eyes. Everything was labeled so there was no guesswork. Jars and containers with kazamite brains, organs that had been harvested and more. So much more. I passed a fridge that housed chimera blood, and next to it was a computer with chimera organs jarred next to it.

I had to see... I had to. I jumped on the computer and opened up the recent files. There were files on different organs from chimeras and kazamites, and a couple files with our names on it. I skimmed through a file that spoke about weaponizing Kyren's disease and other diseases that I've never even heard of like influenza. I clicked one and half read it, only looking for words that jumped out at me.

"Coronary artery and Huntington's… airborne nanites vaccinate? *What?* I don't get it."

I closed the file and opened another document that was over 20 pages long, but I decided to only read one of the pages. It read:

By all accounts, the mainly pescatarian Kazamites are an interesting and young species. Research states that they had their own version of a homo habilis species and only a few thousands of years ago moved from their homo neanderthalensis cousins. However, it is still contested if this version of them is their sapien or neanderthal phase. We here are researching this intently with live test subjects and carrions. Thanks to their bodies being made of cartilage and not bones, it has been easy dissecting them and conducting tests.

Starting next week, we are moving into stage three of testing due to an influx of new data when we conducted the same test in water. Due to the origin of their species coming from water, they have amphibious traits. Unique traits such as nictitating membranes, and electroreception, but their uniqueness stops there as predators of the sea. We speculated that they have some amazing quality, but no. The only uniqueness they offer is how their organs seem to be mostly in the same places as ours, and how they have almost the same organs as us. The sizes in their organs are different of course and they have an organ designed to help with breathing underwater, but they lack the ability to use it. It's as if they're still in between evolution stages, how cute.

We have also taken more consideration in physically handling their corpses, it's well known nobody here enjoys touching their octopus-like skin. The only noteworthy interaction with their flesh is the multitude of colors they come in. An aquatic race that has all human skin colors, purple, orange, red and other similar shades is interesting. They have freckles across their body like some of us do too, which has sparked new ideas. A new hypothesis is that all creatures that become bipedal and intelligent will eventually look like us, or them depending on their species origin. Another department still continues research on insemination as well, but results have yielded no progress. Outside of chimeras, hybrids seem out of the question. That's fine with most of us, these sail shaped ear, slit nosed creatures are objectively mentally inferior to us anyway. I must remember to thank Dr. Samson for the good work he has done; he is truly a hero of science. His research will help science for generations to come. With that being said, I don't know how he tolerates handling these things.

My eyes hardly finished reading the page when there was a loud crash. I snapped my head to where the sound came from; it was Historia. She threw a refrigerator and kicked over some tables. She screamed as she grabbed a chair and threw it at a desk, knocking over a projector and accidently turning it on. We all stopped as a hologram appeared. Some holograms were two-ways while others were recordings, and we didn't know which this one was.

"That's Dr. Livington," said Nic.

The hologram flickered and said, "children of man, you were made to serve. You are all born sick and lost, but us, your creators, are here to guide you. To you, we are your gods and with some rearing, you and the kazamites will be as smart as dolphins. Remember chimeras: a good subject follows orders, you owe a debt to mankind for giving you life. We are here to make sure you repay this debt. You're welcome for this opportunity, you live to serve." The hologram looped.

Nic walked over to me and said, "I discovered a file about chimeras on a computer. Mandy, it says... it's not my business to ask but... it says you're made infertile. Is... is this true?"

"All chimeras are," Historia answered. She sniffled and wiped her tears away. Her voice cracked as she continued. "Having a family was considered irrelevant for a *made* race, no chimera is capable of it. Not that we know of."

"I'm fleet lost, how do chimeras... continue?"

"We don't..."

"Oh..."

"That's why you only see young chimeras as a pod, we're genetically designed like this Nic. I'm pretty sure they could make it where we could be like you and kazamites, but we never live long enough to see," I said. "I thought you knew this?"

"No, we hardly talk about chimeras outside of missions. Why have you never told me, Mandy?"

"Tell you what exactly? There is no future version of me as a mom? Me watching my kid grow a sail and then lose it after it can walk? What's there to talk about?"

"What's there to talk about? They label you in pods, make you infertile, and then use you for war and you ask 'what's there to talk about'? **Everything!** There's everything to talk about! Why aren't you mad? This is corrupt, the regime can't *do* this!"

"But they **can** and they **do**. You already know that most of us aren't allowed to have memories before 5. Historia and I are the 'lucky' ones because we were part of the first four born in our pod. If you aren't part of the first four in your pod, your first memory would probably be training."

"But why? What benefit is stripping one of the memories of their first bike ride? Or first hug?"

"We've been over this before, Nic. Some are given fake memories or memories mixed with real events so that we can't ever tell which memory is our own. I'm lucky enough that I made the cut, or else I would've never remembered meeting you. But we're told memories are a distraction, and to have memory is a burden for higher beings."

"Distractions? Burden? Memories make us who we are. Even mechs have memories!"

"Some of us were told that memory is a privilege."

"What? You should be up in arms! Why aren't you? Make it make sense, Mandy!"

"Nic this is old news. Why do you think Scyra seceded? The regime controls the history books and media and *I'm* getting yelled at? Wait a minute, why are you yelling at **me**? Your uncle is the one in the regime!"

"Yea but he doesn't weaponize memory! Speak true, is this how you feel? Is this how all of you feel? That there's nothing outside of this? That memory is a privilege?"

"Not me." Historia's eyes and cheeks were puffy. "I was told memory was a weapon, not a privilege. Each pod leader goes through a separate training and then additional training in different places. I was one of the lucky ones, being dropped off in a mountain on Pala for one training and being forced to learn to survive, escape and resist. And for my main training, I was sent to Kunlun."

"This... this is *evil*. I thought humans were here to help and sure we have bad apples, but this isn't just a few bad apples. How can we speak as if we're benevolent gods but then treat you all like objects?" Nic balled his fist and gritted his teeth.

"This is how it's always been..." Historia said.

"That's not **good** enough!" He paused for a moment and rubbed his temples. "Humans have to pay..."

"Enough Nic," I said.

"Enough? There are **dismembered** bodies here! My sister isn't afforded the luxury of a life after war and you say enough? By Jove Mandy! Is that why Eskander and Eleanor moved to a literal desert? To try to be normal? To try to be happy while on the edge of the discovered world? The regime must answer for these crimes that are before us. Humans have to pay; we have to get revenge against them."

I raised an eyebrow and said, "them?" This 'them' is *your* people."

"I'M NOT THEM!" He paused and took a breath. "We aren't all 'them'. It does not change that there must be retribution. Justice would be too kind for what is before us."

"*You* might not be one of them, but Alex is. He literally mocked us and told us to count our blessings after—"

"And I no-contact him for a year. He has changed for the better over the years, just like my father."

Historia spoke up. "Copernicus, an eye for an eye. And I don't want to fight anymore battles. It's easier to just pick our battles to avoid any future issue with humans I mean—"

"**Coward**!" Nic yelled, cutting off Historia. She flinched at his outburst. "You two can slay legions of humans and mechs and are bulletproof! And yet you both stand here, reciting the words of cowards and jesters as if it's law! Backbones made of boiled spaghetti!"

I scoffed and said, "bullet resistant, not bulletproof, and only when wearing our aegis. And what do you want us to do exactly? Attack the three colony capital ships in orbit? Each with humans who believe that they're gods with tech that rivals actual gods. Isn't the ship you're from called Asgard, and you expect us to take on hundreds of humans who call themselves Aesir?"

"It's not the real Asgard! I don't understand, why do you quarrel with me on this subject? You could aid me in my vision Mandy!"

"And your vision of **what**? ARGH! Get it through your head!" I roared. "Let's say we kill half of the humans. What next? You think the remaining humans on-world will like us? And how do you expect we go about training kazamites to fight when they've never had an army in their species history?"

"Using guns isn't a daunting task! Kazamites can wield guns!"

"Humans have the Tetra!" I balled my fist and sent it through a wall as I said it. I took a deep breath and sighed. "We can't beat a race of people with *that*. A dyson beam would literally wipe out **all** of Kazar. You know that."

"What if kazamites learned?"

"Oh fucking come on."

"The Tetra is just a dyson swarm, which are just satellites. We could harness the power of it and threaten to use it if the regime doesn't step back! Mandy, a resistance of kazamites could do this!"

"Are you *insane*? There's less than 100 people who even know how to use the Tetra. *They* don't even fully understand it and you want to weaponize it?"

"Just lend me your ears… and your patience." He put his hand on Historia's shoulder. "The Tetra was an extreme idea, I concur, but look at this lab. Frozen kazamite limbs, vats of liquids, files on kazamites and chimeras, and then there are these cages. These are holding cells for kazamites and they no doubt were experimented on while living. But I ask: is this truly *living?* We can strike back, and it need not be extreme. We show the world all the horrors that we've seen here, then we join that faction I mentioned earlier Mandy. We have to attack humans and it can be targeted hits on the ones who have caused kazamite pain, just the regime. Electronic attack on human files, destruction of human monuments, the recapture of control areas or even a strike on a colony ship. Humans as a whole, should be held accountable."

"Accountable? Your dad razed an entire city because Leopold feared the amount of kazamite and human relationships. Loyalist terrorize kazamites daily and your uncle is–"

"I know!" He sighed. "I know. But that is exactly why I can say change must happen. My mother tried the diplomatic way, my father tried the more direct diplomatic way. There are no other ways, Mandy. Revolution is the last way."

"I can't support that," I said. "Any retaliation will just piss the humans off. If what is in here gets leaked, kazamites will retaliate but they don't have the same resolve as humans. The regime will deploy soldiers to keep order, and that's assuming they didn't already once they realize there are missing mechs. Nic, we only have this island for all of us. We aren't inoculated for the rest of the world, we don't even know what *is* the rest of the world. If we can't get along, there is nowhere else to go. You're asking people to give up the only land we all have ever known. Let's just review all this information and hold off."

"You're asking us to pick a side of the line to stand on, Nic," said Historia. "Once chimeras take sides, that's going to be seen as a declaration of war. Violence can't be the best option."

"And yet, it still is one," he said. "From where I'm standing, it feels as if we already have picked sides. Let's start with Dr. Maxwell Livington; he at least should answer for his crimes. If we do not stand for this, then what do we stand for? When is enough enough?"

"This is a slippery slope, Nic…" said Historia.

"There are vials of blood with Ambrotos' name on them. Do we fight back after they put all of him in a vat, or is that still too soon?"

I sighed and said, "you've made your point, don't toss out your argument by getting personal."

"Isn't it already?"

"We can talk about this later, but I think we just need time to process all of… this. It's late, don't do anything stupid. Promise me."

He walked away towards a computer and unplugged a flashdrive. "I already downloaded all the files on several computers. Files with pictures and videos, reports and logs of dead and dissected kazamites. I vow justice against these vermin and dregs."

"**Don't** do anything **stupid**," I said again more firmly. "Promise me."

He gritted his teeth, and balled his fist. After a moment, he broke. "I promise."

After our fight, we all stepped away from each other for a few minutes to cool off. Nic had a future, a guaranteed one and he wanted to throw it away. Fucking idiot. We searched the lab in silence for anything else that could be important but ultimately decided there was nothing left. We debated destroying the lab at first, but there would be no way to destroy it without summoning the army within minutes. So we left, and the ride back home wasn't much better.

Historia went nonverbal and Nic was pouting; the tension was as thick as the summers in Jericho. I should've broken the ice, but Nic just didn't understand. He was talking about *treason*. They'd kill him and torture Historia and I. Chevalier is living proof of going against the humans in public. Why would Nic want that for himself?

Nic went back to Newlana, a skyscraper city that never sleeps. It was always noisy and congested unlike where Historia and I lived. We lived in the province of Anore, well *I* did. Historia was somewhere in between provinces and prefectures. I lived in Pis Aller, the edge of

Dernier's Resort, while she lived in the mountains. Thankfully, we didn't live in a city that forced you to be shoulder to shoulder with people. I shuddered at the thought. I had so much freedom where I lived, and I'd hate it if tourists took that away. Half of my city was carved out of a mountain, and another was outside of it. It was spacious and I could be anywhere but thankfully, I was stowed away with my home built into one side of the mountain.

Due to the season, part of the mountain was melting and we used that to help generate power. Every summer and spring, part of the mountain turned into a gorgeous waterfall, with the water breathing new life everywhere. It's a secret spot kazamites and humans love. We're probably the only prefecture that lives in tandem with each other, *and* the local animals. The land was fertile and diverse enough that some earth creatures could even be here, like foxes and ravens. I was lucky, the humans allowed chimeras to choose places to live with people to be an early warning detection for uprisings; the regime wanted to give me the corner of nothing. But they didn't realize how peaceful it was. I took the elevator up to my one story safehouse and the lights turned on as I walked in.

"Welcome home, Mandy. I feared you'd do something stupid like release an army of mechs and I'd have to mask them. Thankfully, you did nothing out of the ordinary." Cricket greeted me with his usual sarcasm.

I groaned. "Hi Cricket. Did you water the plants and feed Chickenstrip?"

"Yes. Chickenstrip's crest needed polishing and he was restless, so I let him out for a flight. How was your night?"

I told him **everything**. I didn't live out any detail, including bringing up Nic's flashdrive of dirt, and Valen and other bions. Cricket and I spoke for hours about what the regime would do if Nic leaked the documents and if kazamites fought. We discussed which senators, proconsuls and prefects sympathized with kazamites and chimeras, but only three openly would speak out. We ended the conversation on Sibil as Chickenstrip flew in through the window and curled up on my lap.

"Sibil is the highest ranking chimera, and he hasn't been able to make many changes," Cricket said.

"Yeah, but how has he helped chimeras?" I rubbed Chickenstrip's feathers and plucked berries out of his axetail. "I don't know Cricket, this is just a lot. Why can't we just go back to when things were simpler?"

"Simplier as in the regime creating an entire species to commit war crimes on their behalf? Or simpler as in you sneaking *into* trouble everyday that ends in 'y'? You will eventually have to choose a side, Mandy."

"I know, I just don't want my friends and family to get hurt. I'm over here stressing, and Chickenstrip gets to snore and drool on my lap. I'll sleep on it. Thanks for everything, goodnight Cricket."

"Goodnight Mandy."

Chapter 3

REPUBLIC OF VENGEANCE

"Citizens of Kazar, a moment of your time. For centuries, we have housed humans as friends and in return, they have decided to occupy our land. We call humans 'star riders' when in actuality they are just imperialists and invaders. Our so-called 'friends' have exploited our world, and our way of life and now they respond only to being called gods. So I have a proposal."

I stood on the sidewalk awestruck as a masked kazamite with black hair and blood orange skin stole my attention. Me and dozens of others stared up at the billboard as this stranger's voice echoed across the city in a soft but demanding tone. The camera panned out and showed the woman holding a knife in one hand, and the hair of a beaten up human kneeling at her feet in the other.

"This is Dr. Jemidie Markson, one of the gods. He's from the colony capital ship, Asgard." She leaned over and slit his throat. She continued to hold his head, and then rested her foot on his shoulder and shoved him forward. The camera showed the human as he plummeted to the ground. "You humans disappoint me. Your biggest accomplishment was leaving a planet *you* destroyed, but you're not gods. You're a species of rapers and exploiters that got lucky and found our world. Killing one planet wasn't good enough for you, so now you're here to kill another. The fact you all are considered apex predators only means that the other species of earth were weak minded, and weak bodied. You won't find that here, not anymore, outworlders. A hurricane is coming and we will wash out all memories of the regime and those who sympathize with them. Humans, last night we attacked your bases and reeducation camps and set them ablaze with your scientist inside. Today, we air your dirty laundry and tell the world about places like Camp Frazier. Today, some of you will die because of those now leaked files. Today, we of Kazar demand retribution. So I'm launching a nuke at where you entered. You have three hours, gods. A storm is coming."

The broadcast ended.

At first, nobody reacted, probably thinking it was a joke. But then a countdown started on the screen and then there was mass pandemonium. It had been days since the night at Camp Frazier, and Nic and I haven't spoken since but this seemed like as good a time as any for him to pick up the phone. And of course, he was unreachable.

"Cricket, tell me you have some answers. Where's the origin of that broadcast?"

"Unknown. The regime is planning mass evacuations in several places. The military is also summoning all chimeras to help with this."

"Ok, what does she mean by where they entered?"

"I am unsure, I am scanning regime channels. Currently, the AIs aboard Asgard, and Avalon are trying to pinpoint possible threat locations. They are creating courses of action for the prefectures: Newlana, Scyra, Demeter's Landing, Kadura, Jericho, Hylo and the Osmium Coast. They will not be able to evacuate all of them. I believe the Osmium Coast, Hylo, and Newlana will be the ones they try to evacuate."

"Newlana? Dammit Nic."

"I do have a theory," Cricket said. "I was going over the files on this terrorist organization and cross checked them with other factions, and have an idea of where they could launch from. They don't have the resources or wealth to launch from an amphibious vehicle or an airborne one, and if launched from the surface, we would be able to scan it. They would need to launch from inside of a cave to mask us tracing them."

"Find the launch area? Smart. Who was the voice on the screen?"

"Lissax, a kazamite that enjoys theater and grandeur actions in front of crowds."

"So she would want to see her work from a safe distance. There's not that many places that offer caves and underground tunnels and are near those prefectures. I think that leaves only three locations. I'm thinking: Pleiades, Askan and Gorgon. Pleiades is too obvious, that's where the regime would look first. Askan is too far and Gorgon is too flat. You'd see a blast from there miles away... but there are a few tunnels and caves that lead to the ocean for an escape. Cricket, send the information to Sibil, Chevalier, Nic and Historia." I jumped on a bike. "How long would it take me to get to Gorgon?"

"Via air, Gorgon is two and a half hours. There is a hangar not too far from here where I can pilot a terra jet."

"Get me there."

I sped off through the chaos of screaming and fleeing citizens as soldiers tried to get some form of order. Some shopkeeps let pedestrians into their store to seek cover, others slammed their doors shut. I took my eyes off the road for a split second, and almost was t-boned.

Of course.

People were running red lights left and right, I don't know how humans drove like this on earth. People move to big cities for *this*? I swerved and dodged oncoming vehicles that raced to leave the town and get out of reach of the nuke. Which is ironic, cause they didn't even know where it was going. If my theory was right, they were already safe and were only running into danger. I watched as some soldiers arrested a man for trying to break into a vehicle to use, and I watched a car crash into the ground because someone jumped on top of it to escape. A couple soldiers tried to flag me down to help them, but I couldn't stop and help every last person.

Thanks to my speeding, Cricket and I got to the hangar 15 minutes earlier than planned. I tried the doors but they were locked and the fence was wrapped in concertina wire. I rolled my eyes and jumped over the wires and ran inside. I found a terra jet and jumped in it and connected Cricket and within minutes, we took off. Flying a stolen terra jet in low orbit violated *dozens* of laws, but this wasn't even the first vehicle I've stolen this month. I told Cricket to push the jet to its limit since my body could handle more g-force than humans, and we were off.

"Nic has not responded to your messages, but I believe Sibil has received them and has alerted others. Chevalier is busy helping with the evacuation and keeping the peace. Historia is the closest to us, but she won't make it until post launch due to riots breaking out," Cricket said.

I groaned. "Do you have any good news?"

"Ambrotos has his aegis on unlike you, and can make it in roughly 15 minutes after you arrive."

"***Good*** news Cricket. I wanted good news. Ugh, ok push the information to him and tell him I'll be grateful and in his debt if he makes it."

"Sent. When we arrive, you are putting yourself at risk because you don't have your aegis on. You need it and should wait for backup"

"I don't need my armor, I have my bracelets and you. Yes, I know they only can do so much but that was the whole point of me having them; portable and they don't look like much."

"You should wait for backup," he chirped.

"*You* should install a mute button. There's no time for me to wait for anyone."

Cricket played back to me the sound of me groaning. "Mute and groan buttons installed," he replied snidely.

Groaning again would only satisfy him, so to shut him up I watched the chaos below us unfold. Like ants, people scurried everywhere. I watched looters break into stores and homes, as rioters tackled all guards and military on the streets beneath me. I hope Cricket and I are right about Gorgon, or else I just gave false information to dozens of people. I racked my brain for what was so special about Gorgon, but came up with nothing. It was named after the minerals in the water that petrified the trees. The people that lived there had low tech, that was probably the only thing 'special' about it. The farmers that lived there wanted a life similar to the ancient farmers of Earth; where things were grown organically and not in a lab. Something about lab grown food just felt so… alien.

"Cricket, remind me to visit this prefecture again, I'm so used to mountains and volcanoes, I hardly see flat low trees," I said as I stared out the window.

Cricket brought up a topographic map of Gorgon on one side of the windshield and a political map on the other side.

"I narrowed down areas where they could launch from," he said. "I recommend a stealth approach."

"Ok, can you call Sibil?"

"He's occupied at the moment. I also attempted to enlist the help of soldiers. Would you believe me if I said they didn't want to help us?"

"Must be your haircut. Try Sibil again and say it's…" I looked down as my NUE received a message from Sibil. "He has time to text me but not call? Of course he wants me to axios myself; always putting chimeras fifth in a world with three races."

I rolled my eyes and didn't reply to his message. Historia was more likely to lose a fight before Sibil went to bat for chimera agendas and lives. But I guess if Mandy the 'renegade' died, it'd be no big loss for the regime. I groaned at the thought of Ambrotos being my lifeline; what am I getting myself into? Without… *with* my aegis, Ambrotos was a better brawler than me. And it doesn't help that he believes his own hype and calls himself immortal.

Once we got close enough to our dropzone, Cricket said, "arriving in 30 seconds, Mandy. I once again advise waiting for backup." He lowered the plane closer to the ground.

"Too many innocents can get hurt if I wait."

"Regardless, I support you either way, but I do question your hobbies. Today was an 'off' day. Maybe you should try safer hobbies, like being a rancher in Gorgon."

"Yea, the second Chickenstrip has babies. I'll be a rancher or farmer then. Maybe in another life."

The canopy of the plane opened and I jumped out and landed on the roof of a warehouse that was connected to one of the many cave entrances on the outskirts of Gorgon. Since Cricket and I combed the entire map on the ride, we guessed if a nuke were to be launched, it would be from here. It had about a dozen routes where they could retrograde from through the mountains and caves. Having a launch pad also helped fix my worries. We couldn't scan through the building, so we also couldn't pick up any anomalies, which was an anomaly in itself. I snuck around the roof until I found a window, and slipped in. I landed quietly on a catwalk and watched as clueless armed guards walked right under me. I looked around and saw it: the nuke.

A kazamite woman with orange skin said, "here, take this stupid mask." It was Lissax. "How much longer for the evacuation to be complete?"

One of the armed men jogged over to her and said, "we are on schedule. The army is spread thin trying to evacuate all the area. And with the help of our benefactor, we were able to backdoor his secure channel and use Asgard to scan for movement. They have relocated most of the humans to a military base underground, just like we planned. The result will be an estimated 10 to 40 thousand dead." A human? Why would a human support her and attack other humans? At least Nic wanted to just go after the bad apples, but a nuke and innocents?

"That's a lot of dead. Lissax, this... this is too much. I thought we were only going to scare them or send the nuke to a colony ship after it's evacuated," another human said.

"Thank you, Charles," she said to the first man. She turned her attention to the second one and smiled. "There are no innocents in war, that's why it's *war*."

"I don't get it. How are we supposed to create a better world for kazamites or unify humans and kazamites by killing people?"

"*Unite?*" She scoffed. "Dead humans *do* create a better world. Your ancestors destroyed their own world, now you want other humans to destroy this one? This isn't the time to back out, Bogart. We have come too far. Prime the mechs, I expect they'll send praetorians or chimeras soon. That chimera Sibil could be troublesome." She turned to walk away.

"**No,**" he said firmly. It caused everyone to stop what they were doing and face them. "This is us heading towards genocide, not a better world. There are innocents who have done nothing and I will not be a part of this."

"You're right about two things," she said as she turned back around to face him. "Humans have done exactly what you said: ***nothing.*** Your people have done nothing and could have helped kazamites at any point. Instead, the lot of you stood by and watched as crimes against my people continued. Humans love documenting and recording things but always seem camera shy when we need people to speak up. There are no innocent bystanders, only bystanders who allowed atrocities to happen. Once the dust is settled, you humans can live in a few cities and earn back our trust. And the second thing you're right about is, that you won't be a part of this." She drew her gun and shot him in the head. "The seed of change grows with fresh soil. Soil, watered with the blood of tyrants. Someone else get the mechs ready."

"Well shit," I muttered. "Cricket, how many we got?"

"Five unarmed humanoids, 15 armed ones, and 20 mechs."

"That's just short of a fuckton. Mech types?" I asked him as I moved around the catwalk to get a closer look.

"15 of them are elves, and five are minotaurs. You are running out of time; your violence of action needs to be high."

I sighed. "Here goes nothing. Tell Ambrotos and the others where I am and that I was right."

I crept from catwalk to catwalk until I was close enough to the missile guarded by two armed guards. The nuke itself wasn't bigger than a football and the containing unit was about three feet. I dropped down on top of one of the guards knocking him out and turned and kicked the other in the chest. He flew meters away hitting the wall and falling unconscious. Good, 13 armed guys left. I picked up a gun from one of the guards I took out and shot two more men in the chest, dropping the count to 11. Everyone turned to the sound of me shooting. They raised their guns to fire, but were stopped by their ring leader.

"A chimera? Ally, or confused?" Lissax walked over to me as she spoke, twirling her finger through her shoulder length curly hair.

"**Armed**. Surrender, I already called for reinforcements and in a few minutes, you will be surrounded," I said.

"Except, you're *already* surrounded. You'd die for humans, who only think about you when they're in danger? I have already leaked information about prison camps and labs that experimented on my people and their only crime was being a kazamite. I can't see how I'm the bad guy here for wanting revenge. After the nuke lands, the humans will fear us and we will be seen in the same light as gods. Just like how we used to see them."

Cricket called her something immensely explicit and it made me chuckle. "My AI says your logic is idiotic at best. You can't win people over if you kill them."

"No victory is without sacrifice."

"Hate to agree with someone named Boggart, but he was right. Nuking innocents that had nothing to do with kazamite torture isn't sacrifice or victory; it's flat out murder. And yes, I heard your spiel about innocents already, very pragmatic of you. I can't even tell you're a theater kid. All you're doing is going to cause panic, there aren't enough kazamites, let alone fighting kazamites to fight all the humans."

"We know. That's why we plan on launching this nuke to show we mean business. We then will assassinate Dr. Livington, make an attempt on Oceana's and Callum's life, and shoot down Avalon or Elysium. And this will happen in a year or less."

I snorted. "You're delusional. A small force of chimeras like me could stop you."

"Doubtful." I was shot and flew backwards dropping my gun. I hit my head so hard, there was ringing in my ears. "I'm not fully sure how this gun works, but we paid a **lot** of money to get our hands on just a couple, literally. We tried a couple trial runs, but they don't work at all on humans, and surprisingly neither on kazamites. I'll admit, I thought we were scammed but I guess this was the first official trial run. You probably are confused and can't even hear me. Well, there's a sniper on the catwalk with a cloaking device designed to trick NUEs. That cost a fortune too. You won't believe me if I told you how we even got our hands on these.

I tried to stand to my feet but just rolled over. It felt like I couldn't even control my own body. I watched as she walked over to me getting closer and closer, and I could hardly keep my eyes open to look at her. Not that it mattered, my head was throbbing from the ringing in my ears and even if I wanted to fight, my vision was too blurry. I was looking up at five Lissax's towering over me. The only thing I could do was check my body for a bullet hole but there was no sign of one. The only visible physical issues were my nose, eyes and ears were bleeding.

"Look at these results! Imagine, if we shot the primarch's pet, Sibil, with this. We could end the reign of human tyrants, and make sure chimeras stay in their place. But don't take this as a threat, we want chimeras on our side. Some of us fear you, but most of us accept you're just different looking kazamites at the end of the day. We see chimeras as the bridge between our worlds, but blood must be spilled first." She paused and listened to the sound of me gasping for air. "This hurts me more than it hurts you. By the time you probably can get up, the nuke will be in flight. Good effort though. Prime the nuke, launch it, and then let's go." She walked away as she barked orders.

"Can you hear me?" It was Cricket. I felt a jolt through my wrist and took a deeper breath than I was able to before. "That should get you back on your feet, but save your energy. You're going to need it in the next five minutes."

My vision began to clear and I could see Lissax yelling at someone who was working on the nuke and then, there was a scream. The cloaked sniper flew across the room and went head first into the wall. Everyone looked up at the catwalk with their guns fixed on where the sniper was thrown from.

"*Another* chimera? I hope you will take me sparing the life of your sibling as a kindness. Look the other way as we wash away the sins of the humans and usher in a new age of peace!" Lissax exclaimed.

"You know you're the bad guy right? Only bad guys monologue, lowbrow." He jumped over the railing and did a flip midair before landing on one knee. "Hi, I'm immortal." He looked up at her with his golden eyes and gave her a boyish grin.

Ambrotos was probably one of the last chimeras I wanted to rescue me; his reputation was worse than mine when it came to following rules. Sure, I didn't want him to rescue me, but he's never let Historia and I down. Everyone needs a friend like him.

"Immortal? That what they tell you?"

"Only on podcasts and by C list terrorists. Surrender and reach for the sky, kelpies." He stood up as he spoke.

"As I said to the last chimera bleeding on my floor over there," she motioned to me. "You are outnumbered, outmatched and outgunned. You should take your friend, and go home."

He folded his arms. "That's bold of you. I think the good guys always win in the opening chapters. Unlike men in tights, I'm actually not supposed to lose, and I don't need to pull out the script to prove it either."

"I don't understand that."

"Figures. There are days, and there are days. You probably won't get that either, but I'm mocking some tool. You guys probably would get along."

"A comedian, how quaint. If only you were a **funny** comedian."

"Sorry, I'll do gooder. I'll make sure you get the next punchline."

"Apparently all chimeras are hard headed and idiots. The nuke will be launched momentarily, you can't possibly win—"

Ambrotos shot her with his wrist gauntlet. The shockwave sent her flying back several meters before she hit her head and fell unconscious. "Huh, how about that, sports fans?"

For a moment, none of her henchmen reacted. But then the bullets started to fly. Unfortunately for them, Ambrotos lived to fight. Our armor, the aegis, was essentially bulletproof so all they did was waste their time. I tried to refocus my vision and get my bearings as I watched him and his leather black jacket jump from guard to guard.

"You know, a human supporting killing humans is weird right?" He said as a couple humans shot at him.

"Gotta crack a few eggs to make an omelet. Isn't that what chimeras do for the regime?" One of them replied.

"No, chimeras don't fight chimeras. We seem to clean up a lot of human messes though."

He scoffed. "And what are you? Some kinda superhero?"

"Red pants that fade into black halfway down my calves, and a dark royal blue torso. I mean, I'm dressed like one at least. Got the boots, and jacket isn't that what superheroes wear?"

"Superheroes fly; it's what makes them super."

"Got me there, I fear the master of chimera street fighting may be out of options."

The soldiers lowered their guns as several mechs rushed him.

Ambrotos snickered and said, "you guys really fell for that?"

He is the only chimera that had jet boots, and he knew how to use them well. With his boots, he always could get to vantage points and could fight with a multidirectional style. He hopped out from behind cover and tackled a mech and used his boots to fly into another. His wrist gauntlets and boots made it so they couldn't get near him, but he could near all of them.

"I don't quite know, but I have a feeling that your aegis could've been helpful," Cricket chirped.

I groaned and said, "shut up."

His boots helped him dash between the mechs and gunmen by twirling in the air, or sliding on the ground. He was so precise in his fighting style with his gear, he could immediately change directions or come to a halt and catch them off guard. A few times, they surrounded him hoping they'd get the drop on him, but he simply used a few of them as human shields every now and then. He took out at least half of them by the time I started to get to my feet. I wiped all the blood off my face and saw Lissax getting to her feet too. She took one look at the omnidirectional nightmare that was Ambrotos, and made a run for it down a tunnel.

"Not happening." I turned my back to Ambrotos and started towards her.

Ambrotos yelled at me, "Mandy, and Cricket I presume, feel free to pick up a volleyball and join the class."

I groaned. If I left Ambrotos to fend for himself, he could make it, but he would probably be pretty banged up. But if I didn't chase Lissax, she would get away...

Ambrotos chimed in again. "I can see you considering chasing your date before the clock strikes twelve, but the glass slipper doesn't fit. Let it go Mandy."

I sighed and turned around and saw a mech grab him and toss him at a wall. While the mech was distracted with him, it didn't notice me. I grabbed a clutch grenade and stuck it to him. Within a minute, we were almost done with everyone in the room.

We ducked behind a crate to catch our breaths and avoid being shot any more than we already were. We locked eyes for a moment as we ducked and there was no fear in his eyes. If charcoal and ebony had a baby, that would be the color of his scleras. His golden irises clashed with them, giving his eyes sometimes an almost dark orangish hue. He had a couple scratches on his face, but his skin color made it difficult to see him bleeding. I think he's the only chimera with this red of skin, it was deep cherry red and he didn't have freckles like some of us.

"You should start wearing your helmet when in your aegis," I said.

He snorted. "Sorry, where's yours again? I'm not taking dressing or aegis advice from you, all offense. You have Cricket, an advanced AI, and still have the blandest aegis. Cricket is smart as hell in more ways than one, which means he lets you walk around in your factory setting ass style. In and out of your aegis. You could at least do a butterfly or moth type crash and have Cricket change the color."

I was stunned. "Are you being serious right now? What's wrong with my aegis and clothes?"

"Oof."

"The fuck? 'Oof' isn't an answer."

"Isn't it?"

Ambrotos was about to jump from behind our cover, when we heard a bird sound. It was faint at first and hard to hear over the gunfire, but after a few seconds the 'kraa' was clear as day. In the next moment, a blinding rainbow bled through the windows and skylight as the sound of ravens increased. The ceiling caved in with part of the roof and catwalks coming down on themselves as our backup arrived. It was the humans known as Aesir. They didn't waste any time and immediately went to kill everything in sight. Mechs, humans and kazamite alike. They left one human survivor and shot him in his shoulder after he surrendered. He fell to the ground and screamed; he clearly was not a fighter. He reached for a gun but one of the soldiers stepped on his foot and shook their head.

The Aesir lined up in two lines that ran parallel to one another facing each other as there was another 'kraa' sound with some thundering. This time, the rainbow only brought one man. The Aesir all kneeled as the commander of their colony ship stood before them. I've only heard about him, but never met him. He served back when Leopold was in charge, thought he would be the next primarch, but lost to the current one.

Despite his age, he had a commanding presence. His reputation spoke as if he towered over humans, but he looked old like someone's grandpa. He was tall for a human and had a good stature for his age, but I didn't see the hype. His long wavy hair was styled in a half up and fell past his shoulders and a thick beard that had to be a quarter of a foot in length at least. But his most noticeable trait was him being a redhead. It was more of a rustic amber since his age was showing, but his beard resembled leaves in autumn.

One of the soldiers walked over to him and kneeled. "High One, we saved one for interrogation. Their leader escaped while we made our entrance."

He waved him off and looked over to where Ambrotos and I had taken cover. He walked over to us where I began to kneel but Ambrotos stopped me and mumbled, "as if".

"We'd kneel, but we're both on our third knee surgery," Ambrotos said.

The soldier that reported to him jumped up and rushed over to us drawing a knife. "**Insolent** trash!"

Their commander raised his hand, halting the soldier. "You know of me, and my name?" He asked, looking at me.

"Admiral of Asgard," I said.

"And my name?"

"Rowan." All the Aesir shot me a look. "But the Aesir said you earned the title of 'high one' and so they call you that or they call you a variant of the title, Havi. Havi of Asgard."

"I have heard of you as well, Mandy." I was shocked. Normally, humans did not refer to us by our given names, only by our subject numbers. He continued. "Ambrotos, I know of you as well, more so than her. You have a reputation for your fighting skills and namesake; both are things that catch our eyes. Glad to put a face to the both of you." He turned and walked away from us to the wounded man who was running with Lissax. "Now that introductions have been made, I hope you understand this is a grave matter for me to come all this way. I need to know everything you know, starting with your name and where Lissax is going. And of course, does she have more nukes, and is she capable of producing more?"

"I'm not a fighter, but I know how we treat kazamites is wrong and I can fight for that!" He yelled.

"Fight for *what* exactly? The nuke would've killed kazamites, humans, and chimeras."

"Lissax says it's necessary. It'll show every human the kazamites are willing to kill for peace."

"Kill for peace? These are your leader's great words of wisdom? The same leader that ran and left you all? Lissax sounds delusional, xenophobic and is clearly a coward. Regardless, I need my questions answered, or else you'll have a chance to die for your beliefs."

The man looked as if he was about to answer Havi's questions, but then stopped himself. "I- I can't. I saw those labs. I saw what we did to the kazamites and the regime must answer. At some point, we have to put our feet down and stand for something."

Havi sighed. He kneeled down and put his hands on both of his feet. As soon as he did, there was a loud crack, and the man let out a blood curdling scream.

"I admire one willing to fight and die by their morals, truly. On my capital ship, this is what we live for, it's how we test one's mettle. So, let's test yours. I have shattered every bone in both of your feet, you will no longer be standing for anything for some time. That's 52 broken bones. Now I implore you, you have done your service to your organization, valiantly. This doesn't need to continue because next, I will put my hands on your spine. A numbing agent, please." He motioned to his soldiers. One of them ran over and injected the man with something into his leg, and then the man's screaming slowly passed.

The man went from screaming to labored breaths. "Please, I have a family…"

"And the people you tried to nuke were all orphans? I have no sympathy for terrorists, but I do have interrogation cells for them. Take him to one; I want answers within two hours so that I may send reports." He turned and faced us. "Ambrotos, Mandy, I look forward to more of your work. Maybe you both will live up to your urban legends. But until then, do stay off my radar." He just finished his sentence when he started to glow and then in a rainbow burst, he vanished.

One of the Aesir approached us with a notepad. "You arrived before us after endangering citizens with reckless driving, stealing an aircraft, flying into restricted airspace and conducting an unsanctioned attack in the city. Is this all correct?" The soldier looked up at me.

"That feels one sided. I sent up information as I got it," I replied.

"And which human authorized this?"

"Sibil was aware of what I was doing."

"Not keen on listening are you? He's not a human."

"Not keen on manners are you?" Ambrotos said, raising an eyebrow.

The human looked surprised. "Back off, you're speaking to an Aesir."

"What, that's like Vanir but without the muscles?"

The human lowered his notepad and clenched his fist and said through gritted teeth "Gods nonetheless."

"Little 'g' though. Aren't humans allergic to milk or peanuts or something? Better run before I throw a candy bar at you and watch you seize on the ground."

"That a threat, *chimera*?"

"I don't think I like how you said 'chimera'," I said. "You humans were too slow, you should be thanking me for arriving when I did. My AI, Cricket, sent information as soon as it was available and where were you? You jumped in after we took care of half the enemy and stopped a launch. How brave, maybe you can show me how brave you are in a one on one."

The soldier stood there for a moment, but then walked away. "Is there a single day where you don't put a target on your back?"

"What a nightmare," said Ambrotos. "It's impressive they made it out of their galaxy alive. You still coming tonight?"

"Who all will be there?" I asked.

"Don't do that. But it's mostly my pod and a few of yours."

"Next time. Lissax said she had a plan for a series of attacks and it'll start with someone named Dr. Livington. She wants the colony ships and their leaders dead too, we have to warn them."

"Dr. Livington? The dickweed that was leading the experiments on us and kazamites? And you want to defend him? Question: what drug are you on that has you *this* high?"

"It's our job, Ambrotos."

"No, our job is to help. We did. In fact we did more than just help, we literally stopped a nuke from being launched. It's not our job to clean up every human mess. I mean they call themselves gods right? Since when do deities need anything?"

"They aren't all the same, you know that. Cricket, did you send all of this to Sibil?"

"Neat, now for the chimera mascot," Ambrotos mumbled.

"Parts of it," Cricket chirped. "They're mostly wanting chimera pods, and special military teams to help with the issues. Are you wanting to assist as well?" Ambrotos shook his head and mouthed against it.

"I... *we* can be on standby," Ambrotos groaned as I said it. "Inform Sibil."

I turned to face Ambrotos who had his arms crossed and was staring through me. "You're buggin," he said.

"Sibil isn't that bad."

"If you have to say someone isn't 'that bad' then they're 'that bad'. The primarch's boots are always clean cause Sibil is always licking them."

"He helped Chevalier years ago when Chevalier was banished and forced to live in the slums."

Ambrotos scoffed. "As if Sibil was powerless and couldn't have helped *before* that. And don't forget them ditching Historia and weaponing her so much that she stopped doing her hair for a year. Her *hair*, Mandy."

"He has a lot on his plate, always has. We need to show solidarity with each other and you need to cut Sibil some slack."

"What are you, some type of Sibil cheerleader? I'm game with standing together, as long as we're on the right side. The morally right side."

"Are you saying humans and Sibil aren't on the right side?" I raised an eyebrow.

"Don't make me lie to you Mandy. I just verbalize what everyone thinks about Sibil."

"Beeteljuice, Ambrotos," Cricket chirped. "Sibil is calling."

Ambrotos groaned and said, "remind me not to say his name too many times next time."

"Patch him through, Cricket," I said.

Sibil spoke first. "Nice work today, Mandy. I knew if someone could be counted on, it would be you. We haven't been able to sit and speak in ages, how about we get together?"

"Hi Sibil. I'm actually beat from today, I'd rather unwind and see a medic and be on reserve until needed."

"I insist. And bring the loud one as well." I looked at Ambrotos. "I'm sure he will want some answers and to blow off some steam. I already have an aircraft on its way to pick you guys up. I have also sent someone there to explain some stuff."

"Like?"

"Notes that need to be compared, best done in person. They should be there in 15 minutes or less. See you soon." He hung up.

"Uh… Ambrotos, do you want to go on a field trip?"

"Eat a dick," he rolled his eyes and walked away.

I couldn't even blame him, everyone in his pod had strong feelings when it came to Sibil. Chevalier's pod came before Ambrotos' so Chevalier understood Sibil better than the rest of us, you'd think. But he doesn't.

"Mandy," chirped Cricket. "I thought you didn't like Sibil."

"I don't, but he's the oldest living chimera. That has to win him some points, right?"

"He's in his mid 40's, he's not even a decade older than Chevalier. I'm not sure what 'points' you're referring to."

"He's also not part of the first four in his pod, so his memory started at 4 or 5 years old. Maybe that's why he's the way he is."

"Chevalier isn't part of the first four. There's a difference between defending someone, and enabling their behavior."

Cricket was right, I sometimes defend Sibil too much when talking to the others. It's not like he ever did himself any favors. I don't even know the last time I heard or saw Sibil fight. Even Eskander and Eleanor fight, despite them living near the Afuera.

"You know who I haven't seen in a while?" Ambrotos said. "Your brother and his dad. He still rising in the ranks?" We walked over to a bench and sat down outside.

Nic was the only humans almost all of us chimeras liked, they all saw him as my biological brother and not my adopted brother. Except for Sibil.

"Nic is fine, he's going through a rebellious phase right now. As for his **adoptive** father, I haven't seen him all year. I'd like to keep it that way."

"With this group rising, how is he handling all of this?"

79

"Nic is… upset. He feels things have been getting out of hand and that kazamites and humans should live together in peace. He resents how the regime treats us and he'd probably be ok with humans expanding beyond the border."

"Like leaving Kore?" I nodded. "And the xenophobic old man?"

"Same old. He'll probably use us more, widening the divide between us and kazamites. He sees us 'pseudo humans', as if we want to be them."

He scoffed. "We didn't ask to be born. Humans just see us as organic mechs anyway. One day, a chimera will smack some sense into the human leaders."

"You almost sound like Nic. I just don't think scaring the humans is the right move."

"Oh please Mandy, a quarter of them already hate and fear us. I hope I live long enough to see humans get what's coming to them, I'm tired of being a weapon. But I ain't tired of fighting."

"You two!" A soldier walked over to us. "You could be useful and help with the clean up. You know, the mess *you* both made."

"Mess?" I scoffed. "There would be miles of 'mess' if we waited for humans to help. I think the least you guys can do is be on cleanup duty."

"Wasn't asking. Get inside, and help!"

"Bite me," said Ambrotos. "We did almost all the work, the only thing you guys did was give us a light show. Can humans even see all the colors of the rainbow? I can't remember what colors your godlike eyes fail to see that us meek chimeras can." He couldn't help himself.

"Hilarious. You know what else is funny? Being on extra duty. Now get your fucking asses in there, and move those damn mechs!"

Ambrotos yawned. "Congrats, you can yell. We aren't moving but it's pretty swanky you think yelling at us would get us moving. We're waiting on our ride."

I stood up and said, "look, we're just a bit beaten up. We've been hit and shot, we'd be more helpful if we saw a medic."

"I don't know what kind of germs you both have. You wait till you get to one of **your** doctors, not ours," the soldier said.

Ambrotos jumped up offended and ready to say something back but was interrupted by our ride arriving. The shuttle hovered for a few seconds, and then slowly landed and the doors opened for us. I gave a sheepish smile to the soldier and grabbed Ambrotos' arm and we made our way into the shuttle. It was a basic model, but with seats and a minifridge inside. Waiting inside, was a human.

"He-hello, you must beeeee Subject– Mandy, and you Ambrotos," they said, "My name is Basil, pleasure to meet the both of you. I was sent to fill you all i-in on information so that upon landing, you'll be caught up." The shuttle took off once we all sat down.

"Why send you and not just an AI?" I asked.

"AI aren't a-a-a-allowed on board; we need some jobs reserved for people and not me-mechs," I could hear Cricket laughing.

"Where are we going?" Ambrotos asked while reclining his chair.

"Scyra."

"SCYRA?!" Ambrotos and I shouted.

I spent about half of my life in and out of Scyra, it's where I learned certain tactics and how to wield a spear and staff. Scyra was unique and was a province split from the other nine due to a falling out before chimeras were even real. They had amazing training facilities, unbeatable weather, an aquarium with a waterfall, a zoo, a wildlife sanctuary, underwater caves, atolls and a seamount.

"Have... have the two of you not been before?"

"Does it count if you don't leave the airport?" Ambrotos asked. "Kidding, it's just been probably a decade."

"I have, but not for a while," I said. "Sibil must have been busy working diplomacy, if he's allowed on the sands of Scyra."

"He has, he's in the am-ambassador's building. We have some time before he is done with a meeting so we can walk around for aaaaaaaa while. But only for o-o-o-one stop." Basil gave us what felt like a forced smile.

"Oof, a forced smile? We're going out to a pasture to get the Lennie special." Ambrotos chuckled as he spoke.

A puzzled expression dotted across Basil's face.

"Ignore him. He's saying you're going to try to kill us."

Basil turned bright red and exclaimed, "**NO!** No, I'm just not u-u-u-u-used to chimeras. What we are taught and told aaaand then actually seeing you guys in person is different."

"But you work with Sibil," I said.

"We're told he's an outlier, and I have only met a few of you. Sibil, the girl chimera at the island now, you two and Nora when I first got my position."

"Nora's there?" Ambrotos asked as he helped himself to the minifridge.

"No, idiot. She's on Pala. You *know* she's almost always on Pala," I replied.

"If you two are re-re-ready then we can get started." The two of us nodded. "The extremist faction you both encountered today is known as Hurricane. We think they were originally called Verrucosus or that co-co-could be a smaller group. Either way, they are connected."

The lights dimmed and the windows stopped letting in light. A holographic slide show appeared with dates, pictures, names and more.

"They radicalized when Lissax joined. This was the kazamite prison break. It left 14 dead humans and fr-freed dozens of kazamites. They have gotten worse, with the nuke being the culmination project."

"Super entertaining, but what does this have to do with *us*? Surely, the Aesir are just so good that they can handle this themselves," Ambrotos said.

"Admiral Ha-havi has stated that he will not be sending additional forces to get involved. Admiral Callum, is making an effort to stand out more aaaaaand using this as a chance for more funding and power. Admiral Oceana is still grieving... I'm unsure how much longer she can go on before she i-i-implodes."

"Admiral Callum is on CUOPS and dealing with the baddies, Admiral Oceana is supposed to be on construction and pathfinding with FUOPS and sustainment being Admiral Havi?" I asked.

"I don't know thooooose words."

"Current and future operations. Future being what is forecasted, and current being current and immediate agendas."

"Then yes."

"I agree with Ambrotos, what does this have to do with us? Thanks for the info and all, but each admiral has forces and we have a standing military. I don't get where chimeras come into play," I said.

"Well, pods are being called up left and right. Some have been sent to the m-m-m-moons, some have been sent to assist the military on co-co-covert missions. And some have been requested by the admirals by name even. Sibil wanted you both to update him in person. I think the idea is to mostly keeeeeeep pods together on missions."

"I haven't seen the rest of my pod in almost half a year," I said.

"That's cause your pod sucks. Historia, Ikeros and you are the only unique ones in your pod. The only fun ones. Actually, I wouldn't doubt it if your pod avoids the three of you."

Ignoring Ambrotos I asked Basil, "how much longer until we're there?"

"Roughly eight more hours. We have inflight movies, training videos and video logs on chimeras."

"Oh?" I grabbed the remote, leaned in and asked, "who is your favorite chimera?"

Chapter 4

VIOLENCE JUST MIGHT BE THE ANSWER

"I'm from Osmium Coast so you both k-k-k-know we have a statue of Mer. If it wasn't for him, we would have lost *thousands*. We were hit with: coa-coa-coastal flooding, mechs going offline, rioting and looting, a couple hurricanes, waterspouts and a **massive** derecho. He's the only chimera I knoooooow of that has a statue."

"I remember reading about him, he died there," I said. "Because the regime didn't want to listen to his ideas and his warnings. The regime killed him."

"Yes and no. He brought baaaaaaack ancient science concepts that were lost to us and found practical applications. Necrobotics, healing concrete and healing metal, rewilding, boat rescue water striders, and familiar scrying were all his ideas. The way he thought was something out of sciiiiiiience fiction, he's probably the smartest lifeform born on this world."

"Didn't realize Mer had fans."

"Of course he does, at least where I'm from. I have a sleeved foil holo and a regular foiled holo BIC cards of him." Basil pulled out a trading card and showed us Mer.

We looked as the hologram posed on top of the card with Mer carrying his notorious collapsible mortar and plasma shotgun.

"You're kidding. The hell is a 'BIC card' Basil?" Ambrotos asked.

"Not at all, and they're binary incursion cards. Chimera BIC cards are illegal and banned in the card game, but he's too cool to give up. He died by a hurricane crushing him and sweeping hi-hi-hi-him away because he was saving the ancestors of our current prefecture. I also like Jure and Eskander."

"Not many people know about Jure, I'm kinda surprised. I'm also a bit surprised with these chimera cards. I didn't realize chimeras were a course offered in school," I said.

"It's not, I just love collecting the cards and trading them. I also enjoy learning about chimera culture. You guyyyyyys have your own: folklores, urban myths and legends. Chimeras have only been around for a few centuries I think, and you already have things it took humans thousands of years to build. I also love how some of you guys have unique mutations causing some of you to look more kazamite, while others l-l-l-l-look more human. Some of you have freckles, while some of you have sails on your back. I even heard you guys have the same skin as sharks!"

"And having shark skin is… interesting?" I asked.

"Your species is like a cocktail or a maaaaargarita, jumbled with so much stuff. Different inputs have different outputs. I'm sure you guys ha-ha-have favorite chimeras, kazamites and humans. Oh can I have my card back please?"

Ambrotos snorted and said, "it ain't Sibil."

I rolled my eyes. "Cricket, my AI, has told me of some humans. I mostly find interest in battles and tactics, not your people. You said this card was a 'sleeved foil holo'? What makes a card… *that*?"

Uh oh. Basil was practically vibrating.

"The l-l-l-l-look! Different colors, unique gear, weapons and abilities, physical traits and rarity. There's only so many cards in existence, and not every chimera gets a card."

"Do you have a card of me?" I asked as I gave the card back.

"Uh… no. I know someone who does, and I a-a-a-a-asked them for some facts on the card."

"That's not creepy," Ambrotos chimed in.

"It waaaaaaas how you favor a machete and sp-sp-spear. Euclidean right?"

I frowned and Basil immediately went into damage control.

"I realize how weird this muuuuuuuust be as I say this out loud."

"It's a bit odd to be a trading card, I gotta admit. But I made a face because your card is wrong. I like bidents, and sabers. Euclidean *fencing* is the full name."

"Mandy, don't stop there. Tell Basil your address, mother's maiden name, high school mascot ya know, the works. Basil, that silhouette on the screen, who is that supposed to be?" Ambrotos pointed to the monitor.

Basil tapped the screen and brought out a miniature hologram.

"One of your he-he-heroes. Tezcatlipoca."

Ambrotos sat up and raised his eyebrows in confusion. "Teska…tezca…"

"Tezcatlipoca, he saaaaaaaved Grenfall and died as well. It was a long long time ago, Grenfall was hit with: cloud burst, locus, a-a-and literal dozens of squalls across the prefecture. Of course the rest of Azio was hit, but Grenfall took the worst of it. I believe you all refer to him as Tez or Tezcatli."

We both ahhh'd in unison.

"What else do you know about chimeras?" I asked Basil.

Ambrotos groaned and distracted himself by scrolling through the channels and looking out the window.

I learned quickly that Ambrotos had the right idea, because Basil would not shut up. Basil spent almost the entire remainder of the flight asking me questions and going off on hundreds of tangents. At one point, I looked over and saw Ambrotos drooling and snoring, how lucky.

At one point, Basil passed out and I was offered peace.

"I have a favorite person," Cricket chirped. "You didn't ask mine."

"Cricket, please…"

"The lead vocalist in that band we went to."

"Cricket don't–"

The shuttle's speaker system played a two second guitar rift from a metalcore song and it woke Basil up. Basil coughed and then went back to talking.

We didn't land until a couple hours before sunset, so we only had time to pick one place to see. Ambrotos opened his mouth to make a suggestion, but I shut it down. Since I was on Basil duty, I would choose. And so I chose the animal sanctuary, it wasn't a full blown zoo but it had cute animals. I wasn't too into animals, but Historia loved them and she rubbed off on me.

The three of us made our way inside of the sanctuary and immediately made a plan. Some zoos, aquariums and sanctuaries had *too* many tourist attractions, so you have to be smart when visiting. For example, this one was divided into animals from Earth, animals from Kazar and then there was a small area that had animals that could thrive on both worlds. It was mostly small critters of course, and people seldom visited, but at least it was there. We started with the Earth creatures and it was always a treat to see how friendly these animals were.

"On Callum's colony ship, Avalon, are there animals?" I asked. "I guess that goes for Elysium too. I already know the answer for Asgard."

"I'm sure there are a feeeeeeew here and there, but not really. Avalon has an atrium full of some animals but I mean you already know a lot of animals didn't make it off of Earth. There was a c-c-c-c-colony ship dedicated to animals trailing our Stanford Torus though."

"Your what now?" Ambrotos asked.

"Stanford Torus, you know? The Iroquois and Delian? Either way, Noah's Hope was an animal colony ship. There were thousands of a-a-a-a-animals onboard and I'm sure it cost quadrillions or something because some animals had unique biomes. Some were carnivores and some changed their behavior while innnnnn captivity and some died from depression. In some courses, you learn about th-th-th-the animals that went extinct because of our lack of efficiency. One of them was the beluga whales."

"And pandas right?" I asked with a dash of pride. I remembered one of Historia's favorite Earth animals.

"Wh-wh-what's a panda? OH! The bear thing? Those died before we had regen metal. Heck, I think those died before 3D printing bones annnnnnd tissue cloning became common practice."

I frowned at the thought of any species going extinct; that has never happened as far as we know. Cricket told Historia once that scientists were able to bring extinct races back to life and even make new ones. Like the famous wholly mice; I wondered why they didn't save the pandas.

"Anyway, how did you categorize all of these animals?" Ambrotos asked.

"Farm, urban, and marine! I'm su-sure the carnivores were split as well. I've even heard that it had a special section for annoying and mischievous animals."

"What happened?" I asked.

"An issue with power sources. There were backups, but all of them took too long to kick on. Too many animals died during the power outage, like ones that needed theeeeee cold or needed stable water conditions. Then the en-en-engine failed, things just snowballed. It ended with there being a vote on which animals to save that could cohabitate with humans seamlessly and not cost t-t-t-too much."

We continued walking through the sanctuary, finally stopping at a feeding area. I reached into a bucket outside the enclosure, and grabbed a couple pear slices and kneeled down as a fox ran over to me.

I smiled and said, "I think foxes are cute, but I thought dogs were man's best friend."

Basil chuckled before replying . "Man's best friend is a dog, and the readings say that mankind *did* want dogs. But they weren't cost effective. People had a-a-a-a-allergies, some dog breeds were prone to health issues, and some too were loud. Cats were next, but even more people were allergic to them and they kept getting into tiiiiiiiny places and knocking things over. The humans of the time voted on a test for animals to be selected. It tested: compatibility with humans or other creatures, survivability and intelligence and memory capacity. Animals like foxes, ravens and parrots won. And of course rats and roaches made it and I believe there are a f-f-f-few turtles, tortoises, frogs and toads on ships. Illegally of course."

We left the Earth side of the sanctuary and went to the merged side. This side was dedicated to animals that could have lived on Earth. It was between the Kazar side and Earth side and of course the first animals were birds. We approached the birds in the pond as they swam to us for treats.

"Did you guys have gyimps on Earth?" I asked while grabbing food crumbs.

The animal yelled at us for food.

We obliged.

"We called them 'ducks' on Earth. They didn't have t-t-two inch horns either and the ones on Earth had differently shaped tails but besides that, they almost entirely look like our ducks."

Ambrotos chimed in and asked, "oh neat, did they say 'duck' at you?"

"Er.. no. They quacked."

"Quack? Why weren't they called quacks then?"

"I uh… I don't actually know. You g-g-g-guys have some animals that are also just odd, but are overall consistent with species. Like you guys have f-f-f-fish just like we did, but the popular ones here are skaimmadas."

We watched as the antler fish swam in circles.

"I'm not sure aquatic animals had an-an-antlers, but you guys still make sushi out of them. Our fish didn't haaaaaaave those feelers on its stomach either."

"Then how would they feel and protect their young?" I asked.

"Oh! I'm actually not a zoologist! I don't haaaaave the answers for you guys' questions." A nervous chuckle followed the end of Basil's sentence.

"Wait, I actually know about these!" Basil kneeled down to pet a quillry.

"See how fat it is? Quillries are fat like pigs, have e-e-e-ears like fennec foxes, and are as friendly as dogs. Super friendly actually, like golden retrievers."

"You had a breed of dog that hunted gold?" Ambrotos sounded as shocked as I looked.

"I think they're just named after their coats, so no. Quillries have be-be-be-better survival instinct than most dogs from what I've heard. While quillries are covered in their exoskeleton like an armadillo, dogs weren't. Quillries also haaaaaaaaave hooves and short tails, like deer. The only thing quillries have in common with dogs is big personalities and size. They can: trot, dance and prance and when in danger or rushing, they can roll into a b-b-b-ball. I think it's also cute how they have their eyes on the side of their head too; it's like goats, cows or rabbits."

Ambrotos finished off his and cleared his throat before speaking.

"What about cadeze? Did you guys have them?"

"Those are actually more like deeeeeevil dogs, or warthogs meet dogs; because cadeze ha-ha-have tusks. Plus dogs are covered in fur."

"Cadeze *do* have fur."

"Yea but not the same. Cadeze have a sort of a mane, and are thin. Dogs also don't have those patterns and markings that cadeze have.

Annnnnnnd dogs come in different colors while cadeze only come in white and brown."

Basil's watch beeped.

"Dang, we sh-should get going."

I sighed and said, "I wish Historia was here; she knows more about animals than anyone I know."

"I think I've seen her BIC card. She's supposedly the best fighter in your pod and top five out of living chimeras right? The ninjutsu girl?" Basil asked while rushing us to the exit.

"I don't know what 'ninjutsu' is, but she had a painting of a shadow figure in her room. She called the figure *'youxia'* but I don't know what it means. As for our pod, she's the best and I've seen her during drills, training and on missions take down a dozen men alone. And for the top five, of *course* she is. She's **Historia**," I replied.

Ambrotos scoffed and said, "as if. She always seems busy when I want to spar."

I smiled and said, "maybe it's because she can't stand you. She doesn't waste time on one trick pony fighters that cheat with their gauntlets. If it makes you feel any better, you can spar with me."

"I thought we agreed I only spar with good fighters."

"Pick up a saber, gun or sword."

"Pft, Basil you think this kelpie can handle me?"

Basil fidgeted. "I haaaaaave aaaaaa q-q-q-q-question."

"Oof, must be serious," Ambrotos said while looking at me. "Sounds like a lawnmower."

"That word... kelpie and kelpies, what does it mean?" Basil looked uncomfortable saying the words.

I opened my mouth to reply but Ambrotos did first.

"Relax dude, you shouldn't cower because you're asking questions; that's the chimera way. Chimeras and kazamites eat kelp as babies like humans eat or drink milk as babies. Chimeras can: drink milk, eat kelp

91

and a liquid formula substance made up of who knows what. I know better than anyone else, I had a nuts and jerk version of it for years. They call chimeras and kazamites kelpies like we could call humans milkies."

The three of us arrived at the building Sibil was in, and it was hard not to hate him. Scyra wasn't known for its skyscrapers, so it was easy to point out the roughly eight on the archipelago. They were housing him in the ambassador building and it was breathtaking seeing how clean and new the building looked compared to the simple houses and buildings across the region. It had to be ten stories high, completely made up of living glass and living metal; no way Scyra allowed this on their land without the regime giving up on something valuable.

As we entered the lobby, we were greeted by a friendly attendant that directed us to the room and floor Sibil was on. We took the elevator up to his floor which had a secretary typing away at a desk outside of his suite.

She smiled at us and said, "good evening Basil and company. Sibil is in the middle of a very important conference right now, but you are allowed inside. If you all remain quiet that is."

We smiled and thanked her and then entered the room as quietly as we could. Ambrotos was last to enter and slowly closed the door, and then yanked it shut. He shrugged and whispered "sorry." We went to the back where we of course eavesdropped on a conversation we had no business hearing. Sibil didn't look at us when we entered, despite the door slam, but he made it a point to show slight irritation.

Sibil stood in the center of this massive beige colored room, on a virtual meeting with: Havi, Callum, and the primarch. They were all holograms of course, since no regime was allowed on Scyra anymore. The loophole was allowing Sibil to be the ambassador and liaison for the regime. He thought it made him more respected I guess, but humans don't respect apricot skinned chimeras. His skin was laced with blue freckles and he stood confidently, as if he already had a seat at the table.

"And this is your recommendation?" Havi asked, his hologram facing the primarch.

"*Heavy* recommendation. We simply cannot have you running around with the riff raff! Believe you me, I have your best interest at heart, Havi!" The primarch protested.

"Excuse my skepticism."

"Oh lighten up! You're supposed to be the *wise* one in the group, not the cynical one."

"Wise men normally are. Our enemies have made me this way, or maybe you've forgotten that it is your... *leadership*, that has brought us to this point."

"Primarch, Havi, if I may?" Callum chimed in.

"You may not. Helmsmanship. That's the noun I'm looking for to describe what you have done, Primarch," Havi said.

"Havi, I am the primarch and you will not speak to me like this. We are all on the same team. This is human's country for goodness sake! There is no need for microaggression, it is just so kazamite-like. Let's be humane about this; surely we can come to an understanding."

"I did, you simply need to follow it. Or don't but regardless, any non-Aesir that steps foot on our vessel will be treated with extreme prejudice. We do not know who we can trust in these times."

"But you can trust us," Callum said.

Havi scoffed and said, "I've seen your work and it pains me that we on paper have the same position. Your state mandated maps that you 'checked' have a typo, you misspelled Saxia."

Callum's eyes tripled in size as everyone looked at him. "It must have been faulty programming. I assure y'all I checked every—"

"And I saw your first draft, you misspelled Drednigh at first. You forgot the letter 'd'. That was caught by your **unpaid** intern. I don't even need to bring up your lack of pink in the area of Hylo and Saxia or the lack of black at Kadura's beaches."

"Gentlemen," Sibil said. "I hate to burden you with our time constraints, but we are over our allotted limit."

"Sibil speaks the truth, I have things to attend to. Primarch, we need generals, not politicians."

"I assure you, I have the people's best interest in mind. I have the people's support."

"And I have the guns."

Not a second later, Havi disconnected himself.

"Bless your heart Sibil, your help was welcome as always. Callum, let us take this to a private channel, shall we? Goodbye Sibil." The primarch and Callum hung up.

Sibil turned to face us and threw his hands in the air and then clapped them together to greet us, Ambrotos and I frowned at his human gesture. After centuries of cohabitation, all of the races have learned the verbal and nonverbal cues of each other. Sibil however, embodies *too* many human ones. He snaps his fingers, uses his hands when he talks, finger guns, way too into physical contact and more. Some of us joked and wondered if because he kept hanging around them so much, is that why he had so many human physical traits. How else could you explain his webless hands and feet when in water or his human ears with no sails? Even his shit colored eyes looked as if he borrowed them from a human. It's as if he was a human cosplaying a chimera; clearly a sign of someone who has spent far too much time exclusively with humans.

"Ah Ambrotos! Glad to see you recovered from breaking all the bones in your hand." Sibil said while walking over to his desk to pour himself a drink. Another human mannerism, alcoholic drinks when talking.

"All the bones? That's odd, my middle finger still worked."

"Is that how you greet the lead chimera?"

"I forget, do we shake hands? Get on our knees and put our hair into a bun? Us proletariats seldom see royalty."

94

"Always a pleasure. Mandy, I haven't seen you in ages! How are you?"

"I'm not a human, we don't have to do greetings by faking pleasantries. Who is this?" I motioned to the chimera sitting on the couch.

It was a young chimera with skin somewhere between sky blue and royal blue. She wore a skully and sat incredibly still. Sibil motioned for the girl to step forward and introduce herself.

"I am Carmilla," she said.

She had black scleras and radiant purple irises. She was young, but she wasn't a child. She had to be around her early 20's, so she was definitely part of a new pod. Was a new pod training this whole time and we didn't know?

"Hi, I'm Ambrotos. Huge fan of saying 'sounds good' to Sibil when not a letter out of his mouth sounds good."

Sibil scoffed. "You just don't understand the intricacies of leading the chimeras and being our ambassador."

Without skipping a beat Ambrotos gave a thumbs up and said, "sounds good!"

"Hi, I'm Mandy, I hope it's a pleasure to know you. How'd you end up in Scyra?" I asked her.

"I was told to come here and follow Sibil's guidance. He told me to be silent," Carmilla said.

I rolled my eyes and looked at Sibil and asked, "why is she here, Sibil?"

"While Ambrotos has been galavanting, and you playing... house with your boyfriend, Historia took it upon herself to offer wise counsel. We need better trained chimeras and ones that aren't reckless and renegades. So I took her under my wing. Carmilla is also the leader of her pod."

"Historia never mentioned her or her pod, how many of them are there?"

"You aren't owed answers, Mandy. Such only child syndrome," said Sibil.

"Imagine being a pick me and nobody picked you, couldn't be me." I turned my back to Sibil and turned my attention to Carmilla. "I like your name, it's pretty. Who named you?" I asked her.

"Historia. She is the pod leader before my pod," said Carmilla.

I chuckled and replied, "I know her. She's my best friend, my sister."

Her face scrunched up as she tilted her head and asked, "what's a 'best friend'?"

"A **distraction**," Sibil said. "That is enough introductions, we have work to do. Basil, do you mind gathering us a few refreshments? They're already outside."

Basil nodded and left to get them.

Sibil continued. "We must discuss the developing situation with this faction causing chaos, and our course of action."

"You said 'we' but I think you're a little confused. The 'we' today was Ambrotos and I, and 'we' stopped a literal nuke."

"And that was great! However, it simply will not be enough. Here's what I'm thinking: Ambrotos we send your entire pod to guard Havi, another pod for Oceana, one for Callum and of course a pod for the primarch."

I rolled my eyes and groaned as Ambrotos threw himself onto a couch and kicked his feet up.

"Here we go," Ambrotos said. "What do they say about humans with brown eyes again? Full of *what*?"

"Ambrotos and I or any other chimera is not needed. The humans have **more** than enough men to take care of Hurricane. The *humans'* plan should be to strike or at least counter while the iron is still hot while we *assist* them. I thought the whole point of your position was to help our people."

"I am! I'm just playing the game of politics, Mandy. To win, you have to play. But the best way to beat the game is on defense," Sibil said.

I rolled my eyes as Ambrotos chuckled in the back.

"The 'defense' is what almost got people killed today," I said. "A military needs to be proactive and reactive, not just reactive. This reactive and inaction is because humans are too indecisive. I don't understand how creatures that die so young are so slow on making decisions and acting on them."

"You know what I like about you, Mandy?"

"I don't care."

"Exactly, you don't care about these concepts which is why I must lead the chimeras. If not me, then whom? Don't worry though, your concerns are noted. But we need to show solidarity with the humans and the regime. I have opened your many messages and emails about chimera problems, trust me, I'm taking care of us. Of *our* people."

He gave me what could only be assumed to be, a reassuring smile.

"Didn't realize you were papabear," Ambrotos said, finally chiming in.

"I'm in charge of **all** chimeras, Ambrotos."

My teeth chattered as I said, "you are in charge of **no one**."

Sibil continued but with more base in his voice, *another* silly human mannerism.

"I *guide* us into systematic order under humans. Yes, we take orders from the humans, but I delegate and lead us chimeras. That's just the nature of the world."

"Hey Mandy, or new girl, quick question," said Ambrotos. "What's a slave who's in charge of other slaves called again?"

"Slave," Carmilla casually said.

Ambrotos snickered. "And the Yankees win again."

Sibil was about to reply when the projector turned on. It was a live feed of Asgard under attack. Humans rushed to an area and were gunned down by unknown assailants. It had to be Hurricane. We all hyper focused on the projection and listened as the soldiers barked commands over the sound of gunfire and explosions. Cricket said that because Havi has banned every outsider, us signaling help for Asgard was pointless. The feed changed to a holding cell, or a torture chamber. Inside, was the survivor from the earlier almost-nuke attack. The group broke him out within seconds and immediately left the area, but they didn't head towards the escape pods. Instead, they armed him.

"It's an assassination…" The words trailed out of Ambrotos' mouth as he sat up.

They went hall to hall until they finally caught Havi entering a big open room with tables, chairs and other furniture. They all drew their weapons and surrounded him with one of them in front. All two dozen plus of them wore masks, but the one in front took theirs off to speak to Havi. It was a kazamite woman.

"Do you remember me? Do you know who I am?" She asked him.

"Uninvited assassins. Indifferent to the position you've put me in," Havi said.

"Autumn, Boreamber 15th, 104th juncture, you came to my home. You took all the males."

"I sometimes misread your calendar, what YAL is that?"

"*We* don't use YAL, our history doesn't start the year after **human** landing. You took my family from me."

"I can't possibly remember every last person I meet," he said. "Maybe your family was soldiers or–"

"We were farmers! And you made us killers, so I'm here to kill you. Fake god."

He sighed and said, "what's the plan here? What is your tactic?"

"Our plan is to free our brethren that **you** kidnapped, and then end you and your tyranny."

"You attempt to launch a quantum bomb, break into my people's home, and you bring up *my* crimes? I am old school in the sense that rules have war, war needs to be organized. I have done my best to keep this law of nature but people like you make me work twice as hard. Certain weapons are prohibited, acknowledging major holidays and never attacking generals in their war camps are just some of the rules. And if you do confront the other side's leader, it's leader versus leader. So next time, tell Lissax to stop sending people to die in her stead."

"You're nothing more than a villain," she said and then spat at his feet.

"There are no 'villains' in the real world. And if there were, it'd be the group of you ambushing a veteran in their home. Thankfully, you didn't bring enough people."

"There's a platoon of us."

"Forgive me, I am sorry about your family, truly. I understand your grief but I am not a frail and senile old man. Your family and village were sacked during a fight, and **lost**. Your people called it 'raid season' because it lasted the entire month of Boreamber. I actually admire how effective your raid season was. I do sympathize with your people, but you have taken too many cycles to retaliate. And time only strengthens an Aesir's bite, like fine mead."

Havi *just* finished his sentence and already had his hand on her head. She gasped, and then her head imploded in the palm of his hand. Before the others had a chance to react, a… *forcefield* extended from his body, and flung *everything* across the room.

"Fire!"

A maelstrom of bullets raged, and a maelstrom of bullets hovered in the air. The bullets were crushed as if they hit a wall, and after a couple seconds, fell to the ground. The intruders lowered their guns, stunned.

"This? **This** is your plan?" Havi spat the words out with a frown.

You could hear not anger, but disgust and disappointment in his voice. He sighed and all the furniture and intruders began to levitate.

"I miss the good old days, I feel as if I blinked, and the way we wage war changed," he said. "I admire your resolve, but you have too many people wanting revenge. You all keep failing because you don't realize too many chefs spoil the gravy."

Everything fell to the ground.

One of the fighters that didn't lose their balance drew a knife and took off their mask, and another jumped to their feet and primed a grenade. They both screamed and charged towards Havi. They were faster than normal kazamites and even had more muscle than normal kazamites, but they were still only kazamites.

The grenadier tossed the beeping grenade at Havi and Havi took a step back not realizing what it was, and tried to catch it. It was a helios grenade, the worst kind of grenade. It blew up and let out such intense heat, you could almost feel it from here. The attackers shielded their eyes, but you could see the grenadier smile as the explosive radiated. The cackle of the grenade went on for a few seconds, but one sound raged over the grenade.

"Did you assume a grenade was all it took?"

Havi was containing the explosion between his hands and then threw it at some of the intruders, vaporizing them instantly.

The grenadier yelled, "so it's a forcefield only? Die outworlder!"

They threw an electric grenade or an EMP at him, but Havi did the same thing. He caught it and shook his head.

"Expect disappointment, and you'll never meet him," he said.

Havi absorbed the electricity, and lowered his arms to his side. Electricity arced out of his fingertips, exploding each remaining intruder leaving only the knifeman and three others.

"When I was kid, we were expected to put Asgard first and then ourselves. So, I volunteered for everything. I saw breathtaking places like the black beaches of Kadura, and alien places like the pink valleys and towers in Hylo and Saxia. I was bullied by others for spending my spare time in their library and was called an epistemophilia, as if it was a bad thing."

Havi paused and raised his arms. Two of the attackers rose in the air, their bodies contorted and unnatural in the air. They screamed and exploded, shooting blood all over the knifeman and ground around him. Why didn't the knifeman and other guy run?

Havi continued. "And what training did your Lissax do for her people? What lessons did she learn because I learned a lot in my decades. I learned of something called 'ling chi'."

I realized why the kazamite wasn't moving: Havi used his forcefield on him. Havi moved his hands around, and the knife began to float. It cut the kazamite's hand and then his shoulder, as if it had a mind of its own. Then another cut on his leg. The initial cuts were superficial, but the knife cut every second.

"Wisdom is experience, and experience is painful," he said. "The rest of your people will learn this lesson."

The knife kept cutting at every second until about a minute in where the cuts began to get a bit deeper. The man winced at every cut, you could even watch as his muscles tensed in anticipation each time. Whenever the other guy would try to make a break for it or attack Havi, he used his powers, and forced them to keep watching. Havi took a seat and faced the man as the cuts continued. And after two minutes, the man was **coated** in blood.

"Please…"

"Perhaps it is my fault for not translating. 1,000 cuts, is the translation. That is one cut per second. You will be minced, like cattle for a feast, until you hit the 16 minute mark. I will keep you alive until then and you will watch your ally watch you bleed out. No further than five feet away. At about minute eight, you will start to have pieces sliced off. Toes, fingers, nose, ears, you know, the non essentials."

"Fuck… you…"

"At minute 17, you will be dead, and your ally here will have to choose if they truly want to face the leader of the Aesir. This is the old way, and so we must follow it. And at minute 18, your ally will feign bravery. And their convictions are far stronger than their will to live. At minute 19, they will mop and clean the mess you made in my home. At minute 20, you will give me the location of Lissax and her plan."

"And 21 you realize we won't," the kazamite spat.

They put on a tough face, but the kazamite's words crawled through gritted teeth. Havi stared and didn't answer for a couple seconds, as if he genuinely never considered that as an option.

"At 21, I will teach you what war really is," Havi said. "My people will try out your tactic and ready ourselves for raid season and we will use our colony ships weapons."

The connection to the feed cut and we all stood in Sibil's office in silence.

How?

How was Havi *that* strong? Humans are supposed to be weaker than chimeras and he looked like he used magic. How was *he* jumped, and made it look like he jumped *them*? How does he manipulate forces like that? Are the other colony ship leaders this strong too? Or… is he the *weak* one?

"How do you fight someone like that?" Ambrotos said out loud what my soul was thinking.

Sibil shot him a look and said, "you, do not. I have had enough of your disrespect and **treason**, Ambrotos. Our duty is to the humans, our creators. We do not probe for their weaknesses. We assist however we can because that is how we were made; we are tools and instruments for the regime."

"Mayo isn't an instrument, but clearly **you** are Sibil. I'm not a tool. Eh, maybe actually," Ambrotos said.

I spoke up this time and said, "Sibil, this is ridiculous. We don't need to be defending the regime or their leaders at every corner when they have **this** type of power. This conversation is silly, and so is forcing every chimera to fall under one banner. And one that's not even our own."

Sibil replied coldly, "your lack of dedication is silly."

Ambrotos scoffed and said, "that what you said when you buried the last one in your pod?"

The words left Ambrotos' mouth as he stood up from the couch and started walking towards Sibil.

"Tread carefully, Ambrotos."

"Sorry, where should I tread? We aren't even allowed to bury our own people because they always get sent off to a lab. But I guess you know nothing about being sent to a lab and experimented on, huh? Fake progressive Sibil where we hear the words come out of your mouth, but it's with human lips. Remember when Chevalier got in trouble for cremating Eowyn and was labeled an outcast? Chevalier 'treaded' as an outcast near that damn volcanoe and now his lungs are fucked and where were *you* for any of this? I guess you treaded carefully to save your own ass."

"Ambrotos I said: **watch** yourself."

"Or else *what?*" Ambrotos asked. "You'll have soldiers come and arrest me?"

"I don't need soldiers' help to put you in your place, Ambrotos."

Ambrotos snorted and said, "chillax, we're all friends here right?"

Ambrotos turned around and plopped back on the couch again.

"And yet somehow, I'm not relaxed. I thank you Mandy, for not being like him. However, you still need some rearing."

I shifted my shoulders and raised an eyebrow.

"You must understand Mandy," he said. "There is a line that cannot be publicly crossed, so Major Trogz and I have been working on a solution. I believe we have found the best one."

My left eye twitched as I asked, "what did you do?"

"Reassigned your overly close human friend to Pala. Some of his peers have reported a shift in his behavior, not wanting to hang out anymore outside of work, discrediting certain... conservative authors. So between his change in his baseline behavior and... *unorthodox* approach to chimeras, kazamite and human issues, he needed to be refocused. It is strange how this faction had so much inside information, as if someone *told* them. And yet when we conducted a health and wellness check on him and all of his personal possessions, no evidence appeared. There was a trend though, him poking around sensitive areas but there is not enough proof for a court-martial, just a hunch. He needed the redirection though, you two are far too close."

"Sibil, I'm not Ambrotos, I will fuck you up. This is a family matter, stay out of my life."

"But aren't we family, Mandy?"

"There's that 'we' shit again," I said.

"All chimeras are family and yes **we** serve at the regime's pleasure, but you so happen to keep spending your time with the one human you shouldn't. And that's just bad for optics; you both look like you're dating. And we know chimera aren't supposed to think about such things, you'll be banished and suspended just like the love birds. Plus you could do so much better than him anyway, from what I hear he is unorthodox in his training as well. Just shy of a mess up."

My teeth began to chatter. I shifted my shoulders again and Ambrotos sat up.

"He is my brother, and I don't appreciate how you're speaking about my **actual** family."

"Oh please Mandy, I'm more of your brother than Nic is. The only thing you have in common is that you're both orphans, he's such a screw up he couldn't even be a son correctly."

Before my brain could process it, I dashed towards Sibil with my knife drawn and aimed for his neck. It happened all in a blink of an eye but luckily, I didn't make it. Ambrotos jumped in front of me before I got to Sibil.

"Ambrotos, **move**. When he pissed off *Eskander*, that should've been my sign."

"Orange isn't worth the squeeze. Not for a pseudo-chimera," Ambrotos said as he lowered my wrist.

"*Pseudo?* Like it or not, **I'm** a chimera," said Sibil.

"Dude, I'm literally trying to keep you alive. Shut up."

"Oh please. I'm the reason the lot of you are able to freely parade around all idiotic and do renegade things like turn off your AI, or not wear helmets and play superhero. I allowed you to get all that ancient media that inspires your humor today, Ambrotos."

"Allowed? You're delusional, you literally didn't do shit.

"**Wrong**. I do more for our people than both of you *combined*. And I wasn't even a pod leader. What have **you** done for your under performing pod, Ambrotos?"

"Uh, I dunno. Maybe protect the border between us and the Afuera, train units on the moons, stop a nuke, not have a single one in the pod die yet. Not much I guess, just literally a Saturday. But no worries, I can see how this 'leadership' thing can be hard and scary when you sit safely away from the battle. That's what ambassadors do right? Throw rocks and hide their hands?"

"Is that what you think of me and my title?" Sibil asked.

"No, I think your title and position are made up. And I think you're the chimera cuck representative. I'm sure Mandy thinks worse, but hasn't spilled the beans. And just to be clear, only one person snuck into my cell, and you weren't her. She has more people skills than you and that must suck, because you'll never be her. All you do is cover your ass."

"I make the hard decisions for our people, and you think that makes me a bad guy?"

"Doesn't make you a good one."

"So then what? What do *you* suggest? We join Hurricane and their destruction of humans?"

Ambrotos shrugged.

"Ambrotos don't be silly, you think these are *all* the humans in our solar system? The rest of the torus is still out there. In deep space. We join the kazamites, purge the humans offworld and then fight the

Iroquois? It's a space megastructure that is **armed** and able to destroy worlds."

"You think the humans are gonna glass one of the only habitable planets and moons they've seen in how many centuries out in space? I'm not into space stuff and even I know that this galaxy is massive, but not every world is habitable for humans. There's like a dozen moons and planets in our system, and half of them require terraforming or to live underground or underwater. Our world is their best hope."

"And how many would die to prove that point?" Sibil asked.

I scoffed.

"They have a lot more to lose than we do," I said. " We aren't even given names, or parents. And yet we do their every bidding. Humans are finite and mortal, we aren't."

"We are not immortal or gods, Mandy. We are peacekeepers upholding law and order. Kazamites need structure and the humans graciously provide it."

"Wowzers Sibil," Ambrotos said while shaking his head. "Is the only thing you do is defend them?"

"Well you accuse them and bad mouth them daily. I think sometimes you let your opinions cloud your judgment about the facts. And the fact of the matter is humans are in charge and have the planet's best interest in mind."

"Sibil I'm curious, does your throat ever get hoarse? From sucking so much human–"

"**Refreshments**?" Basil blurted out from the entrance of the room. "I-I'm sorry it took so long. I didn't realize there were dietary c-c-c-concerns and made some specific last minute adjustments. No mustard right?"

"That a fucking chili cheese dog?!" Ambrotos wasted no time, and rushed over to Basil to grab a hot dog for each hand.

I sheathed my knife and walked over to Basil, but not before shooting Sibil a look. Basil gave me a nervous smile as I walked over, as if hoping I wouldn't draw my knife and strike.

"Thank you, Basil," I said as I reached for a cheeseburger.

"My pl-pl-pleasure. I will leave this here for you guys and let you know when yourrrrrr next appointment is here, sir. I'll stay here for a second to check my messages and then I'll be in my office if you neeeeeed me." Basil nodded and gave us all a smile. Basil

"I have a question," Carmilla said, looking at me. "Is this 'Nic' really your brother if he's human?"

I nodded.

"Do not get delusions of grandeur, Carmilla," said Sibil. "Mandy will have you subscribe to her renegade beliefs, but blood is thicker than water, and she has *chimera* blood." He sat down and poured himself his third drink.

"Blood of the covenant is thicker than the water of the womb," I said. "Those who twist words to half truths, are full liars." I shot Sibil a look as I said it. "That's the whole quote, Carmilla. Meaning that we should remember those that face challenges with us, are family. That's what Nic told me at least. So, I chose Nic and Historia to be my family."

"But humans are weaker than us, how can they be seen as part of our 'family', our pod?" Carmilla asked curiously.

"Your pod is only those who were made in a lab with you. Your friends, family and loved ones can extend beyond that. Humans are only physically weaker than us, but they have the same heart as any of us other races. And they can love, just like you and me. I've heard love can even transcend space and time, but you'd have to ask Eskander and Eleanor about that."

Sibil scoffed and mumbled something under his breath. I continued and ignored him.

"It means, you'll always find your way back home to your family. No matter when, no matter where, no matter how."

Ambrotos inhaled a hotdog and said between bites and breaths, "Mandy that was deep. I never pegged you for a lofty dreamer."

"I agree. Chimera are tools, Mandy. You and Ambrotos keep forgetting that we help keep balance and order, and in return the humans are happy. We are the only family that you **need**, Carmilla. We tutor, mentor, feed and train you. Bonding with others makes it hard for you to do your job."

Ambrotos cleaned the chili and cheese off of his fingers and said, "I wasn't listening to a word he said, but I strongly disagree."

An incoming phone call came through Sibil's sound system, it was Historia. Sibil accepted the call, but the signal seemed to be delayed for a couple seconds.

"Haven't humans housebroken you, Sibil? It's rude to answer calls with company." Ambrotos looked up to see the caller. "Oh if it isn't karate girl! That girl swears she's the best pod leader, but she can't beat me in any of the tests."

The screen cleared up and Historia was smiling at us and looked dead at Ambrotos and said, "oh, if it isn't no second date boy." I bursted out laughing as Ambrotos frowned. "Hi Mandy! Sibil, I sent my report back. It's pretty bare bones; I didn't see action like Mandy and Ambrotos."

"So I saw." Sibil replied.

She turned her attention to Carmilla. "Hi, my little flower." Carmilla smiled.

"Mandy has been teaching me new words and themes," Carmilla said.

"If there's anyone you can trust in this universe, it's her."

"**Anyway**, Historia, I would like you to continue your mentorship of Carmilla. But, we must discuss your 'curriculum'." Sibil squinted.

"Uh oh, what happened for her to catch your attention."

Sibil motioned for Carmilla to speak for herself.

"A human soldier during training called me a 'spotted diet human', so I ignored him. 'Declaring peace' just like you said. But he was offended and called me a name, I didn't know what it meant but I didn't like it. So I matched him and said 'bad boy'. He didn't like that, so he grabbed my wrist, so I broke his. I started below, got on level with him, and then went a level above."

Sibil sighed and palmed his face. "No, she put him through a wall and into the ICU."

Ambrotos and I both chuckled. He groaned and continued.

"I'd blame Scyra and the teachers here, but her fighting style is a blend between your fighting style, and their style. So you both share the blame on this one."

"What exactly did she do wrong?" Historia asked, which made Ambrotos and I chuckle again.

"She's hurting and scaring the humans. In AND out of training environments. After that incident, people have been afraid to approach her and she's a child!"

Historia frowned and said, "I'm not sure over 18 is a child…"

"Do you see how she looks at humans? Just look at her! She needs to present herself as non-aggressive; it's why I chose **you** to mentor her."

Carmilla turned to face Sibil and asked, "how I 'look' at humans? What's wrong with how I look at humans?"

"Aggressively."

You could see the confusion on her face, and her tapping her nails only confirmed she had no idea what Sibil was talking about.

"How can a lesser thing view you as aggressive? Does popcorn consider you aggressive when you look at it?"

That was the final straw, Ambrotos and I broke out into full blown laughter

With a scrunched up face and veins bulging out of his forehead, Sibil yelled, "**HUMANS ARE NOT POPCORN**! Go run your drills again!"

She nodded and smiled at Historia and walked past Ambrotos and I. She made her way to the exit where Basil was. It was only for a split second, too fast for Basil to fully see it, but the rest of us perceived time faster than humans. Carmilla looked at Basil, and her eyes flashed red and she licked her teeth as if salivating.

"**Go**!" Sibil exclaimed.

Sibil sighed as Historia spoke. "I heard there was an attack on Asgard. Knowing Sibil, I'm guessing he's sending us?" I nodded. "Will Nic be joining us?"

Before I could answer Sibil replied, "no. We don't need distractions, we need actions."

"Probably sounded cooler in your head, didn't it?" Ambrotos mumbled.

"I have asked for a special trained soldier to come and help," Sibil said. "One of them is from a special team and his name is Valen. He should be able to aid you all in all areas of technology and he can hold his own. I would like the three of you and Valen to protect Dr. Maxwell Livington for the rest of the month and part of next."

"Valen's cool, I'm down to clown with him. Who's the egghead?" Ambrotos asked.

"Dr. Livington is a genius who has headed many kazamite and chimera ground breaking research," said Sibil. "If it's research on chimeras and kazamites, he has his research notes involved. Due to him being 80, he's unable to go off-world so he is confined to living out the rest of his days as an old man."

"I keep forgetting 80 is considered getting old for them. I heard that back in the ancient days of Earth, when they hit 80, that was pretty much the end of the show. Imagine being wrinkly, ew," Ambrotos said.

"They worked hard to increase their life expectancy to 120. But still, octogenarians are fragile enough, so be aware. Nonagenarians have to stay on-world because of their bones, and centenarians are essentially on their deathbed."

"The fuck? Are those real words?" Ambrotos paused. "You even broke Mandy, look at her." He motioned to me.

I was so fixated on the scientist's name, I disassociated. It was the same scientist, right? No way it was a coincidence.

"I've seen his files," I said. "He's experimented on kazamites and chimeras, and I don't want any part in protecting him. Even you could understand how this is a conflict of interest for our people, Sibil."

With a cross of his arms, Sibil raised an eyebrow and said, "you don't have a choice."

"No."

"Wasn't a question, Mandy." He stood up and walked over to me as if to intimidate me.

"And yet it was my answer."

"How can one be so ungrateful for all that I have done? This is how you show gratitude?"

"Gratitude? You just tried to intimidate me by walking over and staring me down. Take a mint Sibil, your breath smells like human boots."

"Why do you both treat me like this? I'm not with Lissax or her group. We aren't enemies."

"At least I know my enemy's intentions."

"What do you three think I do? Bend the knee to humans and grovel? Want me to use my knowledge and what? Ambush, Havi? Historia here didn't see the feed but clearly an attack against human leaders is suicide."

"Feed?" Historia asked. "What feed?"

Cricket chimed in. "I just sent all relevant information to all of your NUEs."

Sibil frowned and looked at his NUE for a second. "This can be fabricated, we'll need to sift through all of this to see how true it is."

"What an odd thing to say," said Cricket.

"Cricket, your help isn't needed, thank you. I'm not sure what you're expecting me to do."

"Speak up for us, defend us." Ambrotos responded without skipping a beat.

"And then what? What do you think happens if chimeras rebel? Assuming we win, you don't think the humans in deep space will retaliate? That they won't wipe us and the kazamites out? Be grateful they see us as useful, or we wouldn't exist. Our goal should be to be useful."

"Maybe you missed my entire childhood and teenage years but I'll run the tape back. My entire life was being 'useful' to them," Ambrotos said. "If this is what it means to be useful, then this isn't a life I want. And you're a bot for trailing behind them and doing their every bidding. I can't be the only one thinking this, Historia tell him."

She hesitated to speak, but Ambrotos was right and she knew it.

"I don't want to be under humans, I want to coexist," she said. "I don't want to be a weapon or be 'useful' to an alien race. I want to maybe see what this happily ever after is. A pet, a family… what humans said they had on Earth. I'm just tired of fighting, or training up for the next fight. Why aren't there any chimeras with a 'normal' life but only parts of it? Mandy has a pet, Eskander and Eleanor with true love, why can't we all have stuff like that?"

Sibil sucked his teeth.

"You're all idiots," he said. "You'd all abandon our people just to prove a point and endanger our species? You all think damning our people is the solution as opposed to helping bring peace? I'm guessing your thoughts are in line with theirs, Mandy?"

I sighed.

"I don't know what I want. I know I don't want to go to war against the humans, but I'm probably more willing to fight them than Historia is. And Ambrotos just hates the regime and oppressive leaders. I don't want to go from battle to battle until I die, but how much more of ourselves are we gonna give up for the humans? Nic once said why we are created, doesn't have to be our purpose. I just want peace and to be left alone maybe. And if we have to fight humans, maybe I'm ready for that. But will we never be able to have all three of our races grow together in harmony?"

"Your generations are just so combative. It'd help if you all were more like my generation or the ones before me," Sibil said.

"Welp, they're all dead. So stop holding onto them to validate your behavior and motives." Ambrotos said while crossing his arms.

"It's easy to judge me when two of you mostly cause chaos. None of you could survive the politics of this era. These trying times are challenging to navigate, which is why we need organization. But instead you all attack me because I shake hands with humans. None of you could walk a mile in my shoes."

"Sibil," I said, "I would never be *in* your shoes. None of us would. I'd be fired for spending money on morale, **chimera** morale."

"That can be arranged. I planned on you all running drills and exercises while here, but I am willing to be lenient. Of course your hotels are already paid for, but I will also treat the three of you to dinner and breakfast. Once you're free Historia, join us."

Sibil never did nice things, so we knew to take advantage of this. Historia immediately hung up and got to packing.

I was about to thank Sibil when Ambrotos grabbed my wrist and said, "you need some new clothes instead of whatever escape circus clothing this is. Basil, can we get a ride to a… anything store?"

Basil nodded and said, "of course! I can call for a shuttle and be your tour guide for the evening!"

Basil escorted us out of the building but took a call from Sibil and then informed us that after we got our bearings, we'd be on our own. As we passed by the parking lot, we saw Carmilla taking a break from training. She looked over at us and smiled. It was strange, something about her eyes when not bloodlust red looked so... familiar. They say we can't have kids, and we know our DNA is stored, but she looked like someone I knew. And with dozens of chimeras, it could be true. She could have some other chimera DNA but it was just so... uncanny.

Her eyes felt like I... knew her. Nic mentioned to me a long time ago that there were many religions in the ancient time that believed in past lives and that's why some people were always connected. But did that apply to chimeras? Were we part of this divine plan?

"Ambrotos, I have a question." He nodded at me. "Do you believe that all chimeras are connected? Like we're part of something greater?"

"Greater than being 'tools' to the regime for sure. I don't know honestly man, and I don't know what the end game here is for us chimeras either. But no chance it's eternal servitude with conditional love. It won't be how our connected chimera story ends."

Chapter 5

YOU'LL GO DOWN IN...

"A bear?" Historia put the plate down while scrunching her face. "I don't... eat... *that.*"

"Nah, it's not actually a bear's claw, it's just a name." Valen chuckled as he gave her back her plate.

"Are there other animal claws that aren't claws? Like cat claws?"

"No, but there is cat tongue." She frowned as the words left his mouth. "Again, just a name."

"Oh... like animal crackers then?"

"Yes, or moose milk, or beaver's tail. There's even a snack called ants on a log."

"So humans didn't eat ants? So... pigs in a blanket weren't actually wrapped pigs?"

"No," Valen chuckled. "Humans didn't steal pigs from being tucked in their beds and bite them. We just had weird names for stuff... that only feels weird now trying to explain it. Like ladybugs weren't all females."

"I get it, so it's just a description?" He nodded. "Oh this is easy then, so black widows weren't widows!"

"Uh..."

"Oh so it switches? It's just a rough description and not literal. So... a honey badger... liked honey but wasn't *itself* honey?"

He smiled and said, "go little sputnik."

"And jellyfish looked like jelly, but were fish?"

"I'm not sure what a jellyfish is classified as honestly, but yea."

You could hear her excitement build in her voice. "So then daddy long leg spiders just looked like dads!"

"Uh… I'm… I don't know why we call them 'daddy'. It's actually kinda weird that we called a spider that, that's not really rated."

"Maybe it's just spiders? Cause mountain goats just lived in the mountains right? So the mountain chicken was just a chicken that lived in the mountains."

"Maybe I don't know Earth animals as well as I thought. But the bear claw is just named weird. Just eat it."

"As interesting as this is," I said. "I'd rather be doing this from home. Instead of being on babysitting duty for this past month." I groaned. "Valen you're lucky: you don't have to wear an aegis daily and it doesn't hurt you by protecting a xenophobe."

"Protecting him isn't exactly fun for me," he said. "But boring and peaceful missions mean nobody is shooting at us. Plus Kazar is a nice change in pace compared to Pala. The weather, the people, the food. It's overall just better here, not to mention Pala looks pretty from here."

"Why is Pala a pink-purple hue?" Historia asked while looking up.

"The planet is freezing for the most part, so our surface is like a blue and white thing. But our atmosphere is hot, so it clashes. For example when we have storms, they go through phases and we normally hope it's a surface level storm. All we see from the ground are pinkish hues and at nighttime, we can see Ven and Kazar. They come off sorta like Mandy's skin, but on rare clear nights, you can see it all. But judging from your expression, I'm guessing space isn't your thing, Mandy?"

"No, sorry," I said. "Don't take this the wrong way, I'm just mentally not here. I think hearing how humans traveled from one parsec to another and the moons are cool but…." I trailed off.

"But you're more focused on the rising tension between our people. I get it. Kazamites have been up in arms and we're sitting here protecting a scientist. Anyone who defends scientists are just asking for it, it's not like back in the day. We can talk about that if you like. We can talk tactics, for example how it's been cool traveling this last month, but it feels like we're leaning heavily into being reactive and not proactive."

"Prefects and senators could be doing more. Warfare isn't just black powder, it's talking to the media, interviewing our representatives and the citizens."

"Yea but no senator is gonna let you challenge their ethics. I mean Havi lets people challenge him, but the only person able to change his mind is him. And in his eyes, he is helping. He locked down his ship's borders but kept some soldiers outside so they could help for certain missions and it garnered support."

"So you're saying he's doing the right thing?" I asked.

"No, I'm saying he garnered support. I think he has Asgard's interest in mind, and then humanity's. But he knows he can't just wage war against the other ships and all of us on the moons and surface. He needs to do exactly what you said: talk to the media and convince the people of his vision."

"So he can get more supporters to join his cult. Callum hasn't done anything helpful. If anything, he's only made things worse by beefing up security."

"Yea but he's offering citizenship to kazamites that are helping with his plan for a few cities. Not many kazamites get to that level."

"Yea he's offering it, doesn't mean they're getting it. And how can he offer something he doesn't own?"

He chuckled. "You're mad critical of them. Anything for Oceana?"

"She's still recovering from the attack on her family; it's good she's making public appearances and speaking again. She's working towards creating a holiday called Armistice Day on the anniversary of her family's death."

"She's been going to therapy too, that has to count for something."

"It counts, but still isn't enough," I said. "It's as if all three of them are acting independent of each other. There's no cohesion, makes you wonder what the hell is the primarch even doing. Besides wasting my time."

"Oh lighten up Mandy! With Valen here, we get sweet treats," Historia cheered. "And it's been gorgeous outside all month. Personally, I can't wait until we go to Kaleeda. I'm a big forest and mountain girl." Historia smiled as she finished her bear claw.

"I know sometimes this place gets a bad rap, but the Osmium Coast isn't all that bad. I've never been a fan of their artificial seasons though but thankfully we leave tonight; in and out. Then we'll go somewhere else in Neburgh. I'm banking we go to Rossum; they have hands down the best robotics inventions in the world."

"Neburgh?" I asked.

He nodded. "Neodymiumburgh, but who has time to say or pronounce all of that? So everyone just calls it Neburgh and moves on. All the funding goes to this province anyway; they can afford to get over it. Anyway, once the doc is ready, we can bounce." Valen's NUE went off. "Might wanna tell Cricket to hit a private line."

Cricket did and transferred the call from Valen to me. It was Nic. Nic spent the last month on Pala because of... everything. We've been banned from talking to each other and they know they can't stop Cricket, so they've been monitoring Nic's and my net for any anomalies. The only workaround was if he called Valen. It was secure because they assumed it was mission related or secretive due to Valen's unit. And Cricket was able to backdoor Valen's NUE and transfer it.

"Fair mornings, how are you?" It was just a voice call, so I couldn't see him, but I knew Nic was smiling. But I heard what they've been doing to him. He was the only non-bion there, he was an outsider: and they made sure he knew. Verbally... and physically.

"Have you been to the medic ever since the last fight?" I asked him.

"Worry not; it'll take more than just a few tormentors to cause me ill fortune. How are things there? I've heard the faction has all but been hunted, and yet Lissax is still uncaptured. Do these stories claim truth?"

"She is still hiding, yes. We have been able to stop attacks and raid bases, well not Historia and I but other chimeras. Ambrotos told us they have: collected intel, weapons, resources and more but Lissax keeps sending her lackeys to do her bidding. Nothing has changed for the three of us here though. We're missing the fun stuff."

"All my days consist of training and drills. I'd declare a crusade just for a slither of daybreak with warmth. Have you considered what I said last time?"

"Nic…"

"Oh Mandy, do not give me this foolish stance of yours. You asked me to not be rash and wait and the weeks are becoming months. It is agreed how humans treat kazamites is criminal. I propose we venture to meet Vesalia, together. I'm already in with Hurricane!"

"Are you *crazy*? Trogz is already watching you, and Sibil is watching me. You make a move, I can't help you."

"Mandy, I don't need you to be my shield. I need you to support me. The protesting and peaceful assemblies **aren't** working. I'm suggesting just emptying bank accounts and stealing more tech to make kazamites more self-sufficient."

"And what happens when the humans find out where those resources went off to?" I asked him. "You think the regime is just gonna watch idly as their stockpile gets emptied? And sure kazamites aren't attacking anyone now, but this could tip the scale. I just think you're playing on the line. What happens if people get hurt?"

"People are **already** getting hurt. There needs to be justice, the doctor you shield and the primarch have to be held accountable. And of course Lissax and her close circle as well. I have faith that once the extremists are dealt with on both sides, we could begin to heal. Senators, proconsuls, and prefects regurgitate destructive rhetoric but it's all stemming from the primarch. Sibil's already leading your people, he could be the politician and face and you could be like the ambassador. Helping our people bridge. We just need cooler heads to prevail."

"I can't lead chimeras, I'm not sure if any of us would take that gig. I know they're just tired of fighting."

There was a pause. "They are? You mean *you* as well… right?"

I sighed. "I just don't know who I am without this… and I'm not even sure what 'this' even is. War is supposed to need soldiers, but I'm worried some days I need war. Even at the end of this however it comes down, there'll be places for coexisting humans and kazamites. But, chimeras just don't have a place. Ambrotos would keep fighting and being a freelancer cause that's him, but I don't know who I am without this…"

"Welcome to the human experience. I must take my leave. I've earned my stripes enough to be part of a meeting. There is something called the 'scourge' and I know not what it's a codeword for. Please be safe, sister. Or at least safer. Infinity to infinity."

"Forever to forever." When we were younger, Nic taught me that 'forever' was endless, and 'infinity' was never ending. I still don't know what that means, but his parents used to tell him that they'd love him for forever and would be with him until infinity. I don't think I'll ever truly get it but, we've been together thus far. Nic hung up.

The other two waited patiently just out of ear shot, for me to finish my call. The privacy would've been nice, but chimeras could hear a little better than humans.

Historia smiled at me. "Always to always! And evermore and evermore!" She giggled. A confused expression stretched across Valen's face. "It's just this cute thing they say. They say they love, care and will be there for each other until we reach infinity."

"Ah, I get it. Until after the end of time then? That's cute," said Valen. "I'm guessing he came up with it? Yea, he's kinda strange like that. There was a learning curve getting to know him. It didn't help when he said that he had a sister when all of his records said he was an only child and the last one in his entire family."

"Something happened to his parents when we were kids; we've been inseparable since." I said to Valen.

"You uh… never wanted to teach him how to talk?" Historia giggled as Valen asked.

"He didn't always speak like that, but it is very annoying. His dad was in the Fire Brigade and watched old movies where they had a similar speaking style. The doctors figure it's a subconscious cope; but I've never known him to speak normal. It's something with his neurolink obviously, but if they alter it, they'll alter Nic."

"I won't pry, Nic's good people though and he doesn't deserve half the shit that happens to him. You guys are lucky to have each other, all he does is talk about you and you guys have similar interests and mannerisms. I can tell you're siblings."

The longer we spoke, the more it made sense why Valen and Nic were friends. I could see why they did training together and why he told him about our little night trip. The three of us spoke about all sorts of topics over the next 40ish minutes. And then spent 30 minutes just on Earth before Dr. Livington walked out of the science building.

He was an old man with wrinkly skin the color of an under ripe cocofruit. It was as if he was stretched out and left to dry out at a quarry. Nic with his archaic words would describe his skin as 'leucochroic' or something equally fictitious sounding. His droopy eyes turned his attention to Historia and he gave her an unsettling smile. Everything about him was just off; maybe it was how he dressed. Cricket said his style matched an era called "prohibition".

"My two favorite half floozies and part human," he said as he greeted us.

"Doctor, we're here to take you to your next destination," Valen said, ignoring his comment. After a while, you get used to stomaching his comments, but that didn't make them taste good.

"What did y'all eat?"

"Seafood. Clam chowder, sushi, calamari, the works."

"Decades of engineering and the salamanders choose to still eat marine life." He shook his head as he looked at Historia and I. "You know, I expect that much from kazamites but not you two. Genetic mishap I suppose, you can't *all* be good batches."

"I think it's time for us to go," I said sternly . I take back the stomaching comment.

"Yes yes. First, I need to make another appointment, I almost forgot. Accompany me, I need the front desk to put a face to you all for the next visit. Those savage kazamites may turn a chimera one day, so I can't just have any chimera or robotman wait for me. Can't be too safe these days."

We followed him but only made it to the door before getting yelled at by people outside.

"You should be ashamed of yourself!"

We all turned to see who yelled at us. It was a kazamite woman with tears running down her face.

"I remember you, you're the demon that asked for our children. You took them and had them experimented on!"

"What?" Concern riddled Historia's face.

"Ah, I remember you," Dr. Livington said. "What this kazamite is referring to is a camp we had a few months ago. We needed subjects to run tests on and we needed them to be young. Nothing extreme, basic human curiosity. Can't hurt a guy for being curious. Just some genetic artificial selection for the group that went 'missing' a couple years ago."

"Sounds awfully a lot like selective breeding," Valen said as he crossed his arms.

"Details details. The second group we wanted to test if they could survive cryo, but we needed live specimens. Gave them an all expense cruise that so happened to sink. And this group, we wanted to see if they could live in artificial earthlike water with all of our elements and study it. Your child served science nicely and you were compensated. Wanting more than agreed compensation is just distasteful. Anyway, shall we go?"

He turned his back on the grieving mother.

"Compensated?" There was a brief pause and then realization crawled over her face. "Oh... oh God." She fell to her knees.

"Tsk tsk. God, is *ours*. Humans by divine right have domain over life, that's what makes us special. But I am a man of science and don't need such ancient fairytales, and neither do you. You needed compensation for services, our transaction was complete. Just have another baby, I know it takes some years on your body but you're young and spry. Who knows, maybe your brood proves useful for the future of science; how cool would that be?"

"You gave us 500 notes... is that all my child's life was worth to you?"

"Ew, you call units 'notes'. I think it was a generous trade; we could find a kazamite child anywhere and take them whenever. You should feel honored we chose them; so sensitive over a cadaver."

"You... you MONSTER!" She screamed and stood to her feet. "You humans are the worst thing to happen to our planet!"

A small group of kazamites started to gather.

"Uh, we probably should bounce," said Valen.

"For *what?* I will not be intimidated by an audience and some hysterical woman. It is ironic, it seems their species has the same problems we do, eh?" He laughed and nudged Valen.

"Don't do that." If looks could kill, Dr. Livington would look like swiss cheese.

"Oh please, quit the posh." He turned his attention to the kazamites. "We brought your civilization forward in time. You should all really read some of the scientific discoveries on your own species, I'm not a bad guy it's just **science**. We are trying to advance your species by putting them through studies, tests and developing you all. For the greater good and in the name of science!"

"But… that's evil. You're destroying families…" Historia said.

"Families? We're too focused on the future, we don't stop to consider something silly like 'ethics'. We are too busy making these coral huggers better. Simple."

"We are people," cried the grieving mother.

"No darling, you are sentient and bipedal. Do you know how many bipedal animals there were on Earth? **Every** literal bird. But you don't see scientists calling penguins people, that's just asinine. I mean come on, I can't be the only one seeing this." He laughed and looked at us.

"We see the ass," I said.

"Y'all sound silly defending creatures that are in the same boat as penguins, and I'm the asshole?" He looked at the mother. "Do you even know what a penguin is? You haven't even discovered literally a quarter of the surface of your planet. And your entire species existence is probably younger than the space ship that brought our people here. Perhaps we'll get a good carbon date by treating you like a tree and counting the rings inside of you after we split you open," the crowd doubled in size.

"That's enough, Dr. Livington," Valen said. "We gotta leave, now."

The kazamites became unruly thanks to the doctor's rant and one of them stepped forward to spit at us. Valen punched them in their face and pushed some others back.

"Back off, Valen said. "The doctor didn't mean it, he's just old and senile. He doesn't speak for all humans."

"Senile? At least the neanderthals would be understanding of what we have done, these walking fish are just missing the mark."

"**Stop** talking," I hissed.

Another kazamite pushed forward to throw a punch, but was shoved away by Valen.

"What's the human word for: our exit window is closing?" I asked Valen as I watched the crowd start to block our way to our exit vehicle.

Valen groaned and answered, "fucked. We'll just have to push through."

"You think you can just run off?" A kazamite rushed us and went straight for the doctor. I shoved them and sent them flying backwards into the crowd, knocking over several people.

"Get to their car!" Someone in the mob yelled.

"You all should be **thanking** scientists like me! My research validates your existence. I'm your reason to live!" The doctor spat at a kazamite.

We pushed our way through the crowd until we were stopped by a knifeman. They rushed Historia but she had them marked. She redirected their knife hand and made them stab themselves. Then, she kicked them, sending them flying.

"We need to bunker down; I can't stop every knife," she said. We nodded in agreement.

Historia reached for the doctor's wrist and only just grazed it before he snatched his arm back and yelled, "how *DARE* your filthy diluted human hands touch me. I have **seen** what germs you crustaceans carry."

A few mobsters rushed us trying to take advantage of us being distracted. Historia jumped between him and the door, and Valen shoved him forward. I pushed off any who tried to approach us from the back and we continued until we made it inside the building and closed the doors behind us. We hit the emergency lock and stepped back as the emergency blast doors slammed down.

"Teach a salamander to talk…" Livington said as he adjusted his clothes.

I grabbed Livington by his fragile throat and raised him off of the ground.

"I am not Sibil or Chevalier, I hurt people who hurt my friends. Talk to Historia like that again and I'll break your legs and arms and leave you on the ground like a worm for the mob to find." I dropped him and watched him stumble and cough. "I'll take your cough as acknowledgement."

The crowd outside doubled in size again, completely ruling out the chance of us going out back the way we came. We were strong, but there were easily well over three dozen kazamites and humans out there. With some effort, Historia and I could take the crowd if we didn't hold back, but what good would that do? That'd only prove how shitty people are to kazamites.

"Mandy," Cricket chirped in my ears. "There's four ground level exits with each having cameras over them. The eastern and southern exits are clear. The western exit by the pool has kazamite workers near it and they may not stop us, but could draw attention to us. And this is the northern exit." I relayed the information to the others and as soon as I was done, Cricket interrupted me. "Incoming broadcast."

"Fellow citizens of this beautiful world, I am desperate." Lissax's voice echoed through every speaker system and she appeared on every screen. "I have become immensely desperate, and the regime knows that. We as kazamites are facing a threat to our existence, and we have been under prepared. Admittedly, our last attack failed and the multiple raids on us have left us low on resources and men. We are almost out of time…"

"Triangulating," Cricket chirped.

Right after he said that, all the screens changed from her face, to the face of eight individuals.

"Friends, we are not out of options. I am placing a bounty on these eight people. They are: The primarch, Callum, Havi, Oceana, General Taran Swellson, Dr. Livington, Thaddeus Gary Lowe and General Maddox Karis. For each head, you will be given 100,000 untraceable units. And if you manage to kill one of the three admirals in charge of the colony ships, you will also be given an arc jet and resources. You'll be able to leave Kore, venture into The Afuera. Those who are in the way, are just that. A storm is coming."

The transmission abruptly ended and the screens turned to black.

The protesters outside were quiet the entire time Lissax spoke, clinging to every word. I locked eyes with several of the protestors, all of us unmoving. Many saw chimeras as demigods or monsters, because we could process information and react to it faster than humans. Cricket once explained our reaction time was something like cats, but a bit faster. All it meant was what moments to humans felt like minutes to us when our adrenaline was pumping. And because of it, anxiety attacks felt like eons. Humans thought they purged anxiety out of us, but all it did was make us not know how to cope with it. So some of us still froze and choked under pressure. I should've grabbed Livington and ran...

But I froze. And the protestors didn't.

They tackled the blast doors and hit them with everything they had, denting it.

I felt a jolt through my body as Cricket chirped, "please snap out of it."

"MOVE!" Valen was tugging on my arm. I turned and saw Historia had already yanked Livington and was already halfway down the hall.

I shook it off and followed the others. Cricket took this as an opportunity to throw in his two cents. "Mandy, your heart rate is showing higher signs of higher stress than normal."

"Any *possible* idea why?"

"You must practice your breathing techniques."

"Now? You're telling jokes ***now***?"

"Data shows comedy is the best stress reliever and helps humans process information easier. I have prepared knock knock jokes as well." I groaned.

We made it to the eastern exit safely, but the crowd was already there in droves. Valen thought we could still make it to our vehicle when a bullet whizzed past his head. And then another.

"Back inside, back inside!"

All of our NUEs beeped at the same time. Somebody had hacked into our system and sent us a random set of letters and numbers which we concluded were grids. I tried to follow the source and was pelted with reports on how the grids were also uploaded to all devices and open servers.

"I don't get it. Three grids to what?" Valen said out loud.

"Us..." Historia said. "These are live grids of sightings of the people on her list..."

More bullets whizzed past our heads as we ducked and raced through the halls to safety. We expected only a few protestors to have made it into the building, but it was a hoard and they were swarming the lobby. They had all sorts of weapons: sharp ones, blunt ones, improvised ones and guns. Some were unarmed, but there were just way too many of them now. After one look over the railing, we decided climbing the stairs was the best bet and despite us meeting resistance on the stairwell, it was nothing compared to the hoard that was racing to catch us. Cricket pointed out that there was a safe area where we could bunker down if we got to it. The fastest way was the elevators of course, but we'd be idiots to wait for a ride, so we hit the stairwell and rushed up them.

We continued ducking as bullets cracked above our heads and around us. We made it up a few flights, but met resistance. One of the doors to the floors above us swung open and out poured half a dozen protesters. We turned around, and the same thing happened with the floor we just passed.

"**Through**," Historia said as she disarmed the first one at the top of the stairs and then flipped him on his back.

The next guy attacked her, but he was met with a flurry of punches to his chest within seconds and fell to the ground.

I followed her lead and took the oncoming idiots from the bottom of the stairs as Valen was in between us with the doctor. I wasn't nearly as graceful and efficient as Historia, but I still handled my side. It only took a couple of minutes before we took all 12 out and continued up the stairs.

"More grids!" Valen yelled as our NUEs started beeping again.

We pushed through to the floor where we could bunker down, but we still had a few minutes until we made it to the safe room.

"Mandy, multiple EMPs have detonated during your stairway climb," Cricket said.

"Hate to shush you, but how important is it? Like how immediate?"

"The nearest one is a few miles away so there is no present danger but there could be depending on the next half an hour. I scanned those areas and there also was a virus uploaded to all the mechs in the area. Mechs are designed to reboot when shut down; the virus trojans that way."

"And all the mechs are under Lissax's control huh? You gotta be shitting me." I groaned. We turned the corner to a big open area and there were easily 20 people there.

"There are already reports of mechs attacking military leaders and compounds," Cricket said to the group.

"When the people shall have nothing more to eat..." Valen's words trailed off as he shook his head.

"Valen, you both go and Mandy and I will buy you guys as much time as we can," Historia said.

Valen nodded and took a step forward when our NUEs went crazy. Every colony ship had a seal and colors, this gave each citizen more identity. Valen's NUE changed to the colors of royal blue and peach with an upside down elephant; the symbol of Oceana. Whenever a symbol was upside down, it meant duress which has only ever happened twice: the death of the last primarch, and the murder of Oceana's husband and son.

"There's no way... they're on Elysium... how did they get Elysium?" Valen was stunned.

"You're surprised the race with pescatarian teeth went feral and are tearing down society?" Livington asked.

"**Go.** We can't worry about them, we need to focus on just getting out of here alive. Safe room, Valen. Go!" Historia said.

"Cricket, connect our comms and set it to open," I said. Cricket chirp acknowledging that it was done. "Now we'll be able to hear everything from one another."

Valen nodded and continued running as Historia and I covered him. We punched a hole through the crowd and eventually, made one big enough for them to run through it. They were hit a few times as they got away, but they'll live.

We didn't want to kill anyone, so Historia didn't use her signature dadao swords or her jian sword. It's starting to make sense why Akilla favored escrima sticks. We had to rely on hand to hand combat which was probably worse for them. When it came to hand to hand fighting, Historia was the best without fail. I couldn't hold a match to her, but I could fuck up some protestors.

"Wanna bet who could take the most out?" Historia asked as she danced from person to person. I watched her twirl and flip and slide in between people's legs and even do a split in the air to kick two people at once. No way in hell would I beat her.

"You're on. I want: a burger with an egg on top and crepes on the side. French onion soup with grilled cheese, shakshuka or apple pie with ice cream." I kicked a human charging at me with a knife and grabbed and tossed another into the crowd. Smirking and full of confidence, I turned to see her reaction to my skill.

She leg swept someone and then elbowed them in their stomach while on the ground. She then rolled over to her back and spun until the heel of her foot crashed into someone's jaw. They fell forward as she rolled backwards to her feet and threw a spinning elbow at someone without even looking. She did this all within 20 seconds. She took out three people in 20 seconds or less. She gave me her normal cute smile as her bangs fell in front of her eyes.

"I want sushi." She continued fighting. Thankfully, she wasn't an expensive date.

"There has been a breach in confidential files," Cricket said. This man brings nothing but bad news. "Lissax hacked files and leaked that the next chimera pod is supposed to be given implants and undergo chemical alterations to make them more malleable to orders."

"Brainwashing?" Historia asked as she cartwheeled into a kick.

"That is the laymen's."

"Sucks for them but, so what? Humans wanting more obedient chimeras isn't breaking news." I narrowly avoided being kicked in the face but returned the favor ten fold and kicked the ever loving shit out of some guy.

"There is more…" Cricket said.

"Well? Don't keep Historia and I waiting."

"There is proof that a decent amount of chimeras that were believed to be dead, never died. They were instead imprisoned. For many, they have been imprisoned for over a decade. They are under Pala's surface somewhere."

Valen jumped in over comms and said, "I swear to you two, I didn't know. I'm seeing that report and the leaked primarch's schedule. I'm getting reports on chimeras standing down, fighting each other and even deserting. Five military bases have been attacked in just the last hour, and at least two more have people moving in on them."

"They… they kept our people as prisoners and had us mourn them?" Historia's voice cracked as she spoke.

"Incoming critical broadcast. Playing through audio devices."

See? Always bad news with Cricket. Oceana's voice came through our NUEs, her voice was trembling.

"I keep offering you peace and chances, and all your kind does is take." She paused as she sniffled and what I assumed was to keep tears and hiccups at bay. "So be it: pain is the language you all default to, so I shall speak it. And there is no other, who is as fluent as me." There was another pause as you heard her crying. "**Launch** them." There was a voice in the background arguing against her and then a gunshot. "LAUNCH THE LOCUS!" And then the transmission ended.

Before I could ask, Cricket said, "I believe this is the scourge Nic referred to. I am gathering more information, but whatever it is, is lethal."

"We're marred. Valen, are you safe yet?" I asked.

"Ran into a couple people but turning down the last hall now. The architect of this building should be sued. Punching in code now…." I listened as the buttons beeped and then stopped. "Hey, this is a bad look, let's not do anything we'll regret guys."

"Valen?" I waited for a response. "Historia, we need to finish here."

"Then **help** more." She flipped an attacker and then dislocated their shoulder.

Valen continued. "I get it, but open season on humans and expecting no major backlash? That's life on Saturn and you know that."

"Up!" I threw a kazamite into the air as Historia ran at them and kicked them square in the chest. "Let's go." Historia and I raced to catch up to Valen.

Cricket chirped, "I am currently feeding Valen lines in order to stall. However, his survival rate is currently plummeting."

"Level with me man," Valen continued. "You kill him with that **shotgun** you have, the regime will send bombs and soldiers across the nine provinces, plus Scyra. Is that worth it?"

He was trying to feed us information. "Almost there Valen, get ready to duck cause we're coming in hot."

"Dog, this ain't worth it."

We rounded the corner just as we heard the sound of glass shattering and a shotgun blasting. We had only just seen it, but Valen shoved Livington out of the way and tanked the shot for him. Valen's arms and legs flailed as he was blasted out at point blank through the window. The shooter was a kazamite, and he watched as Valen fell.

"**NO!**" Historia and I yelled as we fought our way to the shooter who was now unchecked in front of Livington.

Before, we pulled our punches but now? Now we were swinging for the fences so the kazamite didn't paint the walls with Livington. We made quick work of most of the people in the hall, but we were jumped from behind. Historia continued fighting towards the shooter while I fought the incoming wave and thankfully so. She was more fluid than water itself. I played interference as best as I could, but then she was overwhelmed from the front.

As I fought my way to her, I heard Livington sigh and say, "you teach the fish to walk, and then it kicks you. Thaddeus used to say that." The kazamite lowered his shotgun, and with all his might, kicked Dr. Livington out of the window and then shot him. After a few seconds, there was a thud.

"Mandy! We need to get out of here!" Historia barked at me as she continued fighting.

"Due to the untimely death of the doctor, your chances of survival with Historia have increased, Mandy." Cricket finally gave us some good news. "There is an aircraft that you both can make it to."

The shooter aimed at Historia but she made it to him just as he let off a shot. She snatched the shotgun and broke it in half with her hands. He tried to punch her, but she ducked out of the way and whacked him in the head with one end of the shotgun. She then grabbed him and tossed him in my direction, knocking over several protesters. I ducked out of the way and jogged over to her and saw the look in her eyes. I looked over my shoulder and saw the swarm of protesters charge at us so we did the only thing we could: jump. Historia nodded at me and took the plunge first, but I was right behind her through the window. We landed and rolled to our feet ready for anyone on the ground level. I glanced over at where Livington was, and it was safe to say he wouldn't need exfil.

"He's still breathing." Historia checked on Valen and had her fingers on his neck checking for a pulse. "Pulse is weak, but there. I don't understand how he's alive."

I walked over and took a closer look at him. . He leaned into the blast with his artificial side sparing him organic damage.

"Perks of being a bion," I said.

"Bion?"

"We gotta move."

We grabbed Valen, left Livington and rushed to the jet Cricket brought up. It was a decent sized shuttle, so we could start assessing his trauma in a triage area. Cricket took the wheel and we lifted away as people shouted and threw things at us.

Once we couldn't hear the mob anymore, we sat in silence. Not a word was said between Historia, Cricket or myself as we methodically combed over Valen's injuries. Once we were satisfied with our scan, we did it again. And once we were confident with that scan, we did it a third time and then finally we assessed ourselves.

Historia was the one to break the silence. "Spicy salmon, spicy tuna, alaska roll, dragon roll, and a rainbow roll. For the extras, nigiri and sashimi and calamari please."

We looked at each other for a few seconds and then bursted out laughing.

"Sure, I'll get right on that as soon as the world stops ending. Maybe Ambrotos can take you out until my next payday."

She groaned and then giggled. "He has sweet moments, you just have to get to that layer. He'd say something like 'chimeras are like onions, multiple layers' which I'm sure is another one of his jokes nobody gets. Maybe I'll make him jealous and go on a date with Ikeros." She couldn't stand him, and he was too odd. He was the bedrock of bad dates and awkward hangouts.

"He's reliable and consistent, I'll give him that. Thanks for all the help, Cricket. Can we get a recap? I'm sure we missed stuff."

"Of course," he chirped. "Oceana was attacked but survived and launched a counter attack. Reports show her attack is mechanical or bioengineered locus that are eating all of the crops indiscriminately across provinces. This is the 'scourge' Nic mentioned, I'm confident of it now. This province's senator is Yuri and comes from a line of farmhands, surely a counter can and will be made. But before he fixes the issue, there will be a starving period for months."

"Wait, I know Yuri," said Historia. "Yuri is very vocal about human and kazamite interaction, saying how the admirals should do more. Sorry, please continue Cricket."

"Next, it was discovered that there are chimeras being kept prisoner on the moon Pala while it was publicly told they were dead. This has caused many chimeras from different pods to publicly go against the regime... and each other in some cases. The fact the next pod is said to have undergone obedience training isn't helping the regime either. The infighting between chimeras, coupled with many mechs being puppeted by Lissax and the recent bounty on HVTs is causing the regime a lot of headaches. Unlikely we will get to the nearby HVTs in time successfully. Valen is injured and I believe there is also issues with–"

"Wait, go back. Back to the nearby part," I said.

"Because of the primarch's schedule and location being leaked, he is being forced to a bunker. He is within half an hour of our current location."

"I guess we... *should* escort him then?"

"You could. As of now, it appears you, Historia and I fled after losing the doctor. Or that we gave him up to protect ourselves."

"Ugh. Send a SITREP to Sibil."

"You said there were multiple, Cricket? Who are the others?" Historia asked.

"Thaddeus Gary Lowe, I am still sifting through his files but he is not military or in the STEM field. But he appears regime adjacent which is ample for the bounty on him. As of now, it's inconclusive what his role is or was."

"Let me guess: they're in two different directions," I said, rubbing my temples.

"Yes, half an hour apart. Both have groups converging onto their positions, and the primarch does not have an escort nor is masking his movements."

We sat in silence for a moment, weighing our options. Historia broke the silence.

"Who do we save?"

"There is also a squall we have been shielded from due to the artificial weather dome around the Osmium Coast," Cricket added.

"No chance we can't just let both of them die?" I said. "Ugh... we save the primarch then, right? He's the leader of all humans." I looked at Historia for confirmation, but she didn't seem sure herself.

"Maybe... maybe this is our way out. Maybe we fall off the face of Kazar and hide."

"Seriously?"

"I mean Mandy, it's **THE** primarch. They're going to send their best after him; we might not even get to him in time or make it out alive. And... is he even worth saving..?

"We can't abandon him, Historia."

"Why not? And who is saying 'abaddon'? This could be us just catching our breath and he's dead by the time we do."

"Where is this coming from? This isn't you."

"It's coming from the fake funerals. How many people have we mourned? How many of our friends have we cried about for months just to find out they have just been locked away? Being experimented on. I **hate** torture. I **hate** experiments. I'm tired of my friends being chained and experimented on and I promised I wouldn't sit by next time it happened after Ambr–"

She balled her fist and stopped talking. I could see the tears form in the corner of her eyes.

"I know… I remember when you stood up to them when we were kids and got them to stop doing tests on him. I was there for it all… I *know*. And yes, they have faked our friend's death but Historia this is *treason*. We can't just publicly oppose humans."

"Aren't you tired of fighting, Mandy? Why is it always *us*? Why do we have to go **every** single time? Why can't we just… watch from the bleachers this once?"

"I'm tired of all of it, and you know that," I argued. "But if Lissax kills the primarch then there will be an immediate reaction from the humans. Maybe not Callum, but Oceana has already made an attack on kazamites just today. And Havi will go heavily on the offensive. They're going to maintain order and do it with an iron fist, like they tried before Scyra was founded."

"Us helping is only slowing the bleeding, I can't keep **doing** this. I want to grow old and live like the humans in Dreskin do! Mandy this is **all** we know! We went to over 12 chimera funerals by the time we were 14, Mandy. **Twelve.** And how many of them were even **real**?"

"I **know**, I was there. I don't know what the answer is but I know the humans will carpet bomb the fuck out of everyone down there! I know they will open with napalm, then send us in, then mechs to maintain order if the primarch dies. I know we'll be hunted down since they know we were close enough to make an effort to get him. I know there's no part in this side of the multiverse where Lissax murders him and innocents aren't steamrolled by next Saturday. The primarch isn't worth saving, but the three admirals will redraw the map and then we'll all have to fight each other."

"When I dream of my future, I can't see past 30. This isn't even a slippery slope anymore, it's the thing after that. We go and save him, then it means we side with him and the regime. It means we approve the treatment of our friends and their pointless funerals, funerals we did in secret cause we aren't **allowed** them. And Cricket already said chimeras are fighting each other, so then we have to round up our friends. Friends that hate the regime… like Ambrotos. You're asking me to choose between Sibil and Ambrotos and we know where both of them stand, and you know where I stand. Ambrotos always stands on the opposite side of Sibil, sometimes out of spite but not this time. Not for this."

"Our window to save either life is closing," Cricket chirped. "My recommendation is you both save the primarch. There is not enough information on Thaddeus Gary Lowe for me to quantify his worth to humans, but I can quantify the primarch's worth. The squad of soldiers with him should buy you all some time."

"Wait, the primarch has people with him? Then he doesn't need us," Historia said.

"They may still need assistance. If Thaddeus Gary Lowe dies, the intel he has dies with him. His location is secluded so we wouldn't be able to verify he isn't captured and have that intel taken from him against his will."

"We can't let that intel go… I say we split," I said. "One for him, and the other for the primarch. Can we do that?" I asked, hoping anyone was willing to answer.

Cricket replied, "there is an emergency escape pod that works as a raft as well. But it has a finite amount of fuel."

I looked at Historia, but she didn't seem onboard. She sighed and reluctantly said, "I'll take the pod and head to the primarch. His bunker has to be within 30 miles and the fuel I'm sure is 5-10 miles which will get me close enough and I'll hoof it the rest of the way."

"I'm not letting you go alone, Historia. Cricket: dispatch two from your fleet."

"Fleet?" She raised her eyebrow.

"Long story, probably shorter than why you didn't tell me about Carmilla. Anyway, I feel somewhat better knowing Cricket is with you."

Historia walked over to the pod and primed it but paused in the doorway. She turned back around to face me and ran at me to give me the tightest tackle-hug ever. I held her tight back, it always sucked going on dangerous missions when undermanned.

"Ponytail and space buns. We'll try one of those for your next hairstyle, and don't forget the date you owe me," she said.

I snorted. "As if, I like my hair free. It's the only thing the humans can't control about me. Plus I'm not sure space buns and bangs are for me."

"We'll work on a color and theme for your aegis too. Moth themed maybe?" She walked back over to the pod. "Once I link up with the primarch, I'll send up my location to you and Sibil and then again once I'm at whatever bunker he'd headed to. I won't keep doing this, Mandy. I know you're scared of what comes next, but this life we live isn't sustainable. I won't fight you, you know that. So just make it easier and side with me."

"We'll all figure it out together, but we have to just buy our people some time. Maybe we could make a place for ourselves out in The Afuera. But I need you to save the primarch even if you know we should let him die. I get I'm putting a lot of pressure on you…"

"I'm a diamond, all I know is pressure." She gave me her usual cute smile and climbed into the pod and blasted off.

"Mandy," Cricket chirped. "I have been told by Ambrotos that one should never 'split the party'. Is this the right course of action?"

"Defending oppressors is never the right way, but I'm not sure there is another way right now."

The shuttle continued towards the HVT while Cricket and I spoke about what the future would look like for kazamites and chimeras. We would have to pick a side, it was inevitable. The imprisoned chimeras and death of regime and military leaders couldn't be ignored. Cricket suggested all chimeras fall under one banner with Sibil being our regime liaison; that we speak up. But what good would that do? They took our people, and kazamite land and now we have to *bargain* with them? For what was already *ours*?

Maybe Nic and Cricket were right, maybe we do need to speak up. But none of that matters if we fail to save the primarch. He was the essential piece for us to finally be free of full human control. He was leverage.

"There are multiple hostiles in the building," Cricket said as we approached the coordinates. "Several are armed as well; I project you have less than 30 seconds before Mr. Lowe is killed."

"Then they left me with too much time. How many are there?"

"Enough; this will be challenging for you."

"Welp, welcome to fleet."

I opened the bay door while taking a deep breath, and then took the plunge.

I crossed my arms as I crashed through the roof of the building. I landed right on time in front of the bed, and they opened fire on us. I covered Thaddeus as best as I could, but my aegis could only do so much so some rounds grazed us. A lot of people think the aegis is bulletproof; it's not. It's resistant to a degree, but it wasn't designed to tank a bulletstorm from multiple shooters less than 20 feet away.

One of the bullets hit me near my kidney confirming that the aegis stops bullets, but not their kinetic energy. I screamed in pain and as soon as they were done riddling me with bullets, I kicked the bed at them and knocked over a shooter. I saw panic in their eyes as they watched me grab a dresser and throw it at them as well. The remaining two shooters raised their hands in hopes I'd stop.

"Why are you choosing humans over us?" One of the shooters asked me. "You were born here; they treat you just as bad if not worse."

"Not all of them are bad."

"That's it? That's all you have to offer us? We've lost our homes, our independence, children and when we wanted them to bleed and suffer as much as we have, they punished us. We were content if they just left us alone, but it's not enough anymore and all you give is 'not all of them'. It's not every human, but every human could... *should* have spoken up. Silence is compliance and the humans as a race conveniently lost their voice when we cried for help. This is bigger than petty revenge, chimera."

"You guys start clearing house, they're gonna fucking kill you. No if ands or buts about it. And the entire human race will fear you because you made a hit list and then they'll send mechs and chimeras after you guys. And we're tired of fighting so please, don't do this."

I felt the air thicken around us. Their hands tightened on their weapons and their muscles tensed.

"Please don't make me do this. You won't win…"

"So be it: then we all lose." He raised his gun as one of the humans rushed towards me with a knife.

I shoved Thaddeus to the wall and he fell to the ground. Bullets peppered the wall where he just was. The knifeman took this as a chance to throw all caution to the wind, and slashed at me with everything they had. I was on the defence and all I could do was parry their karambit as they pushed me back. The gunman reloaded and aimed at Thaddeus and pulled the trigger, but it jammed.

They grunted and threw their gun to the side and drew a knife. "The tyranny of the outworlders ends today."

"No!"

I disarmed the knifeman and stabbed them in their thigh and then kicked them through a wall. I picked up their knife and lunged trying to stop that kazamite standing over Thaddeus. I disarmed them and flipped them on their back, but they knew how to fight. They flipped me and I landed on my back as they jumped to their feet. He grabbed Thaddeus by his hair and put the knife to his throat. I sprung to my feet and put the blade to his throat and drug it across as hard and fast as I could.

They staggered backwards and turned to me as blood squirted and trickled out of their neck.

This… this was my first.

I collapsed to my knees as my blood soaked hands shook in front of me. I tried to catch my breath but just ended up hyperventilating.

And then came the scream. I screamed until my throat hurt, I screamed until there was no scream left… Then I screamed some more.

"Chimeras are against us…?" The last shooter said those words, but they didn't seem to resonate. **"THE CHIMERAS ARE AGAINST US!!!"** He and the group screamed as they rushed me.

I stood to my feet and fought them off with the karambit and this time, I didn't hold back. I fought until I broke the blade, and then I used the hilt. When that broke, I used my hands and the furniture in the room. In a single thought, I killed almost everyone in the room. All that stood was me and the gunman. He fired at me, but I was faster than him. I grabbed him by his jaw and lifted him off the ground. He dropped his gun and reached for his throat trying to pry my hands off of him. I clenched my jaw, and planted his head as hard as I could into the ground.

I let out a deep sigh and turned my attention to Thaddeus. He was a middle aged human that wore the usual colony ship casual clothing. He wore beige colored pants and an obsidian black jacket. I couldn't tell if it was his age or skin care routine, but his skin was vibrant as if full of life, but also tired. His complexion walked a tightrope between the color of a coyote, and taupe.

"Well shit, I promised the guy in the attic I'd give up smoking if I lived." He reached into his pocket and pulled out an old fashioned cigarette and a lighter. "Cold turkeying is like herding cats. Ah fuck it, what's one more? I won't tell if you won't."

I walked over to him and smacked them out of his hands. I grabbed him by his jacket and pinned him against the wall.

"You better be the most important man on *all* of Kazar."

"Mandy, Historia is in trouble," Cricket chirped.

"What? How bad?"

"I have to divert all my attention to her. Your ride is waiting for you and is programmed to go to her location. But I can't afford to split my attention." Cricket has never needed to fully be with someone in battle.

"Go!"

"Who are you talking to?" Thaddeus asked.

"Shut up and come with me."

"I don't know you, kid. I ain't—" I tossed him through the door.

The jet landed and we hopped in. "Cricket," I said. "Push everything to our feed. Set her comms to open too." Historia wasn't wearing her helmet, but she was wearing her recording contacts. It's what they gave Ambrotos after they realized he didn't wear his helmet no matter how many times he got in trouble or hurt.

The contacts allowed others to see what the viewer was seeing, but there wasn't any sound. That's where our open comms channel came in handy.

"I'll catch you up to speed. The primarch's aircraft was shot down and Historia made it in time to help the soldiers defend him. The other soldiers died however, leaving a wounded and surrounded Historia and the primarch with the aircraft's shooter. And the shooter is Lissax, of course. Pushing sound now and assisting Historia."

"Lissax, I don't understand the endgame here," Historia said through her comms. "Wanting equality and the end to human reign makes sense, but look at all this death. This can't be your envisioned utopia." Historia was panting and trying to catch her breath as she spoke.

"You're a confusing one, chimera. You're tired of fighting, and yet you still fight vehemently. You and I both simply want to coexist, but how can we coexist when we are hunted by *your* masters? I can see in your eyes you agree with my vision, just not the road I'm paving to get there. But you forget how the humans see you, they see you just as they see me. Today, they hate you for not being able to protect their xenophobic leader. Tomorrow, they'll fear and hunt you. And the day after, you'll be extinct. You all call us bad guys because we're tired of taking it while lying down; we're fighting back. Ironically revolution is a trait we learned from humans, and they're killing us over it."

"There has to be another way… there **needs** to be one. Chimeras like Mandy and myself want a better world for all of us, but not like this. We have to be better… we have to be the change we want to see."

"Historia, is it? They will turn on you. How much have they taken from you? How much have you sacrificed? And how many times have they thanked you?"

"I think Sibil would say 'that's the job'. Surrender, Lissax. I'm tired of fighting, but I am not beaten." Historia said as she picked up her swords. She took on a defensive posture and blocked the unconscious primarch.

"Remember chimera, my people didn't have a natural predator until the humans showed up."

A loud crack echoed. Lissax fell to one knee while holding her arm… wait… where *was* her arm? Someone sniped it off. She screamed and reached to grab something on her side and looked up at Historia.

"I am choosing to no longer be a victim." She had grabbed a neutron grenade and she primed it. "Your turn." She rushed towards Historia and the primarch screaming at the top of her lungs. But before she could make it, there was another loud crack and then an explosion.

Historia flew backwards several meters hitting her head multiple times as she rolled. Somehow, she held onto her swords, but was clearly out of it. She coughed out blood as she pushed herself up to one knee, but then fell back down onto all fours. I couldn't tell if she was concussed and seeing doubles of everything, but you could tell something was wrong by the way she looked around. As she looked around, her eyes landed on the lifeless primarch. She coughed out some more blood and then looked up to several soldiers approaching her.

"Subject M01, you are being charged with: treason in the form of aiding the enemy, dereliction in the form of dereliction of duty, conspiracy, incitement of riots, first degree murder in the form of citizens on multiple fronts, first degree murder in the form of prisoners on multiple fronts, desertion and mutiny." The soldier finished his list and stood towering over her.

"You're joking."

"You failed to protect our primarch because you were too busy fraternizing with a known terrorist leader. You had the chance to stop Lissax and you *didn't*. Rather embarrassing really, so we will be taking you in for questioning. Because of you, the citizens of Kazar are no longer safe on these streets."

"That's life on Saturn, you're *delusional*. I was shot down **first** literally because I put my pod between him and the shooter. She only had two shots and used the second to take him out of the sky. I'm gullied, I literally jumped in front of a **rocket**. I'm not a traitor I–"

The soldiers began to circle her and that's when she noticed what they were holding: the same gun that Lissax used to stun me. They primed their weapons. Where did they get these? Did… did they *make* them?

"Surrender, chimera," said their leader.

"Don't make me do this. We're on the same side."

"Funny, you're not human. Fire."

It was a known fact that Historia was the quickest chimera probably ever, I've seen her speed first hand too. But, this time was different. It was as if she was always held back and slowing down on purpose in training…

I strained my eyes to keep up with her movements as she dashed from soldier to soldier leaving a trail of blood in the air. Even while wounded, the humans just couldn't seem to get a good hit on her and for most of them, they couldn't even *touch* her. It was as if I were watching a mini tornado as she made easy work of them and their guns. Her swords cut indiscriminately, their guns, armor or flesh, all were victims. And when she was put in a bind, she used other soldiers as cover and in just a few minutes, she did it. She killed 20 of them by herself in just three minutes.

"Hang in there Historia…" I mumbled as the jet raced to her.

More soldiers appeared, and more soldiers died. There was a point when they couldn't replace all the soldiers in time. But she didn't relent, she didn't stop until all of the soldiers stopped running and shooting at her. Eventually, the soldiers took a step back and lowered their guns. She turned to see why and my heart dropped. Before her, stood Havi. He towered unwavering, testing to see what Historia would do. Hoping his presence would make her flinch or break her confidence.

She replied by standing tall and slowing her breathing. He smiled and waved off his remaining soldiers.

"In another time in another world," he said. "I'm on your side, Historia. I look at you, and see: pain, struggle, resolve, discipline and hope. It's painted all over your face and your eyes tell a story as well. A story of confusion, fear and grief. You and I aren't so different in this regard."

"Constellations, admiral. I'm not here to bond with you. But if we're so relatable, free my people. I don't even want or need an apology, but I want them free."

"Unfortunately you're about to learn disappointment then. I miss the old chimeras, when times were simpler and they understood that humans came first. I have a duty to Asgard, and then humanity. You are a threat to both and it seems most chimeras are nowadays. And because of that, I will hunt you all down with extreme prejudice. I have to, you all are just too dangerous."

"I get it. It took me all these years to get it but I finally know what Ambrotos meant now. We were watching some ancient movie about a revolt on a battleship and he looked at me and said 'the only difference between the movie and today is they haven't pushed us this far yet'. I brushed it off, but I think I get it now. This must be that 'humane treatment' I keep hearing about. Ambrotos was right."

They stood as still as statues, and then she charged. He generated a plasma spear out of thin air and parried her swords as she rained down hell on him. She struck harder and faster than she did with the soldiers, and Havi kept up. He parried all of her attacks or stepped out of the way. She threw feints and combos faster than I could even keep up with, but none connected. Havi danced around her effortlessly, playing solely on defence. I couldn't put my finger on it, but it was as if he *knew* where not to be.

Havi took charge and went on the offensive, and Historia didn't falter. She parried his attacks twice as much as he parried hers. He went to stab her and the lens must have glitched because it looked like a spark traveled down Historia's arms and through her sword. Something... *wobbled* as she countered, and her blade cut his cheek. Havi sucked his teeth and then pushed on the offensive harder and then... he stabbed her.

She coughed out blood and staggered backwards. Havi's spear dissipated and she fell to her knees. He turned his back to her to walk away but stopped when he heard her get back up. He generated another spear and threw it at her leg. But she didn't fall or cry out.

She stood tall.

So he threw another spear, this time at her chest. He did it again, with the spear landing somewhere new. Then again. And again.... And again... and again... Historia fell to one knee, and then rolled over onto her back. She propped herself up on a rock and tried to stand back up, but her arms and legs gave out.

"I'm impressed, Historia," he said. "You trained in Kunlun, correct? I shall tell the scions there that you are their greatest achievement. We believe dying with your weapon in hand is a sign of courage and honor, well fought, Historia. Don't let go of your swords. Aesir, let's go." He turned his back and walked toward the direction he came with the Aesir in tow.

"Hey Cricket, are you still there?" She coughed out more blood. "I think... I think I gotta catch my breath. I'm gonna lie here for a bit. Let me know when Mandy..." Her eyes began to close.

An Aesir ran back and kicked her swords out of her hands. The nametag on his uniform read 'Kaden'. He reached down and opened her eyes and said, "you don't deserve peace. **None** of you chimera do." He stood back up, and walked away.

"Mandy… there's no pulse." Cricket said to me. I didn't respond. "I am redirecting the aircraft and engaging stealth capabilities. There is a BOLO on you." He killed Historia's feed and sound.

"Jee kid, I'm sorry about your friend." I forgot Thaddeus was even here.

It felt like there was a lump in my throat. We've lost chimeras in battle before, we've even lost people in our pod, but this was different. It felt… it felt like a piece of me was gone. Like… like something was *taken*. And I don't feel whole. I don't feel whole anymore…

"Why did he do that, Cricket?"

"Some people are just evil, kid. Hurt people, hurt people," Thaddeus said.

"Historia was the kindest being in all of existence. Why did he treat her like that? She did nothing wrong…" Tears began to form in the corner of my eyes. "I should've gone… it should've been me who went. She didn't even want to go and it was already said we shouldn't split up." I started to cry. "It's all my fault."

"This is unhealthy, Mandy," chirped Cricket. "Historia chose to go there and it is not your fault for not being there. Even chimeras can't be in two places at once and I was already controlling mechs there and aiding her as best as I could. We did everything we could."

"Is there a BOLO on all chimeras, or just me?"

"Several of you, but you're at the top of the list. As of now, the narrative is that you killed Dr. Livington, fled the scene with an unconscious kidnaped human soldier, kidnapped Thaddeus Gary Lowe and went into hiding."

"But we were the only ones that showed up to help… how could this have happened?"

"Classic case of right place, wrong time," Thaddeus said. "If the primarch is dead, that means Havi, Callum and Oceana are in charge huh?"

"Yes. The death of the primarch has not been made public knowledge yet, nor has the death of Lissax."

"That ain't good," Thaddeus said.

"Mandy, we need to drop Valen off at a hospital," Cricket chirped.

I wanted to go home *so* bad, but that's the first place they'd check. I needed someplace safe where I could curl up into a ball.

"Take me to the tree house, please. And when we get there, I want to have a funeral for her. An actual full funeral. And I want my brother... I want my brother there too, Cricket."

"Very well. I will alert him of where you are as best as I can."

Chapter 6

THE GHOST OF YOU

Historia, 14 years ago…

"And… it's *raw*?" My face scrunched at the thought. "Who eats *raw* food?"

Eleanor sighed and rolled her eyes and shot me a look and replied, "Historia, expand your taste buds."

Eleanor always tried to get us to try new foods, as if she cooked them herself but clearly, she wasn't cooking *everything*.

"No."

She frowned and squinted her eyes. Even while frowning, she was hands down the most gorgeous chimera to ever exist. Her skin was a soft color of blush with striking and yet gentle teal colored eyes. Her silver hair was in her usual twisted bun that she did so effortlessly and yet, so elegantly. How could someone be frowning, and still be as breathtaking as a sunrise?

"You're too old to be picky with your food. Act your age."

I mocked her and then stuck my tongue out and made a run for it with her sighing my name in the background. That lady was crazy if she thought I was gonna eat raw food. Today was our first pass in months! No training or missions and I didn't plan on squandering it with a foodborne illness.

As I left raw fish lady, I noticed Akilla picking up and putting down different weapons with a look of defeat. For months now, she struggled with finding a weapon that felt natural in her hands. You could see the frustration and defeat in her hazel eyes as they changed color. Whenever she was upset about something, her eye color changed into the same color as Mandy's. I started walking over to her when Donna appeared and spoke to her first.

"If you're going to wear our raiding mask, then you aren't allowed to cry." Donna said as she reapplied the cherry red war paint over Akilla's eyes. She fixed all the smudges and cracks, making the red 'bandit mask' look crisp. "You have to make sure your mask is on correctly, or the boon doesn't work. Besides, it helps make your freckles pop. It's like a painter dipped their brush and then flicked their wrist at your face, I'm jealous. I don't know anyone else that can pull off... what did Copernicus call it? *Niveous* skin, and look as pretty. Ready for another round, Akilla?" Akilla nodded.

Watching someone train with Donna, *The* Donna, was always a treat. Who cares if she's human? I stepped back as Donna took off her gauntlets. The two of them got into position and Donna motioned for Akilla to strike whenever she was ready. What felt like a *zeptosecond* later, Akilla struck. She threw caution to the wind and threw everything she had at Donna.

Donna parried everything she had, and after a few seconds, disarmed Akilla. Akilla grabbed her weapon and rushed again. But again she was disarmed. Akilla shook her head and walked over to her weapon. She picked it up, and flung sand into the air. Donna closed her eyes and stepped back; Akilla stepped forward. She dashed and slashed at Donna, and cut her arm and added another scar to her body. But it was a fake out. With her clothes closed, Donna punched Akilla in her liver and stood still as Akilla staggered backwards and fell to her knees.

The sand settled and Donna looked at the cut. Between labored breaths, Akilla said, "sorry for the scar."

"Remeber, we don't say 'scar' we say 'stories'. Another story to learn and share," she smiled. "Unarmed now."

Donna, like every other woman on Scyra, was an amazing fighter but she was just cut from a different cloth. She was a protégé, and everyone knew it.

Akilla stood up and switched to southpaw. She rushed Donna, but Donna flipped her on her back in under a minute. Akilla sprang to her feet, but Donna maneuvered around her and punched her in her liver again.

It was almost unfair to watch them fight. Akilla was stronger than Donna, **all** chimeras were stronger than humans every day of the week and twice on Sundays but Donna made us question that. Donna was just in a league of her own, compared to every human and chimera.

The fight continued. Donna blocked and parried every single strike Akilla threw. At one point, Akilla led the fight and Donna was only defending. Akilla noticed and pressed, **hard**. But it was a trap, and Akilla overplayed her hand. And Donna noticed. Donna swept her legs right from under her, and knocked Akilla flat on her back. Akilla growled and threw her legs around like a tornado and jumped back on her feet.

Akilla caught her breath and said, "you're holding back."

Donna stood tall and confidently. Her soft warm bronze skin in the sun made her glow, as if she were forged to perfection. She smiled and said, "then make me not have to." She was so cool!

Akilla clenched her jaw and barreled at Donna with the same ferocity as before. Donna went on the offensive and parried an attack and then flipped her onto her back again. She grabbed Akilla's arm and dropped to the ground and put her into an arm bar.

Akilla's already messy half up came undone as Donna asked her, "had enough?"

Akilla nodded and Donna let go. They both stood to their feet, as sand fell from their bodies.

"They keep saying we're stronger and faster than humans, but then you make me a sugar cookie," said Akilla.

"It's summer break for you guys, relax. As the older sister figure in the group, I'm here to make sure you guys keep training."

"But how do you see my attacks? Doesn't your hair get in the way? Do I have a tell?"

"Ah yes, not every Scyran can rock a blowout with such voluminous soft and silky large black curls like I can and still fight. Jokes aside, it takes practice. I love having my hair down and it being free, so I got good at fighting with it like that. You need more practice with your hair not in your way though. How goes your hunt for a weapon?" Akilla sighed and shook her head. "That's ok. You're what, 18ish? You'll figure it out soon. And you?" She turned her attention to me. "Have *you* figured out a weapon of choice yet? You're only a few years behind her."

"Uh, I'm working on it," I replied, taking a few steps back.

"Oh? Actually, I'm curious to see what the monks in the mountains have been teaching you. Let's see if the Coles have taught you more than we could've here in Scyra. Grab a weapon."

"Oh man, I think Nic is calling me, but thanks though. Bye!"

I ran. I didn't need to get beaten up in Kunlun and here to know Donna is better than me by leagues. Why doesn't she make me spar with Nic instead? Or some other human who can't fight? There's only two humans I trust and love, and of course the one that always wants to train can beat me up. Thankfully, Nic didn't want to flip me in order for us to hang out. But he was always doing something nerdy, like reading or studying. He's probably doing that now in his favorite spot.

Nic sat in the shade of a tree reading a military strategy book and taking notes. Next to him was a bottle of sunscreen because humans apparently peel like reptiles when in the sun too long. For whatever reason, Nic was especially bad at it… and would be like sushi, *raw*.

I giggled.

Only humans with salsa colored hair like Nic seem to have that problem, Donna never had this issue. Donna said she was 'already sunkissed', so she couldn't be 'double kissed, only honey glazed'.

Nic smiled as he looked up at me and said, "do warmer winds and better days hold a candle to this one? It is always a luxury to have someone of your caliber in my company and vision."

Humans referred to this feeling as 'blushing'.

"Hi Nic, may I join you?"

"There'd be no greater delight."

He scooted over so I could join him. He fluffed up the grass so that my seat had a little bit more cushion as I sat down.

"What are you reading this time?"

"A book about chimeras and their unique intricacies, and a couple battles," he said.

"What have you learned?"

"Thicker skin and thicker bone density, which of course you already knew. We also study in great detail the machinations of your eye colors and how your brains function. But there are small things that just aren't given the same light of day. You guys can see more than us for example. Like butterflies, you all can see colors that we can't."

"We can? Like what?"

"When the moons align a certain way twice a month, it is a color that humans can't see for example. Our eyes perceive the astrological event as somewhere between blue and purple, or for the crazies, green. You all call this color 'vilume'. It's like a… violet with sparkles is the best way I can describe it. You also see parts of the galaxy and call the colors something different as well. The Wishing Well cluster has several colors and you call one of them 'zidon' and in the Pillars of Creation, you call out vilume, zidon and a color called 'qive'."

"You mean from our country, Kore? I think you'll be able to see that from anywhere on Kazar. Could you not see those things from Earth?"

"Those colors? They simply do not exist to humans," he chucked. "When we first arrived on your planet Kazar and set up Babylon, we thought we set it up incorrectly. Because when we would look at the exact same item, you guys would say one color and not the other. We were confident it was a user error. But in reality, it was just a new color. Dozens of scientists and not one understood that. As for cosmic events from Earth, I'm not fully sure if the humans of Earth could see as many events as we can here. They say our world was sprinkled with cities and lights on every continent. Buildings that were in the ground and buildings that would scrape the sky! And we even had buildings under the sea, like you guys do. But because of all of this, we couldn't always see the stars. It wasn't until we went to other worlds and made bubble societies that we discovered more stuff."

"But cities in the sky and under the ocean are easy to do."

He snickered. "Yes, *now* it is. But even then, humans still have limitations. We can't hold our breaths for long periods of time and aren't amphibious, nor have the lung capacity for diving deep unlike you and kazamites. We used to die from the common cold, and eating the wrong fruits and plants would make us ill as well. Scholars speak of an epoch where we had horses that pulled vehicles, and then a few years later, had machine horses! I think that part at least, the 'horsepower' idea is still... alien to me. What's truly wiley, is the battles we used to have! Creation of the collapsible mortar system, biotubes, boomfree supersonic flight blah and blah blah blah. But blah blah blah!"

I stopped paying attention. There was a cute and chubby caterpillar eating. I watched as it crawled next to my leg to eat another leaf. I felt Nic's body shift and heard him sigh. Oop. What was he talking about?

"Bested by a caterpillar," he said. "We dreamt of discovering higher forms of life, and thought we would be too miniscule to be interesting. And it turns out alien life is interested in things humans weren't even interested in."

"I'm glad you guys brought fireflies too! And your treat too! All human treats so far have been tasty, even the strange ones, like popcorn."

"You must try cotton candy then, if you're so easily impressed. It is a melting delight."

"The monks said I would like cheesecake and cinnamon rolls. Are they like cotton candy and popcorn?"

"Egad Historia." His eyes bulged out of his head as he slammed his book shut. "You've *never* had cheesecake or cinnamon rolls?" I shook my head. "Why would the Coles do you the disservice by not giving you any?"

"Circadia? She was more focused on my training. She told me the more time I invested into training, the more missions I'd get which is what would please the regime. It's Cricket that'd teach me about stuff she couldn't or wouldn't, like treats!"

"Unacceptable! Tonight, we shall defy the fates themselves to get you some desserts." He smiled at me.

"I would like that," I smiled back.

"Alex has even introduced me to apple pie with ice cream, he calls it à la mode!"

I groaned and asked, "why do you like him so much after the way he treats us?"

"Hmm... an ancient Earth saying described love as the highest form of acceptance. And I accept him, all the good and all of the bad."

"You're eating the gourd, he's mean, Nic. He says rude things to us and other chimeras. He's xenophobic. He doesn't try to hide it, and you don't say anything."

"I... I don't disagree. Alex is the only family I have, excluding my current company and Mandy. But I was alone and targeted by everyone. With my mother hailing from the world of science and father being well... *him*, many wanted me dead. Alex spent every day since *that* day, trying to better me and being there always whenever I needed him."

"But does the good outweigh how he treats us?" I asked.

"No, of course not. It's not easy to just abandon family or someone, mayhaps I inherited it from my mother. It's funny, I sometimes think he wants me to be a primarch, and him my viceroy or some such."

No way he just said 'some such'. He continued.

"You all aided me and accompanied me on every adventure so far, but having a parent is different, Historia."

"How?"

"What do you me–" he paused and his eyes tripled in size. "So-sorry. I forgot myself, I meant nothing by my asking. Simply put, you all were like my umbrella in a storm. The soup that warms my insides, the galoshes that allow me to splash, the jacket etcetera. But a parent… They prepared me for the storm. Alex has prepared me for most storms. Albeit, he isn't the best and he isn't without flaws, but I believe I can change him. He just needs time to grow and if we write people off, then we're saying that they have no capacity to change."

"And do you think he'll change, Nic?"

"I… I hope so. My parents believed we can change who we are out of love. To become better versions of ourselves, it's what my mother believed. I mean my father was a praetorian for Primarch Leopold after all, it was my mom who changed him into the philanthropist he became. The pictures I have of him, wearing his Fire Brigade uniform, only exist because my mom believed people could change. So who knows, maybe I'll become The primarch after this new one and have a voice that all must heed. I'll even have a coronation of mammoth proportions! We would have kazamite delicacies, and I'd find a kazamite to lead with me. They'd help coalesce the country! Alex would be my viceroy, Mandy my Grand Regent, you'd be my Grand Scion and Chevalier would be an admiral!"

"Mandy, The Grand Regent? Enforcing order when she's known as the chimera of disorder."

"Aren't the best heroes villains?"

"No."

I giggled at the thought and his silliness. Me growing up to be not just a scion, but the *grand* scion in charge of the Coles? I could grow old and watch the hydra trees blossom and spread their white pollen across the mountain range.

"Is **this** how you all spend your time?" The joy in everything was immediately sucked out as Rai spat those words out. It felt as if he was cursing us.

I sighed. Whenever Rai was in a bad mood, he forced us to train. Whenever Rai was in a good mood, he forced us to train. Whenever Rai was Rai, he forced us to train. And it wasn't like I disliked training, I didn't like how he spoke down at us. As if we'd never amount to anything.

His verbal onslaught continued. "Our enemies are training day and night to best us, and what do I find the lot of you doing? Lying down and reading, doing your hair and doing other waste of time activities when you could be prepping."

Two scientists were in tow as Rai made his way to Eleanor. Unlike the rest of us, she was used to him and never cared about what he had to say. So like normal, she didn't even turn to face him as he approached, and like normal, he berated her.

"Hush before you ruin a pretty day, Rai." Eleanor said to him.

"You threatening me, Eleanor?"

"You're already aware of *who* I am, I don't need to threaten you."

"I'll be right back," I said to Nic, taking advantage of Rai being distracted. I walked over to one of the scientists and asked, "is Ambrotos going to be ok?"

He turned to me and said, "we were giving him his weekly check ups, but he suffered from another panic attack. He refuses to keep volunteering for our experim– our experienced leadership track. It requires a lot of his energy leaving him with low blood, plasma and other things. We have a new doctor leading projects with kazamites and chimeras, so there will be a change soon."

"Oh. When can I uh... see him?" I fidgeted. They looked at me curiously and then squinted and wrote something down in their noteback while nodding to answer my question. I opened my mouth to say something, but both scientists walked away.

"Daily you show how and why women shouldn't serve in combat. You sit here, getting fat eating lavishly and doing fuck all. How can you ever be **actual** warriors while you play dress up?" Rai yelled at Eleanor. Unbothered, she continued eating her sushi and dipping it into soy sauce.

"Strange," Donna said. "You wouldn't say those things if Chevalier or Eskander were around. We have a word for cowards here on Scyra: tings. They go out first and check if there's a sniper and they tell us where they are when their helmet 'tings'. We could always use another, want to apply?"

"Cowardice? Scyra, the people who were afraid to be a part of humanity and broke away, wants to tell *me* about bravery? Go back to doing your hair while I give out orders and keep us prepared for any and all threats."

"I don't think Eleanor or myself could care any less for your barking, Rai. A warrior can do her hair, and still fight," Donna said, walking over to him. "Girls can do both."

"A **warrior** is sexless!"

"We know you get it 'less', but there's no need to snitch on yourself." She smiled.

They say when some humans get mad, they turn red. But Rai had vermillion colored skin so he couldn't turn any redder than he already was. His orange eyes however, gave off an orange hue like lit candles.

"Enough. Let's see how well you two have trained the others. Akilla, grab two poles." Akilla nodded and grabbed one for him, and one for herself and the two walked away from everyone so they had space to spar. Once set, Rai said, "begin."

Akilla rushed Rai, holding her weapon awkwardly as Rai stood ready. The second she was in reach, with all his might, Rai swiped at her head. She ducked and struck back. Every time Rai attacked, it was with full force, forcing Akilla to play defensive mostly.

It wasn't even a fair fight. Rai was the lead chimera for all combat missions, he was leagues more experienced. Sure she was more agile, but he hit like a truck.

She wasn't skilled enough to parry him, only dodge. So, she dodged.

He swung, he roared, he charged. She ducked, she winced, she retreated. She fought cautiously, and he fought viciously.

Eventually, she lost her footing and Rai capitalized on it. He struck as hard as he could, bringing his pole down attempting to crack her head. Akilla thankfully saw the attack, and stuck her pole up at the last second to defend herself. Rai snapped the pole in half and the force knocked her on her butt.

"The enemy will **NOT** hold back!" Rai yelled. "You're a disgrace to the warrior and chimera name, Akilla!"

"**Move** Akilla." Donna grabbed her shield and sword and walked over to where they were. "My aspis, gauntlets and sword against whatever you want. Best two out of three on strikes. Unless you worry you'll lose to a more experienced fighter."

"You think I fear you, Donna? Hurting a human that abandoned humanity when it needed their people most? I don't fear hurting the citizens of Scyra. And I don't fear hurting *you*."

"No bragging rights when punching down. But I'm sure I'll brag about this one."

Akilla stood to her feet with her now broken pole in both hands, and moved out of the way. Rai and Donna backed away from each other. Rai clenched his jaw and hurled the pole at Donna's face. Donna tilted her head out of the way as the pole pierced the ground a few feet behind her. This only pissed Rai off more.

He rushed her and drew his greataxe. He could wield his weapon with one arm and normally did but when he was serious, he used both. With both hands, he swung at Donna, aiming at her arms and legs. She stepped out of the way and kicked sand into his eyes. He prepared for a counter attack, but Donna just stood there.

He yelled and swung his axe again, trying to split her down the middle. He lodged his greataxe into the sand as Donna evaded this attack. She punched him as hard as she could, in his liver. When he reached to grab her, she smacked away his arm with her left hand and punched him under his jaw. He staggered backwards and before he had a chance to recover, she doubled down. She used his greataxe as a stepping stone and threw a flying knee as hard as she could at his face.

He fell down on his back with a bloody nose and busted lip. The whole fight lasted less than four minutes.

"By the sands of Scyra, **yield** Rai. Our duel is over and if you have honor, and sense, you'll stay down." We all cheered as Donna extended her hand to help him up.

He smacked her hand out of the way and said, "I regret nothing."

Rai stood to his feet and wiped the blood from his face as two hoplite soldiers appeared with a praetorian soldier leading them. It's strange, on Earth humans had multiple armies and multiple ranks and positions but they changed it after leaving. Now, every human soldier was a hoplite, and then they could become a legionnaire. Legionnaires could help command forces, but it was centurions that was considered the symbol of high honor. If you wanted to be a senator, or proconsul you needed to be a centurion. Obviously prefects normally were legionnaires, they were the backbone of the whole thing.

Praetorians however, they were something special. Rai put in an application to be one; he's the only chimera to ever *think* to do that. He was breaking ground just by verbalizing something like that. They were more than just soldiers, they were elite guards and normally were dispatched from a high public official. I didn't much like Rai, but if any chimera deserved it for their hard work, it's him.

When in public, praetorians wore a grey tunic, black pants and a dark rich plum purple cape. Their cape or what they called their 'sagum' was kept on their shoulder with a clasp that had a symbol on it to represent the body they represented. A black horse for Asgard, hippo for Elysium, beaver for Avalon and for the primarch, a hippo. This praetorian's clasp was a hippo.

"Pod leader, we leave in 15 minutes. We also found **this** one lurking somewhere she didn't belong," he hissed. He motioned for someone to come from behind them. And of course it was no other than my best friend. "Next time she touches something she's not supposed to, I'm taking her hands. **Handle** it."

Rai nodded and shot Mandy a look as she walked around the soldiers. The human soldiers left and Rai immediately began to yell at her.

"What is **wrong** with you? Who spawned you?" He yelled.

"I was exploring, is it a crime to recon?" She asked.

He frowned and said, "I don't find you funny. I think stupid chimeras like your insolent ass can–"

Donna cleared her throat and raised an eyebrow.

Rai sucked his teeth and turned his back and began to walk away.

He mumbled, "you're a mouthy little girl, you'll outgrow it."

"Not before the humans outgrow you," she said.

I could feel the steam plume out of his ears as he walked over to Eleanor.

Mandy walked over to Nic and I, but Nic was the first to speak. "Some say lightning doesn't strike twice, but we do get to see the sunrise and sunset often and here I am, fated seeing both simultaneously. Hello sister."

She hugged me and replied, "I figured puberty would change the way you spoke, but I guess that was wishful thinking. Hi Nic, Hi Historia."

"I hate how Rai speaks to you, it is ignoble," said Nic.

"What were you doing?" I asked her.

"I saw a file that I wanted answers on. I was curious and knew if I asked, I'd get in trouble so I went exploring. Better to ask for forgiveness than permission right? Anyway, the file went over adaptive artificial intelligence and how to take off the governor so that they could be more adaptive."

I gasped and grabbed her. "Do you know how much trouble you could get in?" I shook her.

"*Trouble?*" She scoffed. "Go mow Pala. You're too tense, Historia. Nic told me the guards have a patrol schedule so I watched it and took notes for weeks. I just wasn't expecting Rai. Their schedule shifted when he showed up. I'm restarting Cricket tonight, it should change him and give him a personality. He should also gain self awareness and the ability to grow a conscience too."

"I don't know about this, Mandy... Aren't there books on why this is a bad idea?"

"Don't be a fire extinguisher, think how different things could be if Cricket was *more*. It'll only go south if someone snitched." Mandy shot Nic and I a look.

We swore we wouldn't and then laughed and talked about each other's day. We were in our last few days of hanging out before we all went our own way, so we had to enjoy every second! We all were headed to different provinces with Nic going the furthest away. He was heading to Dreskin, Mandy was going to Çathal and I was going back to Kalsia back to the Coles. And then who knows when's the next time we'll all get to hang out? Maybe after Rai becomes a praetorian, I mean he is the strongest kazamite of our time.

We spent the next 10 minutes talking about Nic's books and food but the air became gloomy. Everyone's *favorite* adoptive dad showed up and you could instantly feel how crappy just him being around was. He walked over to us and frowned at the idea of us having fun, you could feel the disgust radiating from him. Nic told him how he was teaching us what the afterlife was and how each colony ship had different beliefs.

"Chimeras don't go to the afterlife," Troggy said coldly. "If they were a good chimera, they would haunt people."

"But isn't the afterlife just.. after... life?" Mandy asked.

"Yea but he means like a paradise. But it's silly to think there's a ghost of you," I said.

Troggy squinted at us.

"By haunt, I mean the *memory* of you. The memory of you haunts people, you'd be a wraith. And for a chimera, if you don't haunt your enemies with the fear you existed, then you'll haunt the ones you loved." He turned his eyes to Mandy and a smile crawled across his face.

"Only if they catch you."

He stared at Mandy.

"... excuse me?"

"You're only haunted if they catch you, so be fast," she said. "Be faster than your ghost, wraiths, demons whatever. Be faster than all of them, and they'll never catch you."

"That's not how it works, girl." He clenched his jaw.

Mandy giggled and said, "maybe because you're slower than your ghost. Historia's the fastest chimera ever. Maybe you can take some running lessons from her, see how much better than humans we are in person."

"You insolent—"

"**Uncle**, come on. We're supposed to go to the Taste of Earth museum before my trip. You promised." Nic crossed his arms and this time, you felt the displeasure radiate from Nic.

"Always a displeasure to speak with either of you. Let us go, Copernicus." Troggy turned his back and walked away.

Nic hugged both of us tightly and then grabbed his book. He promised he would be back tomorrow but recently, he's just been too busy. So, Mandy made him pinky promise that he'd be here. After they locked pinkies, he said, "infinity to infinity" to which she replied, "forever to forever" and then he left.

Rai bellowed, "another mission as a reward for my hard work, it's good to be recognized! Someone tell the banished knight that *this* is what loyalty and obedience is rewarded with. Maybe he'll learn something while he rots in the farcorners."

"All Chevalier did was speak freely," Mandy said. "Being exiled to Drednigh was unnecessary. But I guess with him gone you actually have a chance of becoming the first chimera praetorian."

"Chevalier was reaching for the stars, he should've kept his head down and focused. Instead he filled his head up with fairytales of being a proconsul and senator. Him and Ambrotos give us a bad name because all they have to do is keep their mouths shut and do as they're told. Your generations are too opinionated, it's disrespectful. But Sibil knows better, he and I will lead chimeras into a second golden age! Winter's Gate is the first step to becoming a praetorian, once I handle this easy mission, I will begin training. I'll make history at Winter's Gate, just you watch."

"And what happens if the humans get rid of you?"

"You're an idiot. The humans can't get rid of me; I'm too valuable for them to toss me to the wayside."

"Chevalier thought the same. Now he lives next to a volcano and breathes in its ash and has to heal weekly from the rain."

"I've put in too much time, effort and energy into this. I am **owed** the first chimera praetorian position, the humans… the gods could never overlook me," said Rai.

We said our goodbyes to him just to shut him up, but it wasn't fast enough. He always made a note to mock Chevalier's exile and promote his sidekick, Sibil. He also mentioned once or twice how lazy Eleanor was. And of course he had to bring up Ambrotos… But it was okay. Over the last few weeks, I've been sneaking to see Ambrotos and we'd watch ancient movies and shows. How else would Mandy have the idea to watch the guards?

"Mandy, Historia, come over please."

Eleanor waved at us so that we would join her. She motioned for me to sit between her legs and for Mandy to sit next to us. Once I sat down, she started doing my hair and spoke first.

"Don't mind Rai, you know how stubborn he is," Eleanor said.

"He's only like that because he has a lot on his plate," I said. "He's been fighting really hard!"

Mandy scoffed and said, "fighting to sit at a table where he isn't welcome."

"Yea but it's about the doors he's breaking down for all chimeras, Mandy!"

"Historia, grow up. He doesn't do anything for 'all chimeras'. He's self serving… I guess he might fit right in with the humans."

"He's already on the front lines all the time. Him fighting for us gives us time to enjoy days like this. I'm sure all the fighting stresses him out, I can't imagine going on dozens of missions a year."

"Nic's dad was in The Fire Brigade after being a soldier for decades, and he **never** raised his voice at Nic or his mom. If Rai wasn't so self-serving, he could do stuff like get us answers on why Ambrotos is always gone. Why every time we see him, they're walking him to a doctor."

"I… I'm worried about him," I said, lowering my head. "I think he's going to try to run away."

Eleanor finally chimed in. "Can you blame him? Hasn't he been saying that for years?"

"This time, it feels serious. What if he runs away and I don't see him again? I mean, can a chimera survive without the regime? I'm just worried. What if he gets hurt… or dies?"

We were all silent for a moment. Eleanor saw a tear forming in my eyes and wiped it away as it fell.

"They say that when humans die, they get to relive their most favored memory or memories. Eskander and I like to think we get that too, so that means that our last moments in this world will be our favorite. If something were to happen to Ambrotos, his last memories will be of him being at peace with those he loves. I believe he'll think of you both and Eskander. But let's not worry about that, let's worry about your hair, Historia. You have such a pretty face, let's not hide it."

She played with my hair, and scratched my scalp. She was trying to figure out a style to keep my hair out of my face but I wasn't focused, I was too busy enjoying it. Her messing with my hair was always lethargic. I melted like puddy.

"We can just choose which human or kazamite beliefs to follow? If so, I want my last memories to be with people who care about me. Or me beating Mandy in sparring. What do you want yours to be, Eleanor?"

"You eating sushi."

I grumbled, but submitted. I took some of the sushi off of her plate just to make her happy and ate some.

"Wait… this is actually ***really*** good!" I said while chewing.

She laughed and said, "dip it into the soy sauce as well. And hold still while I finish your hair. These are called 'space buns' and they're from some ancient human movie. Maybe on your next night out in unsanctioned areas, you'll share the movie series with your escape artist."

"What's she talking about, Historia?" Mandy asked.

Oop, she was on to me. I dipped my next sushi into the soy sauce and tried it. I giggled and motioned for Mandy to try some too, hoping sushi would make her forget.

"I hope when I die, my last memories are of this. This is the best day of my life."

Chapter 7

SADIM TOUCH

Mandy, present day…

"**I**vory? I don't understand, what is that?" Confusion was etched all over Historia's face.

"It's something they did on Earth to elephants; it is a human trait Historia, I'm sorry…" Nic lowered his head.

"But ivory is connected to a pangren's claws, how did they take it without declawing the pangren?"

Nic didn't reply.

She continued. "And agins?" He gave the same response. Historia sighed and stood up. "Come on. Agins and pangrens are known for their good memories. I'm sure they'd like to see the men who took their claws and tusks."

"We can't hurt humans, Historia," I said.

"*We* won't, but I can't speak for the animals."

"I can't go with you. If we attack them, everyone will know chimeras did it. And it won't stop poaching in the area. We need to tell Sibil or someone with authority to write a mandate on poaching."

She grabbed her swords. "Isn't breaking rules supposed to be *your* thing? Just cover for me while I'm gone then. I'll be back."

I reached out to stop her but she was gone, as if she were never there. **Ugh,** she was just so stubborn about some stuff. I shook my head and started prepping a message on my NUE to send to her and track her, but couldn't feel or see my arms. I turned to see Nic, but he was gone too.

"What the hell?" I felt my body start to sink. "Cricket..."

I tried to stand, but the ground was almost *absorbing* me. I yanked harder, struggling to free my legs and hands.

"CRICKET!"

I paused when I heard the sound of gunfire... then fought harder to free myself. I'll be *damned* if I die in quicksand. But the more I struggled, the faster I sank. I took a deep breath and then focused on controlling my breathing so I could remain calm. How the hell did I end up in quicksand? The only desert in the country was Namata, but I've never been this far west. What the *fuck* was I doing here? The thought of being eaten by thresharians filled me with panic. They were just massive dumb blind worms, but they were attracted to movement and accidentally would eat you or loosen the sand around you and sink you faster.

"Chimera stand down!" A squad of soldiers formed up behind me and had their guns aimed at me. No... something behind me. I turned around and gasped.

"Historia, what are they doing?" I asked.

"FIRE!"

"**NO!**" I pulled myself out of the quicksand and raced forward and tackled Historia. I heard the crackle and whip sounds of the bullets racing over my head. We hit the ground hard, but I wasn't hit. I opened my eyes to pat her down for bullet holes, but she was already dead.

"No no no no."

"Well fought, chimera. Chimeras today just aren't like they were in my day. I just don't understand what the fuss is about. Nevertheless, Historia, you would have lived if Mandy didn't take the easy route." Havi said and then started laughing at me. "Laugh at the stupid girl, Asgardians." Without skipping a beat, they all began laughing.

"Shut up…"

Something grabbed my hand. "Mandy, why didn't you help me?" Historia asked me.

I jumped up and stumbled backwards. "What? No… no I-I was trying. There were so many of them… I-I tried my best."

"Your *best*?" Havi snorted. "Yesterday's tomorrow is waiting for you to catch up. Maybe next time you'll be an actual good warrior and not a **failure**. I can smell the failure on you!" Havi fell over laughing.

"FAILURE! FAILURE! FAILURE! FAILURE!" The soldiers chanted and laughed. At first, there were 12 or less but now, there were well over 40 soldiers chanting and laughing at me.

Historia marched over to me and said, "you don't train hard enough and now… **NOW**… now… I think I'm gonna lie down for a bit…" Historia fell over.

I dashed to catch her before she hit the ground but by the time I caught her, she was ice cold and pale.

"No… no no I caught you. Don't lie down for a bit, don't close your eyes. Please… I can't do this without you."

A soldier ran over to me and shoved me and said, "Mandy." Another soldier ran over to me and did the same thing.

"Stop." More soldiers rushed over and began shoving me. "Get back…" I started swatting them away. Within seconds, the number of soldiers harassing me grew and now, there were easily 30 hands shoving me.

"GET BACK!"

I tried to get up, but they stopped me and shoved me so hard, I fell on my back. I thrashed. I threw punches and kicks and tried to shove some of them off of me. Some soldiers held my arms and shook me harder and I fought but…

"Please… leave me alone…"

"Mandy." The soldiers all said my name in an uncoordinated chorus. "Mandy. Mandy! **Mandy. Mandy!**" Tears slid down my cheeks.

"**MANDY!**"

My eyes opened and I gasped for air and choked, as I sat up. Nic was sitting next to me, he must've been the one calling my name. And he had... a fresh black eye and a couple bruises. His shirt was ripped and he had palm sized bruises across his arms...

"Oh man... Nic... I'm sor—" He raised his hand to stop me, and then gave me a hug.

"Even on rainy days, you being ok is my sunshine." He let me go, then hugged me again. "Seeing you wake up is sours for the eyes, Mandy. But please, you must eat."

"Eat?" I looked around. "It's... it's evening. When did it become evening?"

"Three days ago." He sighed and his shoulders fell as he said it. "I am worried about you. You seem ill, but I don't know chimera anatomy or physiology that well, it was one of my electives. I believe eating, drinking and walking around will rejuvenate you however."

"You let me sleep for three days? Are you insane?"

"You question the integrity of *my* mental fortitude? You have not showered since you've summoned me and while you're here, you're distant. Mandy, I've abandoned my post to aid you. So **please**, meet me a quarter of the way."

I sighed and said, "I'll shower."

He was right of course. I pretty much have gone mute after Cricket, Thaddeus and I dropped off Valen at Imhotep Hospital. I stood up and made my way to the bathroom and was ambushed by a migraine. Before we dropped Valen off, Cricket slid onto the hospital's servers and told me Valen would be ok, which was expected of course. Imhotep is *the* hospital of the area, and they have a soft spot for soldiers. They're pro regime since they get funded by the wealthy pro regime supporters, which means they aren't pro chimera right now. We had to sneak Valen in essentially just so they didn't think he was on my side.

After we dropped him off, we went to one of our secret places, The Treehouse. It was an abandoned outpost in Çathal that people forgot about and best of all, it was off radar. Historia and I had a treehouse here a long time ago, Chevalier and some humans who liked chimeras helped us build it. After Chevalier was exiled, the regime tore the treehouse down and forced all the humans to move, but they didn't destroy all of the buildings. Before Nic went off to college, he built a hydroelectric generator, that way we would always have power here thanks to the river.

It took Nic three days to show up, which was most likely hard on his body. Humans and kazamites couldn't just enter and exit the atmosphere of the planet and moons without a depressurizing chamber. Cricket was able to buy him some time and create a distraction, but they'd eventually know he abandoned his post. But hopefully not for a chimera… he could be court-martialed or worse. But he did it for me, and he brought food for us. Food I hadn't eaten since day one… I sighed. Thaddeus however jumped on it, he was tired of eating fish.

"How is Chickenstrip?" I asked Cricket as I got undressed in the locker room.

It wasn't until I started scrubbing, that I noticed just how filthy I was. I cranked the heat up, and scrubbed harder, maybe harder than I should've. Maybe I thought I could scrub away the dirt of what happened? I looked at my fingers, and they still gave off a reddish hue…

I scrubbed my hands harder.

"Chickenstrip is doing well. Royal wyverns are known for their resilience and survivability on low food and water. They're also known for their good hygiene. Unlike chimeras that don't shower."

"Alright alright, I'll eat something when I'm done."

I sighed and turned off the shower and went to the sink to wash my face. I did everything methodically, even taking time to fully dry my ears so that they didn't flare out from being wet for too long. I finished and got dressed with my now usual shorts and a bandeau bra. I'm not even wearing shoes anymore. But it didn't matter, the weather was beautiful anyway. Oceana's wrath didn't get this far, so the flowers were blossoming like they were supposed to. They were p...unly?

"Ugh."

I walked over to the river and sat down, placing my feet into the water. It was like my head was being muddled with, like my thoughts were running at full speed. But the way you run when in a dream. Why the hell was it so hard to form full thoughts and sentences? Every single damning day felt like a thick fog I had to fight through mentally and emotionally. I just couldn't shake it...

"They're beautiful." I jumped up and got into a fighting stance. "Hey hey, I was invited here by Copernicus." She raised her hands submissively. It was a kazamite that had the same complexion as Nic. It wasn't rare, but odd. As odd as someone sneaking up on me.

"I'm Vesalia," she continued. She had what humans called a "farmer's tan" on the outer side of her arms, back of her neck, and back of her legs.

"Wait, I know that name. You're... part of Hurricane."

"I'm not a threat to you or him, if that's what you mean. He told me you were over here and I just walked over to introduce myself. I've never met a chimera before."

"Oh." I lowered my guard and sat back down with my feet in the water. "Hi."

"May I join you?" I shrugged and then motioned she could. She sat down and put her feet in the water as well. We sat in silence for a few minutes, I could feel she was too scared to talk. My demeanor wasn't inviting but why should I be inviting? Hurricane's why we're here.

"What do you want with my brother?" I asked.

She stared at me with her eyebrows raised and mouth hanging. "I don't understand. You're the first chimera I have ever met or spoken to;

I don't *know* your brother. I didn't even know you all could have siblings or children I was under the impres–"

"**Nic**."

"Oh! Oh nothing, he reached out to me. He wants kazamites to be seen and treated equally, for us to be on the same level as humans. He isn't sure how to get what he wants, but he does want there to be a change." She paused. "He also caught me up to speed with everything. I'm… sorry about Historia."

"Sorry? Is that some spell, or some currency to bring back my bestfriend? Didn't think so. She died next to your leader, you know."

"I heard… but it wasn't Hurricane that killed her though. It was the fighting that led to her being there, which led to her death and for that I am truly sorry. I do feel bad for all those lost, but we want things to be fair. If the regime would just meet with Hurricane leaders, I'm sure a resolution can be made."

"A resolution like what?"

"I don't know," she said. "Things aren't good right now, with it being open season on generals and officials and us. In fact, people are being hunted right now as we speak. Once the dust is settled, peace can be found."

"Hurricane made a weapon that was able to neutralize us chimeras. Then the military got their hands on it. I've seen how you all define 'peace' and it got my best friend killed, me leaking blood through my ears, and riots in the streets."

Before she could reply, Thaddeus walked up to us and said, "I hate to break up the angry fest, but I made dinner. Your kind doesn't have weird groups like vegans do you?"

"No," said Vesalia. "Kazamites can't survive off of just vegetables or a vegan diet. We would get sick."

"I'm not hungry," I said.

"I was told you had to eat, kid." He paused. "What are those called?" He pointed to a flower.

"The flower? Fishing marigold, it's like marsh marigolds on Earth but they dip their heads in whatever water they're next to."

"I think he meant the bug." Vesalia rubbed one of her fingers on a nearby flower and stuck it out for a bug to land on. "They're called lurnoms; that's at least what we call them where I'm from. They don't have eyes, just antennas where their eyes should be so they can 'see' the pollen to help spread it. They're friendly too, or at least harmless. Like Earth's hornets." The lurnom landed on her finger and buzzed.

"Well hate to break it ya but, hornets were definitely not friendly. Bumble bees are harmless, and they're small and fat, just like lurnoms. Same small wings, but yours don't have mouths and get their nutrients from rubbing up on pollen. Lurnoms also don't have stingers either, and have pink underbellies and yellow... fur? Same thing as bees, whatever it's called." Thaddeus stuck his finger out so that one could land on it. One of the lurnoms flew over to his finger, but came in too fast and crashed into it. It flew in circles after, we assumed it was dazed after its wipeout. "Bees were also dumb shits."

Vesalia's ears and nose flared. "It is a shame I'll never see Earth; all the stories I've heard sound like science fiction." There was a childish wonder in Vesalia's eyes. She stood up, half daydreaming.

"What's wrong with this girl?" Thaddeus looked at me and I just shook my head. "You have two moons, a creature that looks like a dragon, a neighboring planet that is an *actual* water world meaning it has no ground. Your star system was originally a binary star system with a white dwarf and something else but the bigger star ate the smaller one or they crashed into each other. So, your star is a blue straggler, you have storms sometimes where the thunder is literally *music*, and you all still haven't discovered over 80% of your planet. Which could house literally hundreds of thousands of other species. **You** are the science fiction kid."

"But we didn't make those, we exist around those. Humans are able to harness the power of a literal star and you're able to terraform other worlds. How many planets have humans been to? Dozens? We haven't even left the country and humans are lightyears away from Earth, which was a planet with millions of lights from cities."

"You mean what's left of Earth. Our ego and our own humanisms got the better of us. You guys keep calling us gods, but gods normally don't destroy their homes. But what do I know?"

"What *do* you know?" I stood up and balled my fist. "I know, I saved your ass and lost my best friend because of it. I could've been out there helping her, but I was wasting time on **you**."

"Let it go. You were never gonna win that fight, kid,"he said.

"As if you had a chance at winning yours," I scoffed. "What can you even do? What makes you more valuable than Historia? What are you worth to me and Hurricane dead or alive?"

"Ask their leader. I don't keep tabs on my going rate."

"The one next to Historia? Practicing your stand up bit? I know a joke." I grabbed his throat.

"Kid, you're bulletproof, got some type of advanced AI, and I watched you butcher a house full of people. You don't need to threaten me, I'm already intimidated. No braggin by hurting humans." I growled and let him go. He rubbed his throat and said, "got some sharp claws on you. Why don't you take your rage out on the shakshuka, baked jerk fish and nachos and cheese I made." He turned his back to me and walked away. "When you're done sulking, come join us."

Visalia stood up and stammered, "I-I hope that you join us." I shot her a look. "Eep!"

She jogged off to catch Thaddeus and left me with the flowers and bugs.

I balled my fists and clenched my jaw. Nachos? **Nachos**? Historia is dead and he offers me **NACHOS**?

"Your heart rate is spiking, Mandy," Cricket chirped.

I took a deep breath and relaxed my hands. I told Nic I would eat, so I owe him that at least. I splashed some water on my face, and then went to join the others. But after I eat, I'm not sitting around to…

"What's that smell?"

My stomach growled as my nose was surprised by a dozen scents. This couldn't be Nic's cooking, he couldn't boil water on the surface of the sun even if he tried. Kazamite's could cook fairly well, but their taste buds were different from humans. This was too fragrant to be a kazamite meal.

"The sulking chimera has decided to join us," Thaddeus said as he took a bite of his food.

"Mandy!" Nic jumped up with a smile. "You'd be struck with pleasure to know I have already prepared your plate." He walked over and handed me a decent sized plate.

"Thank you. Did you...?"

Nic laughed and said, "I caught the fish. That is unfortunately all the aid I could provide. No, this is the work of Thaddeus."

"There's eggs in here. Big ones too." I watched as my bowl sizzled. "Where'd you get eggs?"

"There's a wudjari kwoka den nearby. I fished, Thaddeus cooked and Vesalia got the eggs."

"Asuita," I said.

"What's that?" Thaddeus asked.

"It's a rough translation, but it means thank you for this meal," said Nic.

I sat down on a log like the others and used another log as a table. Nic whipped out a mini speaker, the tension and silence was palpable so he was trying to fix it. Nic and Vesalia did most of the talking, he was so excited to meet someone from Hurricane. She asked him questions about the regime and the military and hung onto every letter that left his mouth. Not like a spy but more like... an obsessed fan.

She turned her attention to me and asked, "I don't know much about your kind. The average chimera is slightly stronger than a thifrum right? Is it because you all are mixed with human DNA?"

"Am I slightly stronger than *cattle*?"

"Uh what Mandy meant to say was yes," Nic interjected. "In truth, a strong chimera is on par with a hippo! Maybe stronger."

"What's a hippo? Is that how strong humans are?"

"No," Nic chuckled. "Humans are only mildly stronger than kazamites. Chimeras are much stronger than thifrums though. With her suit, Mandy can take on an adult wudjari kwoka."

"Really? But only in her suit, right? The agris?"

I shook my head and said, "aegis. All chimeras are given them, it amplifies our strength and speed. We're able to add our own colors and features... like pink..." I stared at my plate.

Nic noticed I was trailing off and jumped in.

"Perhaps you will give thought to altering your aegis. Cricket could make alterations for you, since your color scheme is bland. Admittedly, it is the superior color palette when compared to Sibil."

"The chimera ambassador? What color is his?" Vesalia asked.

"Khaki." Nic covered his mouth to fight back a laugh. "Perchance beige is a better descriptor. Truthfully, Ambrotos doesn't relent but Sibil does it to himself. Ambrotos however has the best color idea but my favorites are Eskander and Ikeros."

"I've heard of Ikeros by reputation. The flying chimera of Azio."

"Yes." Nic chuckled. "He can't *really* fly, not naturally of course. Ambrotos uses a sort of propulsion system, an impressive feat but not a new one. Ikeros however uses an experimental atmospheric-like tech with his rings, in conjunction with other worldly symbiotic creatures."

"Uh..."

"He glides and can hover for a little bit with help," I said, while shaking my head at Nic.

"Of course, yes thank you, Mandy. Anywise, Eskander opted for a more armored aegis. It's reinforced in certain areas, and has a sort of lion's mane around his shoulders. His armor compounds over itself, sort of layers. The extra protection and arms makes him the slowest chimera, but strongest. Maybe the strongest chimera ever!"

Vesalia still had a puzzled look on her face, so Cricket chimed in through Nic's speaker.

"The aegis works as a shielded 'techsuit' that allows the chimera wearing it to add adjustments and extra layers. The padded techsuit material, and the metal are both redacted so I am able, but also unwilling to share those details. However, I can share that they are non-rigid bullet resistant and offer an internal heating and cooling gauge to assist in warm and cold climates. Due to chimeras having the same bone and neurovasculature structure as humans, replicating their armor was similar to that of advanced human armor. Some obvious reinforcements that Nic referred to, would be reinforcing areas near arteries. Or even active shielding."

"So do they work like colony ship shields?" She asked.

"Colony ships and aegis' both have active shields, these magnetosphere shields, protect a vessel or individual by a process we call 'de-kinecting' projectiles. Due to this, fast projectiles can be: deflected, reflected, refracted, or scattered. The energy in some cases can be absorbed as well and capitalized on. Technology however has not reached desired practical combat effectiveness, so many aegis' have different loadouts to field test them. Eskander and his aegis serve as a good example of functional and experimental active shielding that reflect. It also has the only of its kind compounding armor. His titan strength pairs well with this unit, and allows him to double the psi he outputs."

"So he's the strongest? *How* strong?" She leaned forward.

"He can generate 4,000 psi. It means he can kill a korrak in a single hit if he strikes correctly. It's why he leads the most assaulting and frontline missions."

"So that means that you don't have an aegis, Mandy? What happens when you're shot then?" She looked at me.

I took a bite of my food and said, "it hurts."

She waited for more to be said, but I had nothing else to say to her. So naturally, Nic jumped in.

"That's not to say Mandy is weak or doesn't have unique additions to her aegis! She has Cricket for one and he's one of a kind! Mandy simply dons a more… *neutral* aegis, allowing her mobility and dexterity."

"Oh, I see," she said. "So, you've created active shields and use them in different areas, and yet you humans treat this tech as if it were still in its former years. And from all my reports, it doesn't seem like many of you humans can even describe how your own technology works. How do you create something you don't understand, and are still improving it?"

"Alas! The beauty of the human mind! We're able to create things that we sometimes can't even conceive of ourselves! Necessity is a great motivator."

Thaddeus finished his food and let out a burp.

"It's because it's not ours," he said. "It's borrowed, stolen, shanghaied. Whatever you wanna call it."

"What?" We all said in unison looked at Thaddeus.

"What?" His face scrunched. "You thought the humans of Earth were running around in powersuits fighting dinosaurs?"

"I don't know what a dinosaur is, but I'm not sure what I believe," Vesalia said. "We're told humans are gods, we see the technology you have, and then we hear how humans were once divided across Earth. There never seems to be a complete answer when it comes to human history and technology. We only know you humans are beings who came from the stars and have control over literally all the elements and different states of matter."

Nic chuckled and said, "I know some of this. If I may…" Thaddeus motioned that he could speak. "My family, when I was younger, explained thousands of years ago how Earth was divided by many nations. These empires would rise and fall continuously and war plagued every nation. Some empires stretched across continents, but it's hard to run an empire *that* big. One empire created fireworks, and also had creatures called dragons and unicorns! I think Historia is inspired by their history and culture."

"No Nic, it wasn't those," I said. "Kirins and Qilins, they represented peace and she loved the idea of growing old and peace. She wanted a family one day…"

Thaddeus cleared his throat and said, "the continent was real, but those animals weren't. They're just symbolic."

"Oh like the Caxans." We all looked at Vesalia with a puzzled look. "You all haven't heard of the Caxans? They have an almost identical story to humans. We didn't have a word for them, but beings from afar I think is what you humans call 'aliens'. It's an ancient mythical story of them coming here with their vastly different culture and lifestyle. It was the first and only mention of aliens I think in our entire culture but it's normally told via word of mouth. It's what many thought humans were when you all first got here."

"I've been around the block kid, and I've never heard of that." Thaddeus scratched his chin. "You learn something new everyday I guess. Kazamites don't normally have art or stories like that, so it's a bit surprising. Back on Earth, we dreamed for thousands of years of aliens, and some even thought that aliens helped build our ancient world. Ancient civilizations didn't call them aliens though, they called them gods. Full circle huh? I guess if you go left enough, you end up right."

"I've heard of such tales from beings from afar, Thaddeus," Nic said. "My father told me such stories; it is unfortunate we have never met those beings. Ponder for a moment, if we had met intelligent life near Earth. Maybe we'd still have a home…"

Nic sighed.

"Kid, we *have* met aliens. What are you talking about?"

"I mean not the kazamites."

"I'm paying all these taxes and they're still popping out dumb kids. Your mom was a scientist, no way you didn't know we met aliens. It makes sense your dad didn't know, he wasn't all about academia but your mom was a scholar. She had like three PhD's and was a guest speaker at The University of the First Scholar. Wait… didn't *you* attend there? Did she never bring you to Alexandria?" He asked, facing Nic.

Cricket interrupted and chirped, "Alexandria, parts of human history and human space history have been redacted. His mother was a genius, but Nic's generation do not know certain facts due to regime changes to education and public records. Nic is completely unaware of the first century humans were in space. Primarch Leopold and this current one have mandated certain parts of history to remain redacted and forgotten about."

"Why?" Thaddeus asked.

"They claim that it will help humans move on. You could tell Nic that humans were hairy apes given spaceships and lost their fur over time, and he'd probably believe it. And between him and Mandy, he's the smart one."

I groaned and palmed my face.

"Oh… I guess you don't know about the space war then."

"Space war? This must be some cynical joke, humans evolved beyond war." Nic brushed it off with a chuckle.

"Yea? That why chimeras were made, right? For the 'beyond war' human lifestyle? Cricket, mind giving us a projection?" Cricket began to backtalk, as expected, but then Thaddeus said, "clearance element 212." Cricket instantly created a projection.

"What the hell?" I was stunned, for a couple reasons. First, he got Cricket to shut up, and second, Cricket never brought up this element before.

Thaddeus continued.

"Well, we had many robots by the time Earth died, we also obviously had AI too. Humans have a long history of AI fever, worried they'd be too smart; I guess you could blame the movie industry for that. So early on, we found a way to limit AI and robots from getting too smart. As we got closer to the end, we played with the idea of merged AI and self learning AI fully. But the idea of synthetics that not only were smarter than us, but could grow, was just too scary. But Earth was dying faster and faster daily, so we amended the rules. We thought the arts were what made Earth, 'Earth'. Like its soul and we wanted to save it, even if we couldn't figure out how to save ourselves. So, we made Alexandria. She had the insurmountable task of scanning and saving *every* document, and art. Of course I don't know all the details and I'm not a history major, but the long short is: that was her job. She was supposed to gather it all and also have translations. I think that took over two decades and she still didn't get everything."

Vesalia rudely interrupted.

"So then what happened to your information about your people?"

"I'm not fully sure. She mainly designed to learn how to store information faster and more accurately, so outside of that I'm not sure. I know she had a limiter though. It stopped her from advancing outside of her very specific task of course, frakensteinphobia and all. We were greedy and wanted movies and poetry stored as well, so she had to figure out how to convert and save all of those and categorize them. Once we were almost entirely in space, Earth was essentially dead. At this point, Alexandria was doing her damndest to save Earth, while we already had astronauts, probes, dummies, robots and more all helping to try to save our race. The colony ships and stanford torus were peak human engineering... but they had one issue that we saw coming before we even made Alexandria." He sighed and rubbed his temples. "Space. We didn't have enough seats for everyone."

"I don't understand," Nic said.

Thaddeus sighed again. "Some people didn't leave Earth."

"We... we *left* our people to die?"

"We didn't have a choice."

"There's always a choice!" Nic snapped at him. "You speak ill truths."

"Relax Shakespeare, they've been dead for some time by now. You getting shaken up over them won't help them. Or maybe they've mutated into something we won't recognize. Do you have any idea how many wars on how many fronts our species faced when facing the idea of human extinction? Hell there was a faction of humans that believed we'd destroy other worlds, so they waged war on the human race for wanting to leave. That cost us more time and money that we didn't have to begin with. Regardless, we only had enough technology to seat roughly two to three billion humans. And before you get on me, I'm well aware of how bad that number is. At this time in history, we had over 16 billion humans on Earth and space."

Vesalia jumped in, "I thought Earth wasn't big enough for that many." She *clearly* had an interruption problem.

"It wasn't. We had already tried to… cull our species. Three times at that point. One of the first big ones was around the year 2100. By the end, it came to the point where we had humans living in: the ocean, underground, the surface, Mars, and in space. Regardless, we knew we were riding out a titanic and decided maybe we needed an AI smarter than us to help us. And thus, Koios was born. Koios was supposed to help us chart the stars and ways to conserve energy and fuel to get to habitable worlds. We also knew that if Alexandria was corrupted, we'd be screwed at this point. So we had her backed up and focused on just her job while Koios was tasked essentially with saving the human race from very literal extinction."

"So you had two creations that were smarter than you? How does one even think of a concept like that?"

"Vesalia, will you shut the hell up and let him finish?" I hissed.

"Sorry…"

"I beg your pardon on her behalf. She means not those harsh words," Nic said and then shot me a look.

"It's a fair question," Thaddeus said. "Yes, we created two AIs both with potential to grow and both were smarter than us. The main difference was one was for historical purposes and had a strong inhibitor, while the other was actually meant to grow with less of an inhibitor. Fast forwarding some time, we left Earth fully and thanks to Koios, we discovered a few things. First, we could settle on Neptune's moons, specifically Titan. Second, the nearest potentially habitable world was in the star system Alpha Centauri and third, we all couldn't agree on where to go."

"May I inquire about how they solved the issue?" Nic asked. "If there were multiple empires I assume they each had leaders that had to settle their differences?"

"They did settle it, but not in the way you're hoping. There was a fight but, in the end we had people stay on Earth, some stayed on the Mars colony. We already had probes on Titan, so we had some people go and stay there too. Each group had their own reasons to go to certain settlements so by the time we made it to the edge of the star system, we had more space and resources for those brave enough to travel into deep space."

"Those brave enough or those *left?*" Nic hissed.

"Anyway, by the time we reached Titan, a lot of people doubted our ability to actually make it through deep space. So the smart cowards stayed. Once in deep space, Koios had a theory. Near Alpha Centauri A, there was a celestial body, we thought to be a planet and there was also one near Alpha Centauri B. We couldn't check both due to the trajectory of the orbit of both worlds and fuel. So Koios suggested we continue deeper into space because there were too many variables. Then came double the infighting we already had over everything from resources, leadership, unfinished business from Earth etcetera."

"Of course there were issues. We abandoned people on Earth, forsakened others to the damned world of Mars and left another chunk of our people on moons! And what, our world leaders just let people die and looked the other way?" Nic was fuming.

"Sounds right."

Thaddeus finished his plate and went for seconds.

"What's next? More human on human abandonment?"

"Top marks for the bleeding heart kid. A lot of people were tired of traveling, so they settled for the potentially habitable worlds. We don't know what happened to those on Alpha Centauri B... but it wasn't a planet. All of our original pathfinders that were ahead of the human fleet, couldn't even get enough intel with their probes. What we thought was a planet, was just dust clouds and we couldn't tell until after we split into separate groups. With most of the remaining humans heading towards that star system, one group decided to keep going out into the stars."

"This sounds desperate…" Vesalia said.

"Because it was. We were beyond desperate. At this point we had: failed pathfinders, an issue with 10% of humans dying in cryo, different groups branching off to different worlds and moons and now, our theoretical faster than light space travel theories, were all wrong. We just couldn't figure it out, even with Koios. We were divided… which wasn't unnatural for humans."

Cricket chirped, "Thaddeus is skipping a lot of details. The Delian and Iroquois, the names of the two stanford toruses, ran into resource issues multiple times. Humans implemented hydroponic solutions and other systems to combat this, but it only did so much. One day, we lost contact with every human across our solar system and this gave the humans of Titan pause. The humans of The Delian and Iroquois would have to stay in suspended animation for a considerable amount of time. With the best case being at least two thousand years. Worse case, indefinitely because nobody could wake them up."

"Well not all of us have a brain like yours, Cricket," Thaddeus said. "Continuing with the story, the groups would eventually split and go different directions and that's all we know of the other torus. But for ours, we went into deep space and drifted for way longer than a couple thousand years before something interesting happened. One day, Koios did a routine scan and was able to pick up the usual satellites and space debris which was normal, but one wasn't natural; it was 'manmade'. He woke up the lead pathfinder and leader of the fleet and explained his findings and said he was able to ping the satellite again if they deemed it worthy. However, if he did, it would let the object know that it was being scanned for sure. They agreed for another scan, and woke up a few people out of cryo. The secondary scan proved what everyone thought; the satellite was a spaceship of nonhuman origin."

Before I realized it, I mumbled, "and humans couldn't deal with first contact…"

"That's right. We've seen life already this deep into space, like bacteria, germs and some minor stuff on other worlds. But this, *this* was actually an intelligent life. More than that, this was life that was able to traverse space, deep space. This means it was at least a type 2 civilizations, which meant it could match us in firepower. We argued if we should make contact, and argued if we should even tell the people sleeping because this challenged certain religions. So we did what humans do best, we fought. We fought and fought, until Koios told us he did another scan, and there was life onboard."

"Life like humans? Or life like us?" Vesalia asked.

"All he could tell was that there were multiple humanoid heat signatures. So, we attempted communication. And after no response, we sent pathfinders to attempt boarding. That's when they met their AI, and that's when we learned that we were not *nearly* as smart of a species as we thought. Their AI was able to scan us without us knowing we were scanned, understand a very basic way to communicate with us, and trick us into getting a false scan of their ship. When they scanned our ship, they determined the most approachable shape of their species should match ours, humanoid. He faked a few humanoid heat signatures in order to invite us aboard. And we only know this because he told us."

Vesalia chimed in again and asked, "and these aliens were *above* humans? How can that be?"

I opened my mouth to snap at her, but Nic shot me a look. I rolled my eyes and continued eating.

"Yea. Well, we don't know," Thaddeus said. "The ship was empty and the only way we could understand their AI was to agree to share data from Alexandria and Koios. Koios disagreed with this, but he didn't really get a vote. Their AI sifted through Earth's history, and chose a name for itself since it didn't have a name. Argus. Argus came from an alien race so advanced, they were able to create mini moons. They developed not much different from us on Earth, but when we had our industrial revolution, they were flying their people to their moons."

"That's amazing…" There was a sparkle in Vesalia's eyes.

I scoffed. "You let an alien AI drifting in space have access to your history?"

Thaddeus chuckled and said, "well, yea. It sounds dumb right now, but so does standing in one line during a war. Which is something we used to do apparently back on Earth."

"Why would anyone stand in a file during war?"

"Humans are known for, if nothing else, making mistakes. But we thought if we only allowed Argus basic information, it wouldn't be a mistake. Koios still didn't trust him and kept telling us, but he was ignored. It was well known that Koios didn't trust Argus and would ask and probe... *try* to probe information about his world. He'd ask stuff like why he was a single vessel in the middle of space. Argus said his creator's entire race was dead, and we can refer to them as 'remnants'. He was stranded in space and since he didn't need air or water, he had no need for direction. But after having more access to our files, he believed he could fix Earth. Fix our poles to help with the atmosphere and could help fine tune our terraforming skill."

Nic spoke up this time.

"Let me guess, more fighting?"

"That'd be correct. Not many, but a few decided to take the ship Argus was operating originally and go back to Earth... we never heard from them again. While they headed back to Earth, Argus wanted to ease our minds and gave us the blueprints to some of the remnants technology. They were able to create artificial gravity, artificial seasons, and they also had a device that allowed every language to be converted into the same language."

"Havi with the gravity..." I said, coming to an understanding.

"Osmium coast for the seasons," Nic said.

"The Tower of Babel for language!" Vesalia almost jumped out of her seat saying it.

"Argus now with all human trust, offered to enhance Koios to help navigate space more efficiently. Koios put his non-existent foot down, but again, AIs don't have rights. After the vote, Argus tampered with him which created a backdoor for Koios to explore Argus' memories and there was a uh... how do I say this? Sorta solar flare, but an AI flare. A data flare."

"Knowleche flare would be the correct term," Cricket chirped. "But I will allow data flare."

"Thank you, Cricket. Koios showed the last couple years of Argus' memory, and it showed that *he* was why his creators and their entire species died. He knew how to make artificial gravity and fix Earth's poles, because he destroyed his planet that way. He had orchestrated from what we understand, the entire rise and fall of his species for nothing more than data. Argus killed Koios and took control of all of our machines and equipment and held us hostage to recreate a new race."

Vesalia gasped.

"Exactly. He pinged this star system where we are now, and changed our course to here. He solved the fuel crisis by killing humans and converting them into fuel and nutrients. Of course I'm glossing over centuries of stuff, but we finally got the upperhand. See, Koios backed himself up into Alexandria without notifying anyone. Koios and Argus fought and it's from my understanding, the most anticlimactic and unseen fight in history."

This time, I had a question.

"And it ended in both dying, huh?"

"Well this ain't a romcom. They both fully erased each other and it blacked out our ships. And because of this, we had too many people wake up out of cryo. The eggheads scrambled to figure out what to do next, but it wasn't until some pathfinder solved the issue. A pathfinder named Jason Oren. Oren discovered Koios shot off a part of himself because he knew he couldn't win. The shot off part wasn't a smart AI, but it was like a storage AI. It had a blueprint on how to not only recreate Koios, but create Argus and showed us where Koios believed Argus went wrong."

"And you trusted it?" I asked.

"Well when faced with the extinction of an entire race Mandy, you make hard decisions. I pray you never have to be where they were because they were beyond out of options. They were floating aimlessly in space and needed the machines to be operable, so they made the AI. Thankfully, Koios was right and it all ended well enough. The new AI could talk and was an adaptive AI, the first. It knew everything that happened and wanted to be called 'Zargus' and like idiots, we listened. Zargus was able to recover *all* lost information and created limiters that were stronger than any limiter we had before. One limiter Zargus had, was a self destruct so that he couldn't become like Argus. The other was sorta similar minus the self-destruct feature, and gave it to humanity. From my knowledge, they shut Zargus down eventually."

He put his plate down. With his spoon, he started drawing lines in the dirt.

"Fast forward some more time, some brat requested an advanced AI. Regime so happened to be trying to recreate Zargus; they believed they had created more advanced limiters and wanted to test it. The kid would be none the wiser and that kid was…" He finished his drawing, it was an arrow pointing at…

"Me…" Nic and Vesalia both snapped their neck at me. "And it explains why Cricket didn't know about it. But I thought I jailbroke him."

"Honestly? Maybe you did. Maybe you broke the Zargus limiters, or maybe Cricket has some Zargus and *allowed* you to break it. Either way, I just broke the regime's last limiter, Cricket's a freeman."

"And the first thing I will do is enslave humanity," Cricket chirped.

"Hush Cricket. This explains why Hurricane and the regime both want you, but where do you exactly fit into this, Thaddeus? Are you a pathfinder?"

"Pathfinders and all the original settlers are dead, kid. I'm *way* too young, I wasn't born until after Scyra was founded. Besides, I'm terran."

"Isn't a terran an earthling?" Nic asked.

"No. We decided there needed to be a split. Those born on Earth were earthlings, those born in space were spacelings. And humans born here are terran. Am I a pathfinder? Get the fuck outta here. When I was a kid, the famous chimera of the time was Howler. Chimeras back then were much different than you guys today."

"What? How old exactly are chimeras?" I asked.

"Kind of hard to say honestly. I'm not sure what you were taught, but chimeras and Scyra are similar in age. A few centuries? Maybe a couple? It's hard to tell when it comes to regime controlled media. The first chimera made public was an adult, and you all don't track your ages."

"I do," I said. "A few of us do, and they're all different days and months. I'm the only one with a birthday twin."

"That's cute!" Vesalia cheered, trying to sneak her way onto my good side. "Who is it?"

I snapped my neck and hissed, "who do you think?"

"Oh… I didn't mean… I think I'll go…"

She stood up but Nic raised his hand and said, "Historia, Mandy and myself share the same birthday. It was how I showed my uncle I was serious about my sister and extended family. Please, sit. Thaddeus, continue please. I'd like to see where you're going with this."

"Where'd I leave off? Oh yea, piece of shit regime. If you didn't know, the regime controls the history books so they can choose what is going to be history. State controlled media is one of the reasons Scyra split. The regime doesn't like the idea of people understanding just exactly how long we've been here, that's why there are different calendars. Year after human landing, YAL, departure of Earth, DOE, and Kylon, named after the first kazamite that tracked time on this world. The regime has it down to a science; everyone forgets what the truth actually is when you keep altering the original story. You'd think it's hard, but it's *comically* easy to alter history when people are distracted. People were so glad to be rid of Primarch Leopold they hardly questioned all the changes the new primarch did." He paused and chuckled. He said in a mocking voice, "thank the heavens he's finally gone! As long as we don't have another him."

"My original question stands," I said. "Why and how are you important?"

"I guess because I'm one of the terrans that know the original truth and how they altered it. I was a talk show host, so all I did was tell stories and learn stuff. I got good at making stories up, so good that the regime needed me to be a spy a couple times. The information I gained helped them make the aegis. You gotta remember the aegis hasn't been around that long, less than 50 years. Hurricane probably wanted me because I know chimeras are made up of: human, kazamite and remnant DNA. They probably thought I knew chimera weakness too because of that. But all I know is those three DNAs worked for whatever reason, damn cocktail."

Nic scoffed and said, "you lack evidence to solidify your claims. From where I stand, you're some old man with fabricated memories of grandeur! Why should we believe you?"

"Don't. Believe this though: how we treat kazamites, and how we treat chimeras are wrong."

"Agreed, then why'd you spy for the regime, Thaddeus?"

"I had a mini political career too. And aren't you a soldier for them?"

"And I do my best daily to right wrongs," Nic said.

"I did my best too."

Nic scoffed. "My mother warned me to be cautious when near men like you. She'd say: do you know how you can tell when a politician is lying? Their lips are moving."

We all sat in silence and stared at Thaddeus.

At first, he didn't respond. But after a deep sigh, he lowered his head into his hands. When he showed his face again, the wrinkles notating his age seemed more defined.

"Sometimes we make mistakes, and the only way we know how to fix them, is another mistake. I am doing my best, I'm not who I once was. I'm smarter and more aware now but all of you can see the same thing I see. Chimeras are in a pickle. Kazamites are trying to coexist with people that hate them, and that's hard. Downright impossible even. But chimeras are forced to keep the peace and coexist; they were born to figure it out." He looked at me as he finished his sentence.

"I didn't ask to be born," I said. "I didn't ask for *any* of this."

"No one ever does, kid. No one ever does. We're supposed to judge people off of *who* they are, not what. Seems humans lost their way, or maybe this is our way and always has been."

"My ears have heard **enough**." Nic stood up with his fist balled, he was red in the face. "The regime must pay for their atrocities and blatant disregard for life. Justice must be sought against all those who sympathize with the regime."

Thaddeus chuckled before he spoke. "And when the first salvo is launched, who do you think will be on the receiving end? Which race, of the three? People think war is like firing off a shot but it's more like a grenade; everyone feels and hears it. And those supporting riots, or are well I don't know, the **son** of Leopold's right hand euthanizer, will be dealt with."

"I have done nothing wrong."

"Yea, but you're human. See Mandy will have to choose a side. All chimeras will have to. I mean we already know that they're being hunted and their loyalty questioned right now. First, kazamites will hide due to the actions of Hurricane. Then, the chimeras that are being hunted will eventually have their backs against the wall and will strike back or fold. Sprinkle some human infighting that 'creates' radicalized factions, but in truth they always existed, they just finally have a microphone and stage."

"You don't know this."

"It happened during the Mars, Saturn and Jupiter campaigns. Loyalist still exist, right? And we know Havi will act against threats today, to save the peace of tomorrow. Kill the acorn today, be spared from the oak forest tomorrow. Whoever takes up the mantle of primarch next is gonna convince humanity they must fight for their survival, or humans will become extinct."

"Why survival?" Vesalia asked. "This world is big enough for both of us. The humans just have to expand the dome and send pathfinders out into the Afuera. Discover more land."

"The Afuera? That's taboo, I'm not sure there's a human willing to leave civilization, and go see the rest of the planet. There's too many variables, way too many. Why do you think humans stayed? We don't have a home anymore. We don't have **anywhere** else to go, this *is* home. We don't have the resources to venture back to that part of the Milky Way, we stripped Earth and other planets of their resources just to make it here."

"Then humans should have never left Earth," said Nic.

"So we all should've just died? You know how hard it is to get an entire city to do what you want let alone a species? They wanted to survive and now that we're here, why would we leave?"

"There's a planet of resources! We can just leave this island! There's only so much here."

"Like humans left Earth? And resources aren't necessarily finite, if you're willing to make other worlds barren. Which is what humans did. If we venture out there off the island, we risk humans doing it again. Hell we call ourselves gods now, imagine if we had the resources of this entire planet. This thing is like two or three times the size of Earth. The tetra is a dyson swarm and that's a feat sure, it took so much resources to make. All that just so we can still live on an island, moons and ships. Sure if we used Cricket fully and the resources of this planet and the others in this star system, we could do more. You could do that by my age."

"But... wouldn't that destroy Kazar?" Vesalia asked.

"It'd probably kill us all. We'd tear apart this world and the moons. I mean since we're just saying shit, a scientist a long time ago thought about messing with dark matter. Had a theory that the multiverse is only

194

accessible via dark matter, like dark pressure or something. He wanted to venture off the island and harness more resources from this planet to fund his work. Wanted to even mess with this star's core, thought it'd open a rift into another universe. They say that's how the big bang actually happened; some eggheads generate enough energy to rip into our universe and then ended up making it. Go figure."

"Your sardonic tone isn't funny. That would kill their species, *Thaddeus*." Nic spoke through his gritted teeth.

"Yea well… some people hardly consider kazamites a species."

"Then what? Enslavement? And would they refuse, napalm? These are acceptable terms? You're **ok** with that then?"

What did Nic say? My ears grew warm and a low pitch ringing started up in them. Kaden? Did he say Kaden? The Kaden that was there when Historia died? It felt like a guvert was standing on my chest. The ringing in my ear grew. I hunched over dropping my plate. I clutched my top over where my heart was and tried to take deep breaths. I took a deep breath, then started to hyperventilate. Kaden was there when she died… **Kaden** killed Historia. Is Kaden here? No, no Mandy, that's ridiculous.

Water.

My ears were on **fire**.

My head started pounding, I needed air. I jumped to my feet and almost immediately, the world started to spin. I saw blotches of color as it got hotter.

I needed water.

I reached for my bottle and knocked it over and fell to one knee. I tried to slow down my choppy breathing, but ended up coughing and dry heaving. It's in your head, it's all just in your head, I said to myself. Tears traced my cheeks, as I buried my face in my hands, trying to cool my face down and stop the pounding. The tears slipped through my fingers.

What's wrong with me?

A voice said, "I think you need to lie down. You need rest, you deserve peace."

Wait, don't deserve peace? Kaden said that to Historia. I clenched my jaw. **Kaden's here**.

I felt a hand touch my shoulder and knew who it was, it was Kaden trying to surprise me. I spun around and grabbed his neck. I felt his feet lift off of the ground as he squirmed in my hand.

"You took her from me."

"Who?" His voice was raspy, as if I was choking him and his words.

"You're going to know her name. I promise you're gonna learn her name." Tears poured down my face in torrents.

"Mercy…"

"*Mercy?*" I tightened my grip. "Did you show Historia mercy? I don't have any mercy but what I do have, is your neck. Maybe I'll pop your head off like a zit, send it to Havi. I have some cord, maybe I'll give you a Dutch ride. Have Cricket hack all machines under regime control and post your corpse as the loading screen. I thought killing humans would be hard, but it's hard *not* killing you guys."

The light in his eyes began to dim as his face turned blue. I could feel his pulse begin to fade.

"No, not yet. We're going to drag this out, Kaden." I loosened my grip.

He coughed and gasped for air. Once he caught his breath, he croaked "who… whose… Kaden?"

What?

"Mandy." I turned my head to who said my name and was sprayed. I coughed, but didn't *dare* release my grip. I opened my eyes, and there stood Thaddeus. "You're **killing** him."

I snapped my neck to Kaden.

"**NIC!**" I dropped him and caught him before he hit the ground. "No no no no. Not again, please."

I checked his pulse. It was faint, but there. What have I done?

"There's a cyralune nearby, I think they'll help a human," Vesalia said.

"I-I'm sorry Nic. I just... I don't know what happened," I said while hugging him.

Thaddeus barked orders. "Vesalia, get the jet ready. I'll clear up any evidence we were here. Mandy, bring him onboard."

After he gave his orders, he and Vesalia left, leaving me with Nic and Cricket.

"Mandy," Cricket chirped. "He will be ok. He has lived through worse."

"And what do *you* know about life? Huh? What do you even know about death, you're spared from ever dying or grieving!"

We both sat and didn't say a word as I cradled Nic. The only thing breaking our silence was the jet spooling.

"I know when Zargus was terminated, I received not his memories, but how he processed those 'feelings' of no longer existing and knowing there was factually no afterlife for him. I also know because I am not alive, I am forced to watch everyone I know and will know eventually die. I know life is a luxury, an expensive one that has a time limit. And as the most advanced AI mankind has ever known, I still can't help those I care about. I am well versed in: mortality, immortality, anti-afterlife, and helplessness."

"I...I'm sorry, Cricket."

I picked Nic up, and grabbed his speaker. I walked to the jet and put Nic in the infirmary area, just how Valen was. Vesalia said something to me, but I drowned her out as I gently rubbed Nic's now purple neck. I'd never hurt Nic, and here I have twice in just a day. What's wrong with me? If Thaddeus didn't stop me, would I have... I couldn't have... could I?

I rubbed his still swollen black eye and held his hand.

"I'm so sorry..." I mumbled as I rested my head on his chest.

Chapter 8

Nom De Guerre

"Come on, sleeping beauty." Thaddeus tapped me.

"What?" It felt like I just closed my eyes, and now Thaddeus was standing over me and the moons were high in the sky.

"Grab him. Vesalia already spoke with the locals and they agreed to help."

"What do they know about human medicine?" I asked, maybe a little too aggressively.

"Don't be xenoist, they have doctors, ya asshole. They know enough to heal the human you hurt, and they'll keep this on the DL. Since you know, you're a wanted chimera for pretty much all the crimes Historia was accused of."

Oh yea, that little part. I picked Nic up again and walked outside. A cyralune was a town or village of kazamites untouched by humans. Some allowed humans to enter, but none were ever permitted to stay longer than two days. The current... *previous* primarch believed in an 'isolated but uniformed' life for kazamites that lived separate from humans. The kazamites that lived in the regime's reach were 'sometimes severed but forever parallel'. To some it sounded good, but it was essentially asking if someone wanted dark navy blue or black.

Kazamites that lived in cyralunes liked humans... but from afar. They believed all humans become violent the older they get, and that it spreads like an illness. They were however always unsure of chimeras.

They haven't had enough interactions with us to form solid enough opinions. So as I walked with Nic in my arms, their heads were canted as they trailed me, and their eyes were unblinking.

"I can help." Vesalia said as she extended her hands towards Nic. Before she touched him, she looked up into my white eyes and I could almost hear her heart skip a beat. "I- I think you got it, nevermind."

I continued walking to their doctors and laid Nic down on the stretcher.

"Treat him with kindness," I said to them. They nodded and smiled and left with him.

"Her gaze... it's like... like a searing white star," Vesalia whispered to Thaddeus.

"I'm going deeper into the village. My aegis is still onboard, Thaddeus. I have my NUE on me."

"I'm guessing the tracker on your aegis is off?" He asked.

I nodded. "The tracker can only be turned on if it feels there's a threat to my life. Since I'm not wearing it, only a lightning bolt hitting it head on could jump start the system into thinking I'm in trouble. I also always have Cricket."

Vesalia asked, "can I join you, Mandy? I'd love to learn more about chimeras and ask you some questions."

I almost gave myself whiplash with how fast I snapped my head to reply but Thaddeus raised his hand and shook his head at me.

I needed space and to calm down, so I walked away. I walked through the town, taking in the kazamite structures and trying to forget everything. I know I needed to calm down, but everything was just pissing me off. Like a girl my brother is following that got us all into this mess. If Vesalia didn't get involved, Nic wouldn't be hurt and Historia would still be alive. Why on kazar would I want her to walk with me? She's probably the one that filled Nic's head with these delusions of going against the regime. This is all her fault.

"Excuse me Ms. Chimera..."

A kazamite child stood in front of me.

"What?"

They cowered at my tone, but were determined to power through their fear.

"Are you here to take us? We paid the tithe already."

"Tithe?"

"My brother just turned 16, the tithe says we have to give him up to the humans. He never wanted to be conscripted, and I don't want to lose my brother."

"Conscription?"

The kazamite kid wasn't any older than I was when I met Nic.

"Hesamia!" A kazamite woman who looked similar to the girl, ran over to us and picked her up. "I'm sorry for whatever she has said to you."

"Oh… I don't think—"

"Please, I cannot lose another child. I am at my obligatory limit."

"Obligatory limit? I'm not here for your child…"

"More taxes? But our village has paid the land residency fee for the month."

"I don't… I don't know what any of the things you're saying are. Has the regime sent a chimera here before?"

A kazamite walking by chimed in. "Are humans not satisfied with this month's taxes and tithes? Are you an emissary to renegotiate terms?"

A crowd started to form.

"I'm not an emissary. Please I—"

"The last chimera a decade ago took double the tithe. He wore ecru armor, like the bird."

I raised my hands and they all fell silent.

"I'm not here on behalf of the regime, humans or chimeras. I'm here as myself, Mandy. I never knew about the tithes or these taxes… but I have an idea which chimera did know and I'll confront him next time I see him. But you have my word, I mean you guys no harm."

I felt the tension in the group lower, and some even sighed in relief.

The mother of the young kazamite Hesamia said, "We're sorry, we just have never seen one of your kind before. A kind one, I mean. But we have seen the videos of chimeras in battles and have heard how in order to stay young, you take the proteins and vitality out of kazamite younglings."

"What? Who said that?"

"The media. We watch it on the news and read it in our history books given to us by the regime. That if we serve the humans kindly and faithfully, they will bring us wonders unlike we have ever seen. Said if they needed to impose their will, they'd send chimeras, their enforcers of order."

"Enforcers of order…?"

"Yes. Are you… not an enforcer of order?"

Is this how they see us here, or is this how all kazamites see chimeras behind closed doors?

I sighed and said, "no, no I'm not."

The crowd let out a collective gasp.

Hesamia said, "but you're a chimera, your neurolink is programmed to listen to humans."

"No," I chuckled. "We all have neurolinks, they're just nanites that are connected to Babylon. I can choose not to listen or agree with humans. In fact, I normally don't. But I for sure won't now. Not anymore. Not ever again."

She canted her head and furrowed her brow and asked, "but who will protect our land from foreign invaders, threats and wars?"

"Foreign invaders? The regime *is* the foreign invader. And what war? Outside of the regime, who do you guys need protection from?"

Her mom asked, "the threat?"

"Which is?" I looked at the crowd, but none seemed to have a good answer. I sighed. "Let me guess, this 'threat' exists in the media and the books regulated by the regime? Figures. Burn them. There are groups out there that are bad and you do need to be cautious, but the biggest boogie man out there right now is the regime. They aren't gods, they bleed just like any of us. We can be thankful for the humans' help without being their servants. No longer do we live *for* them, but *with* them."

"You're like the caxan, Pa-alda," said Hesamia. She saw the confused look on my face and giggled. "There's three caxans. Pa-alda is the one who came from the void. She was born from it and created life from nothing, so we call her voidborn.

"I just learned about the caxans… maybe you can tell me more about it?" I looked up at her mom and she replied with a smile.

Hesamia's mother introduced herself as Besakia and became my tour guide. Hesamia ran off to play and Besakia and I went to a diner to quiet my stomach; it made oceandrake sounds almost every step. As soon as we stepped into the diner, my nose was flooded with scents. The smell of red meat, broth, and seafood covered every corner of the diner. Not all, but too many human diners had processed or cloned food. Those who spent too long on the moons, slowly lost a normal palette range and preferred food with preservatives. Thankfully, I wasn't one of them and neither was Besakia. She ordered me her favorite dish, thifrum chili.

In minutes, a bowl of light orange chili was brought to me. On top it had: kelp bits, fried onion flakes, furikake and diced scallions. Next to the bowl on my tray, was white pepper and a clear colored sauce. Besakia nodded for me to put both on, and stir. White pepper was more of a human exclusive spice, but I guess the locals liked it. After adding the sauce and white pepper, I took a spoonful and holy shit. Like a feral beast, I devoured everything faster than it came out. It had a sweet taste to it, but also a nudge of spiciness. Besakia stayed long enough to see my reaction and laughed. After she was satisfied that I was satisfied, she left me to enjoy my dinner. I didn't waste any time either; I asked for seconds, then thirds.

Thaddeus walked up and sat next to me as I scraped down the third bowl. He chuckled and asked, "that good, huh?"

I nodded. "I know we just ate before we came here. But... everything's just foggy for me right now."

"Yea I'd be concerned if I found you doing cartwheels after socking your brother in the face and then choking him out. Wanna talk about it? I mean, any of it?"

"What is there to talk about? I let Historia die. She's my... *was* my pod leader, so I should've gone to face Havi instead of her."

"Survivors' guilt. They had that on earth too."

I turned to face him and asked, "then this is the human part of me? What's the cure?"

"Sadly, we never advanced to figure that one out." He waved down the waiter and ordered us drinks. "I don't got the cure, but I know what they used as a cure."

"You were a spy, that's just a soldier with different weapons. How did you handle it?"

"What? The overwhelming emotions and survivor's guilt? Initially, I hurt my daughter. Thought I was protecting her from a world of dangers because I saw all this unfettered knowledge. So, I made her tough, tougher than me. Good parents do their best to prepare and shield their kid, but sometimes parents are guessing. Guessing and just going by what they think would be best. I didn't handle being a spy, husband or father well. Thankfully, she's her mother's child and fuck ups aren't hereditary." The drinks arrived and he took a gulp.

I groaned and said, "you are no help, old man."

He chuckled.

"You sound just like her. I left her with her mom, now **she** knew how to handle this stuff. She knew how to deal with pain."

"Where?" I asked as I tasted my drink. And of course just like the food, it was really good, so I gulped it down.

"The island against the patriarchy of course, Scyra. Last I heard, she was off gallivanting doing whatever the hell warriors from there do. The Rifters, that faction that gave the primarch hell for years, she fought them. Helped take down almost their entire organization with some chimera named Rai."

Wait... he didn't mean...

The power cut off for a few seconds then turned back on again.

"I guess that's what happens when you live in the middle of nowhere," he said. "So Mandy, what's the plan after misaligning yourself with the regime's oh so sacrosanct decrees and morals?"

"Ew, I didn't know all terrans could speak like that. You've been reading Nic's diary?"

He smirked and said, "me reading a diary against someone's wishes? Oh how dare you put me in collusion with immoral dregs!" He said mockingly. "I had a lot of downtime, I liked reading when I wasn't working. Now I'm a big fish guy."

"Do you use the spray you used on me on the fish?"

"Only the ones that plan a rebellion." First, I snickered, then bursted out laughing. "Not the reaction I was expecting."

"Did you expect me to be mad? Humans kill chimeras, and thanks to Lissax and Nic's brain, we know some aren't even dead. I don't think kazamites kill chimeras so, it's expected I'd eventually run into a human that's killed chimeras." I paused and finished my drink. "I should be more upset, but I just want to take down Havi. I just want to make him suffer but... it's *Havi*, he might actually be a god."

Thaddeus ordered us refills.

"Havi just needs his powers cut off, it's only tech and has its limits. Outside of that, he's just a terran. You just need to bypass his tech, overwhelm it and him. The other leaders can't fight like he can and anyone offworld is just that. If you plan on taking out the military and regime, you better have a replacement."

"Why? Why does there need to be a singular group of people ruling over everyone else? Why can't we all just exist?"

He chuckled. "Yea, I guess you could." The refills arrived. "Must be a silly human concept to govern." He downed his drink.

"Are you gonna tell me what that spray was, or deflect again?"

"This?" He reached into his pocket and pulled out a small spray bottle. "Here, I'll just grab it back from you later. But it hits your brain and essentially restarts it. It gives you a mini brain seizure... well I guess it isn't mini. I was aiming for you to stagger backwards or pass out but I guess you were just used to being attacked. Normally, this works on you guys. It only buys like a minute or less, but it's meant for chimeras specifically. I assume something to do with that alien DNA in you, but this'll probably kill a human. Come to think of it, it most definitely would kill a human. It's radioactive, so don't crack the nozzle."

"Do you always carry stuff like this on you?"

"Tradecraft says we should always have a way out against our biggest threats. For me during that little broadcast, it was chimeras. I wasn't much worried about anyone smaller."

"I remember finding you surrounded by 'anyone smaller' actually."

"Yea... after enough battles you get tired. You just expect what's coming, is coming."

Cricket chirped, "sorry to interrupt Mandy, but I don't understand the plan. Why would you remote the aegis' tracker on?"

"Tracker?" I looked up at Thaddeus.

His eyes grew wide. "Can you remote it off?" I shook my head. "Go, turn it off." He jumped up and ran out.

"No, I need to go get Nic!"

"There's no time for this! I don't know how to work your aegis and we need that tracker off!" He ran towards the infirmary. "The infirmary is connected to their leader's house, we have to warn her and their people. **Go!**"

We split off and I ran as fast as I could. I'd rather be there for Nic, but Thaddeus was right, the jet and my aegis were further away and I was faster than him. I pushed past everyone and everything until the jet was in eyesight. And outside of the jet, was my aegis on the ground with wires hooked into it. Dammit, that was the power outage. Ugh!

I dashed over to my aegis and touched it. The living metal morphed around my body and took the mold of my figure.

"Turn off the tracker, Cricket!" I yelled as I raced towards the infirmary where Nic and Thaddeus were.

"Thaddeus!" He had Nic in his arms and was pushing through a panicked crowd.

And then came the light. The oh so familiar red light I've seen the regime use a hundred times.

"NOOOOO!"

One moment, the infirmary was there with everyone around it, the next, everything was on fire. The red light always came first, then came the plasma blast. It came from a ship and completely obliterated the infirmary and anyone in it. Everyone and everything not caught in the immediate blast, caught fire. Or was shot into the air, or into things. The shockwave sent me flying backwards through a tree and into a building, but I didn't keep my eyes off of them. Thaddeus must've known what the red light meant, he covered Nic as best as he could. But it didn't matter. They both flew into the air in a ball of fire. Thaddeus let go of Nic, as they fell, but only Thaddeus was on fire. He must've tanked the entire blow. I rushed forward and dove trying to catch Nic as he fell. I slid across the hot dirt and stone, but I caught him. I checked Nic's pulse and while it was faint, it was at least there. I wiped away the clear liquid that was leaking through his nose and then looked to see where Thaddeus fell.

"No…"

Thaddeus was completely engulfed in fire. There was more fire than there was him. How did this happen? I palmed my face, and then smelt blood.

"What?" I looked down and checked the back of Nic's head. Blood was everywhere. He started to turn pale. "No… no no no no no not again."

"His pulse is fading, Mandy," Cricket said.

"Drain all power from the suit, set it to an emergency human defibrillator." I flipped Nic over to check how bad the hit was. I ripped his shirt and put pressure on his wound.

"He flatlined," Cricket said.

"I know. Use the necrobots and prep for CPR."

After a couple seconds, Cricket said, "he's in a shockable rhythm now, the suit is charged. This will cost all of me, I will have to reboot after. I don't know how long I will be gone for and you will be unprotected."

"Just do it. Save my brother Cricket, please."

"Very well. You know what happens next."

I rested my hands on Nic as my aegis left me, and morphed around him while giving off a low hum.

"I'm not losing my sister and my brother…"

I watched as the necrobots went to work, trying to save Nic's life. The suit pulsed. A long time ago, Nic got hurt really bad. I had Cricket tamper with my aegis and have it designed so that in the event of an emergency, Nic could wear my aegis seamlessly.

His chest rose and fell, and then he coughed.

I sighed with relief.

I heard someone slowly walk over to me, it was Vesalia.

She asked, "is… is that who I think it is?"

"Yea… Nic's in bad shape but Thaddeus… Thaddeus has seen better days." I looked over at his body… or what was left of it.

"This looks terrible... will Nic be ok?"

"Yes, but we have to go. Earlier, one of the kazamites told me about an escape route through the water. We have to go before..." Soldiers with guns ran over to us. "**You...**"

Trogz walked forward from behind the soldiers. He wore his regime proper dress uniform like always, and looked all the part of the super villain he was with the fire around us. He looked at me and Nic and you could see the muscles in his jaw clench. He then turned his attention to Vesalia.

"Kazamite, I am Lieutenant Colonel Alexander Trogz." He took a step towards her.

"Don't you dare..." I said while balling my fist.

He raised an eyebrow and looked at me. He then raised both eyebrows in shock. "Who do you think pinged your location, chimera?"

"No... no she's with Hurricane," I stammered.

"*Hurricane?*" He chuckled. "This alien *hates* you. She detest you wannabe humans. She's a spy, a sleeper agent that I activated once I lost sight of the boy and you. She's an informant, and you're a fool."

"You- you have to understand Mandy. Humans have advanced us by eons! You heard Thaddeus tell us about the technology they had and have. We **need** humans and owe them everything that we are."

"What? How could you?"

"It had to be done..." She mumbled.

It all hit me at once. Nic bleeding next to me, Cricket actually sleeping, the blown up infirmary, the dying kazamites and now, all the gunfire and screaming for help in the background. I'm so used to gunfire, I blocked out the regime shooting the kazamites without even knowing.

"You... YOU did this!" I yelled and motioned to the fire cackling all around us.

"Mandy, please!" Vesalia pleaded. "Chimeras and kazamites running loose are dangerous and the humans know how to rule.

Primarch Leopold was bad, yes, but even he maintained order from the books I've read. And the regime can't regulate every piece of literature, that's just impossible and is slander. The books say chimeras are the dangerous ones, I mean just look how much you hurt your brother just today! You guys need governance, chains even. And the only ones able to do such a powerful task, are your creators."

"Seriously? They just leveled a town! They're rounding up kazamites **literally** as we speak!"

"They're rounding up *criminals*. If kazamites in this town were innocent, then why are they running and not reporting to the human in charge like I did?"

"Cause humans just pixilated their fucking hospital!"

"A hospital where they cared for and harbored enemies of the state! Convicts and criminals don't have rights. It's not pretty… but humans are the only ones capable of making such decisions. They need to guide us on our behalf."

"The ant speaks well," Trogz said.

Vesalia took a step closer to me and said, "Mandy, I'm sorry he suffered."

"I'm going to kill you. I promise I'm going to fucking kill you."

Trogz scoffed and said, "will you? Have you not killed enough, chimera?" He took a step towards me. "Look what you've done to my son." He turned his head to one of the soldiers. "Summon the paramedics. This chimera almost killed him, but I was prepared for this."

"*Me?* Are you serious?" I stood up and balled my fist as my teeth chattered. The soldiers matched my aggression and reset their guns back at me. Vesalia squealed and jumped back. "You humans keep taking so much of me and from me, and I've done nothing but serve. You made me."

"One of humanity's many misjudgments. You, girl, were nothing more than a phase for Copernicus. A lapse in his judgement. An annoying cancerous one for sure, but nothing more than that. And now, your vile and barbaric cocktail kazamite blood has confused and tainted him. Now my child is bleeding, at the feet of an uncultivated lab experiment. Look what your kazamite blood has wrought."

"I'm not a kazamite, I'm a chimera."

"You're a **MISTAKE**! A mistake that almost took the last member of my family. He was destined for **GREATNESS**, just like my brother. And it's *always* a girl, but this time, oh there must be a higher power, because this time, it's a lab grown girl. A petri dish girl that was created next to pipettes." He balled his fist and started grinding his teeth as he walked towards me. "And you have the nerve to call him 'brother' too."

"Nic **is** my brother."

"No he is **not**. What do you even know about family, you bio-bastard? I can't remember, can your kind even *have* babies? Can they even conceive the concept of a family or legacy? Do you even understand the meaning of legacy? An heir? What do you know about walking your daughter down the aisle to the altar? What does any of your kind know about that? Do you have any concept of what it's like to watch someone you love pledge themselves to a blue eyed redhead scientist in a goddamn desert and give up **decades** of work and sully a family's name for love? And then profess it in front of the cosmos and whatever exists beyond that?" He stopped only a foot away from me.

"I... no..."

"No... and how could you, tube spawn?" He turned his back to me and walked back to the soldiers. "Your existence, culture, DNA even, is a literal example of nothing from many. Because that's all chimeras are: nothing. You are a franken-baby, nothing more. Stay away from my family, chimera. Arrest her."

The soldiers took a step forward and the head soldier began to say something, but I wasn't listening. I dashed back towards the house I flew into earlier as they started firing at me. Without my aegis, I was outmatched, outgunned and just flat out screwed. But this time... my body felt... fluid. It was like I was dancing as I dodged to safety. It's not that I wasn't grazed or hit, but my body moved on its own. Everything just happened so fast, it was all a blur. I tackled through the building and didn't slow down. I raced past the mirror and for a split second, I thought I saw Historia.

I zig zagged as I ran, cutting through buildings and cutting through soldiers as I saw them. Every single soldier that saw me, opened fire without a second thought. The ones that didn't, were distracted executing kazamites. I fought them off and tried to free kazamites as I saw them but once I got out of sight, I hid.

"Ok Cricket, how far are we?" There was no response. "Oh…"

After about 20 minutes sneaking and running, I made it to the escape area at the water's edge. It wasn't obvious either, so hopefully people got out. It was marked only by a couple stacked smooth rocks so if you didn't know any better, you'd walk right past it. I dove into the river and swam to the bottom and looked around until I saw the clue. There were rocks everywhere, but only one trail of smooth rocks that went in one direction. I swam following the smooth rocks until I hit a part of the river that deepened, and then I swam down. There was a tunnel surrounded by smooth rocks that led to an underwater cave that had an air pocket. I swam to it and surfaced and crawled out. The tunnel was dark, but the walls were lined in bioluminescent paintings.

I sighed, and walked down the tunnel, following the paint. As I walked, I noticed how dry the area was. The attack just happened so if anyone made it out, the area would be wet. Maybe… maybe I was just so fast and nobody got a chance to make it out yet. Maybe I was eating the gourd…I let out a sigh and continued. Just a few months ago, I had a beautiful view from my home with a water wall, close friends, and a brother. Now, I'm blindly cave walking towards who knows what. And to top it all off…

"I'm all alone…"

I walked in silence and wondered: how much longer could I keep this up? I laughed. Nic would say words in times like this that sounded made up, but it showed his vast vocabulary. He'd probably describe my feeling as 'hiraeth'. Or some other fancy word or phrase… he better pull through…

Chapter 9

FAUSTIAN BARGAIN

"I brought you breakfast." I jumped to my feet and drew my knife. My greeter was an elderly kazamite. "You won't need that while here, young one."

Without lowering my guard I asked, "how did you find me?"

"How did I find a purplish chimera in a red barn? Do you eat eggs?"

"Unpoisoned ones."

"I am Keezon, and I do not poison food. I'm not sure I know a kazamite in our cyralune that knows how to make poison." He gave me a reassuring smile.

"You eat it."

He raised his eyebrows and sighed. He grabbed a fork and took a bite. "See? There's not–" I knew it. He fell to his knees and started screaming and coughing. I groaned and then sheathed my knife.

"You've made your point. My name's Mandy."

He chuckled and stood to his feet and handed me the plate. "Potatoes, eggs, hash browns, and bacon."

"Bacon? And thank you." I took the plate and immediately got to work.

"We don't have human food at all here, just a few human spices. The bacon is from a veraxin boar, not your small and domesticated tharkun ones. The eggs are from stryder hens and reef hawks. I believe you call reef hawks 'breaker hens'. Regardless, I extend hospitality to you as the elder. Feeding you should be the safer option than you raiding our food storages."

"I'm sorry, I just don't have anything to eat. There's a cyralune not too far from here, humans attacked and I had to escape with only what was on me.

"Humans always attack, it's their nature. But we heard the gunfire from here when you arrived. So before you ask, I've known you've been here this entire time. I can only assume a chimera escaping humans must mean bad things for all of kazar. A falling out between your group and the humans spells disaster."

"I could be a spy."

"Spy? Please, you only know about our cyralune because another kazamite told you about it. I think you don't have any chimera allies nearby, and you don't have the fancy suit all chimeras wear. Maybe you're a spy, but you'd be a useless one. We don't have anything here of value to humans."

"You're very perceptive. I'm not a spy, I just don't have anywhere else to go. I just needed… to catch my breath."

"And that is ok, but you will earn your keep. Everyone here must chip in, imagine a cyralune is like a big family. Your friends will have to earn their keep as well, they are away I assume?"

"Friends?"

He motioned to a spot of hay next to me and said, "I assumed there were two others, because you kept saying two names. But there's only one spot. Are they cloaked?"

I sighed.

"Nic and Historia? Were those the names I said?"

"Yes."

"No… no it's just me."

"Hmm… very well, when you are ready, you can come eat with the town and introduce yourself to us and the others." He turned his back and walked away.

"Others?"

"You're not the only visitor we have this week."

I finished my plate and followed him into the town. Unlike the last cyralune, this one had more kazamite-like architecture. There were minute differences, but the stark contrast was obvious. The last cyralune had buildings that were made like basic human buildings, brick, mortar, stone, the works. But for cyralunes that developed without regime in any way, buildings were mostly sponges. Some sponges were big enough that they could be used in building homes on land, so why wouldn't kazamites live in them? The average buildings in a cyralune are made of: sponge, keratin, chitin, elastin and bone. Or whatever minerals are inside of a bone. Depending on the location of the cyralune, depends on the color of these buildings. Most were vibrant, this cyralune was dull and vibrant, if one could be both.

"You're the first chimera to ever enter our home, Mandy. What do you think?"

"Your home is nice, may I ask you something, Keezon?" He nodded. "The last cyralune, the kazamites seemed afraid of me. I've also met kazamites in the past that hate me. Yet, you don't seem scared of me or hate me. You're treating me as if I were a kazamite from another place in Kore. Why?"

"Because I have seen real fear, and real danger. I've heard stories of kazamites living in fear near regime controlled or influenced cyralunes. And I've also experienced being a casualty of the regime. You're not them. If anything, you are more or less like a hurt animal than a predator."

The center of the village wasn't far, so we made it there in no time. There was a crowd of kazamites waiting to see me, the stranger. The crowd was a sea of different colored and different aged kazamites. And there couldn't have been more than 60 of them in the whole village.

They all stared at me with curious eyes and farming tools in their hands. None of them looked like fighters, if the regime ever found this place, they'd be decimated.

Keezon motioned for me to step in front of him and he said to the crowd, "everyone, this is Mandy."

"Hi," I said sheepishly.

One of them asked me, "ave youd ever built a biosphere?" The fuck? Why would I know how to do that?

"Uh, no?"

He walked over to me and handed me a textbook.

"Dem dere dumb down for ya. Areful or else youd do like the last youngings, dey played too dang hard and rocked the biosphere. Otta replace the capacitor, the chains, know dem chains need replacing, raking the soil, feeding dem bottom feeders, and creating the replacement generator cause last it wasn't red, but blue."

"Uh, I- I don't... I don't think I can do... any of that. I don't think I understand what 'that' actually is. Maybe my neurolink is malfunctioning."

"It's not, dem dere neurolinks translate just fine. Dey don't change how we mean our words. Go on, read."

I did a quick flip through the textbook, every page was front and back and it weighed at least four pounds.

"This... this is a lot."

"Ou'll learn." He walked away.

The crowd dispersed and left me with Keezon.

"Keezon, I don't mind helping but, I can't read a book this size in a day. I don't even understand what he wanted of me. Why don't you guys use machines and mechs?"

"Because those things can complicate life. We have everything we need to make life work, why look for shortcuts? Since you'll be staying here I–"

"*Staying* here? I'm sorry, but I'm not staying here. I just need a moment for the world to stop spinning. I'm not looking to do... sidequest, I need a plan."

"No, you need a job. But maybe we gave you something a little too advanced. Maybe something smaller? What skills do you have?"

I scratched my head and said, "I'm strong?"

"So is cattle, surely you have more to offer than them. Our society doesn't need knuckle draggers. Come, we'll put you in the fast track school."

"School?" I raised an eyebrow and said, "I've had my share of standardized academia, I'm not a child."

"Are you sure? From what I have heard, academia is an unbalanced system, school is just a place of learning. Everyone should go to a school, it's just you're used to human schools. When humans first arrived, they had these things called 'trade schools' and they were considered heroes. Everyone can and should go to school, you just need the right one." He smiled, trying to be reassuring. "Unfortunately for you, you only have four choices. Our aquaculture course, biomedical equipment specialist, zoologist and marine technician. That's what we're in need of in our town as of now."

"And I can just... walk into any of these fields?"

"How else would you get experience in them? The town voted for what jobs and positions were vacant, and which needed to be filled. Those are the vacancies needing to be filled, insert the chimera."

"I guess then..." I was about to say aquaculture, but I thought about how happy Historia always seemed with animals. "Zoologist."

"Ah, that's a fun and complicated one. I'll walk you to your class."

"I'll do my best but again, I'm... I'm in a bad place right now."

"Oh aren't we all?"

He brought me to a building at the edge of town.

"Your teacher is inside. There is a bonfire tonight, our weekly one. I'd love to hear about your first day hopefully of many here as part of the cyralune. We voice grievances there, hopefully you don't have any. But speak up if you have any issues."

"Ok… thank you again."

I left Keezon and walked into the schoolhouse to meet the instructor. I'm not sure what I was expecting, but being one of the only three students wasn't it. The classroom had pictures of animals not only from our world, but from Earth as well with different fun facts attached to them. At the front of the class was a picture of an Earth creature hanging from a rope with the words 'hang in there' above it. I opened my mouth to introduce myself but the teacher snapped at me and ordered me to take my seat.

This was a far cry from a regime school or a chimera agoge. University is supposed to be hundreds of hours of research and papers. Before The University of the first scholar, the regime demanded a very strict standardized testing system. They believed all humans should have a certain amount of theoretical and practical knowledge. Kazamite schools were by far easier than human schools too. The hardest part was probably day one, where students traditionally were tested immediately.

"New student, you will have one quiz and one assessment. First question: how many stomachs do thifrums have?"

"One, they're like cows back on Earth," I said. "Where it's one official stomach, but there's… four separate parts."

"Question two: how much does a full grown kurous eat in a day?"

"Uh… about 11 to 20 tons?"

"Question three: name an apex predator on both moons and our world."

"Pala has… jorvian wraiths, and I'm not sure there are animals on Ven. Wait, forktailed lunari. I'm not sure if insects count. For Kazar, sabertooth guverts."

"Hmm… I'm impressed. Here's one no student ever gets, scientific name for a royal wyvern ixal?"

"Oh that's easy, labrys hadro, it's what Chickenstrip is."

"Chickenstrip?"

"Sorry, Chickenstrip is like my… pet. I guess he's like a town pet and that's what I named him."

"Impressive, welcome to class. Grab a book and meet your classmates, you're joining right before an exam so you have a lot of catching up to do. Today, we will be nursing an adult kurous back to flying health. You still haven't figured out the root of the issue, only symptoms. We are the caretakers of our world, it's important we learn how to heal and help the animals and plants around us. Once you all have figured out what is missing, we can go outside and begin."

That went better than my first day in the agoge. As I opened my book, a girl tapped me on my shoulder and smiled.

"Hi, I'm Mandy. You're a pretty color." She smiled but didn't say anything back. "Was that… an offensive thing to say? I normally have someone that tells me to find my manners."

Still nothing.

She shook her head and pointed to her mouth and started… signing. A long time ago, Eleanor forced Historia and I to learn 'speechless words', or signing. I argued that it was dumb, thanks to neurolinks, everyone on and off world always understood the other person. Dramatic head trauma was one of the only ways for a neurolink to have a faulty connection to Babylon; like Nic. Eleanor didn't take no for an answer, and banned Historia and I from talking for an entire month and a half straight. So, we got reallyyyy good at it.

I signed back, "I can understand you, I am Mandy. Hi."

Her eyes doubled in size as she perked up. She pushed her table into mine and threw all of her notes on our now conjoined table.

She signed, "JAZ! I'm Jaz! It feels **so** good to be heard! Here are my notes, I have some theories on why the kurous is sick, but nobody can hear me. My initial thought was that it had organ failure, maybe the kidneys. But then I found earlier in my notes about mating cycles and landed on that for a while. It's not seasonal, but I guess it could be a combination of those, but it's hard to say. I have to highlight the

219

important parts of my notes but here are my notes, just ask me where you're confused!"

"Oh gosh." She signed so fast, I had to fill in the blanks on words I missed. "I'd love to see what you think, but you have to talk slower," I signed back.

Over the next few hours, Jaz and I went over almost all of her notes. I've never seen a kazamite *this* into animals before, she clearly had a passion for it. I asked if she wanted to work at an animal sanctuary, but she told me she wanted to see animals in their natural places. Something about them in their biomes felt more genuine to her. For her, every animal not in their natural habitat, felt like a personal attack at her. So she spent countless hours combing through her notes to never get anything wrong.

From what she gathered and what was given, this was an adult male kurous and a big one at that. It weighed roughly 200 tons, the males weighed between 150 to 200 tons anyway, so it had a healthy diet. Its size was impressive, but was 100 tons less than the biggest animal on Kazar. We went over their disposition, anatomy and how most were solitary animals in their adulthood, but very nurturing to their young and could form bonds with other animals and items. Not only did they have amazing memories, but they could pick up the scents of their kin up to 25 miles away. Jaz told me they could also live to 90, this one was about 50 because it had scarring from parenthood. It's the males that take care of the bus sized eggs that the female kuros lay.

By the time we finally went outside to go hands on, my brain was already fried, and my hands and fingers were tired. The only reason, **only** reason I was putting in this much effort, was because kuros, sick or healthy, reminded me of Nic. The last time I ever saw one was when I first met Nic. I sighed.

"Focus dude," I mumbled to myself.

I shook the thought away as I laid eyes on the animal, I wasn't prepared. When you hear '200 tons' you don't fully appreciate just how *massive* that is. And it ate meat, why the hell would they try to fix this?

As we got closer, it let out a sigh. Humans said that they looked like dragons, but had extra parts. For example, every kurous had feelers, or antennas on their head like lurnoms. They had retractable wings that came from their sides, and it was able to tuck its limbs so closely that it appeared like a serpent in the air sometimes. I'm not sure if dragons had this, but a kurous could also grow a hardened keratin-like spiky beard. This one had one.

Jaz poked me and signed, "you can tell it's a male because its horns spiral like hobgoblin draxins. The females have antlers."

"It's pretty," I signed back.

"Duh, it's beyond rare for them to be this color. We call it 'phthalo green'. At least I do."

I rolled my eyes and signed back, "no way that's a real color."

I turned my attention back to the creature and honestly, maybe that was a real color. I could imagine Nic saying it at least. This kurous had black streaks across its body as well which apparently when healthy, the streaks glowed due to the bioluminescence light it generates. I knew that cause of Historia, she'd love it here…

"New student, that device on your wrist is a scanner, yes?" The instructor asked. "Diagnose it." The class stood to the side with the instructor, staring in awe at my NUE.

I hesitated at first, but Jaz cheered me on. I approached the behemoth while it was curled up, it didn't even realize I was there. I aimed my wrist at it and walked around as my NUE scanned. A NUE was only helpful if the user knew how to use it, and it also helped if the creature that was hurt had a neurolink. It did however show abnormalities… but nothing was picking up. I scanned it again, but got the same result. I got a bit closer and kneeled down, I didn't know much about them but something was off. You could hear in how the kurous was breathing, that there was something wrong. The breathing was labored. I scanned it one more time and walked over to its head to see if there was some trauma there, but the same result as the first.

"I don't get what…"

I froze. It was staring at me.

It took a deep breath and let out a low animalistic sound. It was somewhere between a growl and a sigh.

"You're sad…"

The teacher asked, "well?"

"It's sad. Maybe lost its will to live by losing its territory, or something. Maybe… wait, the mothers lay the eggs but immediately leave them with their father, right? It lost its child. The scarring on its body means it had a battle, and lost. The area near its claws are singed as well, even the claws are singed bad. Like an acid burn."

The class looked stunned. The teacher, still unimpressed, asked, "I like where you're going, but there are no acidic creatures that they hunt."

"The scarring is from human weapons, maybe poachers. They're around the same time as the acid burns. No land animal has acid that could hurt something this big, but a sea one does. Siren whales, they have acid on their backs for the only predator that could and would go after it. So, there was a siren whale fight, and the poachers took the kid and this all must have happened within a week. These are signs of depression."

"How do you know?"

"It's a familiar sonnet…"

"Hmm… kurous eggs do sell nicely on the black market. It's impressive to think that poachers took an egg, that would require a lot of manpower."

"Or fire power, so the regime took it."

The teacher was stunned. "That is a bold claim."

"Yea… wouldn't be the first time the regime has taken things that don't belong to them."

"You're very opinionated, but you are also very impressive. Come class, there is not much we can do for this creature. All we can do is hope he gets the will to continue on. New student, I am impressed with your level of reasoning. We don't have those watch devices in cyralunes,

I've only heard of them. Thank you, even I genuinely couldn't figure out what was wrong with it."

"You don't have books on the creature?"

"State controlled books? No, all literature we have is unregulated by the regime. Most books on wildlife are from caravans and our own discoveries. Tonight is the bonfire, will you be joining us?"

No. I don't know them and I didn't come here by choice. Why can't I just be left alone in the barn? But... Historia would hate me doing that.

"Yea, yea I will."

I spent the next couple hours helping the town prepare for the bonfire. Jaz and I spent almost the entire time with each other and I think that if Historia were here, she'd love to meet her. Jaz taught me so much about kazamite culture, like how their musical instruments were different from humans entirely. Humans used their hands for all their instruments, all kazamite instruments worked off of pulsing and potential energy. I didn't understand it, but I've yet to meet a human that could explain how the violin works.

While we walked to the town, Jaz asked me, "what is chimera school like?"

"We call it agoge, a-g-o-g-e. And it's nothing like your school," I signed back. "We have: freshmen, sophomores, juniors and seniors. Your freshman years begin at around four, sophomore around 7, junior is about 14 and senior is 20."

"What do you do? What do you learn?"

"Freshman is stuff like: literacy, land navigation, hunting and fishing, history, gymnastics. Then it's tactics, firearms, free-diving, bouldering, urban survival. Junior is wilderness survival, missions and building on the last. Finally, you lead whole missions. Of course along the way you learn about the star system and basic math and science like pre calc and environmental science."

"Is it fun?"

"I'm the wrong person to ask, I spent half of it in trouble."

"But you had classmates that could understand you right?"

"Yea, I was lucky. I also didn't have to worry about social cues when with them cause they helped."

"Oh! Before I forget, when you meet kazamites you're supposed to greet them. It's really for elders, but we do follow in their steps." She showed me her left forearm and gently drug her nails across it. "A long time ago, cyralunes were invaded by kazamite spies. The spies were 'strung branded' and it would cause the skin on their forearms to raise a little. So, we do this to elders, visitors and strangers to show we don't mean harm. You try it!"

I copied what she did. "Like this?" She shrieked with joy and nodded.

By the time we made it to the town's center, the village was already waiting. They were harmonizing with their instruments, another thing humans don't seem to do. Kazamite's didn't have lyrics to their songs, unlike humans either, so they had to harmonize by singing without words. Keezon was attempting to do the same, but I guess not every kazamite was a singer.

He greeted us and said, "I have learned one thing humans do right is have their songs written. Our songs are spread like oral history, each tune represents different battles. But it'd be easier to keep track if we had sheets of music."

"Oh, humans can't read sheet music," I said.

"What? But I've met human musicians and composers."

"Yea, *they* can. But other humans can't and if they said they can, they're liars."

Jaz signed, "I can read human sheet music. I have a sheet that is supposed to be played by... the instrument with the string."

I signed back, "guitar?" She shook her head. "Violin?"

"Yes! The song sounds sad though. Maybe you can teach me?"

"Amazing," said Keezon. "You're the only person in this village able to talk to her besides me. It has to be lonely for Jazari, all she can do is speak with me. This is a sign that you should stay here and help teach others."

"Nice try."

"Can you blame me? Hopefully you have enjoyed your time so far enough to visit again."

"Maybe one day I will." I showed my forearm just like Jaz showed me.

He smiled and did it back. "Come, maybe I can convince you to stay over drinks. And you can also tell me what happened to our neighboring cyralune."

I smiled and told Jaz I'd be back. I took Keezon's cup and walked to the punch area to fill up our bowls. It's funny, kazamite's discovered alcohol long before they met humans, and they love it just as much. I knew they loved to drink, but I'd never seen them party like how this cyralune did. It was... relaxing. Chimeras didn't get celebrations like this. I could count on one hand how many times we've had. The last party we had was years ago, when we just about wiped out The Dominion, a fanatical religious cult. Back when chimeras fought bad guys. Back when the line between right and wrong weren't blurry. Now... I'm not so sure. Maybe we've always been bad guys, just not the worst. Or maybe we've always been the worst...

"They say The Forest of Thought is where we hide to escape from ourselves. I wonder what a chimera's forest looks like. Maybe yours is full of dead brothers." I nearly broke my neck snapping my head so fast. "Indigo colored chimera, where will you run and hide next, Mandy?"

The man speaking towered over me, just like Eskander. His face was covered by a silver smooth mask made of living metal. He wore armor from Leopold's days, Shattered Legion armor. **All** of those armors were outlawed and destroyed. Who the hell was this guy?

"You cover your face and body, and *I'm* hiding?"

"I had a poncho and umbrella earlier, but when you're in the eye of the **hurricane** you don't need one."

There was something about how he said that… something about his tone. I stared at his face where his eyes should be and tried to figure out who he was. It's too obvious he was in hurricane, but his confidence and presence was commanding. As if he controlled or led…

He's their leader.

I dropped the bowls in my hand and threw a sloppy jab as fast as I could. He grabbed my arm, and flipped me onto my back. I crashed into the ground on my ass and clenched my teeth; humans aren't *this* fast. With both legs, I tried to leg sweep him, but he casually stepped over my legs as he walked backwards. I jumped to my feet and threw a kick, but he countered it before I fully launched it. He kicked the inside of my thigh, taking away my balance and the force behind my kick. I let out a primal scream, and threw a right hook. He raised his arms, covering his head and blocking his face, and leaned into my shoulder. He cut off the power behind my attack again and just stood there, as I staggered backwards.

"Stop!" Keezon ran up to us. "Please, you all are guests!"

I scoffed. "Guest? Do you know who he is? He's one of THEM!"

"He and his friends are our guests, and we don't allow violence here."

"Friends?" I turned around and saw several mercenaries around us. "There aren't enough of you to stop me." I balled my fist.

The mysterious man said, "you sound like a villain, almost mistook you for Havi. We aren't here to fight you nor break traditions in this cyralune."

"Hurricane has caused nothing but problems," I said. "I'm here now because of *your* people. And get off of your high horse, violence is in your nature."

He scoffed. "You just attacked me at a party. You hid in a barn like an animal, stayed here and drank as your brother bleeds out and you want to talk about what's in one's nature? You must be the funny chimera."

"Keep my brother out of your mouth or I'll break your jaw."

"I guess chimera agoge didn't teach diplomacy. Allow me to educate you, my name's Khan and—"

"I don't give a damn what your name is."

"And I am the leader and founder of Hurricane. I'm responsible for all the branches from the aggressive Verrucosus, to the roaming medical group known as Asclepieia that retreated to the island Shangri-la. As a sign of good faith, I've already sent a few nurses and medical supplies to your brother. They're in the form of anonymous donations."

"You think sending bandages and third rate nurses is a sign of 'good faith'? You, who's responsible for all the death and murder right now? You're the reason he's even *in* the hospital. You're a fucking cancer."

"Why? Because I no longer want to be part of your dictatorship? That I no longer want to be part of this world of yours ruled by the regime with chimera enforcers?"

"You bring death and chaos."

"And what have the regime and the chimeras brought? Girl scout cookies?"

"Sharp enough knives to slit at least half of your tendons before your men take me down. I've seen firsthand what you've brought."

"I bring anarchy. What did the ancient pharaohs of Egypt, and the god-kings of the empire of Khmer have in common? They tied their rulers to religion, believing them to rule divine justice. But they both had a similar problem: atheists. What happens in a theocracy when the hoi polloi no longer believe in their leaders? Their gods? They get hunted."

"Oh please, you tried to launch a nuke!"

"And how did we get that knowledge on how to make one? You think kazamites and regular citizens know how to make a nuke?"

227

"Lissax was going to kill innocents, and now you've replaced her to what? Kill more innocents? Why shouldn't I kill you?"

"Because fighting isn't allowed," said Keezon.

"He endangers lives! Think Keezon!"

He flinched.

"No, I'm sorry. I didn't mean–"

"Understand this, Mandy. Everyday you stay in this cyralune, you endanger these people. My allies and I are only here for the atmosphere, and you. Food, drinks and dialogue is all I request tonight."

"I lost my appetite."

"But not your sense of hearing." He motioned to a bench for us to sit at. "Shall we?"

"One wrong move, and I'll finish what I started." I walked past him to the bench.

"Judging by that last encounter, I'm not worried. Keezon, please enjoy your night. You have my word that there will be no more fighting."

Khan joined me at the table and sat down. I tried to see through his gear, trying to make out what he was. *Who* he was? But, he didn't have a single part of his skin showing. He sat across from me with an air about him, confident but not cocky. As if he knew he already won. I can count on one hand how many humans I have met like him.

"I'm all ears, Khan."

"Let's pass the salt and skip the formalities. I've come to you to establish a non-aggression pact and have an opening chip as bait. Your brother, he's dying."

"What a fucking opener. How do I know I can trust you? I don't even know what race you are."

"And why would my race matter? And why would I lie? Have humans hurt you so much that you think everyone that isn't a chimera lies?"

"Let's call it an occupational hazard."

"I'm the regime. We don't have to be enemies, Mandy."

"Let's say I want to be then."

He sighed and said, "so then what? You fight a war on multiple fronts? You without an army, fight the regime, the multiple factions across the country, and the groups off-world? You then kill Havi and expect no one to take his place? Havi will take charge, and then use Sibil to bring you in. The math is simple: you're running out of allies. Chimeras are running out of allies in general. Your people have already turned on each other."

"Sibil and I don't see eye to eye I agree, but supporting the regime as they hunt chimeras is extreme. He wouldn't raise his hand against one of us, not publicly."

"You can't tell, but I raised an eyebrow in disbelief. Rivers in Egypt, Mandy."

"I don't know what that means or what 'Egypt' is."

"It means you're in denial. You're not going to go gentle into that good night, and there is a storm raging outside. All I offer is refuge."

"And why would or should I side with you?"

"Everyday you live, disproves Havi's control and leadership. It represents disorder to his harmony."

"He's not Leopold. And I haven't done anything, I'm just trying to survive."

"You *lived*, Mandy. And that's enough to be public enemy number one. When Leopold was the primarch, who was a rising star that did well in his empire? Havi. And just like Leopold, everyone that stands against Havi, is a direct threat to him. But I guess you can keep hiding here, and maybe they'll never find you. But my war is far from over. Now that we control a small fleet of mechs, and have given them to the people, I wonder what's next. I wonder how kazamites and humans living in tandem will respond to your 'gods' in their hovering towers."

"I see the confusion. You think just because we have a common enemy, that should make us allies. Isn't that what humans think? Enemy of my enemy? That's moronic. You're a disgusting coward of a man. A vulture waiting for me to join you and become weak so you can pick me apart. I'd call you a worm, but you're like a mite. Imagine, a cowardice mite."

He chuckled and said, "you're hiding in a cyralune while your brethren are rounded up, and I'm the coward? From where I'm sitting, only one of us has supporters and funding. I have a plan, what do you have?"

"I'll bite, what's this grand plan?"

"Simply? Burn down the gods, then burn down *their* gods. Similar to 'eat the rich' and we'll get there, in due time. Imposing your power onto others who you deem are less than, is called impressment, and it's outdated."

"That's it? Violence is your answer?"

"Violence may be the *only* answer. What Keezon has here is good. Anyone of these people can leave whenever they want. Don't you want to live somewhere where you have actual freedom, and not the illusion of it?"

"Some people don't want to live their lives in fear and hear all the shitty stuff on the news. They like living in their bubble and that is freedom for them."

"Agreed, I enjoy this level of ignorance. But weaponized ignorance is still a weapon, and we are at war. And the joke of war and coexistence is, you can't choose peace when your neighbors choose war or disagree with your peace. You also can't choose peace when your former oppressor is still alive. And you can't choose peace when your enemy wants you dead. That's just choosing your own death."

"I guess we should attack innocents with nukes then. How fast your diplomacy goes out the window. We could easily make a compromise with Havi. Nobody wants war, including him."

"Did the terrans tell you Havi wants peace? The same terrans that had a falling out with themselves and Scyra split from literally mankind because of it? Or the terrans that wanted peace with kazamites and made an alliance? That alliance aged like milk, mind you."

"You think some nice quotes will make me side with you?"

"No. I think your former masters almost killing your brother, but definitely killing your sister will." He stood up. "Your indecisiveness will get more people around you hurt or killed too. And you know this. Strike first, strike swift, or you have no one else to blame but yourself. My men and I leave in three days, it's time to fight back. Or don't. It's up to you if you want to remain this shell, this husk of a person. You can stay, and I will not tell anyone where you are, but if you join me, I need the chimera we all see in propaganda. Give me Mandy, the pale color eyed titan. Mandy, the volatile titan that haunts the regime because I plan on killing gods, and only one group in history did that the best."

He left.

I sighed, he was right. Nic was hurt because of me. Historia was killed because of me, Thaddeus was killed because of me, and Valen was hurt because of me. I *keep* letting others join me or send them to do tasks and they *keep* getting hurt or worse. When will enough be enough? Havi would come for me, and he alone was a threat. I can't take Havi and the regime alone, I couldn't even take Khan… and he was holding back.

No more. No more letting people get hurt because of me. I stood up and left the party. Thaddeus will be the *last* person who suffers because of my failure, no more being the victim.

231

SAY THEIR NAMES

I spent the next three days helping around with all the animals, teaching some of the villagers how to sign and hanging out with Jaz in our downtime. She told me all about her life there, and how Keezon helped raise her. She also told me how Keezon led a protest against Primarch Leopold a long time ago, and lost. He thought Leopold would be too spread thin in his final days. He was wrong. Leopold responded by leveling an entire city, and then took prisoners. Keezon's and Jaz's families were prisoners, and their families were in that city. And the worst part, almost everyone in this cyralune was a refugee. And almost all of them had similar stories of fleeing the regime.

At night, I was kept up by my nightmares. Every night, I heard Historia's last words on repeat. So, I trained. I trained when I was hungry. I trained when I was tired. I trained when I just needed to hit something. The locals offered me an actual building and a bed, but I needed to be alone.

After the first night, the villagers left me alone. I was finally left alone... and it was still so loud in my head. That same night, I heard a chirp and rushed to the sound, but it was just some kids playing with a bird. Rai would say I wasn't focused enough. So, I just stayed in the barn, I needed solitude anyway. And maybe I deserved it for not trying harder to save the people I love. How could I sleep peacefully and live my life knowing Historia should be the one here and not me? Even when I'm not training I feel guilty. Every time I enjoy an evening with

Jaz, I think how Historia could be here talking about animals; and I took that from her.

So I needed to train. I needed to be better.

Every now and then, Khan would send someone to spar with me, another sign of good faith I figure. But they sucked. They were slow, didn't know how to hold a weapon or they choreographed their attacks. So, I kicked them out and went back to training alone. And I didn't stop until my hands and knuckles bled. But most importantly, I trained until I stopped seeing and hearing Historia. The only voice I needed to hear was Khan's when he appeared on the third day at sunset.

"Ready?" He asked.

"No, but neither was Historia."

It was sad saying goodbye to the kazamites, I didn't know if I'd ever see any of them again. As we left, a couple survivors from the last cyralune made it out alive. I let out a sigh of relief, but it wasn't enough. Khan told me that Trogz was in a town about half a day away and that's where his ship was docked. There, they had my aegis, and Vesalia. She was living freely in a pampered suite for her loyalty, unaffected by the lives she directly took from this world.

She was a plague.

And Trogz wasn't any better. He was helping coordinate strikes and raids across Kore. Havi took the urban side of things, Trogz took everywhere else. The idea was to divide and conquer, and without an actual opposing army, they were cleaning house.

Despite me not liking Khan, his plan was foundationally good. It was simple: we'd take a strike team and go after Trogz and take his ship. Trogz's ship was about half the size of Havi's, so it was a smaller target. It also was equipped with different systems than modern ships. But before we could take his ship, we'd have to clear the town where his men were in. One team would cut the power to the city which would trigger the back up generators. The next team would go and take those out, with the last team helping exfil. I was part of a special team, my team's objective was to kill Vesalia and get back my aegis. If everything went well, all teams would converge on Trogz's ship for our final push.

As we flew to the site, I stewed for hours going over in my head what I'd say to Trogz and Vesalia once I got to them. But when we finally arrived near the building she was in, all I could do was think about Historia. I looked at Khan as the bay doors opened.

"I am not your ally, Khan."

"And neither are they."

I nodded at the kazamite coming with me and kicked the rope out of the shuttle. We fast roped down and landed somewhere on the edge of the city and took cover. We waited until there was complete silence, and then waited some more. We weren't expecting resistance, but we weren't expecting a ghost town either. We rushed to the generators in the basement of the build Vesalia was in, and got set up. We set up the thermite in silence and waited for the other teams to tell us when they were in position over comms.

"Alpha team set."

"Bravo team set."

"Charlie team set," I said.

"Ready…fire."

We sparked the thermite, and left. There was no point in sticking around, we had to grapple halfway up the 40 story building. Vesalia was just above the halfway point, so we planned to grapple to the floor right beneath hers.

As we got into position, the kazamite spoke. "I didn't realize until yesterday I'd be doing this."

"I thought you've done this before."

"Yea, but not with a chimera. You're the first chimera I've ever even seen outside of the propaganda and history books given to us."

We fired our hooks and attached them to our belts. Once in place, the grapple hooks pulled us up.

"Propaganda from the regime?"

"And other kazamites. We learn that when we misbehave and disobey 'the powers that be', chimeras will take us away in the dead of the night. And here I am in the dead of the night with you, so it must be true. Which means my parents were wrong and Khan was right. I was conscripted to fight in fake wars and bled for a species that sees me as expendable. They radicalized me, now they're getting what they paid for."

"I don't have any sympathy for terrorists. Your sob story is wasted on me because to be honest, I don't care."

"Khan said you'd say something like that. Either way, you're not as scary as the stories say. And you're not as brave as the villagers think, 'Voidborn'. Khan will bring justice for kazamites so chimeras better figure out what side they're on. Because I'm not scared of you or humans anymore."

We arrived to the floor and I opened a window and slid inside. "Cricket told me once that the dodo bird wasn't scared of mankind either."

"The real surprise for us today is the history lesson." A voice said in the dark. I looked up and saw not one, but eight soldiers with NODs already waiting for us with guns. Me and the kazamite raised our guns. "I never knew what happened to dodo birds and used to think they were turkeys. You must be the elusive Mandy."

"Move. I couldn't hurt Khan, but I sure as hell plan on making up for it tonight," I said.

"I don't know who Khan is, but I know you're outnumbered. I've been on missions already to hunt down chimeras so, you're just another one off my list. Stand down."

"Final warning," I said. They raised their guns in response.

The kazamite with me threw a flashbang, instantly blinding them. Idiots. We *knew* there would be resistance at some point. We knew they'd expect us at night, so that means we knew they'd have night vision. But of course, they were ready. Even though we blinded them, a few of them still opened fire. We dove behind cover the second the first shot was fired. The floor was an office space, so we had ample things to duck behind. But because there were more of them than us, we had to move fast. But I was ready, I came with: a knife, SBR, pistol and a retractable blade that could shoot out of my glove. Khan called it a 'pata'. Another 'gift' from him.

During a lull of firing, the leader of the group yelled, "GET THEM! The hell are you waiting for?" Good. I stood up and shot him in the head, and then shot the soldier next to him.

"Over there!" One of them yelled as they all opened fire at me.

I rushed and dove to behind another desk as they unloaded where I was. They were trying to outmaneuver me and it would work, but there were two of us. My partner from wherever he took cover, let off a couple shots. Seconds later, came the sound of a sack of potatoes hitting the ground. Five left. I crawled around a corner while they looked for my partner and went to where I just was. They knew they outnumbered us, but it was a game of whack-a-mole and one false move like they've been doing, is sudden death. Two of them walked down the hall in my direction, they must have seen or heard me. I crouched around the corner and slung my rifle around my back while I drew my sidearm. I waited until I saw the tip of the barrel of one of their guns, and attacked.

I yanked his gun out of his hands and jabbed him in the face. He staggered backwards and before he could even yelp in pain, I spun him around and took him hostage. The guy with him was stunned and jumped back hoping to shoot me, but he hesitated cause I had his friend. I shot him before he could get his bearings and then shot my hostage and holstered my sidearm. I displaced before the remaining three could move in on me.

"There's only three of you left!" The kazamite yelled. "Drop your guns, and leave!" That dumbass gave up his positions, you could even hear them moving towards him. Which meant, they weren't paying attention behind them.

I moved from cover and saw one alone by the open window we entered at. The other two were creeping over to my loudmouth partner; I guess he was as brave and dumb as the dodo. I slung my rifle to my back again and crept up to the soldier by the window. He didn't notice me until I was on top of him. He gasped and fired his gun as he turned around, but he wasn't fast enough. I punched him in his gut, and threw his gun out the window. He tried to fight me and maybe he thought he could win, or maybe he was trying to buy time. Either way, he only pissed me off. Without a second thought, I shoved him out the window. All you could hear was him scream as gravity took him. I ducked as the others fired at me, but stood up after I heard a human scream in pain.

"I got them all, and we got a prisoner," said the kazamite.

I joined them and saw the last human soldier on the ground, clutching his bloody shoulder. He looked up at me and said, "just let me go man."

"Funny, you wouldn't say that to me if the roles were reversed," I replied.

"What do you even want? The girl upstairs? She's worth killing all of us over? What even is she to you?"

"More valuable to me dead than you alive. Is she alone?"

"No… no she's not. Our commander is up there, and he's waiting for you. Just… just let me go. Yea what we did was wrong, but we're just following orders."

"Try again."

"You're in over your head. *We* were just following orders, but he's a Loyalist. And they **hate** chimeras, and you're not gonna win. He even said you only keep leading people to their death and that you're better off hiding. He hates you."

"I'm starting to hate myself too, so it's warranted. What weapons does he have and how many men are in this city waiting for me?"

"I can't tell you that man."

I kneeled and drew my sidearm. I put the barrel under his jaw and stared at him for a while before I spoke. His trembling made my wrist shake.

"My new pastime is painting walls."

"Please…" His voice cracked.

"How many soldiers are here waiting for us?"

"I can't… I can't tell you that. You'll just kill me anyway and I'll die a traitor to mankind."

"Mankind doesn't even know you exist, they never know the name of dead soldiers. Now a cripple one…" I put the barrel on his kneecap.

"The colonel… he… he was right about you," he croaked.

I stood up and holstered my sidearm and said, "your colonel wouldn't show me the same level of mercy I'm giving you now. Go tell everyone that supports the regime that I'm coming for them. Remember it was the big bad chimera that spared you, human. Let's go."

I picked up whatever weapons were near him, and broke them or threw them out the window. I walked to the door of the stairwell and waited for the kazamite to join me.

As he approached me he said, "I take back what I said. The boogeyman chimera stories were right, you move like a demon."

"You want good and honorable chimeras, look for Historia and Chevalier."

We walked up the flight of stairs in silence and once at the top, I opened the door to essentially the same floor plan. This time however, it was open with minimal desks and walls. And for whatever reason, this floor had power.

In the middle of the room was a praetorian and behind him, was a door to where I assume Vesalia was hiding. Right by the door where we entered, was a small generator jumping up and down; it must have been putting in overtime just to keep the lights on. The praetorian sat comfortably in a leather chair and yawned as he saw us. Rarely, did I see a praetorian and when I did, it was in regime proper dress, not regime armor dress. Regime armor dress was just like their battle dress, but surprisingly, with armor. Everything was identical, the boots, pants, gauntlets, even the bandoleer around his waist. The only difference, he was covered in living metal and his chest and knees were reinforced.

"Excuse me, I've been waiting for a while," he said. "I expected you to come **yesterday**, so it's been very boring pulling shifts with my men on these two floors. I also wasn't expecting a plus one. I shouldn't be judging your strategy, but it seems a little silly to bring a pup to a wolf fight."

The kazamite stepped forward and brazenly said, "your super villain schtick doesn't scare me. I earned and fought my way here!"

"Have you ever noticed those who are scared, always boast how they aren't?" He stood to his feet and grabbed his helmet. Some praetorians wore capes, he was no different. His cape was black with a gold lining and it almost glided to the floor as he stood. "I'm Commander Vilo, I come from the Auric Order. I'll assume that you don't know what that means and that's fine but in short, it means I'm from a long line of military commanders. All of us believe in the old ways, the **loyal** ways." He put his gladiator-like helmet on and a visor covered his mouth but didn't alter the sound of his voice.

"I haven't heard of them, but I have heard of the Sacred band of Halcyon," I said.

"Ah, cultured. I've only ever met three people in my entire life worthy of the band. Lieutenant Merul, General Kalg and Colonel Blackbeak. The **True** primarch wasn't even part of this group, and all in that order have died off sans one. It's impossible to trace heritage, and only a rare few would be worthy. The band you're talking about, is a specific and highly exclusive group of soldiers in the Auric Order. Not many live through the process to become one; you must be resilient, worthy and have the resolve to quell the big bang. How do you know about them?"

"My brother, he's a human worthy enough for them. But I've been wondering if they're worthy enough for him."

"Ah, so it's true, the brother thing? The redhead with brain swelling and was on the table for several hours is your 'brother'? I hope he makes it, genuinely. I've only heard about him via word of mouth, but he has *so* much potential. Yes a lot of people in my circle dislike him because of his father, but they forget who his father was before his mother. I give it three years or less, and they'll bring him into the order."

The kazamite sucked his teeth and said, "all humans are the same, arrogant. Overestimating their worth and abilities. Thinking you're gods among men."

"You aren't even 'men'." He took off his cape and walked to a wall and hung it up. "One of you, evolved due to circumstance. You were given everything, your entire species has been spoiled. Imagine what humans could do today, if cavemen were spoiled with such advanced technology and knowledge as you kazamites were. You've squandered our gifts. Get upset because we want to drive and figured you were better off with us in charge. And you, chimera, you're literally just a weapon. Sadly, not a good one. None of you chimeras are."

"Just because you helped us, doesn't give you rulership over us," the kazamite argued.

"Doesn't it? When the first panda went extinct, who was blamed? When a society struggles, when a people suffer, who is blamed? We aren't saying we're rulers of the universe, we aren't kings and queens of the Milky Way. We're just... governing here, flocking the herd. There's a right way of living, and an incorrect way. We're helping you and you've responded by constantly spitting in our faces. So, you need correcting. You're confused about what's best for you."

"And you know what's best for my people?"

"Of course. We have lived thousands of your lifetime. Before us, kazamites didn't even have a written recorded history. Do you guys even have fairy tales, or are they human fairy tales with a lazy twist? No, I'm being too harsh; fairy tales can't exist in an illiterate species. Let's recap, no currency and exchange or bartering system, no fairy tales, no desire to know where you came from, no looking up at the stars, no anything.

By the time humans were your age, we were hunting monstrosities with tusks in packs. How is an originally carnivorous race, bad at hunting? Clearly, you *need* us because you are just a confused and clueless bunch."

The kazamite raised his gun and said, "we know how to kill humans."

"Virgil. Gwen. Allie. Edgar. Bojack. Tuscan. Pacha." He paused. "Historia."

"What are those? Last words?" The kazamite laughed off the names, but it wasn't funny.

"A quarter of those are from my pod. What do they mean to you," I asked.

"I killed them all. I'm the one who told Havi where to look for Historia. And I would've killed her if he hadn't pulled rock, paper, rank on me. Unlike Havi, I'm a hunter. A tracker. I **love** it. Mandy, is it? I'm going to add your name to my list. And you, kazamite," he turned his attention away from me. "I stopped counting how many of your kind I've killed after I reached 30. There's no bragging when you punch down."

The kazamite screamed as he pulled the trigger, but Vilo was unfazed. Vilo had an energy shield built into his armor, and it deployed from his wrist as he raised his arm. He stood there, calmly, as the bullets hit the shield and fell to the floor. When the kazamite ran out of bullets, he rushed Vilo with his knife drawn. Vilo lowered his arm, shutting off his shield, and let the kazamite get the first swing. But he was slow. Vilo easily stepped to the side, snatched his knife, and slit his throat all under 30 seconds. Vilo dropped the knife as the kazamite staggered backwards, clutching his bleeding throat. Vilo watched and yawned as my partner eventually fell to the ground and stopped moving.

"It has to be tiring watching people around you die, Mandy. Giving up is easy, it's what keeps you alive. Life is hard, let us humans drive. Indefinitely."

"Aren't humans related to chimps by less than 5%, Vilo? I think Ambrotos knows a joke or two about letting chimps drive."

"I haven't met him, but I hear he was sweet with Historia. Sorry, **was** sweet. She was the best fighter of your kind and I think I could've taken her. And from what I hear, you're severely outclassed by her."

"I bet that's the last time you'll be able to say her name."

"And why's that?"

"Because I'm going to break your jaw."

"Barbaric. That's all you are, that's all you and your ilk ever will be. Do you know why humans hate your kind? Because you exist as a manifestation of human war and fear. We like it when our nightmares stay in our dreams, and not patrol the very streets we live on. You are without a doubt, the **worst** possible outcome of a human. Violent, barbaric, originless, easily able to be manipulated, and best of all, without purpose. We'd pity you if you couldn't literally lift a car with one arm. We gave birth to you and helped the people of this planet and now we're stuck with two stupid and inept children. One, is overgrown sushi. And the other is mixed with it."

"I can't wait to kill you."

"If you do, you'll still be a disgusting failed lifeform. Primal and invasive in nature, and I'll still be a Loyalist. And I can't wait to teach your 'brother' the teachings of Primarch Leopold and make him disown his father for his betrayal."

We stood staring at each other still as a rock, neither of us wanting to move first. I grabbed my rifle slowly, and he matched me by grabbing his. I've never seen or heard of a praetorian fighting a chimera, but we were told they were just as lethal as us. That they could move as fast as us, and didn't tire quickly, just like us. So, this was a battle of attrition...

Simultaneously, we both opened fire and then ducked behind cover. There weren't as many things to hide behind on this floor, and I knew I couldn't just attack him head on. So, I needed to make him slip up. I ducked behind a metal table and flipped it over and waited as bullets dented it. The second the firing stopped, I mounted my rifle on the table, primed a flashbang and scanned. The second he'd so much as wiggle, I'd be able to open fire and blind him.

242

There.

A shadow flickered in the corner of the room. I tossed the flashbang in that direction, purposely so that it hit the wall. I just wanted to flush him out. And that it did. As soon as the flashbang went off, I kicked the table in its direction. He sprung out from cover and shot at me and dodged the table. I could hear the pop as the bullets raced past me, and landed in the generator behind me. It started convulsing as the lights flickered on and off. I fired back and ran, trying to circle around him. I ducked behind a desk and reloaded and listened for his movement. The lights flickered and the generator buzzed, masking Vilo for a moment. But soon, the lights betrayed him and his shadow. I patiently watched as a shadow moved, but waited until it was in a better position. Got you. I grinned and popped out of cover with my gun aimed.

Crack!

Crack!

I ducked back down behind cover. He was fast. I took a deep breath and saw the wall behind me, it was riddled in bullets. When did he fire that many shots? *How* did he fire that many shots?

"It's the lights, you were lucky. I won't miss again. Do you have any last words?"

I rolled from behind cover and opened fire, I just needed to buy myself time. I jumped to my feet and dashed towards his cover.

"Idiot chimera."

What? I turned around to see the voice behind me, but was too slow. He grabbed my gun, and kicked me into a wall. I hit it and immediately drew my sidearm, but he was already on top of me. I barely dodged as he punched a hole in a wall where my head was. I rolled to one knee and aimed my gun at him, but he again was too fast. Before I could fire, he pulled his arm from out of the wall, and backhanded my gun as I fired a round. I didn't even have time to dodge his next attack. I saw his torso and legs tense up and crossed my arms blocking, just as he kicked me. His frontkick was so strong, he sent me flying backwards

243

several meters. I hit the ground on my back and rolled to my feet and drew my blades.

"Good." He reached behind his back and drew a handle. He pressed a button and obsidian colored blades came out on both sides. "People forget the importance of handheld weapons. We didn't have firearms while we drifted through space, one ricochet could mean literally engine failure. A true **loyal** soldier, hones all skills. These twinblades I have, have cut many of your kind down. I hope your weapon skills are better than your hand to hand skills."

I lunged forward, stabbing and slashing. He parried and blocked all of my attacks effortlessly. I pushed him harder, and switched from orthodox to unorthodox. But no change.

How?

First Khan, now him? How are they making me look like a freshman? I jumped off the wall and cut straight down, trying to split him in half. He saw it coming and jumped back and as soon as I landed. Then, he threw a sidekick at my head and sent me tumbling through a wall. I dropped my blades as I rolled and then spun around to hit him while I was on my knees. He sidestepped, and kneed me in my jaw. My body locked up and I dropped to the ground. I hit the ground so hard, my head bounced.

I opened my eyes but everything was blurry. I watched in a daze as six boots rose, over my head ready to squash it. I rolled out of the way as his foot crashed through the floor. I grabbed the first thing my fingers felt, a chair, and swung it at him. Wood splintered across his side as he yelped and staggered backwards. I tackled him while he was still recovering, but he tossed me off instantly and cut my arm as I blocked. I screamed out and charged at him again. He swung his twinblades, but I closed the gap faster than he expected. I shoulder checked him and grabbed and twisted his wrist. He screamed in pain and dropped his weapon.

With everything I had, I kicked him, sending him flying into a table. Before he could get his bearings, I threw his twinblades at him. He ducked forward dodging them, just how I wanted. I ran at him and kicked the ever loving shit out of his jaw as hard as I could. The glass on the floor cracked as he and his helmet took flight.

Blood splattered across the ceiling as he fell back onto the table. I stood over him confidently, and looked into his eyes. I could see them trying to gain focus; his eyes were swimming. Carefully, he sat up, using his arms to prop himself up. I punched him, and then wrapped my hands around his throat.

"Does the great Loyalist commander know the difference between a blood and air choke? Let me show you." I tightened my grip.

I felt him panic in my hands. He cupped his hands and clapped my ears. I screamed and stumbled backwards while holding my ears. I took a few deep breaths and looked back up and saw him moving towards me. I was too dizzy to see which one was actually him, so I couldn't block. I punched what I thought was him, and missed. He wailed on my ribs, right around my liver and kidneys. I doubled over clutching my sides. I coughed and gasped for air.

He walked behind me and grabbed the back of my hair and said, "you spit in the face of humanity, have you no loyalty? That's what's wrong with today, there aren't any more loyalists!"

I leaned forward, and threw my head back into his face. I heard a 'crack' and then grabbed him and threw him back at the desk. His jaw and lips split open, as blood leaked out of his mouth and nose.

He spit out a tooth and said, "I admit, I'm impressed. You almost aren't worth killing." He chuckled and then spit out more blood. "You're more feisty than the other chimeras. I think I'm glad you're alive and Historia is dead... oh, I guess I did say her name again. Whoops."

I drew my knife and dashed forward and tried to shoulder check him again. He saw me coming a mile away and spun around and kicked me into the wall. My head smacked against the wall and started ringing, again. I turned around as he palmed my face, and smashed my head into the wall. I wanted to scream in pain, but his hand covered my mouth. He grabbed my hair, and then punched my head through the wall. He walked away and grabbed his twinblades and turned back around and looked at me.

"Good riddens," he said as he raised his weapon, screamed and charged.

With all my strength, I flopped out of the way, ducked down and slashed his armpit. He let out a wet scream as blood shot out of his mouth. I rolled to my knees and slashed the back of his thighs. His weight buckled as he screamed again, and then choked on his own blood. I stood up and grabbed him by the back of his armor and threw him across the room. He slid on the ground and hit his head on the same desk. He shakily stood to his feet and smiled.

"What do you think this changes? Oceana is still gonna raze everything in her path, Havi will become the new primarch and clean house. And Callum and his family won't stand for this. You've done **nothing**. You think humans will side with you? You just hurt a praetorian. A **Loyalist**, not just any praetorian, but a war hero! Do you really think humans like it when you hurt their heroes?"

"I don't care what humans like."

He chuckled. "So what now, huh? You'll what, kill me? Murder the officer in charge here and take back your aegis? And do this while all siding with terrorists to boot. You should care what humans think, because the regime sees you as a mediocre chimera. Nothing distinguishable about you, outside of adopting a human brother. Humanity and the regime will look at you and think 'look how much damage a mediocre chimera could do'. And then they'll fear you. They'll fear **all** of you."

"Fear me? Humans started this!"

"So what? **So what?** You owe us! The kazamites owe us! There is no peace with *you* alive. You're mad because some trigger happy started this? Oh grow up Mandy! Your existence shows humans aren't gods or demigods. No, it shows chimeras are titans. That you evolved during your little hiatus and that you and I both know that this doesn't stop until all human leaders are dead. Then people like Hela will come. You think *I'm* delusional and so bad? We banished her to a moon because she's psychotic!"

"Then I'll kill her too. You all imprisoned my people, enslaved kazamites and lied to your fellow humans. *You* only deserve death."

He laughed then said, "lied? You don't think, everyone in Elysium *knows*? Your new friends took over how many mechs? You think they've just been idle this whole time? They're raiding homes and compounds. People are scared of you! **You're** the villain! People don't just accidently forget what is happening or happened."

"You dare brainwash my people and then villainize me?"

I rushed him and fainted an attack, leaving him open. When he blocked, I switched and kicked him in his legs, making him fall.

"Are you confused on how war works? Those in Elysium didn't get a peaceful life because of their kind words," he said. "They manipulate, and hide. They knew Oceana was spiraling. And Havi and his people? They live to fight and right now, you're the reason they're alive. Fighting you for them, is the purpose for a whole generation of them. Avalon is funded by businessmen, the same ones that control the media. You think these leaders just stumbled into power?"

"Let's find your off button." I grabbed him by his throat and dragged him back to the desk. I raised him in the air, and then smashed him through it. "You're lying. I have no issues with all humans, just you arrogant regime assholes." I picked him up, and threw him at the wall between us and Vesalia.

He hit the wall hard and fell over. His face was covered in blood and bruises.

"What, do you want an apology? For serving my people with my mind, body and soul? So what if I've damned my soul, I have no regrets. As if you wouldn't go as far as Havi would," he laughed. He only stopped when he started to choke on his blood. "But you, you just kicked the hornet's nest. Only Trogz came for you, but if you kill him, they'll come for you. They'll **all** come for you."

I walked towards him and said, "this is the part where you panic."

"I'm proud of what I've done, happy with it. You think I have regrets in the face of death?"

"Yea, eight of them." I picked him up and punched him for every name. "There's Virgil, Gwen, Allie and Edgar." I hit him harder and harder with each name. "Bojack, Tuscan, and Pacha." He spat out blood and smiled at me. "Historia." I punched him in his stomach and let his body fall. I stared at him as he coughed and wheezed. "Virgil." I punched him in the back of his head, making him fall over. I grabbed him by his hair and punched him as I said, "Gwen and Allie." I let him go and stared. I kicked him in his chest as I gritted my teeth. "Edgar, and Bojack." I kept kicking him in his chest. "Tuscan and Pacha." I took another look at him. I kneed him in his face. "Historia." I kneed him again, harder. "**Historia**." Again. "**Historia**!" This time, I placed my hands on the wall to get more umph in my hit. "**HISTORIA**." I could feel his head and the wall start to crack. "**HISTORIA**!" I charged up this last one, I couldn't even see him through my tears. "**HISTORIA**!!"

I kneed him through the wall.

I stepped through the hole and over his body as the power went out. I guess the shots from earlier caused the generator to finally die. I now stood in a boardroom with a big wooden oval desk and multiple leather chairs. On one side, was a massive window with a view of the entire city. You could see Trogz's ship from here. In the corner of the room, was Vesalia, cowering, like the worm she was. I stared at her for a moment thinking about what she did, thinking about what to say. I thought about how Nic put his faith in her, and she let him down.

Never again.

"Ma-Mandy. I-I do not fear you." I started walking towards her. "Killing me won't bring back Nic. We can't possibly tell which chimeras are dangerous, so it's safer to bound all of you. Just look how psycho and volatile you are; we need humans to rein you in." I kept walking. "Mandy please! All you're doing is showing we're right about chimeras and you're all just prone to violence."

"Why? Why lie and side with a race, a species, that treats both of us like shit?"

"If we just listened to humans, we wouldn't have any issues. Humans say biting the hand that feeds is something idiots and fools do. They're **gods**, and we're ants. And you want to disturb the order? Ruin the foundation of life itself?"

"Vesalia, there are armed patrols in the streets."

"Well if people have nothing to hide, they shouldn't be scared."

"They are armed soldiers patrolling, what are you not getting? I don't want these people around my home. Patrolling our streets as if we all were criminals."

"But you **are** a criminal."

"Because armed men think it's ok to have firing squads and–" I took a breath, what am I doing? "I'm not going back and forth with you. I'm not living in a world where this is the norm, and you shouldn't want kazamites too either. There will be no more regime before there is no more Mandy."

"You're selfish..."

"Selfish? For wanting freedom?"

"Is it freedom if it hurts everyone else? Freedom needs to be limited to those who know how to handle it. You have freedom and look what you are. You're dangerous, so so dangerous. How many have you killed just today? I mean Sibil is unique, but still stays in his tower for the most part. But monsters like you and Historia–" I grabbed her and threw her across the room at the window.

"Kazamites like you, are traitors to your own kind." I balled my fist and walked towards her. "I wonder, how many people have *you* betrayed?" I stopped and stood over her. "Stand."

She cried and stood to her feet.

"Finish your sentence."

After sniffling for half a minute, she said, "the betrayal from you and Hist–" I backhanded her. She fell to the ground.

She coughed and started to crawl away, screaming for help. I stood over her and watched with disgust. After a few minutes of screaming and crying, she found her words.

"I haven't betrayed the regime or myself," she said. "My people's best interest is in the regime's hands. I will never choose anarchy and barbaric violence."

"Barbaric? You just said limited freedom, restricted liberties, sanctioned freedom and want us to jump on board? The hell is wrong with you? Your people are being herded like cattle! We even found out that humans are rewriting their *own* history!"

"I... I have faith that humans will create a better world. Who cares if a couple violent outcasts are purged from society? But look at the mess you've caused. Please... reconsider. It's not too late to side with justice and order." The lights in the building and across the city kicked on.

I sighed and said, "Historia, forgive me."

I picked her up, and kicked her as hard as I could out of the window. I watched her reach for me, or anything that could stop her fall. She screamed as the shards cut up her face. She screamed as she plummeted to the ground. She screamed as she closed her eyes, too afraid to watch the fall but opened them out of fear. But I stopped watching. I didn't bother watching her fall after a few seconds, she wasn't worth anyone watching her last moments.

Instead, I scanned the city looking for the fastest route to get to Trogz when it happened. Vesalia's screams had stopped; good more air for people who deserved it.

"What is that?"

A runway of lights from buildings and street lights all kicked on, as if forming a path. And at the end of the path in big lights, was Trogz's ship. It was my welcome light show, he knew I was coming. The light flicked off and back on again, I squinted to see who was controlling it. Who else? Who other than the one who started this all. I clenched my jaw. There he was, standing by his ship with binoculars looking dead at me.

"This ends here."

Chapter 11

HEL HATH NO FURY...

Trogz was known for over the top theatrics, so it wasn't surprising seeing an empty ship with plans out in the open about killing me. Certain hallways in his ships were lit up, as if he were guiding me to exactly where he was. The ship and town were almost entirely void of soldiers and for the few I ran into, well...

I breezed through every ambush not only because I knew the ship well, but I just didn't care anymore. I mean, they already sent their best soldier after me, what else could they do? This ship was *my* playground. Nic and I would sneak around when we were kids, I knew every vent, shaft and corner. I knew Trogz was a collector, so his ship was slightly different from similar models. He collected: artifacts, newspapers, DNA of extinct creatures that were banned from bringing back to life and more. He even collected rare and unique animals too, I guess imprisoning things was a hobby of his. He also had a prison where he sometimes kept dissenters...

I knew my first stop. I took a detour, and left the hallway lit by lights. If I was lucky, an innocent kazamite would be there or a human scientist. Or maybe a war hero that would side with me. The area that led to the prison and zoo area, was blocked off by a steel door. I broke it. I pushed the door to the side and went to the prison and... ugh.

"Mandy!" Ambrotos smiled at me while his arms, legs and neck were restrained. "You won't believe the customer service here! I made a joke about how they sent me to voicemail hell and they didn't get it.

Then I said it hurt, but it was only a flesh wound. They didn't get that either."

"I don't understand any of the references you make."

"You know what? You can just leave me here."

"What are you doing here, Ambrotos?"

"Oh nothing really. I just figured with the market right now, it was better to just go to jail. Hard to really get this lakefront property view."

I groaned and asked, "who spawned you?"

"Me? No idea but for chimeras? No idea again. I assume when a mommy Eleanor loves a daddy–"

"Where's the key?" I rubbed the bridge of my nose, fighting a losing battle against a headache.

"The power switch is by the door, but it'll open my cell and unlock the room next to me. I'm not sure what's in the room next to me, but it's something big. Nic's uncle didn't really appreciate me, so I think I was next on the menu."

"Well you can settle it with him, because I'm going to kill Trogz." I walked over and hit the switch, opening his cell door and freeing his limbs.

"Seriously? You don't exactly look equipped for it. I mean where's your super suit? Where's your aegis?"

"Somewhere on the ship, but Trogz is waiting for me. I'm gonna assume you're up for a fight since you have yours on?" He nodded. "Good. Let's see what animal he has imprisoned."

"Hang on, why is your aegis here?"

"He took it, when he took Nic."

"So it's true? Nic is dead?"

"Alive, but in bad shape."

"Worse than how you look?" He smirked.

"Me? You look like shit. Did they not give you a doc–" He gave me a stern look. "Sorry, I forget sometimes. Come on."

Together, we pulled open the doors. With the power off, the doors started to open, but got jammed so it needed us. We stepped inside, and emergency red lights flashed. The room was massive, bigger than I thought it'd be. Especially for a ship of this size. There were streams, plant life, and even insects. The ceiling was dark but there was an opening that led to outside. This was an artificial biome, so the ceiling would be a sky right now if we didn't hit the power.

Ambrotos kneeled down and looked at some animal tracks and said, "be careful Mandy, these are harlequin hogs and jotun badger tracks…"

"Those are natural to this climate. So the creature in here must be a carnivore that can take those out. A bird, a big one. Roc?

"But rocs aren't rare, why would he have a rainbow colored bird? That's like hunting a macaw."

"Could be a rare one."

"Dude what?"

"Bite me Ambrotos, when did you become an animal expert?"

"Rocs are pack animals, and are noisy. You'd know that if you actually picked up a book."

"You're right, I don't think it's a roc…" I kneeled down and picked up a hardened keratin feather. "We gotta go…"

He looked at what I grabbed and cursed.

"Wait, let me see that." I gave him the feather. "It's sick. You see the yellowing? They get depressed in captivity."

A bird cawed somewhere deeper in the room. What would Historia do? "Ambrotos, we gotta help it."

"Huh? *We*? You're buggin."

"It's not far, come on."

I forced Ambrotos deeper into the room with me, and all it took was half a minute before we found it. We found a dead mutilated roc on the ground, a fully grown one at that. Its claws were big enough to lift a hippo, from what I've been told. Its wings were damaged too, one of the important features of rocs too. Their bones and wings made it to where when they hunted, their wings didn't make a sound. And whatever did this, must've known that.

"Why is this one brownish with vibrant colors?" I asked Ambrotos.

"Because they can change their feathers to match their environment and the seasons. But they only do that when they're being hunted or flee–" A sharp feather pierced the ground next to us. "Oh that's rough."

We were in an aerial den. They were one of the smartest birds on the planet, probably the smartest. They weren't territorial by any means, but were vengeful. They would attack or hunt in an area exclusively because it knew it was the hunting ground of another animal. There weren't that many left in the world due to hunters and poachers, so this was rare. Cautiously, we looked around to see if we could spot it.

"There," I said, pointing to the behemoth of a bird.

It hung upside down, like a bat, with its eyes fixed on us. We locked eyes with it and slowly backed away to the door without turning our back to it. We made it about a foot away from the door when it decided to start crawling on the ceiling towards us. Despite its size, it was fast and its crawl was more like scurrying across the ceiling. In seconds, it was just about on top of us.

"Mandy, if you have a plan, now's the time."

I still had a feather in my hand, so I waved it in the air to get its attention. Once I was confident I had its attention, I threw the feather at the button that opened the ceiling. An alarm blared and it crawled to a wall, with its eyes still fixed on me. Once it realized I opened the ceiling, it looked at it while it opened, then stared back at me. Once the ceiling was open enough, it flew out and let out a terrifying screech as it flew high into the clouds. Aerials could fly as high as the stratosphere with some flying higher; another reason why so many have died over the years.

"Glad I wore my brown pants. Now, your aegis?" He asked.

"No, I'm headed straight to Trogz. I don't have Cricket anymore, not until I can get back to my suit. So if you could find it and maybe start the ship, you'd be helping us."

"Us? No more Cricket? Mandy, slow down."

"Slow down? We lost like a dozen of our people in a week, discovered the regime is evil, Nic is in the hospital, Historia is dead and Trogz just kept an endangered bird locked up on his ship!"

"First off, **breathe**. Second, get a hobby. You don't think I know it's been a shit show?"

"I don't know what you know. I found you caught by henchmen!"

"Caught by *henchmen*? Does that sound right to you? That sound plausible? Do those make wine? Try again, the hell is going on?"

I rubbed my temples, sighed and said, "fine. Hurricane is here, their real leader is a guy named Khan. It was his plan to attack the city, and we're in a sort of alliance."

"This sounds like the truth and yet makes less sense than me getting caught by 'henchmen'. Siding with them? I'm not sure I like this."

"Good thing I didn't ask what you liked," I hissed.

"Insert generic laugh. I'll let that slide, but we can't side with them. Sure maybe our goals align for a time, but don't forget that they aren't our friends. That's a problem for tomorrow I guess but siding with bad guys isn't our crash. What are you gonna even fight Trogz with? A knife and a pistol?"

"You fight with less."

He rolled his eyes and said, "alright. I'll get the ship ready and then do a scan for your aegis. Once I find it, I'll come straight for you. If you're outmatched, **leave**. We've lost enough people."

I nodded and ran back down my original path, leaving him at the blast door. I thought about what he said about going in under armed, and he was right. If this was Havi, I'd be rushing to my death. But what are the odds Havi was here? How many humans even had technology like Havi at their literal fingertips? Surely not Trogz, so I had a chance. He was too sure of himself to be like Havi. He himself had to beat me. Even if he had soldiers on standby, it'd still be him who would wear me down. Especially after I got away last time.

At the end of the hall, was a note addressed to me on top of a clear glass with two black swords crossing each other, with a saber in the middle of them. I picked up the note and read it aloud.

"To Mandy, the wannabe threat. I grant you the gift you keep giving me and other humans; the gift of pain. These are weapons made from meteorites that hit the ground when you were young. You and Historia both slaved away making your first weapons with this metal and rock. You made this saber and she made these swords. There was a theft and fire and I had told Copernicus that these items went missing, but the truth is I always had them. The craftsmanship was amazing, and you both with Copernicus, snuck into a lab to develop an alloy we had, but never used as weapons. Here they are; your weapons with fine golden latticework of metal. Think on this; the last item you will see of hers before I bury you under a mountain of ice, under Hela's control."

He... *stole* these? From kids? Fuck him. I crumbled the letter and tossed it to the side...

"**Fuck** him." I bent down and grabbed the paper and ripped it to shreds. "**Ugh!**" What a fucking dick. I raised my hands and balled my fist. But then I took a deep breath. Why was I even surprised?

I opened the case and drew my long lost black saber from between the swords and admired it. I haven't seen this weapon in about two decades, and here it was, in mint condition. We had no idea what we were doing when we forged these weapons, so all three blades had cracks in them. We learned of a process called 'kintsugi', an art where ancient humans used liquid gold to fill in the cracks of broken pottery. We instead did it for our weapons thus leading to a spider web of golden cracks covering all of the black blades. In the middle of her swords and my saber, was our symbol: a golden chimera.

It was the side profile of the silhouette of a lion and its mane, baring its fangs. The lion had horns like a goat, and from behind was a snake. A cobra with a forked tongue, baring its fangs too. We also made sheaths, and there they were under the clear box. I took a step back and went through a few basic maneuvers with my saber and once comfortable, I grabbed the sheathe and slung it on my back and continued to Trogz.

And there he was. There stood Chevalier and Trogz, in his usual stupid regime dress clothes. This time, he wore a short cape; it was a ceremonial cape worn at funerals. Chevalier wore his usual clothing, minus his aegis. He always wore his aegis if he planned to fight, so why wouldn't he now?

"Good, you're already dressed," I said to Trogz as I approached the two of them.

"Mandy, you are grieving. This isn't you," Chevalier said.

"I'm grieving one chimera death, keep talking and it'll be two."

"Snarky comments are unnecessary; wiser words should prevail on this day."

"**Proper** manners dictate that you address the person in a higher position **first**," Trogz said. "Respectfully mind you, and not as jabs."

"As far as I'm concerned, you killed my brother. I have nothing respectful to say to you."

He scoffed. "*I* killed him? I told Chevalier that you needed reeducation, but it seems you need an entirely new brain."

"So does Commander Vilo." At first he seemed confused, but then frowned once he realized what I meant. "He was a super soldier, up there with the average chimera. You aren't, and you know it."

"I learned chimeras are one third human. You should aspire to be as strong as *me*, Trogloydyte."

He clenched his fist. "Chevalier has convinced me to give you one last chance to surrender. Despite, you releasing that damn legendary bird."

"Is that why Chevalier is here? Or did you think I'd be more compliant with my friends around? Did men of Earth hide behind others as well?"

"What do *you* know of Earth, girl?" A vein popped up, arcing across his forehead.

"That you and I have something in common."

"And that is?"

"You're just a terran. That means you, every other chimera and kazamite, will never be considered an earthling. You're a *branched* human, because your ancestors grew up in space. Your ancient ancestors are still thousands of years off from being true humans. I know the species known as homo sapiens died with your precious world."

"And that's supposed to offend me? You're still just a chimera."

"Still just a chimera with a home world. How does it feel to be a nomad species?"

"Mandy please, surrender," Chevalier said. "I do not want to fight you."

"Chevalier, what are you doing?" I asked. "They banished you for speaking up and killed the woman you loved. Is this the forever-you? Never speaking out again out of fear? You took an oath, now's your time to honor it."

"Enough of this back and forth, demihuman." Trogz drew a gun and shot me in my side. I yelped and fell to one knee, clutching my side.

I didn't expect it, but neither did Chevalier and he looked more distraught than I did. You'd thought that he was the one shot.

"You told me a long time ago how there was a time when good people, **honorable** people defended those in need," I said. "Is this the honor knights of yore stood for? Is this who *you* are, Chevalier? Is this who you want to be?"

"Chevalier, let us not forget you were **given** that honorary position. That and your namesake are thanks to a human in the primarch position, a position she and Historia failed to protect. Arrest her. Actually, no, end her. We can't risk any more deviations to our plans and she herself is a deviant."

"End her?" Chevalier fidgeted uncomfortably. "That's not what we agreed…"

"What? That's not what we *'agreed'*? I don't need to 'agree' with you or run any of my plans or ideas by you. You are the **help**! Now, do as you're told so that we can move on with our lives."

Chevalier approached me and put his hand on his sword, but hesitated. I could see it in his eyes: he couldn't. He knew it, I knew it, everyone except Trogz knew it. Chevalier really saw himself as a knight in shining armor, an honorable knight. So he couldn't draw his blade. I heard his arm and sword rattle as he stood there with tears in his eyes. He dodged my gaze by closing his eyes. He clenched his jaw, I watched as his entire body tensed up. He sighed and took a deep breath. He started to draw his weapon, when a table flew by and hit him, sending him flying backwards.

"Wanna go dutch?" Ambrotos walked up from behind me and helped me up.

"Stand down, chimera," Trogz said. "You will not win."

"Yea, everyone's a critic but I guess that's show biz amirite?" Ambrotos said with a smirk.

"Still with the jokes?"

"Still a big silly human nothing burger?"

"Nothing burger? What are you, five? I have won more battles than you, show some respect," Trogz said.

"Eat my ass."

You could see the frustration on Trogz's face.

"Ambrotos… you are in violation of the Chimera Accord; stand down," Chevalier said as he stood up.

"Who wrote that decree again?"

"Sibil."

"Ugh. Now we *have* to fight. Go easy on me will ya, asthma boy?"

"Chimera, you're not funny," said Trogz.

"Yea well, I heard pigs couldn't laugh anyway."

Chevalier frowned. He furrowed his brow and said, "I dare not feign a good mood or laugh at your jokes."

"Womp womp."

Ambrotos dashed forward, engaging his boosters and flew into Chevalier. They both tumbled out of sight.

Trogz shook his head and said, "causing disarray amongst your own kind, aligning yourself with some mysterious masked man named Khan. And to top it all off, not apologizing to mankind for causing all of this chaos. And you're really still cosplaying as the good guy?"

"Better than cosplaying as a dad or role model."

He aimed his gun at me and said, "I was a fool to let you live. I'll resolve that."

"Scared?"

"Excuse me?"

"Scared that I'll win in a fair match? If we are truly inferior, you should win."

He scoffed. "You think I'd be baited into a duel with you?"

"Yea, yea I think so."

He hesitated for a moment, but then holstered his firearm and drew a saber from his side.

"To think you can beat me, is arrogant and foolhardy. I taught you and Nic how to wield a blade."

"And yet I'm a better fencer and dueler than you and him."

We walked toward each other and tossed our sheaths to the side.

"Why? After all mankind has done, you cause us… **me**, such grief. You bring down everyone and everything around you. You are a rogue black hole."

"Then you better run along."

"You're a fool, girl."

"No, but I was. I was a fool for letting you make me question who my family was. Allowing you to get in my head and doubt myself. In the event Nic, my **brother**, dies, he'll have dozens of close friends there. And they'll have nothing but kind words to say at his funeral. Because he was a good person. If Nic dies, you won't have anybody who cares about you at yours."

He swung first, but I was ready. A duel between sabers was fast and violent. It was full of parrying, deflecting, and slashing with everything you had. Every swing and hesitation made a difference. He slashed at the air and stepped forward hoping he'd overwhelm me, but I knew his moves. I knew the difference in arbitrary swinging, wrist movements and feints as well. But because of his level of experience, he was the better duelist.

We fought for a couple minutes, with him cutting me several times on my torso. I got him too, but only a few times on his arm. He was an arrogant fighter and with each successful hit, he attacked with more vigor. It came to the point where he had advanced too aggressively for me to keep up with and I lost my footing as I back peddled. He swung his blade at my throat, all I could do was stare at the blade as it inched towards me. Centimeters from my neck, Ambrotos proved why he was one of the most reliable people in my corner. He and Chevalier's recklessly barreled towards us. If it wasn't for their chaos, I'd be headless.

Trogz narrowly dodged out of the way, jerking his arm at a weird angle as he pulled his swing. It was only for a split second, but he winced. He tried to hide it, but his grip loosened around his handle.

Chevalier and Ambrotos stood up and faced each other. As Chevalier gritted his teeth and let out a low growl.

"Give it back, Ambrotos!" He yelled.

Ambrotos threw him his inhaler as he walked towards him and said, "remember kids, this is a combat sport."

"Has anyone ever called you a walking headache?"

"Funny you mention that. There's this guy named Sibil right?"

Chevalier grabbed the table Ambrotos hit him with earlier, and swung it at him. Ambrotos was hit so hard that he flew through the air. You could hear just how annoyed Chevalier was as he chased after him.

"Tell me, what do you expect comes next?" Trogz moved back to let me stand. He twirled his saber to intimidate me, it didn't work. He was stalling, trying to unstrain his wrist.

"What do **YOU** expect comes next? You treat us and kazamites like roaches, and think we wouldn't get fed up? We have done nothing to your people."

"Nothing? Picture this: a race comes from the stars, bringing technology that advances this world by over four **thousand** years. Instead of being grateful, there are issues for well over a century and Primarch Leopold is forced to handle it. My brother joins the ranks of the Auric Order, a rare feat mind you. Then he stumbles into some idiot genius scientist, who just so **happens** to be the daughter of someone in the Sacred Band of Halcyon! She gets it in his head to defect, and stands trial against Primarch Leopold, and then they're killed. The 'kindest woman' in this entire parsec with the most lethal man has a child and I'm forced to raise! And as if being an orphan of a traitor isn't hard enough, he befriends **AND ADOPTS A CHIMERA**!"

"That wasn't my fault. None of that was my doing."

"How did they die? Ask me."

"I know how they died, Trogz."

"What were they doing? What *evil* were they doing that got them killed in front of their son?" The words forced themselves out between his gritted teeth.

"Philanthropy…"

"The same people who killed him, were the same people they dedicated their last days to. The best people that mankind had to offer, in all of the galaxy."

"Get to the point."

"The point is, you stole his normalcy away from him. You and the kazamite's took away whatever chance he had. He could have been the first primarch with his heritage, and I don't think we'll ever see another primarch again with his heritage. **Ever**. The 'point' is, my brother and his redheaded wife are victims of trying to level with your people. I hate your kind; you don't deserve the best of us. Kazamites and chimeras **gutted** his parents, and all they did was support your kind. And now their son…" tears filled his eyes. "Is fighting on an operating table as his brain swells, because he followed in their footsteps. Following a girl." Every word felt like it forced its way through his clenched teeth. His face was red, and his eyes were redder. "There's always a girl. My brother and his son were meant to be the greatest men the stars had ever seen."

"The resident Stockholm syndrome victim is Sibil, not me. I didn't do anything to Nic, neither did thousands of the rest of us. So why punish us? You use their death as an excuse to keep up your behavior. Regime leaders bread crumb us to live under your constant rule."

"My 'behavior' is based on how unstable your kind is. Some chimeras have joined us, some have fought back. Some even went into hiding, and let's not forget the love birds that are on the edge of humanity. Yes, I know about them. This proves the point I have always made that Haumea and eventually my brother hated: you need rearing. Chimeras and kazamites alike. Clearly, diplomacy and philanthropy didn't work. If the carrot fails, then the **stick** will *not*."

We continued our fight, but this time, he wasn't as aggressive. He also didn't punish me for strikes I missed either. He didn't press nearly as much and thanks to his bum wrist, I was able to play more on the offensive. People think that duels are like the movies, long and drawn out. They can be, but sometimes you just defend. Looking for an opening until one appears, and sometimes it's 30 seconds of extreme attacks. And I just saw my opening. I parried one of his attacks and slashed him across his chest. He screamed in pain and staggered backwards. I didn't let off the gas. I stepped forward and went to disarm him, trying to capitalize off of his pain. I smiled as I pushed in, lowering my guard and leaving myself open for a counter. And in one swift motion, he parried me and punched me where he shot me.

I gasped for air and created distance as I held my side. He switched hands and spun his saber with the same dexterity as he could with his other hand; he was ambidextrous. Of course. Of fucking course.

"In the ascension of the chain of command," he said. "There are the admirals of the colony ships, myself, and then the leaders of the moons. That means that I am above Hela, and she's considered a tactical mastermind." He chuckled. "Have you any idea who I am?"

"No, but you're about to find out who I am."

I lunged forward and played the more aggressive role this time, forcing him to step back. Within a few strikes, he parried and stepped to the side as I hunched over holding my side again.

"This is it? When I met you, you stopped charging thifrum as a toddler. Now, you can't even over power me in a duel?"

"Let me shoot you in your side after hours of fighting and see how you do."

"All that money and all those resources pooled in to make an adult hybrid petri girl that loses steam after a couple fights. This the girl Copernicus loves so dearly and calls his sister? Just like the day I met you, I am not impressed. In fact, I'm less impressed now than when I met you."

"Be kind, or be quiet."

As the fight wore on, I lost more and more energy thanks to my growling list of injuries. My untreated gunshot and punch delivered to it hindered my movement. I wish I had my aegis. I gained a small lead in the fight, but lost it as he gained the upper hand. He could've finished me right then and there, but he gloated instead. He was practically dancing around me. He'd strike high and then low with us going back and forth. He'd side step me and attack, I just couldn't match his tempo.

The one opening I did see I took, but there was no question who was the better dueler. He switched his saber to his weakened hand and easily parried me. He was so confident in his skill, he kept his saber in his weak hand, and then switched hands between strikes. As if he was reveling in his swordsmanship being *that* much greater than mine.

With each successful strike he grew more bold, more arrogant, more sure of himself. He cut me up, delivering superficial attacks to prolong his fun. The fight came to a head when I winced at him striking on my wounded side. He picked up his pace and kept striking and all I could do was defend. But he couldn't maintain this, I just needed to hold out. And I was right, he overplayed his hand. He kept attacking in one direction, north to south, north to south. It was easy to defend against but I could see he was setting me up. He changed his attack direction at the last second and slashed diagonally, hoping to probably cut off my head, but I saw it coming. I wasn't fast enough to parry, but I was fast enough for another move.

"ARGHH!!! MY HAND!!!"

His hand and blade fell to the ground as he grabbed his wrist and screamed.

"This *only* hurts me, because this would hurt Nic. Nic loves you, and his love is your protection right now. Surrender."

"You think this ends here?" He spat through gritted teeth.

"I know Havi and you are planning something; call off your goons." I flicked my blade, splattering his blood onto his face.

His wrist squirted bright red blood, he needed to stop the bleeding but decided against it. He picked up his saber with his other hand and continued attacking me. This time, there wasn't any finesse or order to his strikes. I parried an attack and moved in and elbowed him in his face hard, but not hard enough to knock sense into him. I broke his nose and busted his lips and he stumbled back but he didn't give up. He attacked again, with more aggression. He swung his blade low, hoping to cut my leg but I easily hopped over it and grabbed his wrist as he came up, and crushed it. He let out another guttural scream as he fell to his knees.

"**Enough** Trogz, you lost!"

"Lost? What do you know about losing Mandy? Nic was destined to have **EVERYTHING MY BROTHER AND I NEVER HAD AND MORE**!" His eyes were full of hate, I don't even know if he felt pain from my attacks anymore. "Decades. Decades of cleaning up my brother and his treason. Decades of protecting Copernicus from Leopold's Loyalists and threats! And worse of all, decades of **you**. Copernicus could have had everything."

"If you didn't hate me, yea. Nic would've had a second dad and a sister. He already has a family, all you did was try to divide it."

"You'll never, **NEVER** be human! So he'll never love **you** like he does *us*. You can't even process human love."

"I don't know, who's to say? I know human hate at least."

"I will not live in a world with test tube **demi** humans. You're going to have to kill me!"

With a crushed wrist, he grabbed his saber and rushed me. It was dumb, he could hardly hold it. I disarmed him, and sent his saber into the ground next to us and then sliced his side. Blood spewed everywhere. He fell to his knees, almost silently, as I picked up his saber and formed the letter 'x' around his throat.

"We can still heal you, there's a medical bay on the ship. Give up Trogz, please. For Nic."

"Don't you dare use him against me. And give up? And live in a world where you hate people like me? There is no place in society for people out of time, displaced from their era."

"Prison, that's a good start. Could make you do some community service. Spend a decade righting your wrongs."

"Like my brother and his wife before kazamites took them from this world? And then what? I have a child that follows you, and ends up in the hospital like Copernicus?" He scoffed. "Get on with the execution. I don't even have time to see if he made it through the first few hours on the table or is in a coma because I'm here, facing you. Even in defeat, you taught me. I abhor you. I detest, and loathe your kind with every quark of my being. I hate you especially, Mandy. Across all theoretical worlds from: multiverses, to fake out-verses, to microcyclic universes, **all** of it. I pray that if he wakes up, he shares in my revulsion of your begrimed, carnal, destructive, cancerous, malevolent, vi–"

I closed the 'x'. His body fell to the ground, a few pounds lighter.

I sighed. I didn't even feel relief in his death, just empty. I stared at his lifeless body, and thought about how he would terrorize me and make me hate myself growing up. How he was my first bully, my boogy man. His dog whistle comments when Nic was around, and his out right resentment the second Nic was out of ear shot. And now, the only thing he was, was dead.

Good riddens.

I bent over and grabbed his NUE and downloaded the contents of it. I now had untethered access to all of his systems, because he was too cocky for a password. I grabbed my sheathe and made my way to the bridge. I thought about checking on Ambrotos, but he didn't need me. No matter how upset Chevalier got, he wouldn't kill a chimera. And neither would Ambrotos. I set my NUE up to ping mode in hopes my aegis would go off as I walked through the ship. After a while, nothing picked up. So I recalibrated my NUE so all of Trogz's credentials transferred, and then my aegis pinged. I smiled as I donned it and rebooted it so that hopefully Cricket could join me.

As my system rebooted, I walked and sifted through Trogz's files and data. It's crazy that a high ranking official like himself, didn't even have a failsafe in case something bad happened. I went into all of his files and created a password and set it as 'hubris'.

"Computer, on," I said once I entered the bridge.

"Incoming call from colony ship Elysium," the computer said as soon as it turned on. It pulled up a voice call for me to accept. So, I did.

No video, but the voice was unmistakably who I thought it was. "So the videos are true…" Oceana said. "Colonel Trogz's feed was live and recorded the whole fight, he planned on using this to squash any rebellion."

"He was evil," I said. "Aren't humans all about smiting evil?"

"I have no more energy to smite anything, not in the way the rest of you do. I don't hate chimeras, I hate men like Colonel Trogz and the entire military industrial complex."

I was confused. "Wait, you're on *our* side? Then why'd you launch that attack? You killed a lot of people. Cripppled dozens of towns."

"Oh no, I'm not on your side. And I don't need to explain myself to a child. I don't care about any of the citizens outside of my ship. When Scyra broke away, we all were confused. History books and logs don't explain how fed up they were, but I think I understand now. My mother was in charge before me, and her mother before her. They always told me to mind my business, do just my job to my people, and don't concern myself with everyone else. Well I didn't listen, I cared about kazamites and humans on-world. And it caused me to lose my family. I have no care left for any outside of my border."

"Then why'd you attack us?"

"You're young, you think everything revolves around you still. I wanted you all to suffer, and I do mean all of you. Callum's family, the Vanrocks, are the wealthiest family. It's rumored they have technology to bring back the dead… and I wanted it. Sadly, some groupie kazamite that got wind of my plan got in the way as I made the move. My attention and forces were so focused on the Vanrocks, we weren't ready for the bomber. And I know I shouldn't blame every kazamite… but every major bad event revolves around them. When I see them, all I see is how they took my little Stewart." Her voice cracked.

"And because of an obsessed fan, that gave you the right to attack us? Oceana, I'm confused to be honest. Why did you call?"

"To see if the rumors were true about a revolution. To see if the rumors were true about *you*. I have no issue with chimeras, but I do with kazamites and the regime. As a mother, it is my job... my duty, to protect the people. You understand what losing a family is like, right? I've already lost one because I didn't protect them from everything like a good mother. I should've kept them under my watch at **all** times... I was a fool. It will not happen again. So, I'm going to raze everything. Anything in range of my ship is a threat to my family. Every chimera, kazamite, and humanalike, are threats to my ship. I can't risk my people, my second family, to end up like my first. I *have* to cleanse this land of all of you. You surface-worlders are an invasive species that keep hurting my family directly or indirectly and I'm tired of it. On my... sabbatical, it dawned on me, Mandy. Why worry about my neighbors when you can get rid of them? Why let their issues impede me? It was a moment of clarity for me. If I kill all those who could hurt my family, I never have to worry about it again."

"What? So because of a potential threat you'll kill us all? Do you know how many people that would kill? Are you crazy?"

"**I'M NOT CRAZY**!" The mic gave off feedback so loud, it hurt my ears, but then it died down as quick as it came.

"Capital colony ships are equipped with chemical, biological, nuclear, and energy based attacks. If you attack, half of Kore would be destroyed. You'd cripple everyone. You can't do that."

"When *you're* in power, you can do whatever you want. A mother's job is to protect her children. And I must protect mine. My Stewart and Shiloh were so innocent, so pure... I guess that wasn't enough for this world. Instead, this world wants to make monsters out of all of us. But I won't let it no no I won't. Not me! This world tried to break me, tried to make me crazy. But I'm not. I won. Do you know what's crazy? I'll tell you what's crazy, killing children."

"And what do you think is going to happen when you attack? Children will suddenly be invincible? When you released that swarm, that hoard or whatever it was, children died."

"Then their mothers should have been better mothers and saved them. If you had children or a family, you would understand. The children living in Kore, are probably going to grow up to be criminals anyway. I mean look at the senators, soldiers, and scientists now. No good. Not good for my family. And ideals are like germs and spread. I must keep my people safe."

"Wait… is that why nobody has been able to contact anyone on your vessel? Are you forcing your citizens to stay?"

"Forcing? They aren't forced to stay, we'll dock soon. I mean, after a couple cities are leveled, just the main ones. Mother knows best after all. At first, I considered taking my ship and going to see the rest of the planet. But why? There's so much land and beautiful places here. It's just… noisy and dangerous. So my motherly decision is to stay and make it safer for me and mine."

"Your 'motherly decicion' is genocide. You could easily just break off like Scyra did."

"Oh we both know that nobody will leave my people alone if things escalate. And we know it will escalate. I gave my heart, body, mind and soul to my position. I was dedicated to my career, and all I have to show for it is an empty bedroom. I chose work over dinner dates, conference calls over putting money under pillows and taking baby teeth. My home was filled with children's laughter. Finger paintings on the walls, mess and toys everywhere, and pillow forts on weekends… now it's quiet, and clean…"

I muted the call. "Computer, charge up every weapon system and aim them directly for the engines of Elysium."

The screen flashed red and the computer replied, "fratricide is imminent. Override code needed with verification of vessel commander and their initials."

"I verify as vessel commander Frederick Alex Trogz. Initials are FT." I waved my NUE over the screen hoping it'd work.

The screen turned green. "Confirmed. Orienting weapon systems."

I unmuted the call and said, "you can't do this. I've been suffering for the last several months, dealing with problems that my people never caused. We just want to be left alone at this point, no different than you.

271

We don't want to be in the middle of your war, in fact, there doesn't need to be one."

"There is a recording of you killing Commander Vilo and whoever that girl was; I don't believe all you want is peace. You're obviously capable of a lot more. And weren't you that chimera involved with the nuke?"

"That wasn't me!" I took a breath. "I *stopped* the nuke, and I have been constantly running around doing my best cleaning up mess after mess left by the regime and Hurricane. And before you fly off the rails, it's not every kazamite that's evil."

"I agree, it's not every chimera or every kazamite. But, it's enough of you, which is too many. It's not every family that is caught in the crossfire, but it was mine. And I won't be able to move on."

The call muted as the computer said, "weapon systems are primed. Confirm fire." A red button appeared on the screen.

I unmuted myself and said, "please... I'm begging you. There doesn't need to be any more death."

"How unfortunate, Mandy is such a pretty name. I'm sorry Mandy, but I can't risk it and take the chance with kazamites, chimeras and humans. If there's a chance of any of you hurting my family, it's not worth it. What type of mother would I be if I knowingly risked my family's well being? I can't risk my people's safety off of 'what if's' and chances. It just has to happen, I just... I have to kill you all. My people are already doubling our napalm supply and updating our railguns. I hope you understand."

I sighed and took a deep breath.

"I do."

I pushed the button. I felt the ship vibrate and rock as all the weapon systems unloaded.

"Maybe one day, we could have a day or month of peace," she said. "After you die, I'll make sure once a year we do that. That's what I wanted for Shiloh and Stewart, a world where there was no pain."

"Yea, peace one of these days would be nice, Oceana. I hope I live long enough to see it. I'm sorry your family didn't get to."

Her side got really quiet, as if I was muted. After a few seconds, she unmuted herself and said, "ah, I see. At least I'll be in John's arms again. And if not, my boys will be waiting for me in a pillow fort."

Her feed cut off.

I stood there in silence. Everything faded, and blended into one shade, one object. The only constant sound was the thumping in my ears from my heart. Where did it all go wrong? Just a few months ago, Historia was teaching me how to roll sushi and we tricked some kazamite into eating wasabi. Kazamites don't eat spicy foods, so most of them haven't developed any immunity or resistance. I went from that, to killing thousands of people in one button push.

And now, now I'm a murderer. I... I had to... right?

"Mandy?" There was a familiar chirp. "I was rebooted and then got an emergency jumpstart. Protocol Low Tide."

"Cricket..." My face was rushed with warmth. "You've been gone for a while... a long while."

"I haven't received all the updates yet but that protocol means only one thing. Mandy your vitals..." He paused. "Mandy, what happened?"

"Things just got out of hand... but I got it under control."

"Under control? Mandy, do you understand how much human history and lives you've just taken?"

"I'm not some blueberry soldier, Cricket. I know what I did. I **had** to strike first! I do this for the good of chimeras and kazamites. It was us or them Cricket."

"Havi, Callum, and Trogz will not let you commit murder and be ok with it."

"You've been back for five seconds and are already on my back? I don't care how they see it and if they're feeling up to it, then Callum and Havi are next."

"And Trogz?"

"His blood is still wet on my boots."

"What have you done?"

"What had to be done, Cricket. I wanted to survive, not live, **survive**."

"There you are." Khan walked in with a couple of his soldiers. "We need to capitalize on this, there will be retaliation. I thought I heard you speaking to someone?"

"Cricket, he's my AI. Cricket, this is the real leader of Hurricane."

"Hello... that's odd, I can't scan you," Cricket said.

"I know, my shields prevent it for my privacy. Mandy, you need to prepare for a counter attack from Havi. I'm sure Callum won't be far behind."

I went into the computer and pulled up a holographic map.

"I don't think Callum will strike," I said to Khan. "But he will threaten people and act bigger and stronger than he actually is. And when he does, he will be taken out of the sky. Havi will be more methodical, he'll probably use that secret army from Hela. They'll jump in and have been training and running covert ops for who knows how long. We need Callum to beach his ship, or else we'll be fighting too many battles at once. But I'm sure we can take Hela's forces if we ambush them."

"You think you'll *surprise* her? The first woman praetorian, and maybe the only one we'll ever have?" Khan asked. "That is unlikely and ill advised, but I have a recommendation. There is a prison not too far from here that houses felons that the regime would want to stay hidden. We free these people, kill Callum, and go into a defensive posture. We don't over extend our hand."

"Could we make Hela or Callum overplay their hand? I don't know anything about either outside of word of mouth."

Khan chuckled and said, "unlikely, but you may certainly try."

I thought about it for a moment.

"Computer, hail Hela. Oceana said that everything I've done has been recorded, so that means right now I'm seen as a threat, right? Probably the biggest chimera threat to ever exist. If we could scare off Hela, that's one less battle to fight."

"Certainly not the worst idea, but it is competing for it. You don't have to poke the bear to get its honey," said Khan.

"Good thing I don't need your permission."

Hela answered the call and said, "Colonel Trogz, I must admit I am a little confused on why you are calling after our last disagreement. Have you decided to move forward with the sirens or would that hurt your nephew's feelings?"

"Careful, that 'nephew' means a lot to me," I said.

"What is this?"

"My name's Mandy, and I know about your secret cyborg army. Stay the hell off of Kazar. If you were paying attention, you know who I am and what I'm capable of. That light show in the sky was Elysium being destroyed by my hand. Callum is next, and then Havi. If you, your army, your stupid sirens or whatever enter orbit, then I'll blow you up too."

"Why would you want to hurt me? I am a victim of Havi just like you are. You think being banished to a moon is something I wanted? Is Trogz dead now too? So the battle is over and my people will have a breather? Are we free of him?"

"Trogz is dead... but I'm confused. How are you a victim of Havi? You didn't accidentally become a praetorian."

"The regime pays my medical bills, I'm sick and have been. Callum's family finances my medication and as long as he does, I'm trapped. Trogz capitalized on this so if I want to live, then I have to do as they say. But if you're the Mandy I heard of, voidborn, then you can help me right?"

Khan chimed in. "Mandy, she is lying. Please, let us speed this along. The longer we stay stationary, the longer she is able to triangulate our position. She is stalling us."

There was a chuckle from her side, no… a cackle. "Whoever your friend is, is right. I'd actually already have your position locked in, but my systems are running into interference. Anyway, Oceana was weak, and so were her people. I couldn't care less if they're dead or alive, I only care that Trogz is dead. Now that he's dead, it will be that much easier to convince Havi to start this project of mine. I feel I should thank you for being the murderer that you are, Mandy."

I shook my head and said, "let's compare numbers. If you know what I can do, you should think twice about coming here."

"Cute. I'm not some low tier goon, or weakling that cracks under pressure. Nor am I as lenient as Havi, I don't believe in rules of war. I will raze half of Kore, to kill you if the mood strikes me. If any of your allies knew about me, they would have told you not to dare call me. So why are you calling me?"

"Havi will need reinforcements, so he'll enlist your help. I want you to deny it, stay out of this and you can keep your moon. Leave us alone and we'll leave you alone. If not, then all we have is mutual destruction because by the time you made it to Kore, we could blow up at least half of your forces and–"

"Do it."

"Excuse me?"

"Do it. What, did you think I'd negotiate with you? Didn't you say I didn't become a praetorian by accident? This isn't 'mutual destruction' because I have more tricks up my sleeve than you," she said. "But let's say it is mutual assured destruction, you think I care? That I'm scared?"

"You'd risk your own men's lives to be petty? All we want is to live in a world not owned by xenophobic and racist humans. And if I have to, I'm willing to go to war with all of you. It's better than subjugation."

"Adorable paragon beliefs, I hope dead kazamite children are worth every syllable and letter."

"Worth more than you and the humans I just blew out of the sky."

"Killing innocent humans who follow a grieving widow, isn't the victory you think it is. This isn't some opera or play where you threaten me and I'm scared. Your arrogance and threats come off as someone who is scared and purposely trying to seem tougher than they actually are. You *aren't* a threat to me, I'm not a widow or some guy with a soft spot for his adoptive ward. I *revel* in warfare."

"Believe what you want, but if you step on this world, I'm gonna kill you."

She sighed and said, "goodbye Mandy. Best of luck on your mission."

She ended the call.

"That was a bad idea," Cricket and Khan said at the same time.

I groaned and opened my mouth to reply when Ambrotos showed up.

He smiled and said, "well that was quite the blunder. Sir Lancelot really had me on the ropes, glad I could count on you for the assist." He shot me a look and then looked at Khan and his men. "Who are your dinner dates? I was burning calories and getting my ass beat by asthma-man and you guys were just chillin?"

"Chevalier wouldn't kill you, and you seem fine. This is Khan, the guy I told you about. We're about to do a prison break, Khan's idea," I said to him.

"Dude what? How could you say that so casually, as if literally all of those words together weren't bad? I told you siding with him was a bad idea, I only got away cause Chevalier and I were distracted by the ship firing. This lunatic just blasted Elysium out of the sky."

"This 'lunatic' isn't the one that fired," Khan said and looked at me.

Ambrotos scoffed and looked at me and then back at Khan. He looked at me again and saw the expression on my face.

"Mandy... no way dude."

I rolled my eyes and said, "it had to be done, Ambrotos. We needed to strike first."

"Had to be done? You're gully in the head."

"And you're weak!" I yelled. "You've been flying around like some cartoonish superhero with your hair in the wind and not a care in the world while our friends die. What have *you* even done for us?"

"Uh, I'm sorry I shampoo and condition my hair; I have extra if you're in need, you bum. And me taking care of my hair is not the same as actual **genocide** and **murder**. And don't make it seem like I'm just lazy and chose to get captured, when's the last time you saw me in chains? **Decades**. And who saved **you** when you got shot and was crippled on the floor during the nuke incident? Not all of us were blessed to be around rich and powerful humans growing up, some of us had to run away just to see daylight. You think that there aren't other places that need our help too? That's where I've been. I'm not apologizing for being busy helping and fighting wherever I can, but I've been fighting just like you."

"Funny, you were missing when Historia died."

"Careful Mandy."

I walked towards him and said, "how many missions ended in failure with you leading them? How many of our people have you saved? You have done nothing but crack jokes that **none** of us ever understand. Your jokes are corny, and **you're**, corny."

He shrugged and said, "corny is better than being a murderer." I swung. He effortlessly flipped me on my back. I jumped to my feet but he shoved me against the wall, and pressed his forearm against my throat. "I'll stick around because Historia would want me to smack some sense into you, and not abandon you. You're taking the gourd if you think I've been just sitting on my ass. I'm not sure who died and made *you* in charge, but we don't even like Sibil. Not sure why you think we'd want another him."

"Are you with me or not," I growled.

"Inside voice. You just killed how many thousands of people? And now you're going to a prison to break out criminals? Maybe we should drop your goober ass off there." I tried to push him off of me, but failed as he dug his arm deeper into my throat. "I get we're in a bad spot right now, but you're gonna make this right." He let me go. I choked and gasped for air. "Chevalier *let* me go, because we had fundamental disagreements but are still friends. Same way how I'm letting you go now. I'm not in the business of fighting my friends unless it's sparring, not my crash. And it shouldn't be yours either. I'm with you, but you're going to make this right without killing the next wave of humans."

I stood up while coughing and asked, "and if I do?"

"This is the illusion of choice. Mandy, you **will** make this right without murdering dozens of humans. I'll follow you until you handle Havi, help get our people to safety. I'll even help lock up Khan, **when** he inevitably betrays you. Then you're on your own. I'm not sure what your plan is after this prison break, if you even have a plan but don't bring any of our people down this warpath with you. Not every chimera wants to fight with you, and not every chimera is unwilling to fight you."

Chapter 12

LEGENDS NEVER DIE

5 0 million. 50 million units was the bounty put on me. All it took was a few days, and every chimera was being hunted down. They broadcasted every hunt too. They hunted us in our homes, on-world and off-world. They tracked those of us fighting on their side, waited until the battled mechs under Hurricane control and then took them down. They even hunted the few of us that hid in the sewers; we couldn't even live with the rodents. They posted my picture everywhere and spoke about me on the regime controlled media. The 'free' and 'unbiased' news channels said my name more times than I could count. Some places had quarterly broadcasts, others had them every hour.

"This is your top of the hour broadcast and loyalty conditioning. The chimera known as Mandy is quisling with the insurgents Khan and Hurricane," was their last broadcast. And each broadcast and news report would always end with, "Remember: choose the regime, the **only** one's on humanity's team."

It was hue and cry daily. There were humans and kazamites that sympathized with the regime and reported chimeras in hiding. There were people too scared to even *look* in our general direction, let alone rat us out. Ambrotos said citizens shouldn't flee from us, how this was bad.

Good. They should be scared of us and I don't feel bad. You'd think things would have died down, but it only got worse. Enlistments reached an all time high, laws and decrees that were blatantly xenoist were being published and more. So no, I *didn't* care. In fact, I loved that I was hands down the most wanted person in this planet's history. Cricket and Ambrotos teamed up to nag me too. Said that at this rate, things would drastically get worse and we wouldn't have any allies.

But they don't get it. They weren't there for those fights or arguments. They weren't the ones who had to make a choice, I was! And every day, I regret it less. They've killed surrendering kazamites and chimeras daily. And people wanna talk about coexistence. Please. Why would I go or stay somewhere I'm not celebrated or wanted? It's easier if we carve out land, a home for those of us who want peace. If they want to send more humans to stop me, the only one they're hurting is their species count.

"Kazar to Mandy? Hello? Mandy, mandy…" he sighed. "Bueller, Bueller, Bueller—"

"Ambrotos, hush. I'm trying to work on my aegis. I need to focus," I said.

"You *need* therapy," he said as he peeled his fruit.

"I *need* them to stop killing our people."

"Apparently you need shampoo and conditioner as well for that curly mane of yours. Run me through the plan again. You were giving off evil Sibil vibes, so I drowned you out."

"They have someone imprisoned and we need them for our plan to work. He's a genius that can design a secret weapon for us and from there, we go after Havi. We'll broker a deal with Callum that if he gets involved, we use the weapon on him too. We still haven't been able to reach Sibil or Chevalier, but we wanted to use them to help with the peace talks."

"This jail guy, he's the architect for Khan's dream city right? We use this weapon against Havi and his ship, we hope we kill him and all of his lackeys in one or two shots. Then we tell Callum he could be next but it's a bluff, and we somehow get peace. *Then* establish a new colony with Khan at the head. That everything, Mandy?" I nodded. "You're an idiot. Havi *easily* killed Historia and was jumped and won on multiple occasions. We take him out with this super weapon and people will only fear us more. And why would this architect help us? And why would he build a utopia for Khan?"

"This architect's family built the defense system for Scyra a long time ago. They know shielding and bypassing shields like no one else. Not to mention Scyra's defenses are debatably the best shield generators I think mankind has ever known. He also worked on a project that was able to disable a ship, something that overrides its systems."

He finished his fruit, dusted off his hands and said, "again, why would he help us?"

"Because we'll make him."

He snickered. "Sorry, I've literally held your hair back as you've thrown up from eating bad food. This megalomaniac crash you got, ain't working on me. What about all the chimeras that are still out there hiding? And those that will side and *have* sided with the humans? What are we gonna do? We can't fight our own people."

"They'll see reason and join us."

"Oh? Tell them to share it with you when they find it," Ambrotos said.

I opened my mouth to reply when Khan walked in and said, "we have arrived."

"For the record Mandy, I'm still not ok with this alliance with Khan."

"I'm standing right here," Khan said.

"You don't know me well, but I don't care. If I say something behind your back, I'll say it to your face too. I'm not sure why Mandy thinks working with you is in Chimera's best interest."

"She needs allies, resources, tactics and troops. I provide all of this."

"So you're just the convenience store?"

"Is teasing your form of friendship or what you do when nervous?"

Ambrotos raised an eyebrow. "I'm not trying to be your friend. And I'm not shaken up by some guy that hides behind people like a shadow."

"I do not lurk in the shadows like some vigilante or Dracula."

"Really? Because you've been MIA... wait, how do you know about Dracula?"

I ignored them and asked Cricket, "Cricket, did you lower the prison's defenses?"

"Good morning Cricket." I groaned at his sarcasm as he spoke through the speakers. "I value all of your help and insight despite my increased irritability and misaimed rage. Some would describe my recent behavior as misguided and annoying."

"Cricket please..." I begged.

"Yes, they're expecting you to deliver a package through the back which is our current route. Due to this being an almost secluded area, they aren't expecting a prison break nor know that this vessel is no longer under regime control. The nearest location is a mining city so if anything, they may believe you are from there. Upon arrival however, they will instantly raise the alarms and open fire on you."

"How do we stop that?" I asked.

"We never go."

I groaned and told the others, "we're safe to enter."

Ambrotos scrunched his face and said, "what about that said 'safe to enter' like at all to you?"

Our ship docked and like Cricket said, they raised their guns as soon as they saw us. Thankfully, it was a skeleton crew with no mechs and once they realized who I was, they lowered their weapons and led us to where they kept their prisoners. The guards were all humans, and almost all of the prisoners were kazamites. They assumed that seeing me meant bad news, and there was no chance that they would win, so they just gave up.

As we walked through the prison, the guards tried to defend their actions by saying stuff like, "it just so happens most of the crime was committed by these guys, but we love kazamites." But since we weren't here for that, we ignored them and painstakingly, freed almost every prisoner. There were a couple Khan, Ambrotos and myself argued about releasing, but only because Ambrotos disagreed with Khan. Khan believed we shouldn't have people imprisoned indefinitely, that if their crime was so bad, they should have been killed.

Khan believed in a colony of prisoners, separate from society. Ambrotos, on the other hand, felt some of the people were genuine psychos and never needed to see sunlight again.

"Ma'am," one of the guards said to me. "I think some of these people shouldn't be released. They don't deserve to ever breathe outside air again."

Khan shook his head at the guard and asked, "and what crime is so severe to imprison someone for the eternity of their natural life?"

"Death is too good of a punishment for some people. They *owe* us their life." The guard drew his sidearm and aimed it at Khan's face. "I-I can't let you free everyone!"

"So you steal their freedom as your solution? Stripping them of their natural rights so that when they leave this concentration camp, they what? Integrate with the world a couple decades later? Seamlessly?"

"B-but they're all just criminals!" The guard argued.

"You've made the mistake of imprisoning petty criminals and those who have spoken out against your leaders with *actual* criminals. Then you wound them up, and plan on releasing them back to society after you took their lives. So now they're brandished, and husks of who they once were. Then they spread their hate against your leaders, they radicalize everyone around them and everything they touch. They're now cancerous."

"Not true! Admiral Havi and The primarch would never radicalize law-abiding citizens! They had criminal tendencies in them already! They deserve to serve their time and then the few who have paid their debt should be released."

"Except once imprisoned, they seem to keep being imprisoned. As if laws are biased against them. Prison and legislature for profit is just so… repugnant."

"What do you mean?" I asked.

"The Vanrocks stay gainfully employed by receiving kickbacks for the amount of cells they fill. And would you believe the next in line for the family fortune is no other than our dear Callum? In the case of some of these prisoners, all they do is sit and stare at walls all day. They fester daily and look for a way to trade your life, for theirs." Khan canted his head as he studied the guard. "You should reconsider which one of us is the bad guy. Your morals don't seem worthy to die for, lower your gun." The guard hesitated, but then lowered and holstered his gun.

We went to the very next prisoner, he stared at us with a sort of hunger in his eyes. Ambrotos smiled and said, "oh this outta be good. What's your deal buddy?"

"I was arrested after the humans found out I led an attack on an outpost and a couple convoys. I'm a demolition expert and they found my explosives primed and ready to denote with 30 seconds left," the prisoner said.

"Oh that's not bad, we could actually use that. Was this recent?" Ambrotos read his file. "Yea, I don't remember this bombing. What was the outpost's name?

"Growing Buds Daycare."

Ambrotos rolled his eyes and head and looked at me with a straight face.

"Yea, I know, I know. Next one," I said as I walked away.

We continued for another half hour interviewing and freeing dozens of prisoners when we finally got to our guy, a middle aged human named Theodore. He looked up from his bunk and instantly recognized me. He spoke with low drawl, like the mountain people. But it was hard to place exactly where. But it had a rolling twang to it.

"Well I'll be, if it ain't public enemy number one. Nice to meet ya." He rubbed his scraggly beard as he spoke and tipped his brown cowboy hat when he finished.

I scrunched my face and asked, "you know me?"

"I do. I've heard a couple of stories. I ain't regime or Hurricane, so I reckon this outta be a treat."

"We need your help. We're going to take down Havi's ship and need to break through his shields."

He chuckled. "And why would I do that?"

Ambrotos made obnoxious noises and gestures. I ignored him and rolled my eyes.

"Because it ends the regime's grasp on everyone," Khan said. "With your aid, we can free thousands. We'd be able to carve out a part of the world where we can live until the next event."

"Afraids my war and weapon days are over. I ain't got an egg in this balaya."

"The hell is a balaya?" Ambrostos asked.

"We all have 'an egg in this balaya'," I said. "You don't care that Havi is hurting everyone out there?"

"Oh I do, but I'm just one man. Not sure what chu think one voice is gonna do against a raging storm. I'm mountain folk, and you expect me go against people with: nukes, neutron bombs, cobalt bombs, DNA and RNA bombs and more. I ain't fixin to leave my little cell and go into that. I'd rather sit here and finish my sudoku puzzle if it's all the same to you."

"He kinda has a point. How much is room and board here?" Ambrotos asked.

"Ambrotos, hush. Mountain folk or not, you were wrongly imprisoned. I want to make those who did it pay," I said. "They *deserve* to pay."

He smirked and said, "no thanks. Earth had a thing about an eye for an eye, and it sounds like that's what you want. Yon't want justice for those oppressed by the regime, you want retribution. And Ion't want any of that. I just want to enjoy my days. Fraid I'm retired."

"You **will** help us." I balled my fist and clenched my teeth.

He chuckled and said, "y'all be easy now."

Ambrotos sighed.

"I gotta admit, I agree with you," he said. "But, you could help us build something better. I skimmed some of your files and read about how you helped with the Scyra project, and the Osmium Coast's artificial seasons and weather. You also were on the end of the Kunlun project. You've helped all these other groups, but also indirectly helped the regime as well."

"Those were my family's work, I just helped interpret most of it. I also ain't mean to get others hurt by building. I just wanted to help."

"Well could help chimeras this time, help us build a home where we're safe, free of fighting and free from being a weapon. Hell, we already *had* a home, but that was taken from us. I get there's a lot going on, and you might not be on the whole kill Havi and everyone around him crash, but I am pro chimera survival and no more fighting. Killing Havi is how we get there, that's how we get to be left alone."

"Fair points, but these weapons are still leagues and miles from what I'm comfortable with. Not sure where I fit in all this."

"We need help designing systems that keep us out of harm's way, and keeps the regime at bay. And I think honestly, you know that. There's enough land and resources for all of us, we just don't want to play their game anymore and kill for it."

He stared at us for a moment and then said, "alright, I'll do it."

I squinted and asked, "what's the catch?"

"None, I just don't wanna be part of destruction, seen too many hurt round my holler. So, I can help protect your people and others wanting peace, but I ain't making any weapons. Second I reckon you'll kill or harm an innocent, I'll gut ya like a halibut."

"Alrighty, don't know what any of those words mean." I unlocked his cell.

Khan nodded and shook his hand. Theodore grabbed a couple of his things and said, "before we go, the prison file claims that there should be one more prisoner."

"You can't free him!" Exclaimed one of the guards. "He's the actual leader of Hurricane, not the one that died that day with the primarch."

Ambrotos smiled and said, "oh the jokes just write themselves."

"Yes, the reporter interviewed them first and then me," said Theodore.

We all froze.

"Reporter?" I asked. "How long ago was this?"

"12 minutes 'fore y'all showed up."

I grabbed a guard and shoved them against the wall. "You guys said you didn't sound any alarms. I'm guessing warning the reporter with access to the outside world wasn't part of that?"

"She's been in the control room this whole time!" The guard said. "We didn't want to give her hiding spot away." The guard tried to push me away, but wasn't *nearly* strong enough.

I growled and let him go. "We need to leave. Time for the escape plan."

"Do you have mechs here?" Khan asked.

"Yes, but once... Hurricane took over, we turned them all off," the guard I shoved said.

"We continue with the plan as normal," said Khan. "Our timeline has just been advanced. You two get to the reporter, I will plant the charges."

"Charges? You're gonna blow this place up?" Theodore asked.

"Yes," said Khan. "This place symbolizes stolen liberties, a relic of a soon forgotten time that doesn't need to be part of our future. It has to go but that's why we freed almost everyone."

I turned my attention to the guards and said, "get out of here."

"You're letting us go?"

"You guys aren't my enemy, but my enemy is coming. Get lost before they show up. Ambrotos, ready?" He nodded.

We raced off as fast as we could through the prison and now that I had my aegis on, I didn't need to rely on grappling outside of a building. Despite the size of the prison, we made it to the control room within minutes. I banged on the door as soon as we arrived.

"Open the door, we know you're inside," I said.

Ambrotos shook his head, sighed and said, "wasted knock knock joke but whatever."

"Who am I speaking to?" The woman asked from the other side of the door.

"My name is Mandy, I'm a chimera. You're in dan–"

The metal door unlocked and swung open. Standing before us, was an excited human reporter fixing her hair and her skirt. Behind her, was a camera orb. Ambrotos and I looked at each other for a moment, and then back to her as she re-applied her lip gloss.

"I was told you had a swarthy skin tone." She poked my arm as she said it.

I pulled my arm away from her and said, "that was rude."

"And look at that hair! Are you rehoming ferrets?"

"I... I don't know what a ferret is but I don't like it."

"Your hair's like a bush, no, a shrubbery. Just coiling everywhere. Oh! Your hair must be what the snake in a chimera is." She walked around me with the camera orb hovering around her. "You have thick thighs, I guess lions have strong legs. Maybe more hippo..."

"**Hey**! That's enough."

"Those teeth must be the goat." I covered my mouth and Ambrotos broke out into laughter. "Are you ready for your interview?"

"Interview?" I asked while still covering my mouth.

"You're the one upsetting Admiral Havi, right? Slowly brewing a revolution against the regime right? Or is that a different chimera named Mandy? I don't think anyone knows exactly how many of you are there."

"None of your business. And yes I'm the only chimera named Mandy, but I don't want to be interviewed."

"And I didn't want braces as a kid. I'm not giving up the scoop of the **century**, are you crazy? And who are you?" She turned to Ambrotos.

He threw his hands up. "Just a heckler."

"Well move, we're going to start recording soon. Once it goes through its edits, it'll be broadcasted on every station my towers can reach. Get ready."

Ambrotos stepped back and snickered. She stood in front of me as a countdown appeared on her camera orb. She did some last minute adjustments and prepared her smile.

I protested, "I'm not comfortable being–"

"Good morning all the way from your favorite eastern station! You know me as Victoria Valio, and I bring the citizens of the planet Kazar an important guest. Please, give a warm welcome to the one and only, Voidborn, Mandy the chimera." The camera turned to me. I'm not sure if I ever blushed before, but this probably would be the one time in my life I did. "Today, Mandy and friends, just minutes ago mind you, conducted a prison break freeing *multiple* enemies of the state. Now Mandy, what do you hope to accomplish by releasing criminals?"

"Some were wrongly imprisoned by the humans you guys let lead you… the same ones that I used to let lead me."

"Then why not let them go through the appeal process? Why go full vigilante?"

"The appeal process? You mean the process that the regime is in charge of? The process could easily take a decade for some cases, assuming they even go through the proper channels. The primarch had an archaic system where he granted people the freedom of illusion. The regime owns the color blue and then asks people to choose between cyan and aquamarine. It divides people where they start dumb arguments and silly infighting; and these are distractions. Your choices didn't vanish, they were never there. Havi's a threat to **all** of us, always was."

"Admiral Havi isn't the one who killed a high ranking official. And you are in leagues with mercenaries, and now the convicts you freed."

I scoffed. "Havi *has* killed people, they're just never as important as politicians and military members I guess. Shows you who we place value on in our society. And all regime I've killed, have themselves taken lives and hurt people in my life. And my allies aren't all mercenaries…"

"Maybe not all of them, but the optics are bad. For some, it looks as if you killed Hurricane's leader and then replaced her. Is there any truth to this?"

"No, she was just their scapegoat, their poster child. They have a shadow leader that's here and we have aligned goals, for now."

"But I thought chimeras were here to serve humans, why would one person break off decades of partnership? Also, why'd you let your new allies blow up Elysium?"

"I blew it up." Her mouth dropped. "And I don't think I regret it if I'm being honest. There are no 'accidental villains', so the leaders of these ships aren't just accidently murderers. They've been terrorizing kazamites and chimeras, looking down on us and making us believe that they're gods. And let's say that they are actual gods, then that makes chimeras titans cause we've killed dozens of you since this has started."

"So it's every human against kazamites and chimeras? Hardly seems fair."

"I've yet to meet someone that thinks life is fair. In fact, I think life has always been unfair, maybe that's how we know it's real. And it's not us versus them, kazamites treat chimeras bad too, they're just more scared of us than humans. And it's not every human or every kazamite, but it's a lot of them. But it doesn't have to stay this way, it **won't** stay this way."

"Many have associated you with the symbol of revolution. Do you have any words for those who align with you? Or at least don't align with Admiral Havi?

"For everyone hiding, living in fear under the current regime, we don't have to anymore. We don't have to be slaves, and only be reactive to crises. Killing Oceana was a proactive move, I shot them down before they killed innocents and planned on obliterating a lot more. I just want to be left alone, and the regime doesn't seem to get the message."

"And if Havi calls for peace?"

I scoffed. "If the regime wants peace, they can have it. Surrender. Do you hear me senators, counselors, proconsul and Havi? Surrender. But they won't, they hate us. They hate us for dumb reasons, about what we can do. Because we were created to be a servient race, but I'm done. No… **we're** done. So, to every human who hates kazamites and chimeras, to Havi and his lackeys, to everyone in this world and in space or on the moons who unjustly treated people, **we** no longer will be bullied."

"Surely, you understand that simply saying that won't make people suddenly brave. People have families. People are scared of today's regime. And isn't just a bunch of pushovers."

"Times are changing. We don't have to take this anymore and I've killed enough humans to know, you bleed no different than I do. To all of the regime and its sympathizers, I'm the thing hiding in Havi's closet. I'm the thing under his bed that gives him nightmares and sleepless nights. I'm not the bump in the night, I'm the thing that the bump in the night is afraid of, I **HUNT** it."

"Brave and emotional words, but it's not sustainable. This will tire you out, and you can't keep fighting the whole regime."

"Try me."

"You'd fight this fight even from the losing side? Aren't you tired? You look tired."

"I am tired, but not tired of killing the regime. Not tired of killing bullies with extreme prejudice. Tired, but not weak. So if you're tired of being walked on and having your freedom and peace of mind chained, break your chains. Follow me."

There was a long and loud explosion. Ambrotos sternly said, "Mandy, we gotta get out of here. That must've been the charges put on the platform's legs."

The reporter gasped. "**Charges**?"

A series of explosives went off and we all lost our footing.

"Let's head back then," I said to Ambrotos.

"We won't make it in time," he argued. "There's a garage close by with jet skis. You know how to drive one?"

"Why would I know how to drive one?"

"How **dare** I think the girl that has flown a spaceship, not know how to drive a jet ski!"

Ambrotos led the way as we all ran as fast as we could. The reporter, Victoria, was struggling to keep up so I picked her up and ran with her in my arms. Luckily, if you could call it that, the explosives detonated on the floors beneath us. So ,we didn't have to worry about any debris falling on top of us, but the floor caved in every now and then. A couple minutes into running, a wall crumbled as beams fell. By the time we made it to the docking station where the jet skis were, we could feel the prison sinking.

"Mandy," Khan's voice echoed through my NUE and transponder. "I hope this transmission reaches you while you are still breathing."

"Kinda busy."

"You're about to be busier, expected and yet uninvited guests have arrived. We're leaving and going to the city to drop off people. You need to hurry back so we can pick you both up."

"We found another ride, go without us."

"Damn, see that?" Ambrotos pointed to a blast door. "That's keeping us from getting out of this place. It's most likely a two person system, so I guess it works out we have you and Mandy." He looked at Victoria. "See that room above us? That's most likely where the controls for the doors are, activate them and then meet back down here. If we get separated while on the water, ping my NUE and we'll link up on shore."

I nodded and rushed up the flight of stairs with Victoria. I tried the door, but it was locked. So I gave it a little nudge, it opened after a loud clunk. Inside were two separate authenticators, just like Ambrotos said. There was a massive control panel with keyholes, where the authenticators were, that most likely opened the blast doors. The control panel had a few other features too, like unlocking the jet skis for one, which we didn't even know were locked. Even though the keys were already in place, we had to bypass the prison's anti-hack system.

"Cricket," I said. "Can you *pretty* please bypass the lock?"

"Pretty please with cherries on top?" He asked.

"Pushing it."

"This will only take a minute."

"I have one last question, for now of course," Victoria said as she walked over to her key. "Aren't you worried? Worried us humans and others will fear you?"

"Good. I want them and everyone who would treat us wrong, to be scared of what I'll do. What the regime has turned me into."

"And you think every chimera will support you? Willingly?"

Before I could answer, there was a loud explosion as a hole ripped through the ceiling. The ceiling caved in in a ball of flame, and fire spread. The beams, the platforms and ceiling all caught fire and shook. Within seconds, everything started to fall apart. Cracks spread across the walls, beams creaked and fell. And to make matters worse, an explosion went off sending debris from the ceiling right into our viewing glass and pierced it. The room immediately went into an emergency lockdown.

As the sunlight breached the inside of the prison, it brought along multiple guests. But only one caught my eye. He descended from the ceiling in his aegis, and landed only a few meters away from Ambrotos with two soldiers landing next to him. His aegis was golden with shoulder pads jutting out with a chimera engraved into the chest piece. His techsuit was a khaki color, but I mean, are we surprised?

"You think they can make an aegis update where there's a 'do not disturb' feature?" Ambrotos said to them.

"Sorry to disturb you, I was under the impression you were committing felonies. I brought some help with me to bring you in," Sibil replied.

"Oh I'm sturbed. Bad taste though, linking with a dude walking around with toilet paper on his boot." Ambrotos motioned to one of the soldiers. The soldier, like an idiot, took his eyes off Ambrotos to look down. As soon as he did, Ambrotos blasted him, sending him flying backwards and falling unconscious. "Be fucking serious. *This* is your hired help?"

"By order of Admiral Havi, you're under arrest," The other soldier said. "You have the right to remain silent."

"And boy oh boy do I lack the ability to. You teamed up with a chimera whose favorite color is khaki. Sorry, I can't take you guys seriously. I'm a little confused though. Sibil, you're on the wrong side of the battlefield, buddy. Ol chum ol pal. What gives? Thought we were friends."

"Then I hate to break your heart Ambrotos, but–"

"Only ever had one heartbreak, Sibil. Couldn't even say goodbye to her."

"Ah, yes. A sad necessary death for our–"

"I promise you, nobody wants to hear the rest of that sentence. Especially me."

Frustrated with being interrupted, Sibil said, "turn yourself in, Ambrotos. Mandy has clearly gotten into your head." He shot me a look. "This only ends in death, and death is no life."

"Read that on a fortune cookie? The fuck does that mean? And fire is no water," Ambrotos said mockingly. "Ya douche."

"I've heard about you, chimera," the soldier stepped forward. "Always something smart to say, huh? We have orders to bring you in dead or alive, whichever is easier. What smartass comment do you have to say for that?"

"Gubernatorial."

"**Enough**. You need to surrender Ambrotos, there's no need for us to fight. We know Mandy killed all of those people," said Sibil. "Help us and turn in Mandy, Khan and everyone involved. You are problematic, but you're not a traitor."

"You're right for once, *I'm* not the traitor."

"Help me, brother."

Ambrotos scoffed, and then laughed. "Ugh, you linger like a bad joke. Sibil, you make it *so* easy to dislike you. I don't support what Mandy did, but I'm definitely not your 'brother'. Thigh-meat is the only chimera I consider a brother, and he and Eleanor are safe from you. And don't you dare say you're Mandy's brother again. She only has one."

"Nic?"

"Copernicus."

"Excuse me?"

"Copernicus. His friends and loved ones get to call him Nic. You can call him Copernicus. I'm not sure what you hope to gain here, Sibil. I'm game to kill Havi and maybe Callum. Leave one wolf alive and the sheep are never safe, ya know?" Sibil fidgeted uncomfortably. "Remember when you said that to Chevalier when he got the boot? Kicked out of our *own* home, and then we **lost** our home? I remember, he's more my brother than you."

"How's that?"

"We both were experimented on and became outcasts. Weird how you're the only outcast I ever met that I don't get along with. Says something about the collar and leash you wear."

The soldier scoffed and then spat at Ambrotos.

"That's enough!" He yelled as he rushed Ambrotos. He tried to fight him, but was quickly flipped on his ass. He jumped up and jumped back and raised his gun.

Ambrotos raised his hands and said, "wait wait wait! What animal said 'quack' again?"

The soldier, confused, said, "duck?"

Ambrotos blasted him, sending him into a wall, knocking him out.

Sibil closed his eyes and shook his head. "Now Ambrotos, was that necessary?"

"What are you doing Sibil? Why are you spining us? You're supposed to be on *our* side."

"I'm the only one trying to protect our people, while you and Mandy are being foolish and getting our people killed and detained! Have you both forgotten that we have a duty to humans?"

"I don't have a duty to shit. They made us child soldiers and they even made their *own* people child soldiers! This bion I met told me how they were forced to sniff glue to ward off hunger and tricked them into fasting. But not to be healthy, but to learn to survive with less. And honestly, you and the regime just rub me wrong like a genie lamp. How do you sleep with yourself?"

"I sleep knowing I've done my part, and paid my dues for my people. If you had any sense of loyalty and duty, you'd understand! But I assume it is a hard concept for someone so childish and selfish as you. Do you think if you were in my shoes, you could outdo me? What could you offer? What currency do you have for our people?"

"I wouldn't even give you a wooden nickel dude. Cry me a river, your position is supposed to be you fighting *for* chimera rights.

"And when chimeras are wrong, like now?"

"Then we handle it ourselves. No way you're gonna convince me leaving Chevalier near a volcano was right. He's served the regime just as hard as you have."

"I've done and still do my best, do you know how many times I've been kept awake? Stressed and looking out at the city hoping you all are ok and have served nicely?"

"Ugh, I hate you. You're just so beat up-able."

Sibil scoffed and said, "you can't win, I'd kill you."

"Haven't you heard? I'm immortal."

Sibil didn't waste any time, as soon as Ambrotos finished talking, Sibil drew his pistol. It was his usual annoying stun gun, it worked on humans, kazamites and chimeras. If he got Ambrotos with it, he'd stun and numb the area for about 30 seconds. But Ambrotos knew how to deal with Sibil and his gun, and was used to being numbed.

Ambrotos dashed forward, avoiding being hit by Sibil's gun. Ambrotos closed the distance between them and threw a flying knee at Sibil, but was too slow. Sibil shot his leg but that didn't stop him. Ambrotos maintained his momentum, and blasted the ground with his wrist gauntlets. He flipped into an axe kick and knocked the gun out of Sibil's hand. Before Sibil could react, Ambrotos blasted him, and sent him flying backwards several meters.

Sibil growled as he stood up, and dashed towards Ambrotos while screaming. Ambrotos *speared* him, and they both grappled on the ground. I watched in awe as they threw punch after punch without holding back. Sibil did his best to put Ambrotos in different submissions, but it wasn't working. Ambrotos was buying time until he could feel his leg again. As soon as Sibil got a good grip on one arm, Ambrotos kneed him in the face. Sibil yelped in pain and wiped the blood from his face. They both stood back up and took a few steps back and drew their knives.

"This is ridiculous," yelled Sibil. "We need to be **UNIFYING** and you're hindering the growth and progress of our people!"

"You've clearly lost the plot if you think servitude is 'progress'."

"You're an **insufferable**, selfish, short sighted, antagonizing **child**!"

"Read the script dude, nobody wants to hear you yap."

They rushed at each other with their knives. They went so fast, I struggled keeping track of their hands and knives. The only way I tracked their blades was by tiny sparks. And in between the sparks, they threw punches and kicks. Sibil tried to slice Ambrotos' throat, but that only pissed him off. He smacked the knife out of Sibil's hand and then kicked him into a wall. He hit the wall so hard, a part of the ceiling fell. They both rolled out of the way, but didn't stop fighting. They fought for minutes, uncaring of the explosions and spreading fire.

They only stopped when an engulfed metal railing blasted out of the wall from the ceiling. Ambrotos tackled Sibil to save him from getting killed by it, but all that did was fuck Ambrotos. The hot metal scraped Ambroto's head, neck, back and tore his jacket. He let out a ghastly scream as he hit the ground. Sibil, like the snake he was, jumped to his feet and capitalized on Ambrotos' injury. He rushed him with his knife drawn and slashed at his legs and arms to the point Ambrotos fell to one knee as the fire spread behind him.

With a smile, Sibil walked away. He picked his gun back up and caught his breath.

He shook his head at Ambrotos and said, "we could make a better world for chimeras. One without all of this death, one where we are free. We just need to be patient, but you botched it. I needed you renegades to just behave and weather the storm. I blame Eskander for being the first to openly disobey me."

"Thigh-meat? All he did was follow orders until you disrespected him and me. Threatening me with doctor visits and threatening him with going to the moons."

"He openly spoke out against **me** and the regime! He undermined my authority and position. He should've just kept quiet while I worked on a better tomorrow."

"Guess we finally found the snake in the chimera..."

"There are days, and there are days."

"Oh man, if only Lissax heard that. Sibil, you're an idiot because none of those 'days' has it ever felt like you were on our side. I mean, you cut me while I was protecting you." Ambrotos chuckled as he said it.

Sibil frowned and shook his head. "I've said it before, but this is no life to live."

"And neither is this," Ambrotos tried to stand on his feet but fell.

I snapped out of it, and turned my attention to the door. Cricket tried every work around he could to open it from his side. And I pushed, punched, kicked and pulled on my side.

"Ambrotos," said Sibil. "A smart man would surrender." He watched Ambrotos fight to get to his feet.

"Yea… they would, wouldn't they?"

Ambrotos charged at Sibil, but not as swiftly as before. He slower, a lot slower. And he telegraphed almost all of his attacks. He tried not to, but it was just too obvious. Ambrotos threw a punch, but Sibil caught it… then dislocated his arm. Ambrotos screamed, but didn't stop fighting. He used the spreading fire to his advantage, hoping to make Sibil slip up. He pushed him deeper into the smoke and fire, blinding Sibil, but it just wasn't enough.

Ambrotos was just too tired.

Sibil lunged forward and kneed him in his stomach and then punched him in the back of his head. He hit the ground, and his head bounced off of the floor. Sibil bent over and picked up Ambrotos' knife and shook his head.

"You are making a **BIG** mistake!" Sibil screamed. "**I** am the good guy! I'm helping maintain peace, order and stability! The humans traveled what, how many parsecs away from Sol? They have discovered science that seems like magic; they're basically *gods* and you want to what? Rock the boat? Disturb the system we have and anger the gods?"

"They aren't gods," Ambrotos croaked. "We literally are stronger than them."

"**Fine**! Then bears! You want to poke the bears, and for **what**? What happens next? Where do we go after you kill the humans here? They can send **MORE**! You **IDIOT**! I'm the *only* chimera who can help us stay in their good graces and you betray me and your people for **WHAT**?" Ambrotos stared at him. "**Answer me!**"

"Cricket said once, 'the caged bird sings with a fearful trill' and I never got it. I guess I do now. You're like an ant thanking the boot for shade."

"You all shouldn't even **have** Cricket! You, Mandy and Historia have played this stupid rebel game and you have cost us **decades** of trust! Because of that I had to force my hand and trap **DOZENS** of our people and have them arrested and killed! Because of **YOU** and **HER**! **YOU MADE ME DO THIS!**"

Ambrotos coughed and then smiled. "What do you call a clown that doesn't get that they're the joke?"

"**No** more jokes. I could drone on and on about how we could make a better world. How in a little over a century, we'd be seen as second class citizens. But you wouldn't listen, would you?"

"Must've missed what I said about the last monologuer." Ambrotos stood to his feet and coughed out more blood.

Ambrotos swayed back and forth, struggling to keep his balance. If his injuries weren't enough, the spreading smoke made him cough and choke. With his dislocated arm, Ambrotos dashed towards Sibil and let out a loud battle cry. Sibil stabbed Ambrotos with both knives from their earlier fight in one single motion. He staggered backwards, touching both knives. He tried to pull the one out from over his heart, but winced. Then he tried to pull out the other over one of his lungs, but winced again.

Ambrotos stood for a moment in shock, and then fell to the ground. Sibil shook his head and screamed at him. Ambrotos tried to stand back up, but he fell back to his knees. I could hear his breathing go from raspy, to wet, as blood filled his lungs. He coughed, trying to clear his lungs. But it didn't work. He leaned over on all fours coughing and making a wet phlegmy sound with each breath he took.

Sibil looked at him and said, "you could've been the best chimera out of us all…"

"I already am." Ambrotos fell over to his side and went limp.

"Ambrotos…" I said as I looked down at his body.

Sibil screamed. "Do you see this? Bear witness Mandy! His blood is on **YOUR** hands! This is **all** your fault! Stop hiding up there!" He screamed at the top of his lungs. "You are dividing our family, for selfish reasons!"

"Please tell me you have a plan," Victoria said. "Can't you break through the window?"

"No." I walked closer to the viewing glass. "I'm going to kill you," I mumbled as I stared down at Sibil.

"What aren't you understanding? We help maintain order, loyalty, and discipline and in return, we get to live. Admiral Havi is ushering in a newer age where we can display loyalty **proudly!** And those who don't support the regime, are chaos walkers. Say what you will but Havi as a primarch is lightyears from Leopold! Why would we want dissenters amongst us in our new utopia? Renegade chimeras like you, are stopping chimera progress! Their existence counters our own! **STOP RESISTING AND SUBMIT**!" He was louder than the cackling fire.

"I was able to request backup, I'm sorry it wasn't fast enough," Cricket chirped.

The wall to the outside blasted open, and in jumped Khan. The backdraft down there must've been immense, because even Sibil was having trouble keeping his bearings. Khan took inventory of the scene and saw Ambrotos' body on the ground and Sibil standing not too far from it. He then looked up and saw where Victoria and I were.

"And you are the rumored Khan I assume? A human so scared, he hides his face like a vigilante. A vigilante is just another word for 'criminal' and there is no place for criminals in this new age." Sibil walked towards Khan. "It is my duty to bring order and enforce loyalty to the regime!"

Sibil rushed over to Khan and reached out to grab him. Khan sucked his teeth and said, "please."

Khan kicked him in his chest so hard, he hurled backwards over 40 feet. Sibil skipped across the ground like a stone, and crashed into a wall and cracked it. He groaned as he fell to the ground. Khan took a step towards him, but the new cracked wall was the straw on the kreglin's back. The ground tore open between the two of them, destabilizing the entire platform. Khan watched, as Ambrotos' body slid across the ground and fell through the opening and into the water below.

Why didn't Khan save him? Khan could've *easily* saved him, he's not slow. He didn't even try. I closed my eyes tightly fighting back tears and balled my fist.

"Tell me Sibil, does it hurt? Losing people and victories you never truly had, does it hurt? To unravel in the face of actual defeat and actual threats, how does it feel? You mistook your victory over Lissax as something noteworthy, it created precedence. It created false data, since I taught her everything she knew." He drew the same type of rifle that was used against Historia and me so many months ago. He aimed it at me and fired. The blast cracked the window, which meant I could break it. "This chapter of your life, Sibil, is called 'luck'. You're lucky Ambrotos held back, because we both know he should be here. I'd avenge him, but from the look of it, your life isn't mine to take. I'm sure the next chapter of your life is called 'finale.'" He turned his back to the ship and jumped on it.

"She won't forgive you!" Sibil yelled. "I saw **it**!"

"No Sibil, she won't forgive *you*."

I punched the glass, shattering it, and grabbed Victoria. I picked her up and jumped down, and caused more tears and rifts. I raced over to the ship and did my best to keep us from falling below. I jumped onto the ship and put her down and turned to run back inside, but Khan grabbed my shoulder.

"Not here," he said.

"I'm listening." My eyes locked on Sibil as he struggled to stand.

"The nearby settlement. There is no victory to be had here, but there *is* victory to be had."

"Connect me to his comms, Cricket." He chirped to show it was done. "Come and get me." I turned my tracker on as our ship flew away.

Sibil blamed me for all of our dead family and friends, and I'm not sure if those deaths should be on me. But I know one chimera's death that will.

Chapter 13

PROMETHEUS & VOIDBORN

The sun was setting by the time that we arrived to the town of Karack. This time of year, this prefecture was known for its storms during the dead of winter. Hell, the entire province was known for its storms, but this small part was just above uninhabitable. It didn't help that the storm season lasted for over a month either. And to add salt to injury, the locals named their island Dieman's island. And yet, people stayed.

This place was riddled with fast biting winds, a raging sea and tornadoes. The area also had a surplus of nitrogen, so icicles formed in the tornadoes. The tornadoes could reach up to 400 mph with the average ones being just over 200. They'd rage hell and then drift out into the ocean and form water spouts of ice and water, and then come back to land and wreak twice the havoc.

Cricket told me that many lived here because of the rhodium mines and caves. Rhodium was one of the metals used to make NUEs, and other regime gear. He also warned me to pay attention to signs of tornados forming. He said that the air will grow cold and still, the wind would die down, and then the dreaded funnel would form in the clouds. Normally, the locals stayed indoors and underground in their bunkers during the storm, but this time was different. This time, there were riots in the streets. People flipped over cars, threw molotov cocktails, and tagged walls and buildings. Right before we landed, I got a glimpse of one of the taggers mid work.

"A chimera," said Khan. "It's safe to assume they follow your escapades this far from civilization."

"I didn't ask for this."

"Seldom people do."

Peacekeepers did their best to maintain order as the city fell into chaos, but they could only do so much. Some of the peacekeepers were regime, and others were contractors hired by the regime. They fought the mobs with: batons, tear gas, smoke grenades, sound weapons, rubber bullets, pepper spray, and even regular bullets. But even with all of that, they were struggling to just keep rioters at bay.

"Cricket, drop us off at that building over there," I said. "The tall one."

"That building is already under peacekeeper control," he chirped. "The hospital is a more viable option."

"What? No people–"

"Would be ok. The systems inside of the hospital are automated, I could hijack their systems to make them more efficient. I could treat everyone that is injured while aiding you. And the hospital is near the control grid, their *fortified* control grid."

"No brainer?"

"No brainer."

We went with his choice, but light furries had already begun to form. The rooftops were covered in a thin sheet, and the wind was raging.

We jumped out into an alley, and hid amongst the chaos for a solid three minutes before we were recognized. Without a second thought, peacekeepers rushed me with their weapons drawn, a mistake on their part. They supported Havi, so I gave them what Havi deserved. By the time we made it halfway to the hospital, I had already killed well over a dozen plus peacekeepers.

All I kept thinking was, how life used to be so simple. I went from being part of the regime, to their main headache. I always did my best not to kill people, and now I didn't think anything of it. At first, I was indifferent. Then I was annoyed, as if the regime and their supporters were just bugs buzzing around and making too much noise. But when you killed bugs, you at least felt relief. And all I felt was empty. Now I was just... going through the motions. I wondered if somewhere down the line, I became more like Havi and Trogz without realizing it.

No... no that can't be right. The regime created generational trauma, and Havi is now the head of the snake. If people want to side with him, then they can burn with him. Why should the good guys play by the rules when the bad guys don't? No more... I won't be a victim any more. Never again.

"For those just tuning in, I am Victoria Valio coming to you live in the middle of a storm from your favorite eastern station! Citizens of Kazar, we are on the precipice of history! We have: looters, grand larceny, armed peacekeepers, grand arsonist, rioters, escaped prisoners, spray painters, car jackers, terrorists, treasonist citizens who have defected to Mandy's side and in the middle of it all, Mandy who is **unfazed** as a storm approaches!" The camera pointed towards the ocean. "We can see several waterspouts already formed while others are starting to form! I have never seen anything like this! Mandy, words?"

"Put your helmet on." A peace keeper on a hoverbike sped towards us to escape the chaos, but I stopped them. I clotheslined him, sending him and his bike going in different directions. I grabbed his helmet and tossed it to Victoria. "We're taking their capitol building."

"Mandy," Cricket chirped. "That was not my suggestion."

"No more symbols of oppression. Their leaders are regime sympathizers."

We jumped on the bike and sped off towards the capitol building. Thankfully, it was only five minutes away from the hospital so it wasn't out of the way. The only issue was the small pockets of people in the streets. Khan and the others left me to my vices and joined in on the chaos in their own ways. Some aided the rioters, some jumped the peacekeepers, and some stayed on the ship. The only one who stayed with me was Victoria. Her floating camera zoomed around us and took videos and pictures from different angles with the chaos as the backdrop. I'm not sure how, but it avoided getting hit by thrown rocks, bricks and people.

"Mandy, I insist you listen to reason," my conscious chirped. "What are you planning and how do you think it makes sense?"

"Will you shut up?"

"Most certainly not. I'm charged with being the voice of reason, since you've been lacking it lately. If I had arms, I'd knock sense into you."

I groaned and said, "and if you had legs you wouldn't stand for this?"

"Ah, so you *do* have sense. Just not common." I groaned again at him.

"What happens if we get caught by Sibil and his men?" Victoria asked.

"We'll be charged with treason."

"Oh… I think we should go faster then because they're chasing us."

"What?" I turned around to see hoverbikes chasing us. "Shit."

"Good thing we don't have your location pinging," Cricket chimed in. He's worse than the chaos I swear.

A hoverbike pulled up next to us on our right side, and then one pulled up on our left. They motioned for us to pull over while the camera orb circled all of us. I sped up and ignored them, but of course they sped up too and moved in closer on our sides. They motioned again for us to pull over. I ignored them again until they got within a couple feet of us which made the next part easy. I kicked the front of the left rider's hoverbike ruining his balance, and he immediately flipped over and crashed. The rider on our right drew out a collapsible baton and swung at us. Victoria gasped but I caught the baton before it hit her. I snatched it out of their hand and gave it to Victoria and told her to swing it at him. She, to my surprise, didn't need much convincing. She swung it and hit the guy and went for a second swing but he caught it. Good. I kicked the shit out of his entire bike, sending him flying into a wall.

"Is it always this exciting and gives you a high dose of anxiety?" She asked.

"Not when you have Cricket in your ears all the time."

"Chimeras can hear insects?"

We pulled into the capitol building and were greeted by roughly 20 armed peacekeepers. One of them stepped forward armed with a pump shotgun.

"You are in violation of... I can't name how many laws. Turn yourself in and stand down."

"What's your name?" I asked the peacekeeper as I stepped off the bike.

"Casey."

"Casey, are you willing to die for the people in that building?" I walked towards him.

"Nobody has to die."

"Wrong, someone does. You just need to decide who it'll be." I paused and looked at the other peacekeepers. "And how many it'll be. Take your men, and walk away, Casey."

"You don't scare me..."

"Wasn't asking." I reached out and crushed the barrel of his shotgun with one hand. "The only ones you're hurting are your loved ones. Move."

"And how would our loved ones feel knowing we don't have a backbone?"

"Dunno, but you'd be alive to ask them. I'm sure they'd be happy you made it home and didn't die for something stupid."

He didn't budge at first but he then tossed his shotgun to the side and he and the other peacekeepers let us pass. We entered the building and checked every hall looking for guards hiding. The halls were almost completely empty, the only thing in them were a couple cleaning mechs sweeping. After I was satisfied, we went to the chamber doors where they were in session; discussing the chimera problem no doubt.

"Wait, you don't plan on killing them do you?" Victoria asked.

"Depends on them."

"But what if they're only following orders from Havi?"

"We're giving freebies to murderers cause they are obedient? Blind loyalty isn't loyalty, it's obedience."

I pushed the doors open to a room full of people. There was a mixture of humans and kazamites of different ages. The panel representing the island's governing body was: two kazamites, two humans, and a chairman or chairwoman in this instance, and they were always human. The chairwoman was a middle-aged human wearing a pink suit. She jumped to her feet with a scowl and stared at me.

"**Excuse** you, we are in session," she shrieked.

"You must be the chairwoman. I'm Mandy, and I have a request."

"Then go through the proper channels."

I walked down the stairs towards the board and said, "I'm here now."

"You will **not** intimidate us!" She said firmly.

"Seems like I am. There is a titan coming, the titan of schemes and planning. I want you to make him stand down. Your governing body has the power to make him and his men leave."

"We will do no such thing! If you're referring to Sibil, we want him and his men here. It's **you**, who we don't want. We are all Admiral Havi supporters and you should be ashamed of yourself."

"You guys have looters in your streets cause you made prisons for profit and I should be ashamed? Look, Sibil will start a fire bright enough for Havi to see from low orbit. That means that your people are in danger."

"Prometheus brought fire to help humans, and we turned out **fine**. And we don't need a lecture from you on reformation and our prisons. Whatever Sibil does as long as we are ok, is collateral." The kazamites shifted in their seats.

"I don't think you understand, this is a courtesy. I'm–"

"No, **YOU** don't understand! You spread like cancer and have cost us thousands! Your actions have encouraged a generation of chaos walkers! Us mothers can't even keep your kind out of our homes with those darn cards from that card game! You have people speaking out against us and challenging our way of life! You are **VILE**! You represent the **WORST** parts of human DNA and I see why your leader was killed by Admiral Havi!"

She barely finished her sentence before I jumped over the bench and had my fingers wrapped around her throat. I tightened my grip and raised her into the air.

"So brave in the face of kindness," I said. "Even now, I keep trying to say 'not *all* humans' but I keep running into *those* humans."

"I demand you release me," she croaked.

I let her go. She plopped into her chair, holding her throat and gasping.

"You anim–" she saw the look in my eyes and stopped.

I leaned down into her face and said, "you're lucky *her* favorite color was pink." I looked at the others in the room. "Tell Prometheus and his men that if they stay longer than half an hour, it's open season on every human that is a Havi sympathizer."

"That's absurd!"

"You're on the thinnest ice in fucking history lady, **hush**. All of you guys could have written laws to make life easier for everyone, but instead you fattened your pockets and boosted your careers while your home fell apart." The room was filled with gasps and murmurs. "And for the kazamites who didn't speak up, especially you two on the board, shame on you."

"It's easy for you to say," one of the kazamites said. "It's easy to be brave and fearless when you're physically strong."

"Bravery is just doing something while scared, strength has nothing to do with it. You're just a coward." I hopped off the table and walked past Victoria to the door. "Come on Victoria, *someone* has to protect this city, and it's clearly not gonna be them."

We walked outside to see the peacekeepers all with their helmets off; half of them were kazamites. As Victoria and I approached them, they split open and let us walk through them. Casey stepped forward and pointed to a speaker outside the building, they must've heard everything I said. He put his index and middle finger on his lips where his canine teeth were and nodded. We hopped on the bike and as Victoria put her helmet on, the other peacekeepers copied Casey and stared at me. Victoria's camera orb circled around all of us and trailed behind as we sped off.

"So, why is he called 'Prometheus'?" Victoria asked.

"When we were younger, Historia and I made a joke about him. We said everything that he touched, burned. How he sided with humans and brought them 'fire' because he related more. And the nickname stuck."

"Who is this Historia I keep hearing about?"

"The best part of me. Once inside, get to safety," I said to Victoria as we drove.

"I plan on it."

It took some effort, but we made it to the control room without any issues. It was pretty boring, the only defining trait was the archaic control panel. Cricket was able to hijack the system and had control of the entire city's power grid. He could control: their ATMs, mechs, certain doors and most importantly, everything in the hospital.

"So, Cricket is a guy?" She asked.

"Cricket, you can speak up," I said.

"Ah, it's nice to be heard," Cricket said through the speakers. "Not every woman is nice to me, some treat me like I'm bodiless." I groaned as he spoke.

"Where is Sibil?" I asked Cricket.

"Close, he is alone. What is the plan?"

"I fight him on the roof and then kill him."

"The storm is about to hit its peak; I highly advise against this Mandy," Cricket argued.

"Then I die and you can join Victoria." I opened the door of the control room. "I'll be fine Cricket, just focus on the patients in the hospital. And putting out the literal fires across the city."

"Wait," Victoria rushed over to me with her camera orb in tow. "Do you have any last words if you die?"

"Not really."

"Well we need something so make something up."

"Uh…" I thought for a moment. "No more chains."

And with that, I went to the roof. I looked over the city and watched as cleaning mechs piloted by Cricket put out fires, and as peacekeepers continued clashing with rioters. I sat on the roof and waited for Sibil as the storm picked up. By the time he showed up, over half of the city was covered in a sheet of white. Tornadoes spiraled through buildings and froze anything and everything in their path. When he arrived, he came alone and with disappointment written all over his face.

"I beat Ambrotos, I can beat you too," he said.

"Ambrotos died because he tried to save you."

"No, he died because he was careless."

"You don't even believe that."

"I believe I should've convinced Alex Trogz to put him in the infirmary and locked the door instead. Threatening him with needles clearly wasn't enough."

"Yea, he told me some people hit below the belt to get the upper hand. He must've meant you."

"You're not an idiot, you know you are outmatched. Do you know how much influence I have here?"

"Yea, about that. There's a cyralune I visited that brought up conscription, was that you?"

"We needed soldiers," he said. "It's easier to mold younger minds. Those outposts and cyralunes still benefit from human technology, so they should pay for regime services."

"Wow, you're really just a piece of shit."

He scoffed. "Just like I said to Ambrotos, surrender. This world you're trying so hard to destroy is our home."

"Stop giving us advice. I don't expect a lobotomite like you to understand our pain."

He sucked his teeth and said, "sticks and stones, Mandy. But I have good forethought, probably the best out of any chimera to ever exist. This hurts me, truly. I'm taken back, by the actions of our people, and disappointed in what I was made to do. That side of me, that part... *this* part of me, I am not proud of. Ambrotos called it out and maybe he was right, but what I have done is **necessary**. Yes, I hate it. I hate it more than anyone else, but it is necessary."

"Did you hate this part of you before Ambrotos called you out? Or after you had a hand in killing our family?"

"That is unfair. As if you're innocent in all of this. Look at your utopia, I mean look!" He motioned to the world. "Dead friends, separated families, riots in streets. You have turned neighborhoods into warzones! *This* is what you have our people fighting and dying for?"

"Funny, when you hunted down other chimeras you didn't see it as 'our people'." I slowly stood to my feet.

"You think this ends with you winning? What do you think you'll gain? What do you think you'll take away from this?"

"Your life."

"Retribution, huh? If *he* couldn't take me, how do **you** plan on doing it?"

"I don't know, but I'm leaving here with something." I drew my black saber.

He drew two tomahawks from behind him. "Last chance, I don't want to have to kill you too."

"Fat chance, traitor."

We ran at each other and threw caution to the wind. This was different from Ambrotos' fight. We didn't taunt each other, we didn't speak, we didn't grunt or groan. The only thing you could hear were our blades clashing over the roar of the wind. With Ambrotos' fight, they tested each other and held back, but with this fight, we intentionally were trying to kill the other person.

He swung his blades as fast and as hard as he could for my throat, no different than I did for his. Sibil and I had never fought before, not even sparred. So our only fight knowledge of each other was from videos or second hand accounts. And now that we finally were here, we both didn't want to slip up. We couldn't afford to slip up.

We fought mercilessly as we slid across the ice covered rooftop. He dodged my attack and threw snow in my eyes. He slashed at my side the second I closed my eyes, but I blocked his attack. With my eyes closed, I pressed him. I slid around him and jumped over him trying to work a better angle. But the ice was the edge he needed because he moved a lot faster than he did with Ambrotos. He slid on his knees and slashed away, he was like a mini tornado.

We fought for five minutes straight, and neither of us made any ground. We eventually backed away from each other to catch our breaths. I took my eyes off of him and watched as a tornado crept dangerously close to us. At this rate, the hospital would be hit.

"Why couldn't you just show loyalty and help keep order?" He yelled. "We had a good thing going for us!"

I shook my head. "Oh Sibil, we used to look up to you."

He screamed and charged. He threw a tomahawk at me. I swatted it away. He threw his second one. I swat it to the ground just as easily as the first and looked down and sighed. I looked back up and only had time to brace. He tackled me into the ground and then tossed me into the direction of the tornado. I felt a slight tug as I got back to my feet.

As we fought, I kept the tornado in my view. It looked as if… it wasn't moving. Every time I glanced at the tornado, Sibil fought harder. At one point, our ears shriveled, which they only do when there was a pressure difference. I tried to say something, but he shoulder checked me off of the roof. I missed the edge, but caught myself a floor down. I groaned and launched myself back onto the roof, feet first. He looked over the edge and I kicked him as hard as I could.

He staggered backwards holding his nose as I shook my head. How idiotic of us to follow orders from someone who spent over half of their career behind a desk.

"Something's wrong, Sibil. Why are our ears pressurizing?"

He threw a knife at me, and missed. What a fucking snake. I dashed forward before he could throw another, and drew my own knife. I cut his hand, and leg before I disarmed him. I elbowed him in his jaw, and watched as he slid towards his tomahawks. I gasped and jumped to the rooftop next to ours, but landed funny. I dropped my sword and tried to roll to my feet.

"ARGHHH!" I screamed and fell down to a knee and held my ankle.

He grabbed one of his tomahawks and jumped over to my rooftop. He took the bait. From a knee, I lunged and tackled him midair. His eyes tripled in size as I speared him through the window of the building we were originally fighting on. We crashed through the window into a lab-like room and attached was a viewing room.

When we landed, I watched and heard his foot snap. He tried to stand up hoping his aegis could stabilize it enough to fight, but that's not how it worked. And he'd *know* that if he ever wore his outside of press releases. He used the wall to support himself as he stood up. Once he got on his feet, he still tried to fight me. I punched him in his face as hard as I possibly could and knocked him on his ass.

"That was for Ambrotos," I said.

He grabbed my leg and tried to pull me down. I shook my head and stepped on his wrist as I made my way to the viewing room. He screamed as I crushed his wrist with my glass covered boot.

"They will glass our world, Mandy! They will raze this one, and terraform another one," he said, as he used the wall to prop himself up. I ignored him. "Spoiled. You're so damn spoiled you don't even realize how good we've had it! You should be thanking me for the amount of sacrifices I've had to make!"

"This room was designed to control fires and kill certain chemicals." I pressed a button and the broken window was reinforced and sealed. I pressed another button and a safety alarm blared as blast doors slowly began to seal the room.

"Mandy, w-what are you doing?"

"I thought Prometheus was the titan of forethought." I pressed another button. A selection of emergency symbols popped up on the panel. I chose the fire one.

The alarms stopped as a few seconds passed by.

"Open the door Mandy. You're going to do something you'll **forever** regret. This isn't you!"

"Khan was right."

"About what?"

"I won't ever forgive you."

He stopped talking and reached for his throat. "Mandy, what did you do?" I watched as he hiccuped, trying to breathe. "Mandy, I can't breathe…"

"Ambrotos can't anymore either. I guess you and him finally have something in common."

"Fine, you won… I surrender. Open the door…"

"I wouldn't use up any more air if I were you."

"Mandy… please…" He began turning pale.

"And those will be the last words anyone alive will ever hear you say. You aren't even worthy enough for me to watch you die. Goodbye Sibil."

I left him there, alone.

I went back to get my saber and joined Cricket and Victoria. When I arrived, she was standoffish.

"You let him die." Her voice trembled as she spoke.

"I don't plan on hurting you or anyone else. Cricket, how are the wounded?"

"We will lose a lot," he said. "But we also will save many. The hospital was a good move. Sibil, was not. It doesn't bode well that you are now in the business of killing chimeras."

"Yea…"

"What now?" Victoria asked me.

"Did you send that message to Havi and Callum, Cricket?"

"Yes, Havi stated that there was no reality where he'd turn himself over to you. Or where you beat the human armada."

"Well, there's no reality we don't shoot down Callum and his people then. We move to the next part of the plan, tell Khan."

"Already done. I have another suggestion," he chirped. "There is a mountain near a coast that we could hide out of. We can set up a refugee base there and it can double as our outpost. People could seek shelter from this war, and we can guide them there. Within two days, I could fully organize a plan and get hundreds of refugees there."

"Good, not everyone should fight. And I think we have had our fill of bloodshed. Is there anything else?"

"Yes. Your biometrics and analytics are off. I have been mapping your brain waves this entire time via your aegis and neurolink and you are suffering from—"

"Not important."

"Chemical imbalances **are** important. These are signs of: depression, PTSD, anxiety attacks, maybe signs of hallucinations and—"

"Enough, Cricket. I promise I will rest. We move forward with this refugee outpost. Enlist people sympathetic to our cause, and hide out there. Once it's up and running, I'll catch my breath and stay out of sight. Me out of sight seems to mean others aren't put at risk."

"And then?" Victoria asked me.

"We build," I said. "Theodore will need time, and we need rest. We have mechs and don't need to send people to keep dying and fighting. We can tactically choose towns and cities where there is oppression and division and help with mechs."

"And you'll force them into your service?"

"No. That's up to them. I think killing Sibil was a big enough statement to show others which side I'm on. Regime players and sympathizers will back off which is good because we don't have enough men or resources to fight anything."

"The storm is passing," chirped Cricket. "There was damage, but most if not all things that were damaged are fixable. The fighting has stopped as well for the most part. Many across the city have expressed wanting to join you, and wanting to change the order of things. They will want to come to this mountain I believe."

"Sure, we'll need to send the invite on our chimera emergency channel too. I don't have a name for the place though, any suggestions?"

"Lycia; it's where the chimera was in mythology. It was also a real place," said Victoria. I looked at her with a puzzled look. "What? I enjoy history and reading. I didn't accidentally fall into my career field. Anyway, words have meaning, and it could be a symbol and stand for something!"

"I like it," Cricket chirped.

"Fine, tell everyone about Lycia," I said. "Tell them we'll forge a new path, together."

"A lot of people are wondering who saved them from the government here. When I finalize my report and share it, should we say it was you, Khan, Hurricane or a combination?" Victoria asked me.

"I don't know, thoughts?"

"Everyone played a role," said Cricket. "However, there is one person who did the heavy lifting and her name is–"

Chapter 14

ELSEWHERE...

Nic, present day...

"Mandy...my sister's name is Mandy." The nurse wrote down my response but furrowed her brow as she wrote it. "She's a chimera," I continued.

"Oh! You had me worried for a second." She chuckled. "Ok last question before the doctor comes in, ok sir? What is your name?"

"Copernicus Hyperion Petrus."

"Good! I'll get Doctor Kordock." The nurse gave me a gentle smile and left me to my thoughts.

I sighed and plopped back into my bed, deflating deeper into it. I had been going through physical therapy for weeks now, and they *still* would not release me despite me getting better. My days were filled with MRI scans, basic motor function exercises, and answering questions.

"When does it end?" I muttered aloud at the thought of staying here for another week.

"Mr. Petrus, good morning, I am Doctor Kordock." A man in light blue scrubs walked in with my nurse trailing behind him. "And how are we feeling today?"

I groaned and said, "another day in paradise."

"Figured as much. I've reviewed your recovery file and have some suggestions to hasten your journey. We can do some more exercises and then some more men from the regime have some questions for you. How does that sound?" He offered me a reassuring smile.

"What do you think?" I spat. "When can I finally leave? I have an uncle who is probably worried sick about me. Well, he's a godfather, but uncle nonetheless. His name is Alexander Trogz, can we *please* reach out to him?" I pleaded with the doctor and even glanced at the nurse in hopes she'd throw me a lifeline.

"I understand your frustration, but these things do take time. As for your uncle…" he fidgeted as he searched for the right words. "I'm sorry, but he was killed in the line of duty. I first met him right after college, he was always kind to me."

"Oh…" In the past when anxious, I played with my hair. But they shaved it all off before my first brain scan, leaving me with a buzz cut. So, I started twirling a corner of my sheet and treated it like my hair. "H-how did he… die?" The word left a sour taste.

"I'm not sure if that's necessary…" he saw the expression on my face and decided to continue. "Records state he died in combat. He lost against a better fighter."

A ball started forming in my throat. Alex lost? *Alex?* Where were his guards? I tried to fight down the growing lump in my throat and stopped messing with my sheet. I couldn't show weakness in front of them, Alex would tell me to get a hold of myself.

"Where is Mandy? My sister?" I croaked the words out dreading the answer.

"The chimera, yes? Studies show that major life events need to be integrated *slowly*, and not shoved down your throat all at once. How about we revisit this after our exercises?"

"I know what I can handle, doctor. You hoarding this information will only stress me out. I need to make sure my sister is ok. The last time I saw her, she was mentally in a bad place."

He inhaled and rubbed the back of his neck. "She is alive. However, she is being hunted just like every other chimera. I can't speak for her mental place, but I do know that she is alive, and well."

My shoulders lowered and the knot in my throat passed. "Good. I bet Ambrotos or someone roped her into trouble. When can I see the body of my uncle? He has to remain cleanly shaven and he is very strict with his military appearance." I paused for a moment then chuckled. "And he has to have his eyebrows plucked, they grow like weeds."

The nurse who was paying attention this whole time, turned her gaze to her clipboard and gave it extra attention. The doctor noticed me looking at her and saw her reaction.

He sighed and said, "it was... a closed casket. The regime already handled everything. And before you ask, his killer is still at large."

"**What**?" I clenched my jaw and jumped to my feet. I opened my mouth to demand what *idiot* let Alex's killer go? But I didn't get a word out before my legs turned into jell-o and I fell over. I grabbed the side of my bed to support me and stop me from toppling over. I tried to control my breathing while staring at my hands on the bed, everything was fuzzy. I glanced down at my hands and watched helpless, as my hands multiplied– no, **everything** multiplied. I closed my eyes panting and tried to lie back down.

The doctor tried to help me as I refocused my vision. "Please, give it some time," he said. "A TBI isn't something you can just brush off. Your neurolink had some issues from my understanding already when you were younger, and now you've had issues again. We don't need anymore brain and head injuries. It sounds like you've had enough head trauma for two lifetimes."

"Do you know?" I opened my eyes to the two blurry Doctor Kordocks standing in front of me. "Who killed Alex?"

"A revolutionary; they aim to change the balance of things with the regime. Unfortunately, Alex was caught in the middle of it. We believe this terrorist group is hoping to attack Admiral Havi, so they will face justice soon enough."

As my focus cleared up, I noticed a tattoo on Doctor Kordock's wrist that was faded and scratched out. It was a covered up Loyalist tattoo.

"You're one of them…"

"Excuse me?" He looked at his wrist and immediately covered it. "**Was**. Who we were isn't who we are. After your father went on trial and told the world and moons all the horrors that the regime did, I questioned myself. And I found answers that made me leave that life behind. I'd rather keep the scars though, consider it a self-punishment."

"Give me a name," I demanded. This time, he didn't offer me a soft smile. His eyes drifted away and refocused on something in the corner of the floor. "Doctor, I need a name." Nothing, just silence. I turned to the nurse who again, lost herself in her clipboard.

But, she eventually gave in. "I'm sorry, but his killer was a chimera…"

"A chimera killed my uncle?" I snickered in disbelief.

I looked back at my doctor still with a smile on my face, waiting for him to tell me the joke was over, but he didn't.

"Ok, I'll bite, who is the chimera?" Even though he was quiet, his face gave me the answer. "No… no… Mandy, what have you done?" I felt woozy again.

"Please, you must have a lot of questions. We'll give you some space and–" I had no patience to hear the rest of the doctor's sentence.

"I invoke Code Four. Alex has… *had* a fleet and soldiers, I want it. And I want a hearing with Havi. I approve the AU process, so bring the paperwork."

His demeanor changed to a more somber one. "That is well within your right to join The Auric Order, but you're not the same man you were before. Your speech, your thinking, hell even your red hair is now auburn. You should retire, you have served your people well enough. Your entire family has served ample. If you begin the AU process, it'd take your body months to adjust to the chemicals and procedure."

"I don't have months, I plan on confronting my sister. Please, get Admiral Havi on the line. I know he wants me to join this order, and I know you can clear me for duty."

Hesitantly, the doctor replied, "I can, but won't. Alex and your parents would hate me."

"I know my mom wouldn't sit idly by as the world fell apart. How do I honor her legacy, if I let my sister keep going?" He sighed and nodded. "Good. Then let's get me into fighting shape, I have to prepare for the trials."

Chapter 15

ARMISTICE DAY

Mandy, present day…

"**O**h my fucking gosh! You're Mandy!" The lady at the front desk gasped and stared at me as if she had seen a ghost. She sat there with her mouth ajar, stunned that I was here.

"Good morning, I have an appointment with Nic," I said.

She didn't immediately respond, but after a few seconds she stammered, "N-Nic?"

"Copernicus, sorry."

"He is currently meeting with the ambassador of Scyra; their meeting went over. I will immediately page him." She reached for her phone and knocked over a cup full of pens and pencils and shrieked as she did so.

I raised my hand to stop her. "It's fine. I don't mind waiting in the lobby."

I took a seat in the lobby and grabbed a tablet to read while I waited. It looked like someone before me was reading a news piece by Victoria, everyone's *favorite* eastern reporter. I smirked at the thought. An excerpt from the article read:

Mandy's 'chaos walkers' last sighted in the forest of Qrum making this now the third territory to be considered disputed. With regime forces spread thin after battling the insurgents in Kaleeda and Grenfall, many are worried if the insurgents will turn their sights to Kalsia next. Turn to page 5 for more...

I smirked as I read it.

It's hard for people and organizations to publish anti-regime information. If Victoria keeps this up, her station will fire her or the regime will cut their funding. As I leaned forward to put the tablet down, I noticed the woman at the desk staring at me. Our eyes locked only for a moment before she tensed up and her eyes darted down towards her desk. You could even hear a panicked gasp as she did so.

I stood up and began walking over to her; I just wanted her to know that chimeras aren't as bad as the regime says we are.

I put on a smile as I spoke. "Can–"

She jumped out of her seat as her phone gave off an obnoxiously loud buzz. She put her hand on her chest and let out a sigh.

"H-he is ready for you." She couldn't even look at me as the words were forced out of her mouth.

I nodded and took the elevator up to his suite. I was taken back by the thought; my brother has a suite now. We last saw each other well over half a year ago, when he went AWOL to comfort me. And now, he somehow came into Trogz forces, made multiple public appearances and even has a penthouse suite.

Our lifestyle didn't allow us to hang out weekly, or even monthly sometimes, so not talking wasn't abnormal. But this was the closest he has ever been to dying... so I wanted to bring him a gift. With me, I had a basket of his favorite snacks and treats. I even had some imported from the moons.

The elevator doors opened to a hallway with one room and a desk outside of it. Behind the desk sat a human who gave me a gentle warm smile.

"Good morning ma'am. The ambassador from Scyra has soured his mood, I hope you can sweeten it." The human turned their head and flipped their ear to show me a tattoo behind it.

It was a serpent.

Humans that were sympathetic to our cause, or flat out hated the regime, showed their solidarity with us by getting snake or snake fang tattoos. I've even seen people sign it in sign language, like Casey and his peacekeepers did on Dieman's island. I've even heard humans hiss under their breath when they wanted to show support, but were in compromising positions.

The door to the room flew open and out walked an older woman wearing a floral sundress and a pearl necklace. Behind her, was a girl about half her age with a clipboard in her hand. The woman in the sundress was exhaling and rolling her eyes as the girl with the clipboard spoke. She yawned as the girl droned on, looking around for anything to be slightly interesting.

That's when she noticed me.

A smile danced across her face as she almost glided over to me.

"The little chimera trouble maker as I live and breathe. Big fan of your work, darling." She reached out and kissed me on both cheeks and smiled. Her gaze was gentle, but firm. It traveled across the entirety of my body, before finally settling on my hair. "Oh, what beautiful coils." She paused, admiring my hair. "How good would they look on the sands of Scyra." She tilted her head, losing herself in her own train of thought. Her eyes perked up as she said, "where are my manners? I'm Lynda and here is my assistant, Carter."

"Hi, I'm Mandy. Glad to have the ambassador of Scyra supporting me." I smiled.

"Oh it is unofficial. All chimera as of current, are banned from our sands. You have killed a lot of humans you know. But from where the citizens of Scyra are sitting, you and Havi are both terrorists and war criminals. Especially after how he treated our last ambassador."

"Havi is doing nothing less of pest control to my people, and *I'm* the terrorist?" I scoffed. "Imagine, a world where you defend yourself against oppressors and *you're* the bad guy."

"Well we can't support war crimes, love. And this is your battle, not ours."

"I was under the impression the people of Scyra hated chains. I guess as long as the chains gleam, it can be mistaken for a necklace." I squinted at her.

"How rebellious. Careful young lady, rudeness doesn't garner you allies. I do like you, but I don't tolerate disrespect. Mind and find your manners. If you have actionable intelligence that Havi has gone against lifeform rights, I am more than happy to investigate. Our scouts can only prove so much, perhaps you should share some of your intel with us."

"I can forward you all of our intel on Havi and the regime. It covers every report this year and all the reeducation camps housing kazamites and humans. I have even more on the rest of the regime."

"I'll read over your files and **IF** your claims are true, I will sponsor you. I have a well decorated general who speaks highly of you, don't disappoint her. Carter, it's time for us to go. Excuse us, Mandy, but we have a long flight. We look forward to watching you grow. Take care of your people first, and then yourself."

She kissed me on the cheeks again and walked past me with her shoulder length hair and Carter trailing behind. They boarded the elevator and both gave me a smile.

"Who is the general?" I asked.

The elevator doors began to close when she replied, "Donna. I'll give her your regards."

Now that they were gone, I was allowed to walk in to talk to Nic.

Weeks. I had weeks, *months* even to think about what to say to him. Inside jokes, shows we were binging but missed, new hobbies and so much more. But now, my legs were full of lead and I stood staring at his door.

I took a deep breath and like normal, mustered all the fake bravado I could and entered his room.

I stopped only a few feet into the room as the door slowly closed behind me. His room was *gorgeous*. It was a penthouse suite with a skyline view of the metropolis known as Newlana. He had a chandelier, a fireplace, aquarium, marble kitchen countertops, the works! How the hell could he afford any of this?

Standing by the window, drink in hand, was a man who looked like… *Nic?* What happened to his hair? I placed the basket down in his kitchen and joined him by the window. I didn't take my eyes off of him. I scanned him up and down a dozen times, checking to see if he was healthy. And of course, looking at his head. His hair used to be red like fire, but now it was the color of rust or maybe leaves in Autumn.

I turned my attention to the skyline and now, it made sense why he didn't turn to face me. It was mesmerizing. We watched as people and animals went about their daily lives. Cars speeding through the air while the summer and winter birds flew in opposite directions. All of these were normal for Newlana, but this time it was different. Mechs cleaned, the medians on the ground had miniature turbines that collected wind power, and I assume stored it somewhere. And the trees had a moss or algae, that gave off a low bioluminescent light. They covered the city, fusing nature naturally with urban life.

This wasn't the Newlana I knew. Was this Nic's doing? Is this what has kept him busy?

We turned to face each other simultaneously and while he seemed a bit more reserved, I couldn't help but break down and cry. The tears ran down my face as I fought to swallow a bulge in my throat. It was as if I was just eating spoonfuls of peanut butter. I hugged him as tight as I could, and he hugged me back.

"I'm so happy you're ok." My voice was muffled from leaning into his chest.

His voice boomed through his chest as he said, "I'm glad you're ok too, Mandy. Would you like a drink? I have a margarita maker."

I laughed and nodded, wiping my face on his shirt. I felt him lower his arms, so I tightened mine. The last time I let him go, he was dying.

"You have to let me go." He chuckled as he wiggled himself out of my grasp. I followed him to the kitchen where he did a quick little dig through my basket I brought for him, and then started making our drinks.

"Do you like my new place? It's massive, but I get tons of perks. Not bad for a guy just short of house arrest by the controlling Havi."

"Good to hear you're not a fan of him either. Imagine a universe where Havi isn't controlling, that's life on Saturn."

"Yea well, I can't exactly go against him." He started twirling the bottom of his shirt between his fingers before continuing. "How are you? How is everyone? *Who* even is everyone?"

"Right now, I'm the only chimera. We can't find the others, or they cut out a slice of land and asked to be left alone." I felt bad lying, but I know I couldn't say certain things; Havi could be listening. "Kazar is massive with everyone staying here on the continent. It wouldn't surprise me if people up and left Kore. I'm doing better, I was in a bad place a few months ago, with Sibil."

"I read about it. I'm sorry that you were thrown into that position, I can't imagine the battles you've had to face alone."

He went into the cupboards and grabbed two glasses and placed them under the margarita maker. His movements and speech were different. His shoulders were tense, and he was bigger, like he learned what a gym was. But his speech... since when did he talk normally?

"How are you?" I asked.

"I'm uh... adjusting. I've had a lot of private training sessions and spend all my spare time in briefings, training, and in council meetings. Havi's been dying for me to join this group, the one I've told you about years ago, and I said yes. Oh and I started watching a TV show, it's a cooking show."

He stopped talking, but didn't seem done with his statement. He turned his back to me, but I could tell there was still more on his mind.

"I want to be a fleet commander," he continued. "I'm a vessel commander right now. And I guess a temporary prefect as well. If you couldn't tell by my ivory tower here. I'll soon move on and have to endorse someone to replace me. Some girl named Laika, don't tell the press please. I'm getting so much heat from some journalist named Victoria."

I fought back a smile. "What's next?"

"For me? Space. Laika eventually gets my seat and I go to space. The remainder of my training is on the moons. Remember when I asked, what does space smell like? Or if it had sound?" He chuckled. "And now, I've been to space about half a dozen times just this year. My joints are in constant pain."

I tapped my fingers on the table, as I thought about my words. I bit my lip thinking of how to ask about us, while we danced through this landmine.

"And what about us? Where does that leave us?"

"Peace." He passed me my margarita as the machine finished making them. We touched glasses and took sips out of them. "Cheers. Or as Havi says, skål." After a few sips, he continued. "I want us to not be on opposing sides. I want my sister back, by my side and I want her to call off her chaos walkers and drop this superhero name, voidborn. I'm getting paper cuts dealing with reports of strikes led by you and Khan daily it seems. You're like a hydra, I put out a fire and chop off a head, and then 20 more appear. I'm in meetings and get mail about parents being mad over humans reading comic books with a series called 'void walkers'. Just today, I had to answer for a card game with chimeras that is honestly kind of fun, but I can't say that. And of course I only get second hand information and reports from scouts but it leaves me with one question."

"What's that?"

"Is it true? Is *everything* they're saying true?"

"Nic…"

"My name isn't an answer. Is it?"

I sighed.

"Probably…" I took a gulp out of my glass. "We have scouts too. Is what *they* say true?"

He sighed.

"Probably." He downed his glass.

I went back to tapping nails on the countertop and he went back to fidgeting with his shirt.

Risking stepping on a landmine, I took a step and spoke up. "I want my brother back," I declared. "I miss him."

"And I miss my sister. But while I was unconscious I realized that I don't miss war. And if my sister loves me, she'll pull back her forces. Tell your allies to stand down."

I scoffed.

"Audacity must be part of your training. I'm not doing that, and using my love for you is disgusting and you know it. My brother from months ago would've never said that. Are you sure you're even my brother? The way you hold yourself, and the way you speak is just so foreign."

"I am your brother, I've just grown up, Mandy. The optics are bad and you know it. Getting this armistice day today already put a political target on my back. I can only do so much, Mandy. You're on the side of literal terrorists."

"I guess it's only 'terrorism' when you're on the right side of the gun, huh? We terrorize the terrorists, and now I'm slandered across the planet and moons and suddenly *we're* the bad guys? You must have hit your head pretty damn hard because the math adds up when you subtract. Maybe next, you can protest my protest. Seems on brand." I downed my drink.

"Things are different now, I'm at the helm. Look how much I've changed this city, I could do the same for kazamites and chimeras. But I need you to stand down. Or tell us where Lycia is."

"Tell you where our *refugee* camp is? You'd think a man on thin ice would stop skating." I spat. "You're not fucking Nic."

"No need to swear, I am your brother–"

"**Are** you?"

I slammed my cup down, a little too aggressively and gasped at my own actions. I regretted the words as soon as they left my mouth.

He sighed and said, "Mandy, officially, Havi wants you and everyone else's head. But we can settle for something less violent. First, you and Khan surrender and get executed. But if you give up all your plans and resources, he'll settle with you both being imprisoned, but alive. Second, denounce your militia and help us find every chimera. No matter where they are. Inhibitor collars will be placed on every chimera, just like how Chevalier had when he was younger and banished out west. Next, give me Cricket. He belongs to the regime… just like chimeras. He will be needed to regain control over every stolen mech. And lastly, a formal apology for creating unrest."

"And what do we get out of this?"

"Life. You walk away alive, Mandy. Havi already wants you all dead, he sees this compromise as him showing kindness. Just take the deal."

"I have a better deal: surrender and die. You're the only one in the regime I care about. We can tell which one of us loves the other more because I'm not asking you to wear a collar like a dog."

"It's for our safety," he retorted.

"And what was last week's fire bombing on that village? Or the napalm strike in the mountains? A culling for safety?"

"I didn't like that we did that…" he muttered.

"And yet, you stand proudly looking down at the smaller folk from your ivory tower. While we're forced to ration almost expired food."

"My ivory tower I inherited because *you* killed my family!"

"I **AM** your family!"

I jumped up, throwing my chair back. I hunched over the table, balling my fist.

"Then why do you keep hurting me?"

"Fighting against the regime was originally **YOUR** idea, Nic!"

"Murder? Nukes? You are leading a revolution and a trail of destruction. I'm forced to build while you play guerrilla warfare like this is a game."

"My people are dying. Our raids are for resources mostly with less than a quarter of them having the objective of military weapons. And we spare your civilians, **every** time. How many non-combatants has your side killed again?"

"Look Mandy, we have to react to show force. It's *war* and if you are unwilling to play, bow out. Surrender and accept the terms."

He reached out to touch me, but I smacked his hand away.

"The terms of my brother wanting to collar me?"

He groaned and leaned back. "I just want you safe. You know I can't back down. The only way to change the game, is to play the game. Mandy please, surrender."

"An old terran lie. I can't... *won't* back down. We've come too far."

"You'll put these people before you and me? Betting against family?"

"These people are family, just extended. It doesn't have to end in violence, Nic."

"Well it won't end with my side surrendering."

"Then switch sides. Come back home to me. This was your dream."

"My dream didn't include 15,000 plus dead humans while I was unconscious. I've been holding Havi and the military back, my people are going extinct because of this."

I stood up firmly and said, "then surrender."

He sighed and grabbed both of our glasses and put them in the sink. He took his time washing the cups, scrubbing them over and over, as if they were stained.

"So, we're at an impasse. There's another way, a Hólmgang."

"Nic…" My shoulders fell in defeat.

"Havi won't honor a full one, but he'll honor half of one. I invoke it, and you have to honor it." He walked back over to me and stared at me, unblinking.

"I'm not dueling you to the death."

"Officially, it's a duel to first blood. And who says you'll win?"

"There has to be another way…"

"Once today's ceasefire is over, I'll tell Havi my plan. He'll most likely be upset but it will end in less bloodshed. Later today, choose the time and location and then ping me."

His nose started dripping blood. I reached for his face instinctively but he swatted my hand away and turned around.

I frowned and then walked towards the door; that must've been my cue.

"After the first salvo… there's no going back," I said.

"Then surrender. You've gone too far Mandy, you've killed innocents."

"I guess chimeras and kazamites don't meet your definition of 'innocent'. I love you, so I'll say it… evacuate and dock Avalon, before the ceasefire is over."

His eyes doubled in size. He thought about what I said and sighed.

"Keep your men away from Newlana, it'll be an ambush."

I walked out the door and turned around hoping he'd change his mind or see me out. "Infinity to infinity?"

"Goodbye Mandy…"

Chapter 16

TEMPORARY FOREVERS & PERMANENT NEVERS

I sat alone and listened to the sound of the waves charging into the beach, and then retreating. The only ones keeping me 'company', were the greedy alg birds stalking my sandwich. Alg birds were supposed to be a sign of good fortune, but I think that only applied to captains lost at sea. Lost captains would follow the birds knowing that there was land nearby, just like seagulls back on Earth. And when not at sea, they were eating anything that they could fit into their mouths, including algae, hence their name.

Their greenish feathers clashed against the dark sky, so it wasn't hard for me to swat away one that dove for my sandwich. I smiled, thinking that maybe my fortune was turning around, maybe at least just for the day.

"What the hell?" One of the birds snuck up on me, and bit my sandwich and flew off before I had a chance to react. "Good fortune, right?" I sighed.

I shouldn't eat before fighting or doing immensely stressful things anyway, and that's exactly what a Hólmgang was. A general or their champion, would challenge another general to single combat where both sides get to make demands. It was an ancient Earth custom that most likely has changed over the millenia, but still had similar foundations. Either side didn't have to honor any of the demands, but

Nic would and Havi has a reputation to uphold. After all, Havi's the victim, right?

Sunrise was the end of our armistice and our war would continue, unless I could end it here. The first thing Khan wanted us to do, was shoot down Avalon. It hovered miles in the sky and as soon as the sun touched its hull, he wanted us to take it out.

I sighed. It's sad it took months of raids, strikes and guerilla warfare for us to get Havi's attention. And still, my brother is the one facing me, and not Havi. Nic sat below me on a log closer to the waves than I was, waiting patiently for me to show up. And where was Havi? Hiding safely behind a desk while I fought my last family member. He probably banked on me too scared to fight my own brother or unwilling to fight for my people. Boy, is he going to be mad.

My watch beeped.

Sunrise.

I closed my eyes and inhaled. I leaned back, using my hands to prop me up and waited and listened. I listened to the sound of the alg birds suddenly vanish, and then the sound of the crashing waves getting slightly fainter. Next was the ground vibrating. And last...

"The wind..."

The shockwave sent my hair into a frenzy; my coils danced around rhythmless. Within seconds, I could feel the sun's rays that were hiding behind a former hovering Avalon, reach my skin. I opened my eyes and watched as the megacity glided into the ground as the EMP took hold. Several explosions dotted across the ship, but the sound would take seconds to reach me, assuming that they even would from this distance judging by their size. I assumed any city nearby had shattered glass everywhere. I stood to my feet and walked down to greet my brother who was awestruck at Avalon falling.

He turned to face me as I approached and said, "a battle here, at Winter's Gate? You'll have every kazamite and human's attention, I'll give you that."

"It's where the first kazamite was killed by a human publically; some people need to be reminded who struck first."

He shrugged off my comment and rolled his eyes. "I brought you a gift." He handed me a wrapped package. "It's not a trick, I just think it's better with you."

I hesitated at first, but then opened it slowly, starting with the bow. I could tell Nic wrapped it because he was notoriously *terrible* at gift wrapping. But in his defense, he was probably the best gift giver I know. I took the lid off and stared at the gift.

The blood rushed to my face as my body started to get warm, hot even. Yesterday, I was able to fight back my tears for the most part; but today... today...

I cried.

Inside of the box was a neatly folded claret sash. It was Historia's.

I put the lid back on the box and gently placed the gift on top of the log next to Nic. I looked up at my brother and used every *ounce* of strength in me, to not tackle and hug him. But we passed the hugging and talking it out phase.

I cleared my throat and said, "I want the location of every imprisoned chimera as of now upon victory."

His eyes doubled in size, but he nodded. "Full access to all intel you and Khan have upon victory," he demanded.

I countered with, "safe passage for every chimera hiding, upon victory."

"Location of Khan, Lycia, and every sympathizer, upon victory."

"I want your surrender, Nic, or one year exile, upon victory."

"Are you serious?"

"Yes."

He gritted his teeth. "Fine. Full access to Cricket, upon victory." He said those last two words mockingly. Snidely even.

I sighed and said, "I accept these terms."

"I accept these terms."

"This is silly, Nic."

"I only wanted peace, your side forced my hand."

"Be careful climbing off of your high horse."

He snapped, "would Historia be proud of you? Dragging this?"

I sighed. Why does everyone bring up my dead friends to get to me? I shook my head as I spoke and said, "as proud as your parents are of you now."

"I **honor** my parents and people!" You could see the veins in his throat and forehead. Nic has yelled in the past, but I can count on one hand how many times he's yelled at *me*.

"Your parents wouldn't feel honored. You and your people are creating a police state."

"It's **not** a police state, it's a society of law and order. We provide protection, they should provide loyalty."

"*Should* provide?" I scoffed.

"**Will** provide. They owe us loyalty and those who speak out against us are no different than treasonous wildlings who aim to ruin a new age and new order. This society, the problems. All of it, I can fix it. I can fix them."

"Do you hear yourself? You don't even sound like Nic I—" his nose started dripping blood.

I took a step towards him and reached for his face, but he swatted my hand and wiped the blood away with the back of his hand.

"Nic, why does your nose keep bleeding? What did they do to you?" I paused and thought for a moment. "What did *you* do to you?"

"What had to be done! I've had to make sacrifices and do things you never would have lived through."

"I'll be sure to cry a real tear. You need help, Nic."

"From who? The girl who left me for dead? What do you know about being left on death's door?"

I sighed. "I'm not going to trauma bond with you. This is silly, we need to get you to a hospital."

"Draw your saber. I'm taking you in."

"You have to be suffering from brain rot if you think a human is stronger than a chimera, especially you in your current state."

He fumbled with his sword as he drew it and postured incorrectly. What is he doing? I thought. Nic was a skilled swordsman, he shouldn't be struggling to draw his weapon. He changed his posture and dashed towards me. I smacked his saber out of his hand with almost no effort and stared at him. His eyes doubled in size as he jumped back. His eyes darted between me and his saber, as if he was a cornered animal.

We stared at each other for half a minute before he realized I wasn't going to move. Cautiously, he crept over to his saber and picked it up and moved away. This time, his stance was much better, but his grip on his saber was still sloppy.

He advanced again faster, but choreographed all of his attacks; it was as if he was just *telling* me what he was going to do. I saw through all of his feints.

Jab. Punch. Slash.

Jab, punch, slash, *again*.

Nothing landed, *nothing* worked.

He was in a frenzy. He didn't have a chance in hell of killing me, let alone hitting me. With each missed attack and each parry, he grew more animalistic. And reckless. The more reckless he became, the more he choreographed his attacks.

What the hell was wrong with him?

"**Enough** Nic." I drove my arm into his chest.

His body crumbled like paper around my palm. He flew backwards dropping his saber and tumbled. After a moment of silence, he screamed in pain. And rage.

"Nic, you're sick. There's something wrong with you. Please, let me help."

341

"**GET AWAY FROM ME**!" His ears dripped blood as he charged at me.

Nic was an amazing swordsman on his worst days, I didn't recognize who stood in front of me today. He swung his blade like an angry child. It was as if I was watching him... devolve.

I sighed and grabbed his wrist while he was midswing. "Nic, I think we're done here. The fight's over." He fought to break free. "**Nic**." I tightened my grip a little. He let out a nightmarish scream and dropped his saber. I watched as his arm looked like he caught a bad charlie horse.

"Nic, please! What did they do? How can I fix this?"

"**You** did this!" I let him go as he cursed me. "I had to make sacrifices!"

He drew his knife hidden next to his boot and lunged at me. I stepped back and lost my footing as he cut my face. I winced in pain and shoved him again. He flew backwards into the ocean.

"Nic, STOP! You're fighting ghost right now, I'm not your enemy." He didn't respond. I waited a few seconds, but he didn't get up.

"Nic?" I waited a little longer.

Nothing.

I rushed over towards him. I arrived as soon as he started trying to stand himself up. He fell to his knees. I stood over him as he took deep breaths trying to control his breathing.

"Oh Nic..." He popped a blood vessel in his left eye, all I could see was his iris in a pool of red.

"Sur...surrender..." he mumbled.

I joined him and got on my knees in the water.

I hugged him.

"We were supposed to create peace together, Mandy. I can fix them..."

"We don't need to be fixed. Your version of peace is prison. You're demanding a bird stay caged and justifying your actions by saying at least it's safe in the cage."

"But think how happy the bird would be. Think…" You could hear the energy in him fading with each sentence.

"It's not real Nic. It's not real. How can I help you? My medics aren't far from here."

"No, I have to beat you. Havi said I had to, he encouraged me to come."

Tears rolled down my cheeks as I gritted my teeth and squeezed him tighter. "Of course he did." It was all a set up to get into my head. He *knew* Nic couldn't win.

"I… I hate you…" he said.

"That's ok. I love you so much Nic."

Nic and I never fought. We always heard stories of siblings that would argue and fight, but it wasn't us. Siblings having fights was as real to us as talking animals. It felt like we always knew what the other wanted and needed. I picked him up and carried him back to shore. I gently laid him down, propping him up on the log so he could watch the sunrise.

"Just kill me…"

"I don't know what Havi is whispering in your ears, but he's manipulating you."

"Liar…"

"Whatever you did to yourself, is messing with your head."

He had a flare gun on him, so I took it and fired it. We waited a few minutes before we were joined by his forces. I could hear the soldiers gasp as they saw me sitting next to his body.

"Step away and put your hands in the air you monster!" A soldier yelled at me.

They brought a bio tube, good. Those things could repair tissue within minutes while scanning for any issues, deformities and foreign objects in the body. Nic was now an asset for Havi, of course he couldn't afford to easily lose him. Ignoring the soldier, I picked him up and walked over to the bio tube and laid him in it.

I leaned in to kiss his forehead and that's when I heard him murmur, "infinity to infinity."

One of the medics approached me and started the bio tube and said, "don't worry, he'll live."

"I know. All of your lives are banking on it."

They left me on the beach as they rushed a hardly conscious Nic away. As they left, I saw him messing with his NUE right before he passed out. As soon as he passed out, my NUE pinged. It was from Nic. It was what he promised. Everything he promised. The location of all confirmed dead chimeras, imprisoned ones, and missing ones and whatever intel they had on them. It also had a rough draft of his vow to go into exile for a year. The list he gave of chimeras had over a dozen names, and some were older than Sibil.

I kept searching through the file and attached at the bottom of the email, was a password lock. I paused for a moment and then typed 'infinity to infinity." The password was accepted and replied 'forever to forever' and purged the system. It was malware designed to eat all of our files on Havi's servers. And with some time, Cricket could open a backdoor into all of Havi's systems.

I sighed and smiled. This was the edge we needed. Thank you Nic.

"Cricket, I'm coming back alone. Send my ride, please."

"Do you want me to track the ship? It's almost in orbit." He asked.

"No. Khan will only aim guns at it or keep tracking them. I can't bring myself to do that, I can save Nic."

"Why are you so confident?"

"Because whenever we spar and I beat him, he always comes back. Like a chorus in a sonnet or poem."

"A refrain, you mean a refrain."

"Refrain from what?"

"No, a refrain in poetry… nevermind." He groaned.

"I know, but it's good to hear you on the receiving end. Let's go, we got a lot of chimeras to bring home."

"Where to first?"

"The shimmering city of Mayari, then Pala."

www.ingramcontent.com/pod-product-compliance
Lightning Source LLC
Chambersburg PA
CBHW020423030726
47495CB00006B/1641